The Calling

TM

For more information about Paul Strickler's novels, please visit

www.HorrorPlace.com

The Calling

A NOVEL BY

Paul M. Strickler

For:
My Mouse!
Thanks for everything!
Paul M. Strickler
Hudsonville, MI
12 June 2006
PS

Crystal Dreams Publishing
W1227 East County Road A
Berlin, WI 54923

ISBN 1-59146-039-5

Printed in the United States of America

For Tia

ACKNOWLEDGEMENTS

With gratitude to: William, my father, who always encouraged me; Shirley, my mother, who helped me make the right choices; and Tia, my wonderful wife, who has always put up with all my eccentricities!

Thanks to the staff at Crystal Dreams: Sarah Schwersenska, publisher; Carole Vogt and Martin Vogt, editors.

A special thanks to My Mouse. You helped more than you know.

The following also deserve a special thank you: Sandra Hampton O'Brien, Laura Steele, Jodell Danbert, Judy Follette, Tad Malpass and the late Carlton Follette.

Thanks also to: Marjie Strickler and Chuck Drews, who helped, in differing ways, to guide me down the path.

Thanks to my early readers and supporters: J. Arthur Schmidt, Linda Schmidt, Betty Towne, Moira Martinchek, Russ Coombs, Lynda Gauthier, Kylie Fannon, Tom Stoddard, Henry Vlieg, David Ordiway, Ronda Taggart, Rose Rau, Jackie Capelin, Bonnie Anderson, Lora Sielatycki and Lou Ann Klump.

Thanks to the following family, friends, teachers and those who I met along the way that have contributed to making me the person I am today: William Strickler, Jr., Charles Strickler, Ann Goetz, Mark Goetz, Teresa Strickler, Andrew Drews, Jeff Drews, Peggy Johnson, John Holec, Ron Fuller, Linda McGeorge, David Schmidt, Lewis Lake, the late Willard Lake, Martha Gottlieb, Doug Pell, Bill McClain, Elton Veenstra, Helei Qu, Marcus Cafagna, Jim Fatka, Angie Mickevich, Ronald Schmidt, Bernie Clark, Brad Elm, Michael Fettig, David Gaunt, Jeff Kruzel, Anita Kuhs, Eric Leaman, Elaine Lockman, Joyce Newville, John Pemberton, Andy Place, Lou Ann Schrader, Connie Sherk, Maurie Tomkins, Sharon Solgot, Katie Massey, Kris Whittet, Susan Andras, Alan Baily, Bridget Houston, Cyndy Karlskin, Barry Maginity, Patty Moore, Larry Failing, Dennis Simpson, Mike Roberge, Mike Hansen, Cynthia Dawson and Don Black.

Thanks to Susan Herner for her encouragement.

Thanks also to the following fellow authors who helped inspire, teach and entertain: Peter Straub, Stephen King and Dean Koontz.

PART ONE

The House

Do not fear what you are about to suffer. Behold, the devil is about to throw some of you into prison, that you may be tested, and for ten days you will have tribulation. Be faithful unto death, and I will give you the crown of life.

- Revelation 2:10

Prologue I

Ratingen, Germany
August 10, 1903

The fire gave silent and ceaseless birth to blood-soaked sheets of waving fabric, their color changing as the flames evolved and grew, mesmerizing in their display of persistent transformation that, while apparently random, seemed born for some as yet unknown purpose.

"Do *you* think he's a witch?" Otto said, the words sounding too loud to Hermann in the darkness, despite the roaring bonfire.

"Warlock. A male witch is called a warlock, not a witch," Hermann whispered.

"But mother said—"

"Mother was wrong. Now quiet your mouth before I do it for you."

There was something stranger than witchcraft about their neighbor, Dr. Robert Benjamin Woulfe, whom they were observing in the clearing. Hermann's cousin, Gustav, thought Dr. Woulfe was a sorcerer. Was there a difference?

"Why is he talking to that fire?" Otto asked.

Hermann carefully observed his younger brother Otto as he fidgeted, moving his knees, trying to find a softer place to kneel behind the clumps of poison sumac, watching the fire and the man. It had only been fifteen minutes, but seemed longer.

"I don't know."

Hermann's awkward position had infused his knees and legs with a throbbing numbness, yet he refused to move. He felt a sudden tickle at his neck and brushed something off.

The fire dominating the clearing crackled and spat, feeding on a conical-stacked pile of logs like a ravenous beast. Flames erupted like clawing hands straining to find purchase in the black fabric of the night. At random intervals, smoke drifted toward them. In the dark, Hermann couldn't see it, becoming aware of it only after it had stung his eyes or slithered its way into his mouth.

Dr. Woulfe, now gazing almost exclusively into the fire's heart, began reciting, in an almost musical litany, the words of Calling.

The smooth chorus of the doctor's voice rose and fell in rhythm with the reaching flames. The fire expanded, seeming to draw power from the doctor's words. Firelight painted tree trunks with flickering shapes that jumped and scampered like children made of light and shadow.

An air current immersed Hermann's body within a growing heat subsequently creating a warmth that calmed him until Otto, stretching his leg, rustled a nearby sumac. Hermann, disturbed by the sudden interruption, glared but said nothing before he noticed the fire's light, dancing on the side of Otto's face, had visually transformed his cheek into a rippling sheet of blood-colored tissue.

When the air current ceased, Hermann felt another tickle at the back of his neck. He brushed at it again but this time the irritation remained. He clawed at himself, bending and twisting his arm, digging into his neck with his fingers until the pain from his nails erased the maddening tickle.

The flames suddenly rose higher, seemingly commanded by the doctor's booming oratory as he more vigorously employed increasing emphasis on each repeated stanza of his strange speech. The fire seemed to comply and danced in an orgy of intertwining bodies which wrapped themselves together and then flew apart. The accompanying heat created a rustling in the leaves and a sudden crack of wood echoed loudly back into the forest, startling a large animal somewhere in the darkness. Hermann was relieved when the sounds of breaking branches and snapping twigs faded in a direction leading away from the clearing.

The back of Hermann's neck felt raw and hot.

"Can we go now? I'm tired," Otto said.

Hermann suddenly sensed a change in the shape of the fire, as the fire seemed to be *forming* itself, as if some force were containing the flames, holding them down and together, somehow compacting them.

"A while longer," he whispered, his throat dry and raw.

Otto shifted again, pulling his leg back under himself. Hermann snapped his hand onto Otto's thin forearm. His brother's skin felt dry and cold.

"Sit down fool! You want him to see us?" He winced at the loudness of his voice.

"There's nothing going to happen," Otto whined.

The resolve so manifest in the doctor's words of a moment ago now seemed to melt away as if from the heat. His voice dropped to a murmur and then went silent, replaced by the sounds of whispering leaves and the roaring fire. Perhaps in an attempt to plead for guidance from the stars, the doctor stretched his head aloft. With the doctor's gaze temporarily diverted, Hermann was the first to see the thing that had been Called beginning to take shape within the twisting yellow flames of the bonfire.

"I think something's happening *now*—"

A subset of the fire's flames, those within the heart of the inferno itself, were presently combining themselves into a form noticeably untouched by the wavering, thrusting reach of the rest of the fire. Even from the relatively lengthy distance of his vantage point at the clearing's edge, the materialization was nevertheless immediately apparent. As he looked more discriminately into the fire, his fascination with the shape being born of light and flame was enough to keep his fear restrained—for the moment.

The doctor lowered his head and then staggered back in apparent surprise from the fire and the transformation occurring within it. Almost immediately, he reversed his position and moved once again toward the flames and, with even greater vigor, resumed his commanding litany. Now, as the wood fed the hungry flames, so too did the doctor's renewed commands seem to give fuel to the fire's transformation—hastening it, giving it the strength to wrap and form and create itself into a shape which began, finally, to suggest something familiar.

It was then, when he could no longer hear the rustling leaves, the fire, or the doctor's voice, that Hermann felt the strangeness. At first, he tried turning his head, attempting to look at his brother, but his body refused to cooperate. His eyes, no longer seemingly under his control, remained locked onto the sheets of slow-moving light, the flames no longer frantic or groping.

The Image came to him slowly, stealing away bits of thought and sight, sliding into his consciousness, obscuring the clearing and the fire and . . .

he sees his mother's smiling face—uneven teeth, almond eyes framed by shimmering black hair—then her face contorting, the skin around her eyes pulsing and straining as if about to give birth to some monstrosity, then her orbs bulging, her mouth grimacing in pain and terror, her eyeballs extending from their sockets, the surrounding skin pulling taut with the effort of restraint

. . . he struggled to shut the Image out but could not, there being no eyelids on his mind he could close, so he was forced to watch the grisly performance . . .

and then they do, her eyes bursting in a silent explosion, the sockets producing snake heads, dark green with blazing white and yellow eyes, red tongues extending from black mouths, flicking and searching, the heads waving before her face, snapping and hissing

. . . and then at last he succeeds; he is suddenly free, as if he had previously been held aloft by some giant's grip and now been suddenly dropped to the earth. His head ached as if the Image had been a physical attack against the matter within his skull. As he returned his focus to the clearing, he saw an impossible sight—of the doctor *becoming* a part of the fire, of light and flame and flesh merging into some new, albeit foreign substance—until unannounced, the next Image erupted into his head, the intense pain folding him to the ground, the soil's aroma rich with the smells of rotting wood and fetid leaves . . .

His German shepherd, Mesha, runs toward him, tail wagging, eyes bright and alive—until the fur peels from her snout and, hanging in twisted folds from her head, sloughs from her skull to reveal the pink white of flesh and bone

. . . and as he wrestled against the torment, the unstoppable Image-flow into his mind, it suddenly faded and he could once again visualize Otto through the Image's after-haze. However, there was something else now with Otto. No, not with him, *on* him. He saw Otto fall to the ground, trapped beneath a massive black shape and . . .

the last of his dog's fur peels away, falling to the ground, revealing a pinkish white body, not of flesh and muscle but of bony scales, and then she is upon him, no longer friendly but snarling with foam-drenched mouth, the scales a rippling horde of hard-shelled creatures with small gaping mouths clicking and snapping

. . . he struggled to again see his brother, catching instead only an obscured glimpse of a dark shape and multiple protruding limbs entwined about Otto's body. As the forms writhed together on the ground, he attempted to tell himself that it was simply another vision. He put his hands to his face, rubbed his eyes and . . .

sees a pumpkin patch turn into a field of severed heads, mouths gibbering and sputtering unintelligibly at him, taunting him, spittle and white foam dripping and

. . . then opened them to see his brother, his pale and now imperfect skin streaked and spattered with . . . then before him the shape once again, impossibly large, obscuring . . .

and as the heads talk, black worms pour from slobbering mouths, falling to the ground with sticky plops, then squirm their way toward him

. . . then running from the clearing, screaming his brother's name to mask the breaking sounds, knowing Otto would never, could never, respond again—running harder now, unable to see; the Image stabbing, clawing its way into his skull, twisting and turning within his mind; his body tripping and going down, his knee connecting with rock, wrenching himself up, ignoring the throbbing pain, lurching forward into the black forest, each reflection of the Image delivered in multiple layers of hot pain—he sees nothing that is not the Image, feels nothing but the nearly unendurable agony . . .

and he looks down, sees his feet planted in the ground having become some form of plant, the grass blending, mixing with the color of his skin at his ankles

. . . and runs into a tree, cracking nose and forehead on knotted bark, feeling peripherally the blood soaking into his shirt, warming his cool skin . . .

and then the worm-snakes are there, slithering around his ankles, sliding up his naked legs, their bodies like rough sandpaper coated with sticky hot saliva

. . . and then sinking to his knees, holding his head, trying to physically squeeze and push the Image out of his mind but cannot . . .

and his dog Mesha is with the pumpkin heads, jumping, snarling, the double punch of paws on his chest, the smell of hot, dead-animal breath, saliva drops spraying across his face and into his mouth and eyes—feeling his throat tear—then the dog's momentum knocking him down and

. . . he feels his throat tear, the subsequent loss of breath and voice as the creature, now a heavy mass covered with thick fur, slams into him, knocking him into the sumac, broken trunks and limbs puncturing his skin . . . all of it slowly fading into the welcoming blackness and . . .

finds himself floating into darkness where there are no Images or visions and he welcomes the soothing embrace of sleep, of the darkness free from pain

. . . hears, as if from a great distance, an inhuman scream echo through the forest like a beast in the last agony of giving birth . . .

then he is drifting . . . out and away, then down . . . sinking into the cold . . . the pain dimming, then gone, replaced by the dark . . . and the cold . . .

. . . everything fading into black . . . blackness promising freedom from the pain . . . the Image fading . . . the pain sliding out and away . . . the blackness filling the void . . . coldness . . . sleep . . . the black.

1

Boyne City, Michigan
June 16, 1995 • Friday

1

The emerald eyes of the man Michael Sarasin would in time call the Mysterious Stranger, reminded him of the looks of fear and horror he had previously seen on the faces of people who stood gawking at the car accident he and his family had witnessed the day before. They were eyes which simultaneously seemed to conceal and betray a lurking madness beneath their surface. Eyes so intense they seemed alive, as if they were entities apart from their owner and were somehow reaching out to snatch his parents' Jeep Cherokee and slow it down, pull it back, hold on to it. The kind of eyes that could talk.

Michael, his younger sister and parents, were less than a mile from Woulfe House when he saw the stranger for the first time. The man was standing on the side of the country blacktop, disheveled and wild with his long hair and sporting an olive canvas coat in the pre-summer heat. The man, leaning against a ten-speed bicycle that may have been red once, probed Michael, turning his head slowly as they passed.

They were about three-quarters of a mile from the house when Michael first noticed the mammoth Victorian structure named after its builder, Dr. Robert Benjamin Woulfe.

Michael's mother, Samantha, or Sam as she liked to be called, was driving, following the blue sedan of Mary, their real-estate agent. As they arrived at the top of a hill, they noticed that from this vantage point to the house lay an open field interrupted only by a large, strangely-twisted tree while behind the house was a forest, covering the length of the lumpy earth all the way to the horizon.

While his family's attention was focused on the distant house, Michael's, however, shifted to a closer examination of what he considered the oddly-shaped tree. This particular willow had a dark, if not completely black bark, and appeared nearly leafless. It also sported a thick, straight trunk branching off into four crooked appendages shaped like arthritis-twisted fingers. Michael thought these same four branches, while contorted in a way that projected the appearance of jointed fingers, seemed instead to be rather than simply appendages which had grown naturally into such a gnarled configuration had instead been intentionally shaped that way—broken and twisted by some force larger than itself.

As his mother drove past the odd-looking tree, the illusion didn't diminish. To Michael, the tree actually seemed to command the field like a black fist. The tree's rough bark was gouged in excruciating furrows, like twisted ropy veins and tendons pulled taut against release from the ground. Swollen knots bulged along its trunk and branches. Although the tree was located at least several hundred feet from the roadway, Michael was able to note its every detail as if he were standing beside it.

"Look at that weird tree!" Amanda, his younger sister, suddenly announced as they floated past it. As she leaned over him, her blond hair swept casually across his lap and for a moment he was reminded of Cindy, the girlfriend he would probably never see again. He pushed his sister away and she glared at him but said nothing.

Michael was alone in his resistance to the idea of The Move. With his mother in charge, however, the deal was as good as done. He refused, though, to give in. It wouldn't be like last year.

On their way to Boyne City, or "Up North" as their neighbors in Farmington Hills called it, he began creating in his journal a list of all the things he thought he was going to miss out on by moving to rural northern Michigan. So far his list included "hick-town paperback library," "no local Internet access" and "no cable." Sam switched off the car radio just as the DJ announced it was 90 degrees in "Boyne Country."

More like Boring Country. And, once again, off to another great summer.

"It looks like a hand

(claw)

doesn't it?" his father, Alan, said; then he leaned toward Sam, the sun glinting off the gold rim of his glasses.

"I asked Mary about that tree the first time she brought me out here," Sam said. "Some of the locals are superstitious about it. They call it The Claw."

Michael smiled at the name and then at his mother's voice—the latter sounding the part of a tour guide in some national forest.

And over here, ladies and gentlemen, for the final attraction on our tour of the Great Forest, we have The Claw. Dating back to the first century A.D., The Claw has stood the test of time and people's imaginations. During the Middle Ages, the locals of nearby Nowhereville told their children that if they didn't behave, The Claw would grab them in the middle of the night and bury them in the earth beneath its life-draining roots. And not only did the poor children believe this, but most of their parents who told the tale did as well.

As Sam turned the Cherokee into the driveway of the house she had decided would be the next residence of the Sarasin family, Michael's attention shifted to the lawn, which he noticed had been mown recently, and he wondered who had done it. He thought again about the man with green eyes, but something besides the grass had sparked his attention. A second later, he realized what it was. There was no "For Sale" sign. His uneasiness, which had begun when he first saw the green-eyed stranger and was then compounded by the tree, further intensified—making his breath come in short, quick gasps. When his mother stopped the car, he clambered out. As soon as he stepped into the hot sun, his head began to throb with a dull ache and he noticed the air smelled strangely . . . old.

"Wow! It's *huge!*"

Michael dimly heard his sister's exclamation, the pain in his head insistently clamoring for attention. Steadfast, he reached for the still-open car door as the ground swayed in front of him. He waited for the dizziness to pass and then, as quickly as it had come, the pain faded to a distant rumble somewhere in the back of his head. Yet even as the pain drifted away, he knew it was only a brief respite as he could feel its promise to return manifested in the form of a faint pressure which remained deep behind his forehead.

Back in control of his faculties, he studied the house more carefully. He gazed upward and there, at one of the second story windows, he saw a face—the face of a man with long hair and brilliantly green eyes.

2

"I had no idea it was going to be so big," Alan said. They stood now on the white gravel driveway lying along the right, or south side of the house, a driveway that ended at a small barn in a corner of the backyard. Just before reaching the barn, a short section of the driveway ran perpendicular to the main road and led to a carriage house nestled in the woods. While the architecture of the carriage house matched that of the house, the barn was clearly modern. Both the barn and carriage house were painted white like the house, though the barn's coat was peeling in several places.

Alan hated to admit, even to himself, that he was already impressed. The house wasn't just big, it was grand. It wouldn't even be much of a stretch, perhaps, to call it a mansion. It was one of those rare types that, unfortunately he thought, were increasingly being made into B&B's. From the massive fieldstone foundation, to the leaded-glass windows, to the expansive front porch, to the exquisite corbels supporting a roof jutting defiantly into the sky—the house was a solid and incredible piece of work. Even with all this, though, his enthusiasm was tempered when he remembered the question that had been nagging him since the beginning.

If this place is so wonderful, why the cheap price?

And, as he stood looking upon what, if only from the outside (a valid consideration at this point he thought) appeared to be a truly magnificent home, he again reflected.

Why hadn't it sold in over two years on the market?

The house was Victorian in every respect, from the narrow wood siding to the ornate trim, roofline and front porch columns. Woulfe House was indeed an imposing structure—imposing even to the full-grown maples and oaks surrounding it on two sides. And, although the terrain was flat, the house seemed to rest on a rise and Alan felt the sense of a cliff-top castle eschewing dominance over its surroundings.

They decided to tour the outside first, and in his wife's conversation with the real estate agent he sensed joy in his wife's voice and was refreshingly moved by it. As they neared the front of the house, he wondered how bad the interior would have to be to dull their interest.

"Why would anyone build such a magnificent house way out here in the country?" he asked no one in particular. "It seems kind of strange. Usually one only finds houses of this type making up the main 'old' quarter of most towns." They were now halfway around the house, moving toward the backyard while off to their left was the open field—and The Tree.

"I don't know for sure," Mary said. "The original builder came from Germany. He was a doctor of some sort I believe. Guess he wanted the solitude."

"He didn't have a family?"

"Yes, I think so; later on he did," she said, frowning and touching her cheek.

When Sam came over to Alan and grasped his arm, her face looked like one gigantic smile.

"So, what do you think so far? Isn't this just incredible?"

"I'm having a hard time believing it's as genuine as it looks," he heard himself say and, upon a moment's reflection, decided that really was how he felt.

Sam looked at him as if about to ask another question when he noticed a thin blade of grass in her blonde hair. As he brushed away the errant strand, her eyes following his hand, he wondered how it had gotten there. She then abruptly let go of his arm and hurried to catch up with Mary.

A classical garden covered most of the backyard. Surprisingly, the garden showed little in the way of overgrowth despite years of neglect and Alan fondly recalled the master gardener classes he had attended at Sam's behest two summers ago. A cobblestone path, starting at the corner in front of them, wound its way through sedum, spotted lamium, lily of the valley and Ajuga to the other corner of the garden near the barn. Farther off the path, mounds of Siberian iris, stonecrop and hostas grew like isolated islands while periwinkle hugged the bases of several medium-sized Douglas firs and European hornbeams in the back corners. As the path further snaked its way along, it featured side pathways leading to a gazebo, a rock garden (hosting growths of wall rock cress, mountain sandwort and baby's breath and crowned by a pedestal-mounted sundial) and a patio. This patio in turn spread itself forth from the base of a cement stairway which led down from a small porch occupying the corner of the house closest to them.

Alan playfully asked Sam, "Does this mean I can finally persuade you to get rid of some of your house plants?"

"Perhaps," she said, smiling like a child who has suddenly stepped into a candy store where everything is free. He wondered if she had really heard his question. Then he smiled too, at her seemingly genuine happiness, and the thought that perhaps everything was truly going to turn out as wonderful as she seemed convinced it was.

"I'm gonna check out the gazebo!" Amanda cried and immediately set off at a run.

When Alan heard Michael approaching from behind him, he turned, and noted the expression on his son's face.

"Don't look so glum, son. Just think of it this way—you won't have hardly any grass to mow."

Michael glared, then turned and shuffled toward the patio where a black iron patio set—a round table and three chairs—had been conveniently left behind.

Near the start of the path, a cement rabbit coyly peered out at them from a clump of wormwood. Nearby, a simulated dry creek bed wound its way through the corner of the garden in front of them—a wooden walking bridge spanned the creek where the path intersected it.

After Amanda had reached the gazebo, Alan happily watched her short, bare legs piston her body up the steps.

"I think this is almost the best part," Sam began and turned to look up at him, "this garden. It's going to be so peaceful and relaxing on a day like this. I can see myself sitting out here for hours."

Mary replied, "Yes, beautiful isn't it? With a little upkeep, you'll soon have your own piece of Eden."

Alan turned back to his wife for a moment and then, as he swiveled to look once again toward the gazebo, he realized he couldn't see Amanda. Mary had started talking again, then paused, almost as if she were *expecting* something to happen.

A thin scream punctured the air, mixed with and followed by the sound of splitting, breaking wood.

Without hesitation, Alan raced down the path, nearly tripping on the wooden bridge, stumbling down the bridge's other side and back onto the path, cutting across a corner, finally trampling his way through the hosta. When he reached the gazebo, he discovered Amanda on the floor—her left leg seemingly swallowed by a hole in the floor's center.

"It hurts!" she cried.

"I'll get your leg out . . . hang on now; I'll be as careful as I can, I promise!" But first he knelt to get a closer look at the damage. Conscious of the danger of driving splinters into her, he carefully took hold of her leg with one hand, one of the boards with the other, and gently pulled. He soon heard Sam and Mary arriving behind him. Amanda whimpered initially but made no other protest as he safely extracted her leg.

As Michael pushed past Mary into the gazebo, Alan felt the floor move.

"What happened?" Michael asked.

"Just some rotted boards. She's got a few scratches, I don't think they're too serious though."

Amanda hobbled over to one of the benches lining the inside perimeter of the gazebo and sat down. Alan shuffled over to her on his knees to further examine her wounds. He noticed several long, red scratches which stretched from her knee to her ankle.

"Looks like you're going to live," he said facetiously. Since he'd confirmed to his satisfaction that there didn't appear to be any splinters, he stood up and walked across the floor, stomping and checking for more weak spots.

"We'll get you cleaned up inside dear," Sam said.

"Looks like it was just in the middle here," he said. "Seems kinda strange . . . I would have thought the middle to be strongest."

"Well, there you go," Sam said.

When Alan turned to look at his wife, he stopped when he saw Michael who was staring at Amanda's legs as if they had turned into something hideous.

"There I go, what?" he said, forcing himself to turn his attention back to Sam.

"Your first project. A new floor for the gazebo." She smiled and turned to leave. "Well, time's a wasting! I can't wait to show you guys the *inside!*"

Mary was already halfway along the path leading to the other corner of the yard, so Sam had to run to catch up.

"Yes, let's," Alan said, though fairly certain he was now only talking to himself. He was pleased, though, when Amanda got up and jogged after her mother, nursing only a barely noticeable limp.

Refocusing, he departed the gazebo, leaving Michael behind, having forgotten his son's strange reaction.

3

Michael was certain that the man he had seen on the side of the road staring at him was the same man he had seen staring at him from the house's upstairs window. But then Michael had blinked, and just that quickly the man with green eyes was gone. His reaction to Amanda's accident however was easier to explain—simple déjà vu.

Inside the house, the family split up. His parents followed Mary on a tour of the first floor while he and Amanda decided to investigate the basement. Climbing down the basement's bare wooden steps was like entering a lightless catacomb. As they descended, the temperature dropped, and goose bumps sprouted on his arms before he reached the bottom where an open door swung onto darkness. Having completed the descent, he stopped and carefully examined the door; he had never before seen anything like it. In a word, it was massive. Made of solid oak, it appeared homemade—and was at least three inches thick.

He turned away from the door and entered the darkness. Fumbling around at first, he eventually found a light switch which activated a single bare bulb located approximately in the middle of what was the main open area. Next, he noticed four small rooms built from rough, whitewashed lumber that had been constructed in each of the corners. Over the course of time, most of the whitewash had fallen or rubbed off and had settled as a thin white layer of dust on the floor.

"Creepy," Amanda said.

"No argument here. Kind of neat though."

"Looks like a dungeon."

The perimeter walls marked the inside surface of the fieldstone visible in the foundation outside. Consequently, the natural gray and black rock lent much to creating the dungeon-like atmosphere.

Overall, the layout of the floor plan appeared balanced—one small room in each of the corners; the middle area left open. Secondary, free-standing walls surrounded the middle, thereby creating a type of hallway around the perimeter, broken at each corner by the respective rooms. The floor was bare cement, and the low-hanging ceiling was a spaghetti-like patchwork of insulated pipes and wiring. Overall, it smelled like musty sawdust—or something long dead.

Michael walked cautiously into the center of the room.

Something's not right here.

The thought seemed to speak itself within his mind like the unbidden memory of some distant conversation.

"What's the matter?"

Before answering, he searched for the cause of his sudden uneasiness but saw and heard nothing.

Like something left behind . . . something bad or rotten . . .

"I don't know. I just had the strangest feeling—I don't even know how to describe it. Like something *bad*, as if I'd just smelled a dead animal." His eyes continued their search, scanning and probing the deep shadows. "Spoiled, but yet . . . like the feeling you have when you've forgotten something . . .

that if you don't remember soon . . . a bad thing will happen as a result of your forgetting." After a pause he added, "Understand?"

"Nope." Amanda turned away and neither of them spoke again until Amanda pointed at the floor and said, "What's that drain for?"

She was pointing at a circular grate about eight inches in diameter. Michael scanned the rest of the floor and counted—one, two, three . . . six, seven . . . eight drains in all.

More and more curious. Why would anyone have so many drains in a basement? Did it get that *wet down here?*

He didn't especially like this explanation but under the present circumstances, he could think of nothing better. And yet, there seemed to be another reason just beyond his grasp, the feeling that he had seen something like this before. About to suggest to Amanda that there might be a water problem and it would be worthwhile reporting it to their parents, a memory came to him in a sudden burst of color and sound much like a TV blaring to life inside his head. This scenario, he realized, was what he had seen at his uncle's ranch in Texas almost four years ago.

He remembered that it had been fall and it was the first time Michael had been to his father's childhood home. The trip, an attempt by his father to patch things up with his family, had only partly succeeded. The resentment of Alan's brothers for his not wanting to help them run the ranch after their parents had died in a freak electrical accident, could not easily be forgiven in their eyes. To them, his behavior was a disrespect for family bordering on treason.

What Michael remembered most though about the trip occurred on the second to last day when his uncles began butchering cattle. He had stumbled upon the sight of the slaughter after having been awakened by strange, pre-dawn sounds. For nearly half an hour he intently watched the process through a grimy side window until his uncles spotted him. He would never, however, forget what he had seen that day—the severed heads on hooks, the raw, dripping meat . . . the endless blood draining away, seeping through grates in the floor . . .

"Hello, Michael? Anybody there?"

He heard his sister's question as if it had come from somewhere far away.

"Oh . . . yeah. I was just thinking . . . it probably gets wet down here in the spring. All the drains are for letting the water

(blood)

drain so the basement doesn't flood

(stink with the smell of death as the men in their black rubber boots wade through the thick liquid, the blood getting deeper because the drains are plugged and the blood can't drain away and so it gets deeper and deeper until it's an inch deep, a four-inch high cement levee keeping the blood enclosed within the . . . then two inches . . . killing room as it gets deeper . . . three inches . . .)

with water when it rains."

"Oh," Amanda said. He ignored her quizzical look.

Following the perimeter, they found one of the corner rooms that had once been used as a coal storage room. The room's walls forever blackened, it reinforced the image that they were indeed in a castle dungeon, this room one of its prison cells. Against one wall, they noticed that someone had built what Michael guessed was intended to have been a lumber rack—a wooden framework about ten feet long. A single two-by-four, now gray with dust, rested on the framework's bottom shelf. The room's blackness, in contrast with the whitewash, seemed like a magnet—like a room which wanted to draw him in to where the dark could consume him.

Turning away, he noticed an unexpected movement—something small and dark near the floor in one of the corners. He turned and stared into the darkness.

Then Amanda yelled, "Hey, I found something!"

Michael turned and saw Amanda standing about ten feet away, near one of the wooden walls, bending over and picking up a piece of paper.

"What is it?"

"Newspaper."

He went over to her and, without a word, plucked it quickly from her hand. To his surprise, he discovered there were actually two pieces, both newsprint, both yellowed and badly faded. The articles in each were short and the first appeared incomplete. Forgetting for a moment about the strange dark shape, he read the articles twice.

***Boyne City Eagle*—Monday, June 20, 1955**
Religious Group Disbanded in Raid—3 Dead, 2 Missing
BOYNE CITY, MI—A religious society, which some local residents refer to as the New Moon Society, begun by Dr. Sylvia Woulfe of 5444 Pleasant Valley Road, was raided by local law enforcement authorities and a volunteer deputy contingent early Sunday morning. Killed in the raid were Alfred H. Parsons, Henry Goldsmith, and George Montgomery. Six of the society's members and two sheriff's deputies were wounded and taken to Petoskey-Harbor General Hospital. Missing and presumed dead are Dr. Sylvia Woulfe and Warren Halstead, son of Boyne City mayor, Franklin Halstead.

Details as to the reason behind the raid are sketchy. However, one local resident, a friend of George Montgomery who wished to remain anonymous, said that several members of the religious society had murdered George Montgomery earlier in the evening and that this had sparked the raid on the society by the sheriff's department. Neither Sheriff Greg Kelly nor Mayor Halstead could be reached for comment.

The second article was slightly longer and from the same newspaper. It was dated one day later.

Death of Cult Leader Disputed
BOYNE CITY, MI—The death of Dr. Sylvia Woulfe, founder of the religious cult raided during the early hours of Sunday morning, still remains in doubt today due to the fact that no body has yet been recovered.

Sheriff Greg Kelly, contacted this morning by the *Eagle*, said, "Because the body of Ms. Woulfe has not been found, it is the opinion of the Sheriff's department that she escaped. State authorities have been contacted regarding her disappearance and a warrant issued for her immediate apprehension."

> Jeff Wainwright, who participated as one of the volunteer deputies in the raid, said he saw Ms. Woulfe shot "at least four or five times" and that shortly after the raid claims to have seen her "lying on the ground, [and] blood everywhere." Mr. Wainwright went on to say that "...she [Ms. Woulfe] was dead and that's all there is to it." Sheriff Kelly declined to comment on Mr. Wainwright's account, saying only that "a full investigation is in progress." Deputy Jason Black, alleged by Mr. Wainwright to have been the one to have shot Sylvia Woulfe, also refused comment.

"So . . . what do they say?" Amanda asked.

"Nothing." He ignored his sister's scowl and, carefully folding the news articles, put them in his pocket.

"Ready to go find Mom and Dad?" he said.

"Guess so," she said, then suddenly brightened, "Yeah! Let's go see the bedrooms!"

Racing each other for the stairs, they were halfway there when they were suddenly startled by a strange noise behind them which caused them to stop. The sound, like a motor starting up under the floor, continued for about fifteen seconds before ending abruptly with a loud double bang—similar to someone pounding on a door in an attempt to be let in.

"Just a sump pump," he whispered, initially feeling foolish for whispering but for some reason feeling right about it just the same.

If there's an operating sump down here, then those floor drains weren't designed for any water problem.

As a result, he tried to think of perhaps another explanation for the existence of the strange floor drains. Instead, all he could see was the picture of the killing room at his uncle's ranch in Texas . . . of the blood getting deeper and deeper across the floor . . . threatening eventually to engulf them all.

4

Michael and his sister hurried to the second floor where Alan, Sam and Mary were presently descending from the third-story attic. Michael and Amanda joined them in the hallway.

"There, now about the only thing you haven't seen is the basement," Mary said. Michael, however, chose to tune her out as she droned on about how they could fix up the basement into work and recreation rooms.

"Where you guys been?" Sam asked.

Michael felt his headache, absent since they'd arrived, suddenly return. It once again pressed in on his skull as if this time it was actually trying to squeeze its way into the center of his brain. His mother stared at him, her face wrinkling and compacting into a look of concern as she waited for an answer.

"We were in the basement," Amanda answered, to Michael's relief.

"You've been down there this entire time?" She looked first at Amanda, then turned back to him. He tried to smile—more in an attempt to mask his pain than as a response to her inquiry. In the next moment, however, her facial expression went blank and she turned toward the stairs, intent with renewed focus upon the house once again.

The relentless pounding in Michael's head continued.

"Yeah, we—" Amanda began, but their mother was already descending the stairs, alternately taking a step and looking back at them. "We looked around for a while. It's kind of neat," she finished.

His mother looked at him again, but Michael had little room for any concern other than the incessant pain attempting to drill itself into the center of his brain.

Mary and Alan were now halfway down the stairway. He was conscious of his father's conversation with the real estate agent but had been unable to actively follow it. Even though he didn't want to, a part of him still struggled to hear it though. The previously unwelcome effort to concentrate on listening unfortunately only increased the tightening pressure in his head.

". . . 5350 square feet . . . natural gas heat—one of the main pipelines runs just beyond the lilac hedge . . ."

As Sam disappeared around the landing, Michael heard his father and the realtor downstairs talking about insulation and R-values . . . when finally the pain eased as if a pressure relief valve had suddenly been opened on his head. As Amanda went downstairs, he closed his eyes.

What's wrong with me? Never had a headache like this before . . . what the hell's going on?

(Wake up time Michael! Time to face it—it's the house, don't you see? Can't you feel it?)

Give me a break will you? That's utter crap and you know it!

(So what are those drains for? Or how about that door? A real piece of work that! And then that thing you saw in the corner . . .)

Inside his mind he laughed at himself and instead of attempting to stop it, he let it go—allowing his internal conversation to dispel the last of his headache.

Slowly, he opened his eyes and started downstairs. He took a left at the bottom, passing the stairs leading to the side entrance and ultimately the basement, and entered the kitchen where Mary and his parents were still deep in conversation. Through an oak doorway, he saw Amanda in the dining room, looking at the backyard through a lead-paned window.

"Well, I'll leave you two here to talk it over," Mary said and turned to go. When she saw Michael, she hesitated before smiling, then walked past him to the stairs. "Take your time!" she called and then was quickly down the stairs and outside. The screen door shut behind her, a broken spring causing it to bang with a loud clap. Michael edged his way farther into the kitchen where Amanda was now standing in the doorway which led to the dining room. Alan was leaning against the metal kitchen sink staring out the window. Sam moved beside him and put her hand on his shoulder.

"So, what do you think?" she asked, her face turned towards the afternoon sunlight. Her voice was calm—barely expectant—almost drowsy.

Mom's already made up her mind—she wants it—and she's turning on all the charm to get it. Now it's up to Dad . . .

but he hasn't gone down into the basement yet. Go down in the basement, Dad, go down and then you'll see—you'll feel *it—you'll . . .*

His stomach suddenly began turning upon itself, spinning and rolling.

"I don't know," Alan began, "I guess I'd still like to go down and look in the basement yet."

Yes! Do it, Dad, do it!

Michael's headache began knocking again, impatient to be let back in, angry perhaps at having been shut out.

"Well, sure, of course," Sam said. "But what do you think about it so far? You must have an opinion by *now.*" She followed him as he turned from the sink and walked in the direction of the stairs which led to the basement.

Michael turned in front of them.

"It's a big house—" his father said behind him.

"I know, but just think of all the room we'll have! We'll both be able to have our own offices—you can even set up a work room in the basement."

"I suppose . . . but it's old, Sam, almost a hundred—"

Michael reached the stairs and started down.

"And did you see those windows in the dining room? Did you *see* them, Alan? Leaded, and the glass is original; you can still see the air bubbles in them—that's how you can tell they're the real thing."

Michael was now at the side door and put his hand on the knob. His mother and father had reached the stairs; then he was outside, bathing in the fresh air, feeling the sun warming his face. Behind him he heard his parents stop on the landing. His father was talking.

"I guess what I feel is that it's too good to be true. I keep asking myself—'What's the catch?' For the size and quality of this house, not to mention the hundred and twenty acres—why only a hundred and sixty thousand? There's got to be something else . . . something we haven't found out about yet."

. . . it's the killing room in the basement Dad, where the blood stands so deep you need to wear boots, that's what's bothering you . . . the killing room . . . check out the drains, they're for draining off the blood you know . . . but of course

every once in a while they get clogged and then the blood just gets deeper . . . and deeper . . . and . . .

"... something someone's not telling us."

"Like what?"

"That's just it—I don't know and that's what's bothering me—I just . . ."

And then they were gone, the basement swallowing

(their souls)

the sound of their voices.

And then Michael was running out into the backyard, stopping, then gulping air like a swimmer who'd been caught in an undertow who has finally managed to break the surface and is deliciously attempting to relieve the aching pain in his lungs. He stood at the start of the garden path where Mary was standing a short distance away, staring at him.

"Hey there, Michael . . . say, you don't look too good, kind of pale . . . you feeling all right?" She began walking toward him.

Talking to the real estate agent was the last thing he felt like doing.

"I'm all right, thanks. Just needed a breath of fresh air, that's all." He still felt out of breath, as if he had been jogging.

"That's good. So, what do you think of the place?"

(the place is evil—evil waiting for them to step into its lair)

. . . the place is weird and creepy and too big and too old and too far out in the country.

"I . . . I don't know. It's pretty big," he said and, turning his back to her, walked onto the path, not pausing to stop until he'd reached the gazebo. After he sat down and had glanced back toward the yard, he realized Mary hadn't followed and was instead moving toward the patio.

As he was beginning to relax, feeling the headache fading away once again, he looked down at the hole in the middle of the gazebo floor and suddenly wished that he could stuff his mouthy little sister down into it entirely. He looked up and turned toward the house just as Amanda burst out the side door as if something were chasing her. He sat up and started out of the gazebo but before he reached the stairs he heard her shouts, not of fear, but joy.

"We're going to buy it! We're going to buy it!"

Spotting him, she ran in his direction, yelling the entire way, "We're going to buy it, Michael! We're going to buy it!"

His knees suddenly weak, he sat back down. Amanda didn't stop but ran past the gazebo, along the path and across the bridge which spanned the artificial creek bed. Back in the yard, she did cartwheels as Mary looked on, laughing and clapping.

I think my real headache is just beginning.

2

Friday Afternoon

1

Alan thought the Boyne Street Inn, sitting on the blue lap of Lake Charlevoix, looked more like a condominium than a hotel. Each room jutted out individually from those surrounding it and each sported an external balcony. Spotting a dozen sea gulls perched atop the building's red-shingled roof, they were so still he initially mistook them as part of the building's decoration.

Striding confidently from the Cherokee to the hotel, Alan smiled as Amanda did cartwheels in the grass. On their way back from the house, Amanda and her mother had talked nonstop about gardening, interior decorating and bug collecting. Excited at the opportunities offered by their new residence, Amanda hoped to greatly increase the size of her bug collection which already contained several dozen butterflies, nearly twenty beetles, half a dozen spiders and a dozen or so other insects. She had started her collection almost two years ago but the going had been slow due to their living in a suburb near Detroit.

As Amanda fell sideways out of a cartwheel to land laughing in the grass, Alan realized that for the first time in a long while he was truly happy. Although never one for rushing into things, he and Sam's relatively quick decision to buy the house felt good to him; it felt somehow *right.* He had never before seen his family so happy; everyone that is, except Michael. But hopefully, he too would come around in time.

When they entered the hotel's small but comfortable lobby, he immediately noticed a large wooden model of a clipper ship sitting on a table near the green marble expanse of the front desk. In addition, reddish-brown Oriental rugs were strategically placed to cushion their feet against the granite-slab floor, while framed photographs of local lake scenes tastefully created artificial windows in the walls.

"Hello, may I help you?" a young woman in a dark navy suit asked him. Her brass nametag read "Tammy Harris."

"Yes, Alan Sarasin—we have a reservation." He smiled at the woman, whom he thought looked to be in her early twenties—probably a temp hired on for the beginning of the busy summer season or perhaps a local home from college, majoring in liberal arts or elementary education.

As a college computer science teacher, Alan enjoyed guessing students' majors by studying the way they acted, talked and/or dressed. The hotel clerk quickly demonstrated that she was, at least, no stranger to computers as her fingers danced their way across the plastic keys faster than his eyes could follow.

As she typed, she talked, the two activities seeming to race against one another.

"Here on vacation, or just for the weekend?" she asked, following this almost immediately with, "Ah, here we go—Alan and Samantha Sarasin."

"Actually, we're going to be moving here. We just bought—or actually offered to buy—a house south of town."

"Really? That's wonderful! Whereabouts, if you don't mind my asking?" Tammy's smile was huge and sincere.

"Not in the least," Alan said and smiled. He turned just enough to notice Sam eyeing him—each eyebrow descending upon an eye until the two seemed to become one. He knew the look well. Then he turned his attention back to Tammy. "I'm sure you know it, big Victorian, sits all by itself in the country south of town on Pleasant Valley?"

"Oh *sure*, I know that place. Been a *lot* of people out there."

"A lot? . . ."

"Lot of owners I mean." Her smile wilted and then disappeared. "It's sorta got a reputation."

"Oh? What kind?"

Her eyes dropped. At the same time, a woman who had previously been occupying herself unnoticed in a back corner behind the counter, suddenly emerged to stand next to Tammy. She was much older than Tammy, her white hair a mass of tightly curled knots. She was also considerably shorter than her co-worker and many pounds heavier.

"Okay, I've got you down for Room two seventeen." Alan thought Tammy's voice now sounded strained.

"Did you say you're buying Woulfe House?" the older woman asked, fixing Alan with a dark, unwavering stare that made Samantha's look of a moment before now seem almost like a happy clown's face. Alan glanced at Tammy for support but she was seemingly preoccupied, studying her computer screen.

"Built by Dr. Woulfe in the early 1900s, I believe," she continued, not bothering to wait for his answer. "There's a story to that place, did you know?" Her gaze probed him, as if she could see into his mind and know immediately all of his thoughts. Meanwhile, her eyes appeared impossibly dark and yet alive and prominent in the midst of her pale, wrinkled face and white hair. Though she wore almost the same navy suit as Tammy, their similarity was severely eclipsed by their different demeanors.

Grandma from hell, Alan thought, then looked down at the counter, temporarily allowing his attention to be diverted by the swirl pattern in the marble. Nevertheless, he felt the intensity of the woman's gaze as it seemed to bore itself into the top of his head.

"No, I'm afraid we don't know any of its history. It was built by a doctor you say?" he said and looked up at the woman again. He realized he hadn't yet seen her blink.

"A doctor?" she said and her tone reminded Alan of the witch from Hansel and Gretel.

"He wasn't a *medical* doctor if that's what you're thinking. In fact, I don't know exactly *what* kind of doctor he was, but it wasn't that." she said and temporarily released him from her fixating stare as now she seemed to be searching for her own answer in the marble swirl of the counter.

A door, presumably leading to a manager's office, opened behind the counter and a man stuck his half-bald head out, "Lori, could I see you for a minute?" he said, then closed the door without waiting for an acknowledgment. Alan wondered if the woman had heard him. She was looking at him again and then, amazingly, she blinked for the first time. For some reason her gesture reminded him of a cat.

"No, he was no medical doctor, that Woulfe . . . what *he* taught was . . ." she said and her voice trailed off, as she seemed to slip into some kind of daze while Tammy quietly stood by, half-smiling, her eyes darting from Alan to the computer, then back to Alan, then finally to the counter. The computer made a noise and Tammy almost jumped to reach behind her, turn, and quickly slap a plastic room key onto the counter. The sudden noise also seemed to startle the old woman and, blinking several times in quick succession, she concluded, talking as much to herself it seemed, as to him. "What he taught wasn't the *living* . . . it was the *dying,*" she continued and while the words seemed to hang, echoing in the air, she turned and disappeared into the doorway from which she had been summoned.

Alan suddenly felt cold. He looked at Tammy again but her face was directed toward her computer. Had he heard the old woman correctly—or had he imagined it?

"Sorry about that," Tammy said. She turned and glanced up at him, her face glowing with embarrassment. "She gets a little funny like that sometimes." Tammy held out her hand, looking down as she did so. "I'll need to swipe your credit card."

What he taught wasn't the living . . . *it was the* dying. The phrase started repeating itself in his mind like the chorus of a maddening song.

"Huh? . . . oh . . . just a minute." He tried convincing himself that he must have heard her incorrectly. Then he tried—and failed—to come up with a possible alternate interpretation of what she'd said.

What he taught wasn't the living, *it was the* dying.

He pulled out his wallet and handed Tammy his Visa Gold card. Looking behind him, he noticed Sam and the kids at the opposite end of the lobby, examining a display of local craft items on the wall near the ship model. He hoped they hadn't heard the old woman.

If that's what she had even said.

(you know damn well that's what she said!)

Tammy took the card from him, her finger brushing momentarily against his.

His eyes followed her hand as she ran his card through a slot at the top of her computer keyboard. She returned the card without looking at him. "It'll just be a moment for the authorization to come back."

As they waited, Tammy raised her head and smiled at him. Alan, however, was by this time looking straight through her.

Had she really said their house's builder was a doctor of the dying? What did that *mean? Was he a mortician?*

"All set, Mr. Sarasin," Tammy interjected, breaking him free from his thoughts. "You're on the second floor, room two seventeen. Take the elevator, then a left on the second floor. May I suggest a rollaway bed?" He stared blankly at her and tried to remember what she'd said.

"Uh . . . yeah, that would be great."

"I'll have it delivered to your room within the hour. Have a nice stay, Mr. Sarasin," she said and smiled again. Instead of returning her smile, though, he turned away, looking but not actually seeing the room key in his palm.

What he taught wasn't the living . . . it was the dying . . .

2

"Can I have the room with the balcony?" Amanda asked.

They had just ordered dinner at the Pied Piper, a restaurant near their hotel. Michael thought the place looked like a restaurant trying to appear upscale, but falling seriously short. The tables and chairs were just a little too cheap, the framed wall art just a little out-of-theme and their waitress just a little too flippant.

"Good choice. That would have been my pick," Alan said.

"Well then, that's settled, easy enough," Sam said and paused. Michael saw her glance briefly at his father for a moment before continuing. "Tomorrow I'll give the movers a call and see if we can get them rolling. I should probably go back down . . . visit Grandpa . . . and Grandma . . . and pick up Ghost." Ghost was the family cat; all-white and so-called because the Patrick Swayze-Demi Moore movie of the same name had been playing when they had received her as a gift from a friend of Alan's.

"By yourself?" Alan asked, trying to sound casual, but Michael noted the alarm in his father's voice as easily as he could see his suddenly wide, searching eyes.

"Well, how else are we going to do it? Someone'll need to be there when the movers arrive. And . . . I might as well try and talk to her again," she said, and she began playing with her square napkin, folding the corner of each layer into the center, staring deeply into it as if it were a magic portal that could somehow transport her to a different time, a time when the idea of a simple visit to her mother's was not a prospect to be evaluated with caution and trepidation.

"That's what I meant; facing your mother alone may not be a good idea right now."

Michael continued to watch his mother's napkin folding while at the same time hearing his father take a drink of ice water. He watched her fastidiously turn the final corner of her napkin into the center as if what she was doing was the most important thing in the world.

"Why's Grandma so mean?" Amanda asked.

Sam looked up, holding the napkin tightly so it wouldn't unfold. "Oh, honey, she's not mean, just—extremely practical. She doesn't leave much room for her feelings. She likes to think life is just another business." She glanced down at her napkin again, delicately moved her water glass on top of it, and then took it off again. "There's black and white, and dollars and cents, and by those measurements, whatever path gets you the furthest ahead, that's the one you should follow. Every question has an answer that is more logical and more practical than the others and once you've determined which one that is, that's the path you follow, regardless of anything else . . . or whose toes you step on while getting there." Sam glanced at Amanda, then Alan.

Michael watched as his mother's napkin folding continued—realizing now what it meant. Next, she began turning up the second layer in an identical fashion to the first, though this time only folding each corner in half as far.

"So, when will you be leaving?" Alan asked.

The napkin folding suddenly stopped, but Sam didn't look up. "First thing in the morning. Better to get an early start," she said, then turned to him for a moment before recapturing her water glass.

"We won't have a vehicle," he said.

She took a drink. "You can rent one at the car dealer in town. Mary mentioned it—that Chevy dealership across from the real estate office."

Lifting her water glass again, she observed the pattern it had left behind.

Michael also regarded his mother's napkin, thinking it looked like an abstract origami piece. Then he looked at Amanda and for a moment, too brief for him to tell if it had been real or only his imagination, he thought he'd noticed Amanda's eyes flash green.

3

Friday Evening

1

"I'm going out," Michael announced and stood up. Their hotel room having been equipped with a VCR, Alan and Amanda had gone on a walk to a nearby video store earlier to rent some videos. Michael's mother was presently sitting on one of the beds, watching the TV news.

"Where are you going?"

Michael wondered if the sound of alarm in her voice was a reflection of her motherly concern or the hurt she felt at not being able to talk to him. Since she hadn't turned away from the TV when voicing the question, he decided it was probably neither.

"Thought I'd take a walk along the lake. Back in a bit." He'd gotten to the door and placed his hand on the knob before she spoke again.

"All right. Be careful. Just because this is a small town doesn't mean—"

"I'll be fine," he interrupted, then opened the door and left.

2

Outside, the air was still warm, though it had cooled enough to make the prospect of a walk an enjoyable one. From the north, sea gull cries sounded like the distant raucous of a school-yard full of children. Michael was glad to be outside—away from the hotel—away from the house.

He remembered the old woman's face from the hotel. In his mind, though, he felt that when she spoke she was speaking to him, not his father as her finger, its yellowed nail a meshwork of fine gray cracks, waved up and down in front of his face.

Woulfe House, BOY. It's called Woulfe House and don't ya be fergettin' it, ya hear?

He stopped walking and looked again in the direction of the gull sounds. Then he continued his walk and farther down the shore, he happened upon a park containing a band shell, several slides, a large swing set, a teeter-totter and a plastic sandbox shaped like a turtle. The park had not been entirely visible at first because of the city marina. Something, almost like a strange odor or unusual sound—though it was neither of these—kept his gaze fastened upon the marina and park. Fortunately, the smell of the nearby water brought forth a pleasant, clean aroma, a much-needed contrast to what he was feeling.

Then he saw him. Between two silver boat masts conspicuously framing him like the bars of a jail cell, stood the stranger. Michael's pulse quickened and the early evening air instantly felt colder. He tried to tell himself it wasn't the same man, that the distance was too great for him to be sure. However, the man stood still until, like a slow-motion movie, his arm waved outward and up. Gulls swooped, landed. The stranger was feeding them and, Michael felt certain, looking in his direction—staring, in fact, directly at him.

Michael turned briefly in the direction of the hotel. Now in shadow, its multiple jutting balconies appeared like black mouths with their bottom jaws sticking out, waiting to be fed.

Now what do I do? Follow him? Ignore him?

The first idea seemed terribly wrong and yet right at the same time.

Though it seemed only seconds before Michael faced the marina again, when he did so, as before, the stranger had vanished.

3

Michael was relieved at so far successfully having avoided the possibility of a conversation with his mother concerning the house or the move. He wanted to avoid such a conversation not because he was generally against both ideas, but because he was still unsure of just *how* he felt. The source of this uncertainty, at least in terms of the house, he couldn't specifically identify, only felt, it being instinctually-based rather than simply a list of negatives he could rattle off like a grocery list. He needed more time to think about some things.

(like last summer?)

As the sun descended to the horizon and a cool breeze arrived off the lake's shadowy orange surface, Michael, with head bowed, shuffled along the new white sidewalk before straying across the grass, moving north this time, toward the marina. The grass, already long and thick from a generous spring, felt like sheepskin and his tennis-shoe clad feet plowed furrows through it like ships racing through a heavy sea.

Reaching the lakeshore where it ended abruptly at a four-foot bank of piled boulders, Michael watched wind-born ripples gently float in and lap at the rocks with a kissing sound. Like the stranger, the gulls too had disappeared and but for the occasional drone of a car engine from the town behind him, it was quiet.

He stood near the water, finding comfort in the sounds of the waves and in the view of the sunset, watching the sky color deepening with interlaced bands of red and purple.

Then, in an instant and without reason, his serenity evaporated. Everything came back to him, not the memories of the events, but rather the feelings surrounding them: his girlfriend Cindy, the house, the stranger on the side of the road, the incident of last summer. As a sudden despair subsequently seeped into his body, he tried imagining what it would feel like to step forward into the water and experience the cold welcoming caress of the lake's embrace. And then, just as quickly, he was back, looking hopefully toward the sunset and admiring its beauty.

His thoughts shifted back to their new house. He didn't like it; that much was certain. Exactly *why* he didn't though was a question he couldn't quite answer yet. But he knew he felt *something*—something not altogether right about the place, and although he wasn't sure, he thought his father had felt at least some of it, too.

Then there was the question of the newspaper articles, but even more worrisome was the basement and its strange drains. The idea sparked by his memory, he knew, was nevertheless preposterous. No one would butcher livestock in the basement of a house and yet . . . why were the drains there? Was the sump pump perhaps a later addition and the drains simply never removed? That seemed a reasonable explanation, but then again, there had been an awful *lot* of drains.

Michael felt a longing for his computer. He longed for the black and white logic of it. With computers, things either worked or they didn't; and when they didn't, there was something wrong that usually could be fixed—incorrect settings, improperly seated adapter boards, incorrect hardware device drivers, loose wires—the list was endless. Usually, though, after the first one or two attempts, he inevitably found a solution. Not so however with the questions surrounding their new house. Not so with life in general, or especially in his relationship with his mother.

He began to think again about last summer and what was supposed to have been the vacation of a lifetime. Three weeks in the western United States catching the major sights—the Grand Canyon, Grand Teton, Sequoia National Park, Devil's Tower . . . Yellowstone. It was at Yellowstone, on the return segment of their loop, about halfway into their vacation, that it happened. He felt the incident had been as much Amanda's fault as his, maybe more, but his mother never saw it that way.

It was early evening of their first night at the Blue Springs campground and Amanda was bored.

"Come on, let's go exploring!" she said.

So they set off on an adventure on one of the walking trails which led away from the campground like spokes on a wheel.

Their parents, of course, provided the usual warnings—stay on the trails, don't go too far, don't stay away too long, it would be suppertime soon, etc. It was Amanda who broke the first rule and that, as they say, was all it took.

They'd walked for almost half an hour and he was thinking it was close to the time when they should be heading back when they saw it.

"Michael, look! A wild mustang!"

"That's not a horse, retard—it's a moose."

The animal must have heard them or been spooked, for almost immediately it began moving off, grazing its way back into the woods.

"Let's follow it," Amanda said.

"No way! You're crazy. Mom and Dad said—"

Without the slightest hesitation, she ignored him and took off, leaving him little choice but to follow. They tracked the moose, keeping well behind it, following it as much by sound as by sight. Michael wasn't sure how far they'd walked but it must have been farther than he would have guessed when they eventually came to the clearing. For there, right before their eyes in an open circle, surrounded by aspens and lodgepole pines, was an entire moose herd: four bulls, at least a dozen females and a half-dozen juveniles.

Not entirely unprecedented, the spectacular sight nevertheless kept them in the woods, fixated on the animals, as time slipped away unnoticed. Finally, Michael realized the growing dimness wasn't the result of passing cloud cover, but rather a lowering sun. Now genuinely concerned for their safety, they set off in the direction of the campground. Or so they thought.

Almost immediately he knew they were in trouble, as now a changed and suddenly unfamiliar landscape accompanied the growing darkness. Shadows existed where before there had been none. Colors were muted, trees and rocks and plants taking on the same uniform hue. Within minutes, he knew they were lost.

As the light rapidly faded, the wind increased and they soon heard the far-off rumblings of thunder. After some initially futile searching, they found a pile of fallen trees to take shelter under. When they were found at noon the next day by a park ranger on horseback, Amanda had already begun to display the first signs of sickness. Pneumonia was the diagnosis by the doctor in Jackson. Three days in the local hospital had been the cure.

"How could you have been so *irresponsible?*" his mother had said upon their return. During those three days of Amanda's hospitalization it seemed like she said it to him nearly every hour, like some sort of chime marking out the installments of his sentence. There was more though to the story than just the moose chase, but Michael never bothered to tell his mother—she was beyond listening to anything he had to say about it, her rhetorical questions falling upon him like the rain he and his sister had endured for more than ten hours.

His silence unfortunately only infuriated her more. He could have answered, he could have said it was Amanda who had left the trail, that it was he who had been forced to chase her into the woods . . . and he could have told her about the bear.

But he didn't.

Michael found returning from the memory difficult and when he finally did, he noticed the lake water at his feet was now a rippling black sheet like a mirror that didn't reflect but instead pulled light into itself. He thought once again about what it would feel like to simply step forward.

The coward's way out. I may be a lot of things—but I'm no coward. As someone once said—this too shall pass.

Turning, he continued his tenuous walk along the lake's edge, a sudden, unknown sense of urgency propelling him onward. It was getting darker, but this wasn't the cause of his haste. He followed the lakeshore for several hundred feet until he was forced landward by the mouth of the Boyne River whose course flowed through town, emptying itself into the lake in front of him. Right along the riverbank the grass was gone, probably trodden into dust by the feet of fishermen who lined the river's banks throughout the summer. A boy, several years younger than Michael, wearing jeans and a red shirt that for a moment reminded him of Cindy, fished from the other side of the river. Michael watched the boy make two casts with a black rod and a shiny metal bait. The boy never once looked at him.

While crossing the bridge, Michael took a moment to glance down once again into the black water, before continuing along the riverbank on the opposite side until he'd reached the lakeshore again. From the riverbank, he walked on the sidewalk, which led to the park ahead with the city marina on his left. There were only a few small boats left in the marina but he noticed that the two sailboats he had seen earlier were gone.

Am I just paranoid or what? Probably just a guy down on his luck. This isn't a big town—just a coincidence. A guy like that probably knows everybody. He sees us and we're the strangers to him. He was just curious. No harm done.

Yet even as he tried to rationalize the man's appearances, a second voice began to speak in his mind, quiet yet insistent—*Oh sure, that's right, say he's just a poor guy down on his luck, a menace to no one, just some little old guy who would never hurt anybody. Yeah, and won't you be surprised when you finally meet up with this guy in some dark alley somewhere . . .*

Michael argued with himself—this is Boyne City, there *are* no dark alleys.

. . . and pulls out this big meat cleaver and you catch a glimpse of the dried blood on the blade before it suddenly comes down on your neck . . .

Furthermore, if the guy was a murderer, he would have been locked up a long time ago.

. . . and you finally get to find out for yourself the answer to that ageless question: When your head gets cut off, for how long afterwards are you still alive?

Yeah, and where would a guy like that get a meat cleaver? He probably doesn't even have the change to buy a cup of coffee.

The "argument" ended as Michael, walking toward town, recrossed what a small plaque attached to its cement side indicated was the Water Street Bridge. Moments later, he reached the main T-intersection where the town ended at the lake's edge. He stopped on the corner and waited for the light to change, more out of habit from having lived in the city than out of any real concern for traffic. Once again, an unnatural coldness caressed his body, sweeping across his skin like water. He shivered and felt the now familiar and unwelcome sense of haste again—that he needed to get moving, to get back to the hotel. Turning around, he moved rapidly several yards up Main Street, then stopped. On the street corner a block farther up and situated diagonally from him, walked a young couple. As they strolled across Main toward Michael's side of the street, a familiar presence revealed himself behind them—the stranger. The man, now clearly looking directly at Michael, didn't move. In the fading daylight, his eyes looked as dark as cannon barrels.

Without the slightest hesitation or even a second thought, Michael marched directly up the street toward the mysterious man, intent on what he didn't know; *to confront him? Maybe. Or just to see what the man's reaction would be to his advance?* With these questions barely having been contemplated, he had his answer—the man turned and walked down the side street away from him. A moment later, he disappeared.

Driven now, Michael pursued him furiously, walking as fast as he could without actually running. Halfway up the block, he cut diagonally across Main, recklessly running in front of a black pickup which didn't slow down. He ultimately came to the corner where the stranger had stood but a few seconds before.

Michael then continued at a fast pace up the deserted side street and came to an alley that hadn't originally been visible from the corner.

So, Boyne City has dark alleys after all, he thought before a flash of olive green caught his eye—someone standing at the far end.

He turned into the alley. Between the tall brick walls, it was dark and felt even colder. For a brief moment, he felt as if he had entered another world—that he would reach the end of the alley and instead of the south business district, he would be somewhere else—a land of brick and concrete where people with eyes that could change from green to black to green again lurked behind every corner.

When he reached the end of the alley near the town's theater, he turned in both directions but saw nothing. As he veered back toward the hotel something made him turn around again. Peering into the growing dimness along the street which led out of town, he again saw the stranger, this time standing at the next corner.

Once again Michael began walking, but this time the stranger didn't move. When Michael had covered half the distance between them, a teenager on a bike suddenly whipped by him from behind, consequently stopping his breath for a moment as if a small fist had been punched down his throat. When he eventually recovered from the shock, he wasn't surprised to see that the stranger had disappeared yet again.

Nevertheless, he continued walking, noticing the large maples which grew between the sidewalk and the street, several of the trees pushing up the sidewalk plates with their bulging roots. It wasn't long though before he spotted him again. The stranger continued playing with him, always leading him onward, heading south and east. When the stranger disappeared for what would be in this encounter the last time, Michael found himself at the foot of what a faded wooden sign proclaimed to be Avalanche Mountain. Next to this, but slightly farther off the road, was another sign. The second one, metal and green with yellow letters, read: "Historical site of Sedgwick-Davey Copper Mine. In operation 1915-1928."

The nearby darkness on his left revealed a gray weathered shed which leaned awkwardly under its own weight, its broken windows protected by glass daggers. Michael renewed his search again, but this time saw no further evidence of the stranger.

From the shed came a sudden whispered sound similar to that of a snake sliding over the surface of a weathered gravestone. Out of the darkness, a single word floated . . . quiet and surreal . . . *Michael.*

4

Later, back in the hotel room, Michael said nothing about the stranger. Amanda and his mother were watching a rental movie while his father was reading a Frank Herbert novel.

Instead, Michael simply recorded the events of the last several days in his journal. It was funny, he thought, that as he wrote about seeing the house and running into the strange man, the events seemed to lose their earlier significance. Through the act of writing, his thoughts took on a new reality, a reality that in the light of black words on white paper didn't seem quite as menacing. Still, he couldn't shake the uneasiness he had felt when seeing, for the third time, the Mysterious Stranger—a name he had just given him. Furthermore, he realized that when he was downtown and seen from such a short distance as opposed to the earlier sighting of him in the park, there had been no doubt—the man had been staring directly and intently at him. Michael didn't think he would ever forget those black eyes in such vivid contrast to the bright green he remembered from the roadside.

Later that evening, lying in bed (Amanda had been given the rollaway, thank God) thoughts of the mysterious stranger continued to persist much like a bothersome mosquito buzzing around his ear.

If the man had no home, then where did he sleep? What did he do in the winter? Who was he and why did he hang around Boyne City? Was he a ghost?

He discarded this last idea almost as soon as it had formed—though he wondered briefly where it had come from. To his exasperation, he discovered he could answer none of these questions—only guess at answers—answers for the most part that on the surface seemed ridiculous. But he resolved to find out exactly who the stranger was and what connection he might have to their new house.

Is there a connection?

(But of course, Michael . . . the floor drains! Don't you see?)

Give me a break.

(Maybe it's where he took his victims? Took them into the basement, cut their throats, bled them on the floor—kept things tidy that way.)

He pushed the thoughts from his mind. He was tired of thinking about them—the house, the stranger—it was enough. Then he remembered his walk and the boy at the river, the boy in jeans and a red T-shirt and he thought once more about Cindy.

Cindy always wore jeans and preferred bright-colored t-shirts—usually tight, he remembered—and suddenly felt himself stirred by the memory of their last time alone. It was the first and only time he had ever touched her. She had surprisingly been bigger than she looked, more solid too, a heavy roundness he could not forget. It was soon after this however that he learned his family was moving to Boyne City. Once he made this announcement to her, Cindy had promptly cooled to him. Prior to this, she had promised him much during the summer ahead—that she might even let him go all the way. She had said she was tired of waiting and that she wanted him to be her first. Then, when he told her he was moving it was as if he had become invisible to her. He called her a couple of times after that, but her interest had evaporated.

That night, sleep was a long time coming and when it finally did . . . he dreamed.

4

Friday Night
Michael's First Dream

In the dream, Michael awakens. He hears water running downstairs, as if a water pipe has broken and water is gushing onto the floor. He creeps downstairs. The sound of the water stops. He goes into a back room that serves as a washing room. It is a small white room containing a white washer and dryer. Everything in the room is white. The sunlight, shining in through a single small window above a white plastic utility sink, looks muted, as if partially eclipsed. Looking down he sees the floor—white tile speckled with flecks of gold, like spilled breadcrumbs. Turning around, he sees a pool of water on the floor. The water looks black. Suddenly his shirt, jeans and socks are gone and he is wearing shorts. The floor suddenly feels cool beneath his feet—like a slab of refrigerated meat.

Stepping into the water is like wading into a heated pool. The pool is black because of its depth. Then he is immersed, swimming freely under the water without any apparent need for air. Beneath the surface, the water is as clear as pool water and full of waving green plants rising from a bottom he cannot see.

A man appears. It is the Mysterious Stranger. His canvas coat, which he still wears, doesn't appear to impede his progress within the water. The man swims toward him and he feels he must get away—get away and not let the man catch him. He swims frantically toward a surface he cannot see. Swimming for what seems hours, he rises but still cannot see the surface. Exhausted, he stops and looks behind him.

The man is gone. Michael floats alone in the water. The plants are gone and the water is a beautiful Caribbean blue. He sees the sun above. Continuing to float, he feels warm and strangely contented.

Then he is standing knee-deep in swirling surf before a white sand beach. Farther in from the beach is an entangled grove of palms and banana trees. He strides out of the water and lies on hot sand which soon bakes the water from his skin. Hearing the lap of ocean waves mingled with the distant chorus of a seagull flock, he closes his eyes.

Sensing the return of the man, he opens his eyes. He sits up and looks around the beach. It is now sunset and the air is cold. There is no one on the beach. Nevertheless, footprints in the sand lead to where he sits. The tracks come from farther down the beach, turning a few feet from him only to lead back to where they started. The tracks make two perfectly straight lines in the sand and he shivers at the sight of them and closes his eyes.

After what seems merely seconds, he opens his eyes but sees nothing. Everything is now black. The sound of the water and gulls has been replaced by a far-off screaming. The screams are singular and distinct—of men, women and children. Then he hears the roaring of some beast followed by more screams, several of which are cut off abruptly. Silence follows but does not last. He is conscious of a sound like a hundred people eating cooked, unpeeled shrimp—a crunching noise which makes him afraid. Then the screams begin again—this time louder and closer.

Now he is in a woods and it is no longer night. The light is dim because of a thick tree canopy and a dark, cloudy sky. The forest colors are muted and grayish. Behind him, he hears thunder and feels the ground shake as the beast stalks him. It is a different beast from the one on the island, although he does not understand how he knows this. Trees splinter and snap with each thunderous footstep.

Now he is above the trees, floating, watching himself running on the ground below, being chased by a tyrannosaurus-like dinosaur twice the height of the tallest tree. He runs like a gazelle while the monster takes one ponderous step after another—and quickly closes the gap between them.

Then he is back in his body and the stranger is running beside him. For awhile, they run side by side and then the stranger is gone. Although the beast is nearly upon him, Michael stops and turns. In a bright clearing, he watches the dinosaur eat the stranger in a single gulp, crunching once and swallowing

Then he is home, standing in the living room with his family around him. He tries explaining the scratches and bruises on his body to his mother. "Monsters don't exist in real life, Michael, you know that—I think you're *the only monster here."*

"But I saw it, Mom, it was real! It was after me!"

And then the dream is over.

5

June 17 • Saturday

1

In the hotel lobby, Sam grabbed a breakfast of coffee cake and orange juice.

"You don't need to do this by yourself you know," Alan said. Michael and Amanda had already said their goodbyes and gone to check out the hotel pool.

"But I think I do. If you know what I mean."

Alan stared at the plastic orange juice container in her hand, then into her eyes.

"I guess I do."

Sam stared back, more being conveyed by their silent gazes than could have ever been spoken in words.

"Just be careful, okay? Don't let her give you any crap, right?"

"You can count on it."

Alan saw the commitment in his wife's eyes and something else he had seen only a few times before in their years together—a dark strength that was almost frightening in its intensity.

"I love you Samantha Sarasin."

"And I love you Alan Sarasin."

They kissed and then she walked quickly across the lobby, opened the hotel door, and left without looking back.

2

When Sam reached the Cherokee, she hopped in with an exuberance she hadn't felt in years. A part of her, though, gently prodded that at least some of her enthusiasm was no more than an act—for her family and herself. Smart enough to know this, she was also smart enough to know that she wasn't fooling either completely.

While driving, she followed the same roads she had traveled so many times before in recent weeks—twice for interviews, twice more for house-hunting visits. The first interview, she had thought at the time, had gone poorly. But when the call came for the second, she astonished even herself with her eagerness. She understood now that it was not so much the job she had been excited about, but the chance to finally distance herself from her mother, if only physically.

Her familiarity with the drive made it easy for her mind to wander just as the road wandered in its twisting, winding path through the northern Michigan hills and valleys. As always in the case of an impending visit with her mother, she spent more time worrying and preparing for the visit than she would actually spend in her mother's presence and then she thought immediately about Kevin—always her mother's primary choice of conversation topic. It never mattered what Samantha had come to talk about; it seemed her destiny was to be forever eclipsed by the shadow of her brother—at least as perceived through her mother's eyes.

She remembered one of her more recent visits with a shudder. She had tried explaining to her mother what had happened at Ackerman, Maskin and Smith, her former employer, but it was like talking to a television set. Her mother simply ignored her, continuing instead to spew "As the World Turns Around Kevin." This time the story concerned Kevin's latest success—a glowing review in the *Detroit Times Magazine*. The magazine article indeed *had* been impressive—Kevin making the cover ("How an enterprising young dentist made it big through his own unique technique . . . blah, blah, blah")—but to hear it recanted over and over again was too much for her. The article proved an immediate success and its results positive and instantaneous—calls for appointments at Kevin's four offices soon came pouring in as if people were booking a Caribbean cruise getaway on a half-price special. Sam's mother, as expected, quickly lavished a gushing flood of maternal pride conjoined with an obvious undertow of disappointment aimed at Sam who seemed to her mother to be a failure in comparison. So it had been all their lives, as far back as she could remember.

Sam often thought of Kevin as a vase. On the outside there was beauty, refinement, class, even a sort of nobility; Kevin was a Ming of exquisite craftsmanship. But, on the inside, a view for which only she seemed to possess the requisite height to behold, the picture was altogether different. Inside, she saw a fermenting pile of refuse—a putrid mass writhing with the maggots of immorality, contempt and disrespect. And while everyone else stood in awe, admiring the beautiful exterior of the vase prominently held aloft on its pedestal of motherly pride, Sam stood alone, ready with rock in hand—able, but so far unwilling—to shatter the false image. With but one toss, she knew she could readily spill the truth into a vile mess at the feet of the worshippers.

But only, my dear Sam, if they believed you.

3

Sam arrived at her parents' house in the early afternoon. Her father surprised her by meeting her at the door, a task usually performed by Johnathan, one of the five full-time staff at the main residence.

"Samantha, hi!" he said. With that welcome he then grabbed her hand as if he were trying to drag her into the house before she could escape.

"Happy early Father's Day," she said, then, unexpectedly for them both, hugged him. He took a step back, then pulled her close, making her wince at his sudden intensity. He closed the door and together they strode into the main hall. Despite his warm greeting, Sam sensed a note of sadness in her father. Though, in her eyes, he was downcast most times on account of the subservient role he allowed himself to be cast into—this time it seemed different, deeper somehow—but then again, maybe it was just her imagination.

Sam nevertheless was thankful for the opportunity to speak with him this time free from the chains her mother normally kept him shackled in. She tried not to pity him, and tried even harder not to despise his weakness. Fortunately, most of the time it was easy—she only had to think of her own secrets which had been suppressed by the force and power that her mother wielded with such callous abandon over all those around her. To her credit, Sam thought wryly, she at least wielded it consistently—from the lowliest servant to her own daughter and husband; the exception of course, being Kevin. Kevin had always played under a different set of rules.

"Back so soon?" her father asked, his voice echoing in the huge room. "I trust everything's all right? Have you found a house?"

As they crossed the white marble floor, the smell of clean stone somehow made the room seem more real to Sam than its opulent richness. She knew the extent of the energy expended every day to keep up its appearance. The main hall alone was an open expanse rising three stories with two curving staircases which provided access to the second and third floors. The stairs were white Italian marble and twelve feet wide. For a moment, Sam saw herself as a child again, racing her brother up the staircases to see who could reach the top first. She suddenly realized she could no longer remember the number of steps it took to reach the upper floors.

"Yes to both actually. Everything's fine; and we've found the most beautiful house."

They moved across the main hall, toward the west wing and into one of the large den areas where they stopped. Her father suddenly turned to her with the same face she had seen earlier—something definitely missing from his eyes, she thought.

"I see," he began. When he continued this time, it was in an odd, neutral tone, as if relating the day's financials, "Your mother's upstairs in her office."

Sam stared at her father, as if suddenly mesmerized by the valleys and craters that now sculpted his face after so many years of self-imposed servitude. She noted his hair, though whiter, was still thick. The navy pinstripe suit he wore smelled faintly of cigar smoke, a habit he had supposedly given up four years ago. And he didn't so much stand up as hang upon himself—as if flesh and muscle were wet clay slapped upon a thin framework already bending under the strain.

She'd been hoping her mother was still at work; she had been planning on having the afternoon to prepare.

Then she remembered one of the other rare occasions when her mother had been home waiting for her—it had been when she first visited home after marrying Alan. After the diatribe about irresponsibility and reckless disregard for the family had left the walls—and herself—trembling, she had stayed away from her mother for more than a year.

Then she remembered the cat. "Ghost?"

"Never better. Took a liking right away to Wendy. She's been feeding him. Even gone to sleeping in her room at night too, as I recall." He smiled, then stared at the floor.

"Sounds like Ghost all right. I'm glad he didn't make a pest of himself."

The house seemed unnaturally quiet. She suddenly wanted to run away—right now—fly out the door, across the expanse of the ten-acre back lawn and into a particular copse of willows which grew near a pond in a remote section of the estate—her childhood secret place. It was the same place to which she'd run after the incident with Kevin.

"Not at all, of course your mother on the other hand—"

"Yes, yes I know. She wasn't thrilled with the idea."

"She demanded that I install it within a kennel."

Sam didn't have to ask any more. She knew her father hadn't stood up to Augustine. Not only that, but she also knew the real reason Ghost had stayed in Wendy's room—to hide him so her father could give the appearance that he had complied with his wife's wishes.

As she slowly began climbing the stairs to her mother's third floor office, she felt the old anger growing inside her once again.

4

"I've been driving all morning from—"

"Ah, yes, where is it you're moving to? Boyne something or other."

Augustine had pronounced it "boyne-ee."

Her mother's office was a room probably larger than most people's homes and looked like a library. Every wall but the one behind her desk was covered from floor-to-ceiling with bookcases. Everything was dark—the bookcases, the hardwood floor, her mother's colossal desk. The wood floor was stained so dark it was nearly black, though its starkness was relieved periodically by several deep-red Oriental rugs of exquisite design. A gray suit of armor, a massive halberd clutched in one metal hand, stood as perpetual guard in a corner.

As intended, Sam's gaze was drawn to the picture of her grandfather whose visage glared down at her from the wall behind the desk. It was therefore, that to stand before Augustine was to be at audience before them both.

"*Boyne* City. We've found a house. I came back to oversee the final arrangements for moving—"

"A house? That's nice." Augustine looked up from several stacks of papers strewn across the length of her desk, as if only then realizing Sam was in the room. "Kevin called an hour ago." She smiled.

Sam thought it looked like the smile of a hungry shark and steeled herself for the inevitable bite.

"He's going to be opening a fifth office in Fredericksburg. Two weeks before it opens and he's already booked four months ahead. Quite amazing, really."

Sam felt her control slipping once again. She thought she had been prepared but quickly realized she'd forgotten how well her mother played the game.

"Wow, that's something," Sam managed. "Anyway, like I was telling you," Sam continued as Augustine's gaze dropped back to the papers on her desk, "we just bought a house in the country. A beautiful Victorian, five bedrooms . . ." Sam let her voice fade away at the same time she was forming fists with her hands so strenuously that her wrists were beginning to ache.

"Kevin says they originally planned to open in late July or early August, but he was able to put pressure on the contractor and they think they can swing a July 5th opening," Augustine said as she looked up again, her Cheshire-cat smile still in place. A gold pen gleamed in her hand and made Sam think of glowing radiation. "Like I told him, those contractors, that's part of the game they play and you've got to be firm or they'll just jerk you around for as long as you're willing to hang on."

"As I was *saying*," Sam was unable to keep from emphasizing the last word and noticed her mother's eye twitch slightly, "we've managed to get our hands on a restored Victorian; I could hardly believe the price after I saw it." She forced herself to go on, as if she were a guest at someone's table trying to swallow the last chunk of something horrible, "A deal even *you* would be proud of." Having said this, she finally relaxed her hands and felt a tingle as the flow of blood resumed.

"When are you moving?" came the brusque reply. Her mother had switched tactics and Sam again felt herself losing ground, being surrounded, as if the source of the final, killing blow lurked somewhere in the shadows of her mother's office. She valiantly tried to match her mother's icy tone.

"Immediately. That's why I came down. The movers are going to get the last of our stuff together and be up to Boyne City the beginning of next week."

Augustine's pen was now moving methodically up and down in her hand—the gold plating seemingly winking at Sam.

"Kevin and Jennifer are taking a vacation—did you know? Three weeks to Australia once the new office gets off to a good start as I've no doubt it will." As the pen bobbed up and down Sam felt herself mesmerized by it. "Last weekend he bought Jennifer a new car to celebrate. One of those new Jaguars, silver I think, maybe white, I don't know, but he just went out and bought it, just like that." She looked up at this last remark and Sam could still feel the smile even though it was no longer there, like a familiar shape hidden beneath a blanket.

Sam watched as the gold pen now moved from her mother's right hand to her left.

"With my new job, I don't know if we'll have a chance to get down here too often for awhile—"

"Ah, yes, what's this new job you're taking, Accountant . . . or something? . . ."

"Office Manager." Sam stood up. "Why don't you ever *listen* to me?"

"Excuse me?" Augustine looked up, the smile now not even a memory. "A bit testy today are we? I still don't understand why you're even leaving that other—"

Now it was Sam's turn to interrupt, her voice rising with each word like a roller coaster on the downside of a big climb, "I *told* you already, why can't you understand? You weren't listening then and you aren't listening now." Sam took a step back.

Augustine looked down at her desk, then put her pen down carefully as if it had suddenly become a fragile piece of art. Sam watched it roll to the edge of the desk and fall off without a sound.

"You could have just said no. If you were actually *capable*, there would have been no need for you to acquiesce in such a situation."

Her mother folded her hands as if about to pray.

Sam was incensed. She had left her former employer because of the sexual advances that had been made toward her by one of its partners, advances which, instead of ignoring, she had brought to the attention of the entire firm.

"How *dare* you, how can you possibly sit there and spout such filthy . . . *crap?*"

Augustine rushed up out of her chair, planting her hands firmly on the huge desk. When she spoke, her words came out clear and slow—with no trace of the anger surely lurking beneath the surface—but full of the command she was used to. It was the tone she used whenever she expected to be unquestionably obeyed.

"Watch your mouth dear—I'm still your mother. I don't need to listen to that kind of disrespect. All my life I've worked—"

"Oh *please . . . mother,*" Sam began, spitting out the last word, making it sound like something rotten. "Spare me the I've-always-worked-so-hard-so-you-could-live-nice *bullshit!* I've heard it enough. You do what you do for *you*—not for me. And certainly not for Dad. And no, not even for Kevin. It's always been just *you, you, you . . .* so why don't you just give us a break and admit it for once?" Sam realized she had been waving her arms and forced herself to drop them to her sides.

Augustine glared at Samantha as if the housekeeper had just told her she could go clean her own damn toilets from now on. But, just as suddenly as the rage was there it was gone, replaced by her practiced mask of civility. She looked down again at the papers on her desk. "I think I've heard enough. If you cannot treat me with so much as common respect, I think—"

"*I* think it's time to go. You've made it more than obvious there's no getting through that thick head of yours." Sam turned and marched toward the door.

"I think you can find your own way out, yes?"

Sam could sense the return of her mother's leering smile. She stopped, remained facing the door, her back still to her mother.

"Your concern is so touching, *mother,*" she said, and abruptly left.

6

1

After his mother had left, Michael hoped he would be able to have some quiet time alone. Within two hours of her departure, though, his father had rented a car, convinced their real-estate agent to loan him the key to Woulfe House and purchased several bags of cleaning supplies at the local grocery store.

The drive to the house was quiet and uneventful. When they crested the final hill, Michael, upon seeing the tree again, experienced a sudden, sharp pain in his head.

Not again.

His prayer seemed to help this time, for as quick as it had come the pain faded. By the time they pulled into the driveway, the pain had gone.

As he examined again the front of the house with its yawning porch and bulbous bay windows, Michael was reminded of the face of some Cubist beast.

All right, here we go again. Try any funny stuff though and I'll be ready. You're just a house and pretty soon you're going to be our house. Maybe you don't like that much, maybe you don't even like people that much, but this is the way it's going to be. Mess with me or my family and I can burn your rotted carcass to the ground.

It never occurred to Michael as strange that he had suddenly begun thinking of their new house as being alive.

2

At the house, they divided up the chores: Alan would work on the first floor, mainly in the kitchen; Amanda would take the second floor and clean the bedrooms and bathroom; Michael was assigned the basement.

Michael began his assignment by sweeping the cement floor with a broom he found leaning in one of the corners. The old broom's deteriorating bristles, however, unfortunately left behind as much debris as they swept up. As he worked, he consciously avoided the floor drains, telling himself he didn't want to accidentally sweep any dirt into them.

From upstairs, he heard Amanda singing. Sweeping with fast, short strokes, he attempted to drown her out. Without a dustpan though, he was forced to sweep the dirt into piles; he had already left half a dozen.

For Michael, the reality of what the future would hold for him, for all of them for that matter, was becoming more apparent with each passing minute. It was based in the hardening reality that this strange house that made him uncomfortable for reasons he couldn't quite explain, was soon going to be their new home. He would soon be living in it, eating in it—sleeping in it.

He stopped sweeping and leaned on the broom handle. His gaze sought out one of the floor drains.

Okay, good joke, ha ha. But it's all over now, right? We can we go back home now, right? Right?

Then he heard a noise—like a whisper or the soft rustle a dried leaf might make sliding across cement. The sound, he realized, had come from the floor drain directly in front of him.

No, not a joke, more like a nightmare—a nightmare only just getting underway. Hang onto your seats, ladies and gentlemen, it's gonna be a hell of a ride.

After several minutes waiting for the sound to repeat itself, he forced himself to turn his back on the drain and finish sweeping. A few minutes later, he stopped to survey what he had accomplished while at the same time consciously avoiding any further glances toward the floor drains.

All right, this is ridiculous. These things were never used for draining off blood and there isn't anything inside them that could have made a noise like I thought I'd heard. So let's just pry one of these suckers up and see what we've got. Once I prove to myself that it's nothing but an empty pipe in the floor, everything will be fine.

He knew he was treating himself like a child, but it didn't bother him; he even thought he deserved it. Crouching, he set the broom down beside himself and tried to pry up one of the drain covers. No success. In one of the piles of dirt he had swept up, he found a broken stick a little smaller than a pencil. He inserted this splinter into one of the drain holes and lifted the cover just far enough to be able to get a finger underneath the lip and pull it free.

Upstairs, Amanda stopped singing.

He put his hand on the cement floor and felt its coolness. Then he touched the drain cover. It was colder than the cement. Much colder.

When he put his hand over the exposed drainpipe, an icy column of air slid between his spread fingers, caressing them like the draft from a freezer.

(That's what death feels like Michael. You're feeling the caress of death that's come to shake your hand, a sort of how-do-ya-do-might-as-well-get-acquainted-since-we're-going-to-be-seeing-a-lot-of-each-other kind of thing.)

Grabbing the drain cover again, he tried putting it back in place. The cover, however, didn't quite sit all the way down, so he used the broom handle to slide it flush. He tried putting the broom back in the corner but it fell over. He ignored it and left the basement, taking the stairs two at a time.

3

Michael found Amanda in the upstairs bathroom where she was cleaning the bathtub with a bottle of 409 Professional that looked like grape soda. Other cleaners were scattered nearby, along with several sponges and brushes. The air reeked of bleach.

"Looks like *you're* having fun," he said from the doorway.

Amanda stopped scrubbing for a moment and sat down on the edge of the tub with a sigh. She frowned and wiped her brow with her forearm. "So how's the basement? Find any ghosts yet?" She smiled.

"Not quite. I did find something pretty interesting, though."

"Oh?" She put her brush down and grasped the sides of the tub.

Michael thought she was trying hard not to sound interested.

He paused a moment for effect, making sure her curiosity was fully engaged before he continued.

"Want to see it?" he said, asking the question with hopefully enough nonchalance to mask his own fear, but without, he hoped, enough detachment to dampen her curiosity.

She crossed her arms and stared down at her feet. "What is it?"

"Come down and find out for yourself," he said, then turned and left, not waiting to see if she would follow. He knew she would.

4

Downstairs, Michael pried the cover back up on the drain he had opened previously.

"Put your hand over it."

"Why?" She looked at him with narrowed eyes and then crossed her arms.

"It's not a trick. In fact I wish it was, but the truth is I don't know how to explain it. Just hold your hand over it and you'll understand."

"I don't know—"

"It's not going to hurt you."

She walked over to the drain and stared into it. Then she looked back at him but he couldn't interpret her expression. Turning her attention to the drain, she crouched and quickly waved her hand over the pipe. At the first sensation, she snatched her hand back. A second later though, she was holding her hand fully over the pipe, joyously raising it up and down within the rising column of cold.

"Neat!"

"So where's the cold coming from, Miss Smarty?"

He crouched down beside her. She frowned, her hand still held over the pipe.

"Underground. When you go underground it gets colder, right?"

"Yeah, but not *this* cold."

"Well . . . what's your explanation then?"

"That's my problem . . . I don't have one."

7

June 19 • Monday

1

Michael saw the Mysterious Stranger again on Sunday.

Michael, his sister and father had spent the day exploring Boyne City and its surrounding communities, swimming at the hotel pool and generally taking it easy. They had not visited the house. However, it was while driving back into town that Michael spotted him. This time, the stranger was in the cemetery, standing between one of the few mausoleums and a gravestone canted so severely it appeared in danger of toppling over. As before, the stranger appeared to stare directly at him; his green eyes unmistakable.

Now, in the hotel room, they were getting ready to go to the bank and begin the mortgage paperwork.

"Dad?" Michael asked.

"Yes, Michael?" Alan was sitting at the desk reading *Information Week.*

Michael leaned forward on the edge of the bed, then sat up and walked over to the entertainment center. Leafing through the cable TV guide he said, "Can I go to the library instead?"

He sensed his father looking at him.

"Sounds like an excellent idea. Amanda can go with you too."

Great, just what I need, little miss tag-along of the never-ending mouth.

That settled, Alan closed his magazine, stood up, stretched his arms above his head and yawned silently. He dropped his arms and looked at his watch.

"Well, hop to it then; I'm supposed to be down at the bank in thirty minutes."

"Anything beats sitting around here." Michael quickly threw the guide down and started to search for his shoes.

"Just don't expect *too* much. This isn't Farmington Hills. They're probably not going to have much."

"I'll *go,*" Michael said.

2

"Do you even know where the library is?" Alan asked as they were leaving the hotel.

"Of course," Michael said. "We saw it yesterday. From downtown you just take that street between the drugstore and hardware store."

His father looked at him for a moment and Michael wondered what he was thinking.

"All right. We'll split up at the intersection and I'll meet you back at the hotel, okay?"

"Sure."

"And keep an eye on your sister, all right?"

Michael gave his father a hard stare but he pretended not to notice.

"Oh, Dad," Amanda said.

"Don't worry, I will," Michael said with as much ice as he could put into the words. It apparently worked, for his father turned around.

"I didn't mean . . . I mean, that's not what I—"

"It's okay, Dad. I understand."

Alan was staring at him and Michael could see he wanted to say more. He was glad, though, when he didn't.

3

Fifteen minutes later, they reached the main intersection in town. Michael noticed it was a few degrees cooler than it had been the last couple of days. Nevertheless, the seagulls were still maintaining their normal rowdy presence near the lake and could still be heard from the middle of town.

Standing at the intersection, Michael paused briefly to reflect on his last experience, when he had seen the stranger in this same place. He realized they would even be traversing part of the same route he had previously used to follow him. So, naturally, Michael couldn't help but take a moment to scan the street corners and sidewalks, but of course there was no sign of him.

"All right, I'll see you two later. I have no idea how long this is going to take, so—"

"Don't *worry*, Dad."

"I know, I know," Alan said and handed Michael the room key. Again he hesitated, but only briefly, then left.

As his father headed across the street, Michael set off quickly in the direction of the library.

4

Her brother took off like someone was chasing him and soon Amanda found herself having to jog to keep up.

"Slow down, will ya? Geez, I'm running just to keep up," she complained as they passed the entrance to the alley behind Packard Drugs—the same alley Michael had followed in his chase of the stranger two days before.

Staying ahead of her, Michael continued to say nothing, only further increased his pace to reach the next corner. Amanda finally caught up with him. They waited patiently for several cars to pass before crossing but as Michael strode off the curb, he broke into a half-run which lasted until he'd reached the other side of the street.

"Come on, Michael, slow down!"

"Will you just *come on!*" he said, no longer bothering to even look behind him. She scowled at his back.

"Fine, run all the way there if you want, but I'm walking." Having concluded her simple act of defiance, Amanda slowed her pace to a leisurely walk. She could see the library now, a tall brick building standing across from what looked like an elementary schoolyard. She wondered if this was the school she would be going to in the fall. Despite this new distraction she remained determined to keep her pace steady—and of course, slow.

Michael was already at the library and bounding up the front steps as she neared the end of the second block. Stopping on the corner, she waited for a slow-moving car to pass. There actually would have been no real danger in crossing, but she purposely decided to wait so as to further increase the distance between herself and Michael. As the car slid by, she noticed a missing front hubcap and several dents in the driver's-side door. Belatedly, she also noticed that the driver, a large woman with tangled black hair, had waved to her.

After the car passed, she looked again toward the library but now Michael was gone.

5

From the outside, the library appeared to be much bigger than Michael had expected. It might even have been called imposing, at least by small-town standards. The brick building was graced with ornate cement trim on the front, around the windows, and along the roofline. In addition, large cement columns surrounded a magnificent set of double front doors. To Michael, the building's architecture seemed more suggestive of a courthouse or other government structure such as a post office or city hall. Furthermore, although the building appeared to contain only one story, it seemed to possess the height of a two-story structure.

He climbed a short flight of cement steps to the wooden front doors. Pulling on one of the heavy doors, an incredible ear-piercing screech announced his presence to whomever might reside inside, and at that same moment his perception changed; he no longer felt he was entering a government building, but rather a haunted castle.

And then, as if to accentuate the aural atmosphere, the door violently banged shut behind him, its weak spring slapping twice against the door's top. Immediately, the odor assaulted him—the musty, yet dry smell of a building that had been around for many years. Directly in front of him was another set of stairs—wooden and steep. Climbing them produced a series of loud creaks that rose with him, further announcing his arrival to the librarian on duty.

The nameplate on the desk, which greeted his arrival at the top of the stairs, proclaimed the librarian to be a Mr. Tedric Bentley. Michael's first impression was that Mr. Bentley's age probably matched that of the building.

The librarian's stark white hair was in sharp contrast to the weathered, black skin of his face. Watching him at first from a distance—for the librarian didn't immediately raise his head from the task he was busily concentrating on—Michael was initially put off by the man's apparent indifference to his presence. And so, he searched the shadows between the towering cases of books for another potential source of help, but saw no one. Then he wondered if perhaps the old man was hard of hearing. And so, as he approached the desk, Michael cleared his throat.

His initial impression of the librarian's aloofness was dispelled however when the man, his head still bowed and his hands working diligently at something on his desk, spoke without looking up.

"This darn screw came out of my glasses again and I . . . just . . . about . . . got the little bastard back in there." His face twisted and bunched as if his will alone could accomplish the task. The man reminded Michael of a little black elf, and so he tried to see exactly what it was he was working on, but the librarian was hunched too closely over his work.

"There! That should do it!" he proudly exclaimed. With an obvious sense of satisfaction, he raised his head triumphantly and proceeded to slide a pair of silver wire-framed glasses onto a bulbous nose. He looked at Michael for the first time. "Now then, what can I help you with?"

Michael felt the man examining him through his recently repaired spectacles. However, instead of feeling uncomfortable, he felt strangely at ease.

"Say, I don't quite remember seeing the likes of you in here before. Maybe it's a library card you be coming after?"

"Well. Actually, I—"

"Because if you be wanting to check anything out, you're gonna need a card to check 'em out with, now aren't ya? Am I right, or am I right?" he said.

The old man continued studying him, waiting for a response.

"You're absolutely right, sir." Michael by now had edged his way a half-step closer to the desk.

"Well then, come on over and we'll see if we can't fix ya right up."

He went over to the librarian's desk where the librarian pushed a small yellow index card and pen across the dark wood to him. Michael hadn't seen where the items had come from.

"All you do is fill out this little application, and we can get you a card. I'll be needing your name, address, age if you want—but if you be less than sixteen I'll need to have you take it home so's one of your parents can co-sign."

"I'm only fifteen," Michael said and picked up the pen which felt surprisingly warm and wrote his name on the card.

"Oh, well's in that case you might as well take it on home then and, like I said, just get one of your parents to sign it at the bottom there and we'll be all set." Michael's disappointment must have shown on his face, because the librarian continued, "But don't you worry now, cause if you's gotta have something right today, that's no problem either. I can let you have up to three things today to last you until you bring back the application for your card."

"Okay, thanks. I guess I'll look around then." Michael picked up the application form and moved in the direction of what he thought was the reference and general non-fiction area. As he did, a familiar screech came from the front door followed by the loud protestations of the wooden stairs. Without turning around, he listened to Tedric's greeting.

"Well, hello there, young lady. I must say I'm not familiar with your pretty face neither. How can I help you?"

Michael, now several yards from the desk, turned to look at his sister.

Amanda was standing a few feet in front of the librarian, hands clasped in front of her. "I'm here with my brother," she said as she glanced to her right, spotted Michael and quickly hurried over to him. However Michael turned away just before she reached him, continuing on his way to investigate a small island bookcase filled with what looked like dictionaries, encyclopedias and other reference books. When he heard the footsteps of the librarian following them, he looked behind him to see Tedric carrying a yellow card prominently in front of himself like a determined autograph seeker.

"Here you go, little lady, you'll be needing this. I already explained to your brother what you need to do with it. But you can check out up to three items today, okay?"

"All right," Amanda said and snatched the card. She then moved toward the other side of the library where Michael had spotted a children's and young adult's section in a small alcove area. Leaving her there to browse, he turned back to the island bookcase and began to scan the titles. A minute had passed when he sensed the presence of Tedric standing nearby, watching him.

"Anything I can help you find, young man?"

Michael found himself suddenly annoyed at the man's friendliness, but then became sidetracked when he realized what he was looking for wasn't going to be found in an encyclopedia. Nevertheless, a part of him was reluctant to show a stranger the news articles he had found in their basement. What if the librarian had been a part of it? Or, maybe the librarian would laugh at his interest in what may have been nothing more than a bunch of crazy loons chanting around a bonfire.

(Except that people had died. A lot of people. And did anyone ever find out what happened to Sylvia Woulfe? Maybe she haunts that dear little house you'll soon be moving into, eh?)

Michael quickly forgot his annoyance and found himself suddenly liking the librarian; there was a sense of trustworthiness about him. He knew he was going to need some friends sooner or later and a librarian would be as good as any and maybe even better than most.

"Maybe you can. I have these newspaper clippings I found." He fumbled with his billfold, almost dropping it, then extracted and carefully unfolded the two newspaper articles. For a moment, he held them back, wondering again if he was doing the right thing. So when he ultimately decided to hand them to the librarian it was as if he were handing over a fragile and rare antique document. "Know anything about these?"

With a blank expression, Tedric carefully read the articles detailing the raid on the cult. Waiting for his response, Michael looked at the back of the man's hands where tufts of white hair had formed patterns like drifted snow. Turning back to the reference books as a distraction, he began reading their titles again but without actually registering the names.

"So, what's your interest in the Woulfe family?" the librarian inquired. The tone of his voice was unlike that which Michael had heard previously—mournful almost—as if speaking of a great tragedy.

"We're buying their house," Michael replied, trying to interpret as best he could what the librarian was thinking, but Tedric kept his eyes downcast, staring at the articles in his hands as if he were still reading them.

"I see," he said, in the same lifeless, yet seemingly almost concerned tone.

"You wouldn't happen to have any old copies of newspapers from 1955?"

Tedric seemed to return from his trance and looked up at Michael.

"Yes . . . sure," he said slowly, his voice then gathering momentum like a truck attempting to gain speed on an uphill grade. "We keep them downstairs. And, yes, I know a little bit about the Woulfes," he said, talking again in the same loud and friendly voice he had used when Michael first entered the library. "This cult . . . and the raid . . . big news for a small town back in fifty-five. But you won't find much in the newspapers. Hushed up pretty good it was."

Tedric glanced at the articles again and now Michael was afraid he wasn't going to give them back to him. He wanted to reach out and grab them but the librarian's tone kept him still.

"Sheriff put a clamp on the newspaper after these here articles were published. It was something people didn't want to talk about, let alone splash across the town paper for all the world to see. No sir, Sheriff put a clamp on them newspaper folks right quick after that. Then there was nothing left but the whisperings and the gossip. The ol' grapevine was still healthy and hearty back then and so the news got round just the same—o' course as it made the rounds, it got embellished quite a bit along the route." Tedric briefly peeked up at him for a moment to see if he still had his attention before going on. "Fact is, story got so twisted, it got to the point I don't think anybody, 'cept maybe the ones that were there of course, ever *really* knew what happened that night."

Tedric looked up again and this time as their gazes locked, Michael sensed the presence of something else in Tedric's small, black eyes.

Fear? Nostalgia? Regret? So what was it all about then? Will I be able to find out? Do I even want to?

"Come on, I'll take you downstairs. I have something better than the papers."

His interest piqued, Michael followed Tedric down a narrow side staircase. As they descended, the odor of dust and antiquity grew stronger. Having reached the basement, Tedric flipped a switch, turning on a single set of fluorescent lights on the ceiling of a small room. Michael was immediately reminded of Woulfe House and couldn't help but make a quick visual scan of the floor, looking for floor drains. Huge bookcases to their left and right served as makeshift walls. And at the corners of the room, the open spaces between the cases appeared to lead into still other areas of the basement shrouded in darkness.

Tedric walked directly over to a row of four-drawer file cabinets that lined the back wall. Crouching, he pulled open one of the bottom drawers.

"This here's my private collection," he said; then he turned slowly back to Michael, and lowered his voice. "I don't show it to just no one, mind you."

"Oh." Michael didn't know what to say. "I really appreciate it."

As Tedric flipped through numerous file folders in the over-stuffed drawer, Michael moved closer.

"I've got articles, letters, writings and what have you on all the people around here." Michael could see people's names carefully handprinted on the folder tabs. "Anybody that was somebody I've got a folder on 'em in here. News stories, pictures, whatever I could, got put in their folder. Some of this stuff goes back a long ways, early 1900s."

"You collected all this yourself?"

Tedric laughed. "Well, not really. Actually, it was my mom that started it. After I started working here, in 1962 that was, I brought it all from home and assembled it here, adding to it along the way, best I could."

With renewed interest, Michael surveyed the row of file cabinets. There were at least a dozen.

"You've got stuff on the Woulfes?"

"As I recall, I believe my mom took a special interest in the father." Tedric stopped his search and pulled out a folder labeled WOULFE. "Here we go." Opening the folder, he began handing things to Michael.

The first was a newspaper clipping from the *Boyne City Eagle*. It was dated January 10, 1918:

> BOYNE CITY, MI—Dr. Robert Benjamin Woulfe, formerly of Ratingen, Germany and Miss Marion Albany of Boyne City announce their engagement. A small wedding ceremony has been planned for July 30.
>
> The bride-to-be is the daughter of Mr. and Mrs. Jack Albany of Harbor Springs. Jack Albany owns and operates the Boyne City General Store on south Water Street. Miss Albany is employed as a part-time assistant librarian at the Boyne City Public Library.
>
> Dr. Woulfe was previously Professor of Special Religious Studies at Gerhard-Mercator University in Duisburg where he taught and performed research in Asian and Middle Eastern religions for six years. Dr. Woulfe is currently pursuing individual research studies at his residence south of Boyne City.

Tedric then handed him another article, also from the *Eagle*. This one was dated December 9, 1920. It was badly faded and ripped nearly in half.

> BOYNE CITY, MI—With great joy, Dr. and Mrs. Robert Benjamin Woulfe announce the birth of their daughter, Sylvia Marion Woulfe, on Tuesday, December 7, 1920.

The next article was dated six days later—December 13, 1920—and was in better condition.

> **OBITUARIES**
> *Marion Albany, 35*
> Marion Albany, wife of Dr. Robert Benjamin Woulfe of Boyne City, died December 11, 1920 from complications resulting from childbirth. A memorial service will be held at St. Mary's Church in Boyne City on December 16.

The remaining article, source unknown, was not printed in English. A piece of notebook paper however was attached to the clipping with a rusty paper clip. Handwritten on the paper was what appeared to be a partial translation. The article was dated September 2, 1903, while the note had August 16, 1925 printed at the top. Michael read the translation, finding it the most interesting piece of the group:

> Translation of a newspaper article appearing in the Duisburg Nachrichten as sent to me by Gustav Jensen.
>
> Ratingen, Germany. Accused of practicing the black arts and linking him to the strange mutilation deaths of several livestock near his country home, Dr. Robert Benjamin Woulfe has been driven from his estate by an angry coalition of neighbors. Likewise shunned by his family, Dr. Woulfe left directly for the University where he has been teaching religious studies for the past six years. There, he announced the resignation of his post and his immediate departure for the

> Netherlands and possible eventual passage to the United States.
>
> A special council of the town's leaders decreed the special verdict against Dr. Woulfe earlier in the week based on evidence and protestations from several of

Michael found it odd that the translation ended so abruptly. He glanced over to look at Tedric, but the man wouldn't meet his eyes. He handed the articles back, watching wordlessly as Tedric carefully replaced them in the file. Michael's head was suddenly bursting with questions—questions he was not entirely sure he wanted answers to.

Black arts? Strange mutilation deaths of livestock? What the hell was this guy into, anyway? So if he got driven out of Germany and came here, what happened then?

But uncover such answers, he resolved to do.

(Yeah, and then what, Sherlock? By then you'll be all moved in comfy cozy—living in the devil-cult house.)

Michael had no idea where to start.

(Just do me one favor though, will you? Stop pretending you don't know what all those drains are for. You did *catch that, right? Livestock Mutilation Deaths?)*

With Michael's new resolve, they returned upstairs where he thanked Tedric for his help, gathered up Amanda, and left the library.

As he walked, he watched the sidewalk pass under his feet and kept imagining that every cement square was suddenly fitted with a large, black drain in its center like a gaping mouth, wanting to engulf him.

8

June 20 & 21
Tuesday & Wednesday

1

"Mommy's home! And she brought Ghost!" Amanda's joyous squeal resonated throughout their hotel room.

Samantha had slipped in quietly during the night, not wishing to wake the children and had likewise slipped their cat in as well, no doubt against hotel policy. Upon her return, Alan found himself only able to whisper a few words of greeting and so as yet had been unable to accurately assess her current emotional health. Upon waking, however, her mood became immediately apparent. After a few perfunctory greetings, she began to act like a prisoner getting ready to work on a chain gang. Alan watched her, knowing the cause of her mood, and feeling helpless at the same time.

Their morning routines successfully completed in the midst of an uneasy silence, they left the room together and took the elevator to the lobby. From there, they headed down a long hallway in the direction of the hotel restaurant. As they walked, Alan found himself becoming angry.

I wonder what she said this time? Must have been pretty bad to dampen Sam's enthusiasm this much. I swear, putting some distance between us and that spiteful woman will be the best thing to come out of this move.

“That bad?” Alan said. They were alone in the hallway, Michael and Amanda having gone on ahead of them.

“Yes,” Sam replied with more emotion in that single word than could have been expressed in a thousand. As they stopped and looked at each other, Alan could see the thick wetness in his wife’s eyes that signaled oncoming tears.

Damn that Augustine! Where does she get off acting like this to her own flesh-and-blood daughter? Sometimes, I think I could actually murder that woman.

“Want to talk about it?” he said, surprising himself at his restraint.

He could see her calculating, considering. “Maybe a little later.”

Soon after, they arrived at the restaurant, rejoining Michael and Amanda. The restaurant was empty but for a man in a tan business suit reading a newspaper, and a white-haired couple sipping orange juices. A waiter, undoubtedly another college student on summer break, Alan thought, seated them with a mumbled remark Alan was unable to catch but for the last word “. . . shortly.”

“Well, you’ll never guess what we did while you were gone,” Alan said, perhaps a little too loudly—and perhaps, based on the atmosphere, a little too lively. But the direct approach had failed, as it almost always did and so it was time for Plan B.

“No idea,” she said, picking up her menu in the same methodical way she had exhibited earlier as she laboriously made her way through her routine back in the room. It was not going to be easy, he saw, but then again, it never was.

“Yeah, Mom, you’ll never guess what we did!” Amanda said.

“Saturday, I was able to convince Mary to loan us the keys—” Alan began and thought he saw the hint of an eyebrow lift a fraction of an inch, “so we spent the day at the new house cleaning.”

“Really?” This time she actually glanced up at him, if only for a second. In that single glance, though, he had been able to see a renewed interest peeking out from behind the previously self-constructed walls of her misery.

It was sad that each of Sam's visits to her mother always brought about the same result. And each time it was up to Alan to grab her by the arms and lift her back up to her feet again. Sometimes though, he slipped, and then it took a while longer. At other times though, she was able to do most of the work herself. Either way, it was always painful to watch, and each time it happened it only added to the growing pile of anger he tried to keep dammed up inside.

"Yeah, I even cleaned the bathroom upstairs and the bedrooms too," Amanda said.

"Hey, that's great!"

Alan was genuinely relieved to see her starting to come out of it—this would be one of the better times. He knew it was the house that was responsible for her change in attitude and so he was glad for it and for what it represented. He was genuinely pleased it had made her happy and was hopeful that now—perhaps for the first time—they could finally begin living their own lives. He knew that distance alone wasn't going to solve everything, but at least it would be up to them when—and if—they decided to grapple with Sam's mother again.

Alan started to relax as Sam and Amanda talked. Even Michael was finally able to bring himself to put in a few words in an attempt to help lift his mother's spirits. Alan watched as his wife's countenance transformed—almost like one of those time-lapse photography films on the Discovery Channel of a flower opening its petals—from a closed bud to an open flower in what seemed to be a matter of five seconds. For Sam, it was minutes; on the other hand, previous occasions had required days.

"While you were in the shower, I called Mary about signing the final mortgage papers—she said she'd meet us at the bank at ten tomorrow. I tried to set it up for today, but they just couldn't swing it."

"Guess you guys were pretty handy while I was away. I'm impressed." Sam leaned over and kissed him. Amanda blushed while Michael pretended to read his menu. "Actually, you guys are all pretty great!" she said and—for the first time that morning—smiled.

"I really think this is going to all work out," he said.

"I told you it would," Sam replied with a glowing smile Alan had missed more than he'd realized over the last several days.

He grinned back at her, then looked around the table, still smiling—until he saw Michael. The rare grin that had been on his son's face a minute ago was now gone. In its place was a vacant look of . . .

What? Sadness?

(you know exactly what it is)

tiredness? . . .

(it's the look of fear—the unquestionable visage of someone so terrified that for the moment they have withdrawn from the outside world)

Alan tried to respond to this thought but found he couldn't. It was, he realized, the truth, and before he could reflect on the subject further, the look was gone. As they ordered breakfast, Alan tried to convince himself that perhaps it had never really been there at all.

2

For Michael, the rest of Tuesday passed for him as if he were walking around in a nightmare with sporadic panic attacks striking him without warning. Fortunately, the attacks never lasted long—usually only a minute or two. Each one, though, left him shaking—and beginning to question his own sanity. During the rest of the morning the intensity of the attacks wore him steadily down and by the afternoon he wanted to do nothing but sleep. Lying down for a nap around one, he didn't rise again until awakened by his father at 5:30.

From then on, he was fine. His nap had left him feeling refreshed and alert.

After supper, Michael tried telling his parents about the news articles and Dr. Woulfe having been a suspected practitioner of Black Magic. His mother, however, was quick to dismiss the whole thing. Michael thought he did at least detect some interest from his father, but he was easily swayed by Sam and was soon agreeing with her that it was probably nothing to worry about.

"Even if it's true," Alan began, "it was what, forty years ago?"

But Michael could only think about his panic attacks and the image of eight basement floor drains that looked like black mouths.

3

The next morning, Wednesday, they checked out of the hotel at ten minutes before ten to go to the bank. It took nearly an hour to finish up the paperwork and after what would come to affectionately be known as The Great Paper Signing, Mary gave Sam the keys and that had been the end of it.

Or the beginning? Michael thought. *Depends on your perspective I suppose.*

From the bank they drove to the hotel parking lot where Alan retrieved the rental car. Sam, Amanda and Michael followed him in the Cherokee, then waited for him at the car dealership while he returned it. Next stop was BC Electric where Sam was going to work. While there, they transferred the house's electric account into their name after which Sam called the movers and the phone company.

On their way to their new house, Alan, Michael and Amanda hung onto their door handles and seats as Sam took corners marked 35 mph at speeds closer to 60.

"Mom, aren't you driving just a *little* bit fast?" Michael asked.

She just grinned at him in the rearview mirror.

The Cherokee emerged from the trees on Pleasant Valley Road and Michael looked once again in the direction he had the first time they had come down this road, not at the house still half a mile or more away, but at the misshapen tree—The Claw. Even in bright sunlight, he thought the tree looked strangely dark.

One of the first things I'm going to do once we get settled is take a good, hard look at that tree.

At the house they divided, as before, into work teams. This time, Amanda was put in charge of vacuuming (Sam had possessed the foresight to bring their vacuum cleaner). Alan assigned himself the basement because Michael had adamantly refused it opting for the attic (since it was the farthest space removed from the basement). Sam was left to "float"—going wherever she was needed to clean or to help someone else. Michael assumed this was because she was so excited she wouldn't be able to stay in one spot.

They'd worked for an hour before their stomachs began to complain. When they'd regrouped in the kitchen, Sam volunteered to make a McDonald's run.

As Michael was listening to his mother backing the car out of the driveway, he heard his father call out.

"Hey, kids! Come here and take a look at this!"

Michael gave Amanda a might-as-well-go-see-what-Dad's-gotten-himself-into-now kind of look and dragged himself toward the stairs. Amanda followed closely behind.

Downstairs, Michael realized his father had managed to turn on every operating light he could find. Despite the lights, he still couldn't see his father and it was actually Alan who spotted them first.

He was crouched near one of the wooden walls which served as a boundary for what once had been a laundry room in the northwest corner of the basement. It was the opposite corner from the spot where Michael had found the newspaper articles. Next to him, a board had come loose or had been removed and was lying on the floor with a single bent and rusty nail sticking up. Alan held up what looked to be a book.

"It's some sort of book—there's a title here on the first page."

Michael, with some degree of trepidation, peered over his father's shoulder and read the single word centered near the top—"Tagebuch." Although the word sounded familiar to him, somehow he couldn't immediately place it. Slightly below this and also centered on the page was a name, a name he easily and immediately recognized—and that made him feel suddenly cold—"Robert Woulfe." Underneath was a date: "Februar 23, 1895."

"What is it?" Michael whispered.

"I'm not sure." Alan turned the book over before opening it and after flipping several pages said, "Looks like some kind of journal—pretty old too, if that date's any indication.

Spelled February wrong though." He continued riffling pages, stopping near the end. "Most of it's written in some foreign—"

"It's German," Michael said with sudden understanding. "Februar is German for February. And tagebuch means journal."

"Oh. Okay. I've found one entry here though that's in English. January 20, 1898. 'Still no closer to the vehicle. My researches have continued with the original works of Jerod. Deciphering now entries of spring and summer, 1526—' Whoa, *1526?* Is this for real?"

"Go on," Michael said, trying his best to read over his father's shoulder but to his frustration he was unable to see more than the top of the page.

"Yeah, well let's see. 'The language is difficult and meanings confusing, but I think that fire may be the answer. It will take several weeks to be certain and my studies have suffered. Dr. R—,' some name here I can't make out, 'has talked to me most concernedly about this. Perhaps I will attend to my work until summer.'"

"That's the end of the entry. The next one's in German."

"Can I have it?" Michael asked, already reaching for it.

"Well . . . sure, I guess so. Maybe you could translate it? That would be a challenge for you—might keep you out of trouble for a while. Looks like it'd make for some pretty interesting reading."

At first Michael thought his father seemed reluctant to hand the book over. Finally, he did, handing him the dusty leather tome as if handing over the keys to the family car.

Michael left the basement and returned to the attic carrying the journal like a prized possession, his head filled with new questions and renewed speculation.

All the answers could be right here—in this book! What was Dr. Woulfe's cult about? Did they really use this house? What was their purpose? What did he mean about fire—and a vehicle? I just have to translate it. Maybe Mrs. Wright's German classes hadn't been such a waste after all?

It seemed he had been looking at the book only a few minutes when, from downstairs, he heard his mother return. Reluctantly, he put the book down, feeling, for some reason he couldn't quite explain, suddenly averse to leaving it on the floor. It was almost as if such an act were in some way disrespectful. Finally, though, the pangs of hunger prevailed, he left the book, and rushed downstairs to eat lunch.

4

After his children had left, Alan reached into his pocket and brought out the other object he had found along with the old book. It was a gold medallion about three inches in diameter, on a heavy gold chain. Inscribed on both sides of the medallion were markings that Alan thought looked familiar, and yet were like nothing he had ever seen before. On one side was a star with small symbols contained within each of its six points. In the star's center was what looked like an eye. On the reverse side were two concentric squares. In the border between the squares were what appeared to be several more symbols similar to those inside the star. Around the edges of the circle on both sides were words—neither in German nor in any other language he recognized.

He carefully replaced the medallion in his pocket, thinking it best to keep this particular token to himself—at least for now. Later, he would try to find out what the symbols meant.

He wondered briefly why he'd felt the need to hide the medallion when he had already given Michael the journal. Before he could contemplate this dilemma further, he heard the door on the landing open and close—Sam was home.

One thing he knew for certain, though. Finding the medallion—for reasons he couldn't presently fathom—had both scared and exhilarated him.

9

Wednesday Night
Alan's First Dream

In the dream he stands in a museum, its ceiling high above his head. The room is expansive, almost as free and open as the outdoors. He looks at the white walls, the white floors—he hears nothing. Everything is white and the room is empty; a museum with no paintings or sculptures. He is alone in the museum and the building is big; four, five, maybe six stories—it consumes an entire city block.

His thoughts return from outside to inside and he stares at a white wall. Paintings appear and disappear, flashing as rapidly as a movie film in which each frame reveals a different image. The scintillating images create a maelstrom of color. The room however remains silent as death even as the paintings flash by, occasionally stopping for a fraction of a second on a particular one before moving on, giving him the barest impression of a single color and nothing more. All he knows is that the paintings are abstracts—wild blazes of prominent dark colors. The paintings come to an abrupt stop—and a single rectangular canvas remains and the floor has now turned black, its surface so polished that he can see a clear, reflected image of the painting at his feet.

The painting is red and at first he interprets it as an extreme close-up of a cut-open tomato, but it is not.

Suddenly, there are people in the room; six or seven, they stand still like trees or statues and stare at the painting. The room is huge, though, and they stand far away.

His attention returns to the wall, and he turns his head back toward the painting without remembering having turned away to look at the people. This time the painting is a deep ocean blue with aqua speckles dotting its dark background like algae.

Now there are 20 or 25 people in the room but they are still far away and nobody crowds him. The strangers all stand motionless staring in rapt attention at the art on the wall. All of the men wear suits and hold briefcases; one man holds a portable computer, cradling it like a baby in the crook of his arm. The women wear skirts and dresses; several wear suits. One woman holds a handled shopping bag full of rolled papers which might be architectural drawings or maps. She wears a gray suit with a bright red blouse. A gold chain sparkles around her neck like a ring of fire.

Now the painting on the wall is purple, but so dark it is nearly black. Yellow streaks emblazoned upon it look like lightning. Outside, he hears thunder, far off and booming. As the sound of the thunder rumbles away he hears raindrops dancing on metal and glass.

The people in the room now number at least a hundred. This time, however, many of them are closer and the room suddenly feels crowded and hot. None of the people move or breathe or talk or cough—they just stare—now at a pine-green painting with small red boxes of different sizes scattered over it like the design of a contemporary Christmas card.

He suddenly feels angry—angry at the crowd invading his privacy—invading his intimate moment with the art.

Now there are too many people to count, creating an image similar to Magritte's "The Time of the Wine Harvest" *although, unlike Magritte's version, the people in the museum are distinct individuals. There are no gaps between them—they stand as tight and close as vertically stacked logs at a paper mill. There is little air now and he fights for each breath and fidgets uncontrollably. He can no longer hear the rain and the people stand as if frozen in place. He, himself, stands within a small circle of the people—less than a foot away from the nearest person-statue. Sweat runs off his forehead, stinging his eyes and the heat is nearly unbearable. On the wall, the paintings have become a flashing blur of kaleidoscopic colors.*

His air is nearly gone and he longs for death as a release but fears the pain of it. His anger is immense, directed at the people surrounding him who seem not to breathe. At the same time, he senses the people in the room are actually consuming the remaining air as if they are air sponges—sucking in the air through the pores of their dry skin. He realizes he has moved, and finds himself standing in front of the paintings, which are now a blur of indistinguishable colors. Looking at the paintings, he doesn't know whether he feels or only imagines a breeze on his face. Behind him he feels the stare of the crowd like a knife-point in his back, pushing him toward the wall and the flashing paintings. He is afraid and so he turns his head to avoid having his nose pushed into the paintings, fearing that touching them would be like touching a saw blade.

And then he is suddenly through—like Alice through the mirror—he is through the painting, the wall, and the museum. He can breathe once again and discovers he is now alone outside on a bright summer day standing in knee-high grass on the side of a small hill. He frantically gulps the sweet air. A dozen yards to his right stands a large maple tree, shading him from the glare of the sun, which is high and warm in a sky colored blue like the ocean.

He looks at the maple and then it is gone, replaced by the four-armed willow from the field near their new home. As he looks down he sees that the grass is black, as if it has been tarred. At the same time the sky becomes overcast—painted with gray clouds. The tree is leafless.

Evening arrives in a gush and pale human hands begin to sprout from the black ground, their fingers outstretched and groping. There are hundreds of them. It would be impossible to walk anywhere without putting himself within the range of one of the hands. He looks once again at the tree.

There is a cold wind, so cold it brings tears to his eyes, blurring his vision. The wind, like a precursor to winter, causes a rope hanging from one of the massive branches

(fingers)

of the great willow to swing like a pendulum. The sky becomes even darker, almost night-like, and he sees a body hanging from the rope, swinging in the cold breeze, each swing causing a violent creak in the wooden branch. A full moon is alternately revealed and hidden by the motion of the swinging body while in the ground the hands continue their constant groping as the body swings back and forth: creak, creak, creak.

He finds himself standing near the tree close to what appears to be the body of a teenage girl. He feels somehow he should know her, but he doesn't. He is actually close enough to touch her. She is dead, her skin a pale grayish-white like the color of wood smoke and similar to the pallor of the hands that wave at him from out of the ground.

The girl's eyelids open and a pair of green eyes as brilliant as malachite chips stare back into his own. She speaks: "What he taught wasn't the living . . . it was the dying," and she continues to repeat the phrase after each pair of swings: creak, creak, ". . . what he taught was the dying," creak, creak, "what he taught wasn't the living . . . it was the DYING . . ."

He runs, stepping without regard on the groping hands which dissolve beneath his feet like wet mushrooms and he nearly falls. He is intensely terrified of the thought of falling into the hands, even more terrified of this than of the dead girl.

He runs through a fog so thick he can see only a few feet in front of him. The fog is choking and gray and the black grass shatters under his footfalls with a sound and a feel like eggshells.

Then, suddenly, the fog is gone. The sky becomes lighter, the grass less brittle, and he is back in the green field once again, and the sun is shining and the sky is blue like the ocean. He looks and sees their house in the distance.

10

June 23 • Friday Morning

1

"We're leaving now!" Sam called.

Alan, ready at the side door, waited while Sam stood at the top of the stairs fumbling with her day planner. They were going into town to pick up some items for the house and garden, and to put in an order for the wood to replace the gazebo floor. It had been a while since Alan had tackled a home repair project and the idea, coupled with the business of settling into their new house, had infused him with a renewed enthusiasm.

"We'll be back in a while," Alan announced to Amanda and Michael, who were now standing next to Samantha. "You and your brother stay out of trouble, okay?"

"We will," Amanda replied, an impish smile on her face.

Alan noticed something else in the smile that had crossed his daughter's face. At first he couldn't place it. It wasn't until he had left the house and climbed into the Cherokee however that he remembered where he had seen it before—it was the same expression he sometimes saw when she was putting an insect into her chloroform-filled killing jar.

2

"Come on, let's go outside," Amanda said.

Before Michael could reply, she'd rushed down the stairs and out the side door. At first, he thought about simply ignoring her but with their parents gone, he knew he would be the one blamed if she got into trouble. And he surely didn't need to relive the Yellowstone incident again to remind him what *that* would be like.

Despite his initial reluctance, he walked quickly down the stairs and opened the side door—Amanda was, to his surprise, nowhere in sight. His stomach began to tighten—then he heard something in the backyard.

As he ran towards the sound, his imagination played tricks with him, conjuring up images of accidents and tragedy. A few seconds later he was relieved when he saw her in the gazebo running in circles, engaged in some unknown game.

Entering the garden, following the cobblestone path, he was startled when a large brown toad hopped onto one of the stones in front of him. The toad hesitated briefly as if sizing him up then continued on its way in a series of heavy, awkward bounds. The toad reminded him of another animal that had crossed his path not so long ago—a dog of the same color—a dog he had since been struggling to forget, though even the dog's death had not halted the sound of its pitiful whimpering which remained etched in his mind. He shook his head, hoping he might shake himself loose of the memory, then continued on to the gazebo. By the time he stepped inside, he was sweating profusely but was careful to stay away from the still uncovered hole in the floor. Amanda was now sitting on the other side and asked, "Want to go down that path—see where it goes?"

"What path?"

"The one over there that goes into the woods." She pointed behind them to a spot where a faint track faded into shadow between two maples.

"Sure, why not?" he said, but before he could caution her about sticking to the trail, Amanda had jumped up and run out of the gazebo and onto the path. This time, she had gone a good fifty yards before he was able to catch up with her.

"Slow down! What are you trying to do?"

"Chill out, I can take care of myself! Besides, you were doing the same thing when we went to the library, so now *you* can see what it feels like."

"Yeah, whatever." Nevertheless, she did slow down and soon they were walking together in single file, Amanda leading. Michael found the forest unnaturally quiet—and extremely dark. The farther they traveled into the woods, the darker it seemed to become.

Although having not been used in a long time, it was evident the path had once been well trodden. Worn down to a depth of nearly two inches into the hard humus, most of the trail was still bare though not very wide—only a foot or two in most places.

After several minutes of walking, Michael noticed what seemed to be an unusually large variety of mushrooms growing alongside the path. Most of them were types he had never seen before.

Walking past a rotted stump, he spotted several small clumps of fire-engine red mushrooms which looked almost like small teacups littering the ground. Also, in the same location, he found a white shell-like mushroom, a yellow toadstool as tall as the top of his Nike high-tops, a brown sticky lump that must have at one time been a fungus of some kind but now looked like something left behind by a large forest animal and, finally, a clump of about a dozen, tall, gray-white mushrooms that looked remarkably like eggs on stalks.

Farther down the path, Amanda found a mushroom the size of a dinner plate. It was growing out of a stump about a dozen feet off the path to their left.

Michael caught up to his sister just as she was approaching the unusual-looking mushroom. Consisting of a stem as big around as Amanda's leg, the mushroom grew horizontally out of the stump's side before curving upward to where it sprouted a large cup—dark brown at the center and white everywhere else. On the surface, it looked like a coffee-stained bowl, except that its edges were ruffled like the hem of a fancy dress.

"It's huge! Maybe we should pick it and take it back to show Mom and Dad," Amanda said, then grabbed a nearby stick and poked at the thick stem.

"Let's not. Who knows what kind of poison could be on that thing and then you'd have it all over your hands. And . . . the way you're always picking your nose, your nose would probably rot off before we could—"

"I do *not* pick my nose! *You* probably do that . . . and eat your boogers too!" Amanda threw down the stick and stomped back toward the path.

As they resumed their walk, Amanda continued to grumble under her breath while Michael followed closely behind her. A few minutes later, he assumed the lead.

"So, where do you think this goes?" Amanda asked.

"How should I know?"

"I don't know—just asking! Do you think we're still on our property?"

"*Yes*, we're still on our property. We've got a hundred and twenty acres—that's a lot of ground."

The path had now dipped sharply into a small valley before rising up on the other side to a height at least twice as high as that of the original descent. At the top of the hill, the trail took a sharp turn to the left, then skirted down the side of an even larger, steeper hill covered with white pines. The dirt on the path, carpeted with a thick layer of dead pine needles, was soft and slippery. Michael was cautiously proceeding down when he heard a sudden crash of brush followed by an inexplicable sound like a heavy rug being spanked with a rug beater several times in quick succession. Just then, a vague black shape detached itself from a clump of bushes from farther down the hill and propelled itself up and out of the trees.

"Geez . . . what was that?" Amanda whispered.

"Just a pheasant . . . probably," Michael said, though whatever kind of bird it was, if a bird at all, had been bigger than any pheasant he had ever read about.

"Oh," Amanda said. She steadied herself the rest of the way down the hill by tightly clutching his shirttail.

At the bottom, the ground leveled into a marshy bog full of scraggly evergreens, many of them dead and having toppled against each other to create a seemingly impassable jungle. In several locations there was a wet sheen on the ground and their feet subsequently made squishing noises whenever they stepped on one of the wet spots. Farther off the trail, between the evergreens, Michael could see pools of standing water.

Moments later they came across a spot in the path where the shoring had given way and they were forced to walk through a long patch of black mud several inches deep.

"These mosquitoes sure are bloodthirsty all of a sudden," Michael said, swatting at one of the insects as it tried to land on his arm, then at yet another on the back of his neck. He thought it strange that they hadn't been bothered earlier.

"You're telling me—I'm getting eaten alive back here!"

Michael looked back at his sister just in time to see her left foot sink into the syrupy mud. Fortunately, however, by slowly and carefully wiggling her foot as she pulled, she managed to keep from losing her shoe.

"Careful," he reminded her. About ten feet ahead there appeared to be the last segment of the mud patch.

"I'm trying! How much farther we going anyhow?"

"Until we get somewhere."

"So where's *somewhere?*"

"Somewhere up ahead," he said, stopping to point in the general direction of the trail.

Amanda grunted. "Oh, *that* helps a lot. Or maybe you just think it's *your* turn to get us lost this time. Mom's going to kill us when she sees our shoes."

"Don't worry. There's an outside faucet on the house. The mud'll wash off."

He began walking again, but a wall had been breached as Amanda's comment brought the memory of last summer hurtling back into the forefront of his thoughts yet again. Yellowstone National Park. The campground. The trail. The moose herd.

On that fateful night, realizing they were lost and with darkness quickly approaching, Michael had managed to successfully construct a crude lean-to of logs that had fallen into the V of two pines. Unfortunately, it was during this construction that the rain started.

Inside the shelter, with a sense of renewed safety, Amanda had shared the two 3-Musketeers bars that she had brought with her in a small fanny pack. He still remembered the earthy smell of the chocolate mixed with the rain—and then the unexpected arrival of the bear.

Whether it was the call to action, any type of action, that the boredom of being lost tended to instill, or perhaps even a heroic urging, Michael didn't take the time to consider. Instead, he left the lean-to and recklessly stepped into what was now a hammering rain. The bear noticed him immediately and for a second Michael thought he had made a perilous mistake—that had he elected to stay put, the bear might never have noticed them at all.

At first, the large black bear did nothing but stare at Michael; and Michael hoped that perhaps his presence alone would be enough to send it running. But then the bear did run, but unfortunately not away. Michael first sensed he was in real trouble when it growled, a growl which grew deeper just before the animal rose up onto its back legs, let out what felt like a paralyzing roar, and charged him. Michael had never run faster in his life.

But even as he ran, he knew the bear would be quicker. So as he ran, he searched. From TV, he knew bears could climb trees, but under the circumstances he couldn't think of a better alternative. So, when he finally spotted one with enough branches to make climbing easy—no small task in the near darkness—he didn't hesitate.

The tree, thick and gnarled, was on the edge of a small clearing. It was at this same instant that as he jumped into the first level of branches that the bear caught up with him. He climbed until he was at least thirty feet up before he stopped and looked below him. To Michael's alarm, the bear had followed and was already close enough for Michael to smell its rotted-fish breath. He realized he had only one other choice—to venture onto a branch large enough to support his weight, yet small enough to discourage the bear—if he could find such a thing.

His legs trembled as he inched his way onto a branch only a few inches in diameter. Behind him though, along with the fish smell, he caught a whiff of wet musty fur and, and what was worse, something else, something he dared not think about.

As he waited to see what the bear would do next, the rain slackened, then stopped. The bear, breathing heavily, seemed to stop momentarily to reconsider its decision. The sound of the bear's panting was like a small engine running. Then the beast made one final growl and started to descend.

Within twenty minutes after the bear had appeared to climb out of the tree, the rain started again. Due to the combination of darkness and rain, Michael didn't know for sure if the animal was really gone. There was the distinct possibility it had, instead, only gone a short distance away to wait for him to climb down. He listened intently, but heard only the rain and an occasional owl hoot from somewhere off to his left. Then he remembered Amanda—no doubt alone and terrified, wondering what had happened to him—and so he started to climb down out of the tree.

Somehow, even though he'd been previously unable to find his way from the moose clearing in the daylight, he was somehow able to find his way back to Amanda in the darkness. Perhaps God had finally found it in his heart to show him some mercy, but, whatever the reason, within what he judged to be less than twenty minutes, he was relieved when he heard Amanda crying, a sound which now made everything that had come before seem a distant memory. He raced the last several yards and rushed into their makeshift shelter. Her sobbing immediately brought tears to his eyes.

"Michael?"

"It's me. It's okay now. The bear's gone."

He held her tightly in the darkness for several long minutes, allowing time for her crying to pass and for his heart to stop thumping.

In the end, he never knew if he'd saved their lives, or if he'd only taken an unnecessary risk. Regardless, the details of the story had remained, at least so far, a secret shared only between him and Amanda. He was especially grateful that Amanda hadn't mentioned the incident in relating the particulars of the story to any of their rescuers. In the year since, it had created a special unspoken bond between them—an experience they had lived through together—something no one else could ever share. To Michael, it would bind them forever. As strange as it might sound to others, he knew he would probably willingly give his life before he would ever again let anything happen to his sister.

Back on the path again, which continued onto drier ground before weaving itself through the cedars lining the marsh, Michael dwelled on this idea—wondering if there would be an opportunity to test such a commitment in the near future.

As the path rose before him the cedars gave way to maples and oaks. The thick underbrush, now present along their route, made any attempt at straying from the path next to impossible. Walking through this stretch, they were startled several times by the sounds of animals scampering away unseen under the dense cover. The thick woods continued for another hundred yards before the path gently dipped into an open area which then led to the bank of a small creek. A single two-by-ten plank lay across the bubbling water.

"I'm hungry!" Amanda said as they crossed. "Mom and Dad are probably home by now and wondering where we are. We're definitely going to get in trouble."

"Relax worrywart. If anyone's going to get in trouble, it's going to be me."

After crossing the stream, they were back into thick woods and Michael experienced the strange feeling of unnatural darkness again. The path, now twisting and turning around several big maples, straightened for a stretch of several hundred feet to end at what appeared to be a large clearing situated beyond two enormous boulders. The path at this point was also considerably wider—about five or six feet across—and appeared level and clean.

"What's that?" Amanda asked, pointing toward the area ahead of them.

"How should I know?" Michael said; then he experienced a curious feeling—as if another voice had suddenly spoken and told him he *did* indeed know the place they were headed to. His trepidation gradually increased with each step until some part of him was shouting at him inside his head to turn around and run. As they neared the two boulders, the title of a Dean Koontz novel whispered its name inside his mind.

The Bad Place. That's where they were . . . The Bad Place.

They stepped between the two boulders and stopped, uncomprehending for several moments what they were seeing. The sight was just too magnificent, too strange—too impossible.

"Wow," Amanda said slowly and quietly, like a one-word TV commentary usually uttered while looking upon a scene of mass destruction. In this instance, it was delivered with a reserved tone of respect—and awe.

From their vantage point the clearing appeared to be a perfect circle roughly two hundred feet in diameter. The circle was defined by massive boulders, the smallest the size of a compact car; the biggest, a bakery truck. The boulders also appeared to surround the clearing equally, each boulder approximately ten feet from its neighbor on either side. Michael knew though that such obvious and careful placement of boulders weighing thousands of pounds was inexplicable in a clearing surrounded by dense forest and located more than half a mile from the nearest road.

Stepping farther inside the stone circle, Michael couldn't help but marvel at its near-perfect symmetry. As he contemplated its seemingly impossible construction, he found himself speechless. He traversed the perimeter, carefully examining each boulder for some evidence of machinery in an effort to ascertain how they might have been moved—but there was nothing. He stopped again, then watched as Amanda ventured toward the center.

"Check this out!"

She was bent over, staring at something on the ground. As he strode toward the center of the circle he found yet another stone circle. This secondary circle was also ringed by stones, but these were of smaller size, the largest no bigger than a basketball. And, unlike their larger counterparts, these stones were placed adjacent to one another, forming a complete and unbroken circle of rock, about ten feet in diameter. These discoveries, though, were of secondary importance when compared to what he noticed next. For inside the smaller circle, the ground appeared to be completely lifeless.

Like one of those spots where people were always claiming a UFO had landed.

Not a single blade of grass, speck of moss, nor even a weed was in evidence anywhere inside the smaller circle. Inside the large circle there was grass, but there it was short, as if it had been mown.

But how? And if so . . . by whom?

It was as if the grass struggled to grow in the soil located within the confines of the circle.

He stepped away from the small circle like someone retreating from a compost pile after having taken in its vile fragrance.

I know this place . . . this is where they met . . . where the cult met . . . where the raid occurred . . . where those people died . . .

(livestock mutilations)

where Sylvia and her friends used to hang out and . . .

(talk to the dead)

And then, for the first time since the episodes that had occurred on the day his mother had returned, Michael experienced another panic attack. The feeling came without preface and without mercy. He began sweating while his heart pounded rapidly inside his chest as if it were struggling to be let out. At the same time, his stomach felt like it was trying to imitate one of Amanda's cartwheels. In the next moment, an intense, unexplainable, and yet undeniable fear took hold of his body—squeezing, twisting and pulling—and he knew he had to leave—now.

"Come on, let's go!" he said sharply.

Amanda however gave him an annoyed look and was starting to offer a retort when he abruptly cut her off.

"I said, *let's go! NOW!*"

Grabbing her firmly by the arm, she nearly fell as he pulled her behind him back toward the place where the trail led back into the woods. "I know what this place *is*, maybe not all that they did here, but I can imagine it well enough," he said, and it was as if he was now talking to himself. In his panic and desperation to leave the stone circle—even though her small hand was tightly clasped within his own—he had for a moment forgotten that Amanda was with him.

Michael nevertheless continued clutching Amanda's arm even after they'd stepped between the two boulders and left the circle behind. Amanda, unable to keep up with him, stumbled repeatedly but didn't offer any protest.

They continued their "escape" until they'd successfully reached the bank of the small stream they had crossed earlier. Here, he decided to stop and let go of his sister's hand; she immediately began rubbing it like a prisoner who'd been released from the unyielding grip of the handcuff.

The Stone Circle.

He was unable to get its image out of his head. But the image he saw wasn't that of the sunlit emptiness of what they had just experienced, but instead contained the vision of a chanting group of black-robed cultists standing in front of a blazing bonfire. In his particular vision, men suddenly break forth from out of the forest on all sides of the Circle, screaming begins, and blood flows freely across the ground, poisoning it forever, making it impossible for the grass to grow . . .

because it remembers . . .

Michael stood with his eyes closed until the vision cleared. Opening his eyes, he raced across the stream, leaving Amanda to keep up on her own. However, as she was crossing the stream behind him, a sound of crashing, breaking underbrush suddenly stopped them both.

Whatever that *was*, he thought, *it was definitely one* hell *of a lot bigger than a pheasant.*

3

Michael and Amanda were now standing in the middle of the path, neither of them daring to move.

"What was that?" Amanda whispered.

Michael felt his sister press close against him, then her small hand clasp onto his arm.

"I don't know," he whispered.

He remained still, listening, straining to hear the slightest sound. They were startled by a commotion in the brush behind them, about thirty yards off the path. Michael whirled about in an attempt to discover its source, carefully scrutinizing the tangled masses of dead and live evergreens, but saw nothing.

In his sudden movement, Amanda temporarily lost her grip but quickly re-established it again, only harder this time, making him wince as her sharp nails dug into his arm.

"Michael—" Amanda's voice faltered, then broke.

"Quiet!" he hissed. "Come on."

He somehow managed to shake Amanda's vice-like grasp and grab her hand instead. Together, they walked quietly, inching their way down the path, continually moving closer to the place where he felt the sound had come from.

Someone—or something—was definitely in the brush. As they got closer, they could hear it moving, then sloshing its way through a patch of water.

They stopped. "Hello? Who's there?" Michael called out. The sounds from the brush immediately ceased. He waited several seconds, then called out again. "Who's there?"

This time when the commotion began again, it was moving in their direction. Michael searched even more diligently, but still he could see no one—the bushes were simply too high and too thick.

"What is it?" Amanda whispered.

"How should I know?" Michael shot back with a sharp whisper. Then, out loud, he proclaimed, "This is private property!"

The sounds continued, still moving closer.

Stumbling out of the brush that served as a transition between the forest and the open creek bed, a man emerged. He wore jean coveralls, faded to where they were almost nearly white. He carried a thick walking stick, was mostly bald and had pale, nearly paper-white, skin. Michael immediately thought of albinos and guessed the man's age as late 50's or early 60's.

Michael and Amanda stood still. Only fifteen yards separated them from the man on the path.

"Oh . . . hello . . . who are you?" the man said.

Amanda, emboldened by his seemingly frail appearance, replied, "We're the Sarasins. We just bought this land. *You're* trespassing."

"Sarasins?" He scratched his head. "You shouldn't be back here."

As Michael started to say something, he was cut off by Amanda, "Yes we *can*—this is *our* land now."

The man continued staring at them. Michael didn't know what to do. Finally, the man turned away. He seemed to be searching for something.

"One of my sheep . . . lost . . . on your land . . . I didn't know," he said. His hands clasped and unclasped themselves on his walking stick. "We didn't know . . . the club, we didn't know . . . how could we? . . ."

"Are you all right?" Michael asked, and took a small step forward. The man seemed suddenly oblivious to their presence.

". . . it came out of the fire, I saw it . . . *they* didn't, but *I* did . . . it came and took her . . . that's why they never—" His head suddenly snapped up and he looked at them again. "Sarasins did you say?"

"That's right. We just bought . . . the house," Michael said and gestured behind him.

"You mean Woulfe House," the man said, as if correcting his grammar. "Well then, welcome to the neighborhood. I'm your neighbor—Scott Farley."

The man held out a pale, wrinkled hand.

11

1

"We're home!" Alan announced as he put a white paper bag containing sub sandwiches and colas on the kitchen table—a brown Formica relic they had found in the attic, along with some old metal folding chairs. There was no answer. "I wonder where the kids are now?"

"Probably running around in the backyard or something," Sam said as she followed him into the kitchen, putting her purse down on the counter.

Alan unpacked the food while Sam retrieved paper plates and plastic silverware.

"Coming!" Amanda yelled from upstairs. A second later, Alan heard the sound of small feet bouncing down oak stairs. In less time than it took him to walk to the sink and wash his hands, his daughter was seated at the table.

"Where's Michael?" Sam asked while putting colas at each place setting.

"Don't know. He might be out at that clearing we found. He seemed pretty interested in it."

As Alan turned on the water he wondered if Amanda was referring to the field where he'd seen the strange claw-like tree growing.

Amanda then proceeded to recap for them her and Michael's entire adventure from walking down the path to finding the clearing.

"Michael called it the Stone Circle," she noted when she had finished.

"Stone Circle, huh?" Alan said as Sam sat down.

They heard the side door open and close and a minute later, just as Amanda was unwrapping her sandwich, Michael ambled into the kitchen. Alan thought he looked tired.

"Lunchtime, Michael," Sam said. She handed Alan one of the sandwiches, then put the last one where Michael would be sitting.

Michael took the last seat at the table, sitting down with a small sigh.

As Alan was taking a bite of his ham and cheese sub, he was also carefully observing his son.

He's acting weird again.

(yeah, but what's weird for a fifteen-year-old?)

Alan swallowed and said, "Your sister was just telling us of your adventure."

Michael was unwrapping his food like someone opening a Christmas present while trying to preserve the paper.

"We followed that trail from the backyard," Michael said. "It turned out that it's actually pretty long." He had now pulled back the last corner of the paper which held his sandwich and was picking at the bits of lettuce left clinging to the wrapping.

Alan thought he looked nervous—as if trying . . .

to conceal something?

Next, his son lifted the top off his sandwich. Following this, he wrinkled his nose as if he had just experienced the odor or flavor of something distasteful.

"She said you found some kind of clearing . . . that you called it the 'Stone Circle'."

"That's because that's what it was," he said. "A big . . . stone circle with rocks placed around the outside that were as big as cars." To this point, he hadn't looked at anyone as he talked, consciously opting instead to stare at his food as if trying to decide whether to eat it or wrap it back up.

"Sounds intriguing," Sam said.

"Yeah," Amanda said, "it was *totally* cool until—"

"Are you *sure?*" Alan interrupted. "How could anyone have created it? If the rocks were that big, they'd have weighed tons."

"You got me, I couldn't figure it out either," Michael said, carefully replacing the top half of his sandwich.

"You sure you guys aren't exaggerating?" Sam asked.

"I bet I know!" Amanda said, smiling around a mouthful of ham and pepperoni.

"Let's hear it then," Alan said.

"It's probably an alien landing site and the aliens used a tractor beam from their spaceship to move the rocks and put them in a circle, like landing markers."

Michael rolled his eyes.

"Hmm, possible, I suppose." Alan said, trying to project a serious tone, but realizing he probably hadn't quite made it. When he noticed Amanda frowning, he wondered if she had intentionally been trying to poke fun at her brother.

"Are you guys *really* sure? I mean maybe the rocks weren't *quite* as big as you thought, or this circle as you call it wasn't *exactly* a circle." Sam continued.

"Well, does anybody *else* have any bright ideas then?" Amanda said. Alan looked at his daughter and tried to offer a reassuring smile before glancing over at Michael again.

However, before anyone could offer any other alternatives, they heard a gentle tinkling sound from the front of the house. Startled, no one moved. When it came again, it sounded like the quiet ringing of a maid's bell.

"It's the doorbell. I'll get it," Alan volunteered. On his way out of his chair he wiped his hands on a hastily grabbed napkin.

Alan saw there was someone at the side door. As he opened the door to a woman in a blue uniform and cap, he thought at first she was a police officer.

"Good afternoon . . . Mr. Sarasin? Jackie DeJohn, Ameriphone. We tried to re-connect your service but had a dead line. We believe there's a disconnect somewhere in the house. A Samantha Sarasin authorized us for an on-site call."

It took him several moments to process what she'd said.

"I'm here to check it out," she prodded.

"Oh, yes. Of course. The phone company. Sorry about that. Come in, come in. I think the line comes in through the basement." Alan held the door open. As Jackie entered, Alan's arm accidentally brushed against her breast. Jackie however didn't seem to notice. "Follow me," he said quickly to hide his embarrassment and together they descended to the basement.

2

As Alan led Jackie into the darkness, he stopped briefly, fumbling before finding the light. Just as the hanging bulb evaporated the blackness, he thought he saw something dark scurry across the floor in a far not-so-well-lit corner.

He led the phone company technician over to the wall near the front of the house.

"Sure is quite a house you have here, Mr. Sarasin," she said. Turning on a flashlight, she moved ahead of him to more closely inspect the wall near the ceiling.

Alan stopped. "Uh, if you don't mind, we were just in the middle of lunch and—"

"Oh, I'm sorry!" she said and abruptly turned away from her inspection of the wall. "I can come back later if you want . . . it'd be no trouble."

Surprised, Alan was slightly taken aback at her sudden and, he thought, too eager reaction.

"Oh no, no, it's quite all right, it's no bother . . . really . . . it's just—"

"Are you sure? I really can come back later; it wouldn't be a problem. I have another call just a couple of miles from here. I could swing on over there and then come back later in the afternoon."

"Please, really it's fine," Alan said and slowly began inching his way back toward the stairs. "Go ahead and continue. And if you need anything just give a holler—we'll be upstairs."

Something about the woman made Alan nervous.

"All right then. It shouldn't take more than a few minutes anyway," she said and swung her flashlight back toward the wall. Her back now turned to him, she explained, "It's probably just been disconnected inside here. There hasn't been service out here in a long time—couple of years I think. Probably a critter chewed through a line somewhere . . . not to imply you might have such an infestation . . . I didn't mean *that,* you understand."

Alan continued to inch farther back, moving closer to the stairs.

"No problem. Like I said, we'll be upstairs if you need us," he said, relieved at finally being able to get away. As what he considered a courtesy, he hesitated at the bottom of the stairway once more to see if the woman was going to need him any longer. When she didn't say anything more, he happily climbed the stairs—and emerged into the "light" once again.

3

Jackie DeJohn knew the good humor she'd projected towards Mr. Sarasin was entirely forced. She also knew he had, in the short time they had spent together, sensed some part of this, or at the very least, received a vague impression that something was not quite right. She was also certain he didn't know her forced civility was a somewhat desperate attempt to conceal and cope with her almost overwhelming fear of The House.

The House—Woulfe House—had, during the course of her lifetime spent in the Boyne City area, rightfully earned its reputation as a place to avoid. It was a place death and misfortune had visited often and, it was a community consensus, that to come too near its domain was thought to risk infection from its unhealthiness.

When the work order had come across her desk two days ago she did at first what most people do when faced with an unpleasant task—procrastinated. But her supervisor got wind of it faster than she had expected; and so, today she had resigned herself to accepting her responsibility and tackling the task. Otherwise, she knew, it would have haunted her all weekend.

She had come close to revealing her true emotions to Mr. Sarasin, she thought. While the story about another service call in the area was true, the part about returning was probably not.

Now, inside the house and working, she decided that perhaps it wasn't so bad. She had to admit to herself though that when she first knocked on the door, she had been as afraid to venture down into the Sarasins' basement as much as, when a little girl, she had been afraid to look into the dark, ominous closet where she "knew" the monsters were hiding.

Working determinedly, she relaxed and soon located the place where the phone wire entered through a metal conduit stuffed with fiberglass insulation. The wire, itself a single gray strand, came in at ceiling level and followed the length of the floor under the kitchen. Then, at a point about six inches inside the wall, the wire was dangling. Examining it closer, she discovered that it had been neatly cut.

The cut wire, for reasons she didn't understand at the moment, suddenly made her uneasiness return in force. The uneasiness though, soon evolved into fear and before she had time to think, panic had slithered into her body like a cold, electric current. She became lightheaded, then dizzy. The walls started spinning as shadows, visible in the corners, began moving in disturbing, suggestive ways. To avoid falling in a dizzying faint, she sat down on the concrete floor. Her hands, wet with perspiration and cold at the same time, caused her to nearly drop the flashlight. She put the light down, drew her knees to her chest, and hugged herself. Her racing heart felt like an engine missing on one piston while revved to full throttle. She closed her eyes and tried to will the fear away.

God, please don't let Mr. Sarasin come back down here and find me like this!

Her body, soaked with perspiration, made her shiver as her skin dried in the coolness of the basement. Somewhat composed, she wiped her forehead on her sleeve and took a long, deep breath.

A few minutes later, the attack had thankfully subsided. Her heart had slowed but it still felt like its pace had doubled.

Come on now God, I'm only 44, I'm not ready to die of a heart attack just yet. I think you can loan me at least a few more years, huh?

She continued to remain in that same position, sitting and resting, while listening to her heart as it gradually struggled to reach a more steady rhythm. Then she decided to try and stand, but it was too soon and fast and she had to steady herself against one of the floor posts until the dizziness passed. Not many times in her life could she remember such a severe attack having plagued her. The worst she could recall had been when, at the age of 12, her mother received the phone call from the police informing her that her husband—Jackie's father—had been killed in an automobile accident at the age of 32.

However, she couldn't quite understand what had brought on so violent an attack now other than perhaps a dredging up and magnification of her childhood fears nurtured through years of listening to the town gossip about the "special" house on Pleasant Valley Road. The house, which was known as the place where the Satanists used to live, was also near the place where her older sister's classmate had committed suicide by hanging herself from the strange, twisted willow that grew in the field next to the house.

This is ridiculous. It's always been just a bunch of superstitious nonsense. I'm acting like a foolish child. Maybe Mr. Sarasin should *have come down the stairs and seen me a minute ago—would have served me right to be laughed at.*

She carefully let go of the floor post and felt like she was finally able to go back to work. In less than five minutes, she had completed the splice on the phone wire and then wasted no more time making her "escape." Dashing up the stairs, she startled and nearly collided with Mrs. Sarasin who just happened to be coming down the stairs at the same time.

"Anything wrong?" Sam asked with a look of concern. "I was just coming down to see how you were doing."

Jackie couldn't help but notice the strange look in the woman's eyes. She could only imagine what sort of wild look she must have had on her own face while vaulting out of the basement.

"No, no, everything's fine. All set. Everything's all set. I'm done," she replied, mentally wincing at what seemed to her to be the babbling sound of her conversation. She steeled herself, attempting to regain control.

"That didn't take long," Sam said.

"Yep, no problem," Jackie said and moved purposefully toward the door, forcing Sam to step back. "Oh, and one more thing. I know you just moved in; I've got a loaner phone in my truck you can use in the meantime if you need it."

"Sure, that would be wonderful, at least until our stuff from downstate arrives."

"Great. If you'll just wait here I'll get it. Back in a jiffy," Jackie said and went up another step. With Sam now safely moved out of her way, Jackie felt tears welling up in her eyes as she stepped into the welcoming sunshine outside the house.

Once outside in the fresh air, she didn't want to go back inside, even to step inside the door. For a moment she actually considered getting into her truck and leaving, but she resisted. With a deep, calming breath, she grabbed one of the phones she always kept with her from an outside storage compartment on her truck. She then walked briskly, and determinedly, back to the house where she was greatly relieved to find Sam waiting for her at the door.

"Here you go. All we ask is that when you get your own phone you drop this one off at our office in town."

"How long then can we have it?"

"As long as you need," Jackie said, already backing away from the house toward her truck.

"We should have our stuff moved up here by the end of this week."

Jackie was now halfway to freedom.

"Thank you!" Sam added.

"No problem." Jackie, who had now reached her truck, replied, "You have a nice day now and welcome to Boyne City. I'm sure you're going to love it here!"

As Jackie got into her truck and started it, she was almost giddy with relief. However, as she drove out of the Sarasins' driveway she wasn't able to completely shake the odd feeling she had felt upon discovering the cut wire in the basement. She knew the wire could have been cut in any number of ways, yet the image of it continued bothering her for no apparent reason she could define.

Her uneasiness remained with her long after she'd left the Sarasins and as it seemed to grow in strength in her mind the rest of the day, it gradually transformed itself from a simple anxiety about a cut wire into a genuine fear for the safety of the Sarasin family. She couldn't quite explain how or why she felt this way but she was nevertheless convinced something bad was going to happen to them.

You're just thinking this way because of what happened in the past. That's all it is, nothing more and nothing less. Cycles of misfortune like that don't go on forever.

(maybe not, but who says it's going to stop any time soon?)

Later that night, with these same horrific thoughts accompanied by unanswered questions still very much on her mind, she drifted into an uneasy sleep. And later that same night, for the first time in 24 years, Jackie DeJohn dreamed again about her father on his way to work careening off the road to his death in the early dawn hours of an autumn day—seeing once again the blue Chevrolet pickup shatter and fold itself tragically around an unyielding oak on the corner of Harris and Atkins Roads.

This particular dream had haunted her for several years after her father's untimely death, and now it had returned. But . . . why?

4

"I think I'll call Dad, see how he's doing; give him our number," Sam said.

"Sounds like a good idea," Alan replied as Sam reached for the phone, a simple tan touch-tone. She picked up the receiver and listened. "There's a dial tone, so I guess it works."

As she dialed, Alan left the kitchen and went into the sitting room where he would be out of the way but still able to hear Sam's side of the conversation.

5

"Oh, hello Wendy. This is Samantha. Is my Dad home?"

"Oh, yes ma'am! Mr. W's been trying to get you for days now!"

"Really?" Sam was immediately concerned—something was wrong, but what?

"Just a moment and I'll connect you," Wendy said. There was a faint click followed by a long pause, then another click.

"Hello?"

"Dad? It's Samantha. What's wrong?" Sam said, unable to contain her impatience.

"Well . . . I guess I'll just tell you. You deserve to know," he said then paused, clearly reluctant to go on. "Your brother's been arrested. For rape."

In the pause following this announcement, a multitude of images and questions suddenly took flight inside Sam's head. She was dizzy, sick and elated all at the same time. For a second she almost didn't believe it, thinking perhaps she was dreaming. The news however was too . . . real.

In her mind she could envision hefting the rock before the vase. Then, before she realized it, she was smiling with relief. Its weight, for the first time that she could remember, actually felt good.

PART TWO

The Haunting

And when the thousand years are ended, Satan will be loosed from his prison and will come out to deceive the nations . . . to gather them for battle; their number . . . like the sand of the sea.

- Revelation 20:7-8

Prologue II

Boyne City
June 20, 1955 • Monday

"Geez, *this* is weird," Scott Farley said. His two friends Raymond Withers and George Montgomery remained silent beside him, hiding behind a large thicket of wild raspberry and blackberry bushes. Needle-like thorns had already scratched Scott's bare arms to such a degree that he would wake up the next morning with a patchwork of red lines stretched across his skin like the tracks of a rail yard laid out by a drunken engineer. So entranced was he, though, with the events going on in the clearing behind Woulfe House that he remained oblivious to his physical discomforts.

The three founding members of the East Jordan Dare Club had ridden in Scott's 1949 Buick Roadmaster to within a half mile of the Woulfe estate, having followed, for the last mile, a small overgrown road through thick woods. Finding a secluded turnoff, they parked the car and began their trek through the dark forest. Using only Raymond's penlight as a source of illumination, it took them over half an hour to follow in the darkness what amounted to little more than a deer path to the edge of the clearing known throughout the area as The Stone Circle. The purpose of their adventure on this particular night was nothing more than an attempt to fulfill yet another of the reckless dares which were required by their unique club's mandate. But it was also, although none of them would admit it, being done out of genuine concern for their classmate, Warren Halstead, whom each of them considered their personal friend and a promising future member of their club. Warren was also the mayor's son.

When the rumors first began making the rounds at school several months ago, it wasn't long of course before the club took interest. Rumors about a strange new religious society and unnatural midnight meetings behind the house of the late Dr. Woulfe during the dark moon of each month had run the gamut from mildly amusing to wildly outrageous.

Kenny Thompson, a bug-eyed kid in Scott's math class, had postulated the theory that the cult was performing animal sacrifices in an attempt to obtain immortality. Kenny's father, Gerald, ran the Thompson Grocery, and Kenny said his father had told him that Sylvia Woulfe had been receiving monthly shipments of live cattle at her house, but that no one could recall seeing any of the beasts alive after the deliveries.

Then, Lisa Burgess, while talking with Raymond and George at lunch last week, claimed that Sylvia was actually a vampire and was killing the cows for their blood. No one, though, put much faith into this version since Lisa and her mother Helena had always been social outcasts on account of Helena's avowed public devotion to the Druid religion. In addition, the Burgess family's status as pariahs had been exacerbated by other circumstances as well. Lisa and her mother lived alone in a house without electricity deep in the woods southeast of town. The lack of electricity had come about not because of any special religious disdain for the conveniences of the modern world, but because when the electric company came out to the Burgess' house to install the service, they had indicated that they needed to first trim several trees. Helena, upon learning this and not about to let any such desecration occur on her property, came running out of the house waving a revolver in the air and threatening the work crew. Subsequent stories differed as to whether or not she actually fired a shot, but the electric company nevertheless refused to return, and the Burgess' application was subsequently cancelled after Helena failed to provide any acceptable compromise to the situation. To further complicate matters, later that year, Lisa's father died while trying to run his own wiring to the house from the top of a utility pole.

Helena, upon finding his charred body, decided to bury him herself. After initially refusing to disclose to anyone the location where she'd performed the burial, she was finally forced into divulging the details surrounding her husband's demise when Sheriff Kelly threatened to arrest her on suspicion of murder.

And so it was that the members of the East Jordan Dare Club couldn't pass up the opportunity of adding yet another successful exploit to their club's list of accomplishments which included: breaking into the confines of the forbidden Sedgwick-Davey Copper Mine, "trestling" on the wooden train bridge spanning the Jordan River (an activity requiring members to hold onto the timbers of the bridge-supported rail bed while the 11:30 PM from Alanson made its thunderous run above them), and most recently, staying a full night at the famed local haunted house on Crane Street downtown. This last adventure however had seen the unfortunate dropping out of one of the club's members after he claimed to have been slapped on the back of the head while alone in an empty room on the second floor causing him to run, yelling, down the stairs and out the front door.

"What in the world are they *doing*, anyhow? It looks like some sort of African tribal dance or something," Raymond said.

Scott looked over at Raymond but didn't say anything. The glow from the bonfire was casting strange patterns of flickering orange light and shadow across Raymond's dark features.

From their vantage point a short distance from the edge of the circle, they were now able to see a ring of some three-dozen people encircling the fire. The people within the circle—assumed to be members of Sylvia Woulfe's cult—were all clothed in white full-length robes with black belts tied around their waists—with one notable exception. A lone member of the group was completely garbed in black and sported a bright red belt.

"What kind of people has Warren gotten himself mixed up with? I don't think these people are *right,"* George said.

"You're telling me," Raymond said, obviously concerned. "Maybe they're doing—you know—drugs or something."

"*Yeah*, that might be it. I've heard about religious groups like these. They have some leader who gets them all laced up with drugs and then they brainwash 'em," George added, his normally brown eyes now appearing black in the gloom. Having said this, he reached down and scratched his ankle.

"Look. Warren's moving toward the fire," Scott said.

"If nothing else," Raymond continued, "I would think this at least qualifies Warren for membership, don't you think?"

"You're sick, Raymond," George replied.

"There's that creepy woman too," Raymond said, "over on the other side, away from Warren. She must be their leader."

George scratched his leg again. He was the only one of them wearing shorts and mosquitoes, jokingly known by many as the Michigan state bird, had been feasting on them ever since they'd stopped moving. Scott thought it strange however that the smoke from the fire didn't seem to bother the insects.

Scott and his friends had positioned themselves about thirty feet outside the Stone Circle. The members of the cult gathering were assembled about fifty or sixty feet farther away inside the ring of boulders. Scott thought the cultists resembled a rally of Ku Klux Klansmen.

Scott began to wonder what he and his friends were doing here. In the six years between the death of Dr. Woulfe and the arrival of his daughter Sylvia, the Stone Circle behind the house on Pleasant Valley Road had been used exclusively either as a favorite meeting place for high school couples seeking privacy or as a site for hosting weekend drinking parties. It was also during these years that the trail Scott and his friends had just used had been blazed from a largely forgotten two-track road running near the property line of the Woulfe estate. The road itself, with various turnoffs into the woods along its course, conveniently provided perfect hiding places for vehicles.

After the arrival in 1950 of Sylvia, Robert Woulfe's only heir, such activity however had come to an abrupt halt. During the course of the five years in which Sylvia occupied Woulfe House, some adventurous sorts were still bold enough to make the trek to the clearing and it was these adventurers whose stories initiated the recent rumors at the high school, sparking new interest. Finally, Scott's curiosity had been piqued to such a degree that it emboldened him to see firsthand what all the whispering was about. So this, along with the premise on which his club had been formed, placed him, Raymond and George in their current position.

Still, based on the present circumstances, Scott wondered if this was such a great idea. Nothing seemed really to be happening and yet . . .

something is definitely wrong here . . . something almost . . . what?

(evil)

"Maybe she's a witch," Raymond said, breaking the self-imposed silence as he turned around.

"Huh?" George replied.

"You know . . . a witch."

"Oh man, that's crazy," George said. "That's really crazy. And we're even crazier for being here. Why don't we just leave? I don't think this one's even good enough to count."

"Give it a rest, George," Scott replied. "We've come this far; we might as well stay and see what they do next. Who knows, things might still get interesting."

"Yeah, stay here and get caught. Do the words trespassing or private property mean anything to you guys?" George answered.

"Come on, George, what about the Crane house—what's the difference? I think Scott's right. We've come this far; it'd be a waste to leave now. Besides, I wanna see what they're going to do with those cows," Raymond said and pointed toward another section of the clearing.

"Cows? What—" Scott said. Then he spotted them at the far side of the clearing: two Black Angus cattle tied at the edge of the circle opposite them and nearly invisible within the tree shadow.

"Maybe Lisa was right . . . eh, George?" Raymond said.

"Oh, yeah. I didn't see them before," Scott replied.

"Maybe they're going to sacrifice them," Raymond said around a silent yawn.

"That's not funny, Raymond," George said. "If they start cutting up live cows—"

Although he couldn't admit it, Scott agreed. But to show fear wasn't a desirable option. As leader of a club he himself had begun—a club whose entire purpose was rooted in facing fear—he couldn't succumb so easily.

Several of the cult members were now adding more logs onto the bonfire. The addition of the wood immediately released a shower of sparks which glowed like a bucketful of fireflies set free into the night sky. In addition, the crackling and sizzling sounds of the green logs reminded Scott of bacon cooking in a hot skillet and surprisingly the thought made him suddenly hungry. He also wondered why the cultists had added more fuel—now reaching even closer toward the sky, the flames were already half as tall as some of the largest trees which surrounded the clearing.

Then the cultist whom they believed to be Sylvia Woulfe—the only one dressed in black—stepped closer to the fire. Two of the other cult members followed her, each leading a single cow on a short length of rope. A few feet from Sylvia, Warren stood alone.

"Oh geez, here it comes; they're going to cut up those cows I bet," George said, shifting his position on the ground, preparing, Scott thought, to leave. A short distance to their left they heard a cricket chirp and Scott, at that moment, realized that somehow the huge bonfire had become quiet.

Scott's pulse quickened and he felt cold, as if the fire's sudden loss of sound had also been accompanied by a loss of heat.

"Quiet—she's saying something!" he whispered to the others.

Over the muted, almost distant-sounding roar of the fire, they were able, to a limited extent, to distinguish that the woman whom they believed to be Sylvia had now begun speaking. Although they were unable to hear her words clearly, it made little difference as it was soon obvious she was speaking in a language other than English.

"I think it's German," Scott whispered, so quietly he might have been talking to himself. Behind him, he noticed that the cricket had stopped chirping.

"German? Are you kidding? This is getting weirder and weirder," George interjected, his voice level rising higher with each word.

Scott worried that his friends were nearing their breaking points. Even Raymond, who was normally the cool one, was having a difficult time.

"Scott . . . can you make out any of the words?" Raymond whispered.

"What am I, a translator?" he said, sensing a nervous quiver in his voice which he hoped the others hadn't heard.

"I think there's something happening in the fire," George added.

The unexpected calmness he heard in George's voice made Scott look closer at him. Although he could discern little in the darkness, he sensed not so much the calmness that George's quiet statement implied, but instead, the burgeoning of something close to genuine fear.

"Yeah . . . it's like some sort of—" Raymond started to say, but was cut off by George, his voice reminding Scott of a whimpering dog locked outside his master's house on a winter night.

"What's . . . happening?"

On the face of it, Scott thought, nothing. Yet, there was nevertheless an eerie feeling in the air, like a physical tension and expectation of danger that seemed to be pouring into them by the second, subsequently filling them with a cold fear that threatened to dissolve their tenuous grip on reason. It was a growing pressure that, if not eased quickly, Scott believed, would soon send them all running back through the woods like screaming lunatics.

Scott stared at George. Although George had never been one of their strongest members, Scott had never seen nor heard him so terrified.

He turned back to look again at the clearing. The cultists could now be seen moving their hands and making strange gestures as Sylvia continued to speak while Warren edged ever closer to the fire.

The cows too were also nearing the fire, directly opposite the positions of Sylvia and Warren.

None of them, George least of all, were prepared for what happened next.

"Oh geez, oh God . . . let's get out of here . . . oh my God!" George blubbered, now tottering on the high edge of hysteria.

As George rose, Scott grabbed his arm. "Wait!" he said, though his own fear now gnawed at his stomach like a big hungry rat gone berserk. He felt they needed to stay just a little longer—to make sure that what they were seeing wasn't just some kind of trick.

Despite his nearly overpowering fear, the mood in the air somehow and suddenly changed, conversely becoming more soothing—even reassuring. It was a feeling, Scott realized as he remained sitting and watching the strange events, as if another presence had suddenly entered the clearing. A moment later, he saw the source of this premonition and immediately wished he hadn't.

A transformation was now occurring within the bonfire. Flames, that had previously been random and fleeting, now appeared cohesive and directed. At the same time, a shape was forming from within the twisting yellow and orange strands of fire—molding itself into something that looked like . . .

Captivated by the vision, neither Scott nor his companions were able to speak as the "fire shape" seemed to physically extract itself from out of the bonfire and then lunge toward Warren, leaving only a single connecting tendril, like a fiery umbilical cord, a shape which seemed first to caress, then surround and ultimately *blend* itself into the body of their classmate. Warren, to their astonishment, welcomed the strange apparition with outstretched arms.

At the moment of contact, Scott initially closed his eyes, then opened them a moment later. What he saw in the center of the clearing he could no longer adequately describe in words and to further contemplate its existence would be, he thought, a stimulus to open his mind to the cold hand of a mind-numbing insanity.

And still, with all that was happening, it wasn't until the final dying bellows of the cattle boomed over their heads like thunder that Scott and his friends finally acted.

As the transformations occurred, George's fear had grown to the point where he was mesmerized—similar to that of a rabbit caught in the headlights of an oncoming car.

Consequently, George was unable to do anything else but stare, even as Raymond ran, blindly and screaming, into the lightless woods behind them. However, Scott, following close behind Raymond, stopped at the last moment to spin and try to pull George to his feet.

"Come on, George, run damnit . . . RUN!" Scott screamed, inches away from his friend's unseeing face, but George didn't move nor seem to hear him.

Scott then realized that for his own survival he needed to run and so he did, his fear finally overpowering concern for his friend. Seconds later, the sound of George's screams shattered the night, a sound which pierced Scott's body like a fusillade of tiny, hot arrows. And then, in some fashion he didn't comprehend, he was able to *see* the particulars of George's death—the scene playing inside his mind so forcefully and with such realism that it blocked out everything else. Scott, falling to the ground, sought relief from the horrible reality, but, unable to shut his mind's eye to it, helplessly watched the nightmare of his friend's death. He saw, as clearly as if George were still beside him, as his friend's body was torn apart by creatures that, even as he looked upon them, he knew he could never acknowledge their existence.

Scott, in a futile attempt to stop the terrible flow of pictures into his mind, slammed his forehead to the ground and held his hands against the sides of his head. As the Image continued to assert its presence, he considered even more rash options to drive it out—then it suddenly stopped. At the same time, the terrifying screaming also stopped, and though he couldn't be sure, he suspected the cessation of the Image had coincided with the tragic end of George Montgomery's life.

A second later though a new sound began—a multitude of high-pitched screams which probed at him, coming out of the woods like sensors. Instantly, he knew that they—the things he had somehow seen kill George—were now coming after him.

As he lifted his head, he felt something grab his arm. Terrified, he jerked his arm sideways. However, as the grip loosened, he fell hard onto his side where a branch bruised him painfully as it entered his ribs. When he looked up again he saw a small, bright light burning into his eyes.

"Scott! Scott, it's me—Raymond! Come on, pal, we gotta get outta here! I think they're after us!"

Scott needed no further encouragement and struggled to his feet. Sprinting through the black forest, he was unconcerned with the wild briars that tore mercilessly at his clothes and skin. After having run for what seemed hours, Scott was finally able to convince himself that he could no longer hear the cacophony of frenzied inhuman cries—like a chorus of wailing banshees—that seemed to have been chasing them.

12

Tuesday Night

Michael awakens, startled out of a dreamless slumber by an unaccounted-for noise. When he hears it again, it sounds like it is coming from downstairs, perhaps from under the house. A sound like digging and—vaguely—like voices. Is he dreaming? He sits up, swings his legs out from his sleeping bag and tentatively plants his feet on the hardwood floor. He is shivering—but he ignores this and stands and listens—the muscles in his neck strain to put his head closer to the sounds. Should he check it out? Has anyone else heard? If he waits, will his Dad then hear them and go investigate? Is it a break-in?

Or something else?

He is now physically afraid to move and remains standing as he anxiously ponders the numerous questions his still somewhat sleepy brain puts forth. His pajamas consist of shorts and a T-shirt and his bare legs are chilled and tense. He mulls over whether he should go and investigate or continue to wait. Then the sounds *(voices)* come again. Now, they remind him more of murmuring, like the sound of people chanting from under a gurgling brook. The word-like sounds are suggestive, yet indecipherable. Straining harder now, he struggles to hear, attempting to make some sense of the strange murmurings, but fails.

Holding his breath, the ache for fresh air burns inside his aching lungs. He rapidly gulps a mouthful of air and takes a step forward. The floorboards moan their protest while at the same time the noises stop, seemingly severed in mid-murmur. He waits, listening for the sounds to resume.

Dried sweat holds his bare feet to the floor. As he lifts his right foot, the skin slowly detaches itself from the wood with a sticky, sucking sound. He decides to leave his bedroom, using the hallway night-light to guide him to the top of the stairs. With the night-light behind him, an enormous shadow of himself is subsequently projected on the ceiling and walls. He slowly begins his descent down the dark stairs, all the while listening carefully again for the sounds; and as he descends, the oak stairs fortunately remain silent until he is halfway down, when one of them lets out a groan similar to the sound of a dying animal.

He freezes, wanting desperately to go upstairs as quickly as possible and climb back into his sleeping bag. Then something—a quiet, yet powerful voice inside his head—tells him it's okay. The voice also seems to comfort him, telling him he doesn't need to be afraid. He wonders about the source of this voice only briefly, then continues, albeit uncertainly, downward.

At the bottom of the staircase, he hesitates again for a moment, but still hears nothing. At this point, he decides to return to his room, but the voice returns once again, urging him to go on, telling him it's all right and that there's nothing to be afraid of. The words somehow soothe him.

He continues into the basement where the cold air makes him shiver even more and his skin prickles with goose bumps. At first, he sees nothing out of place in the darkness, but then he hears the voice again. Only this time, the voice isn't inside his head and his earlier rationalizations are subsequently swept from his mind much like the first light snowflakes which fall on a black roadway are at once visible and then gone in a swirl, leaving one wondering if they had really been there at all.

Then, from out of the darkness, the voice whispers a single word . . .

Michael

The voice comes again, his repeated name floating towards him from out of the darkness.

He responds instantly—turning, running, taking the stairs two and three at a time, up the four levels to his bedroom. Once in his doorway he stops, still breathing hard, but listening to hear if the voice has followed him. Over the sound of his labored breathing he hears nothing.

By the glow of the night-light he can see the closed doors of Amanda's and his parents' rooms. He doesn't immediately leave the doorway but instead stands outside his bedroom for four minutes, counting the time off by the glow of his bedside clock radio. Finally, he steps into his room and closes the door softly behind him. Gently padding over to his makeshift bed, he climbs in quietly, fearing that the slightest noise might somehow betray his presence and once again awaken the voice downstairs.

Restless from his endeavor, he lies awake. An hour passes but the memory of the sound, of its soft quiet voice gently drifting like a soughing wind from across a calm lake, stays with him, repeating over and over his name, staying the hand of sleep.

13

Amanda's First Dream

In the dream she is running through tall grass in the field next to their new house. The brown grass smells like wet straw and within it are hundreds of insects to collect. Dozens of them are new species and she imagines they will one day be named after her. By merely seeing them, and imagining their capture, they are instantly instilled within a jar, one of many sitting in her wagon which is also at the edge of the field.

She stops at the edge of a small pond. Its water is as clear as the air itself and full of dozens of colorful tropical fish. She thinks how nice it would be to have an aquarium in her new room in her new house. And then she is in her room, standing before an enormous glass tank teeming with a dozen of the brightest, most vividly-colored fish she has ever seen. She knows they have come from the pond in the field and that they are, like the insects, previously unknown and unrecorded species. She imagines these too will be named after her.

On the wall of her room are newly constructed shelves—pine boards supported by white metal wall brackets. She can smell the fresh-cut pine which to her is like a perfume. Covering the shelves are more than sixty quart jars serving as the individual habitats of a like number of live insects. Twenty-three of the jars contain new species recently collected from the field.

It is night and she lies in her bed, thick covers tucked up to her chin. It is cold outside; the wind whispers softly at the window to be let in. Above the whispering, she hears the clicking and crawling and flapping and scratching of sixty insects in sixty jars. One of the lids—a canning ring holding a circle of plastic mesh—suddenly unscrews itself with a sliding sound like bare skin moving on sand. Next, a second lid unscrews . . . then a third . . . and a fourth . . . until sixty lids on sixty jars are unscrewing themselves of their own accord in the middle of the night. The lids sound like knife blades sliding against each other and then she is dreaming within her dream, this time of a field of knives waving and sliding against each other, driven by the whim of an unseen wind. Then the field fades and she returns to her room. It is quiet again, as even the wind now seems to sleep . . .

. . . until she hears them walking and crawling across the hardwood floor of her bedroom, then climbing up the bedposts—digging and clawing for purchase on the smooth wood, then scurrying across the sheets. She can feel the weight of their small bodies scampering upon her from underneath the covers as they climb the twin peaks of her feet to march along the ridges of her shins and up to her thighs. Scrambling and pulling themselves over her stomach and chest, they march toward her face. She is afraid, but unable to move. Several of them become entangled in her hair, writhing and clawing. Then they explore her—a small beetle crawls into her right ear, a caterpillar navigates the ridge of her throat . . . a wasp investigates the cave of her open mouth . . .

. . . And then she is flying, borne aloft in a cloudless sky by massive purple and green butterfly wings which grow out of her back. She circles above their new house and, in the field below, sees the pond once again. She also now sees what previously had been hidden—a shaft of infinite depth in the center of the water. The pond with the hole in its center looks like one of the hot springs she had seen in Yellowstone National Park a year ago.

She leaves the area of the pond and circles above the willow tree. She feels the four-fingered claw the tree resembles straining upward, trying to capture her, to add her to its *collection—human bodies neatly laid out in a mowed square of the field. The bodies are arranged in rows and columns six wide by six long—with a single vacancy in the corner closest to the tree. The bodies lay spread-eagled, a large black stake protruding from each caved-in chest. There is no blood; the bodies appear shriveled and dry. For a brief moment, she actually sees herself pinning the bodies, slamming home stakes into people she knows but dislikes; then the image is just as quickly gone. She recognizes none of the people while at the same time realizing she has now come closer to the ground.*

The ground is hot and she can feel its heat pulsing up at her like a stove burner that has been turned to its highest setting. She also feels the tree wanting to possess her—pulling her down like a powerful magnet. It pulls her farther and therefore closer, and she can do nothing. As she sinks almost into its bower, she feels the tree reaching up for her rather than her sinking down into it. And then she is suddenly within its gnarled branches, her wings a tattered shambles like a busted kite. Against her skin, the tree's bark feels warm like flesh but its texture is as rough and sharp as gravel.

She is hanging in the tree by the tatters of her wings, feeling certain the wings will soon tear and she will consequently plunge to her death. She tries to look down but finds she cannot turn her head.

Now she is being wrapped in thread—round and round like an insect caught in a spider's web—around and around tighter and tighter starting from her feet up.

Trapped like this, all she can see is the setting sun, a brilliant orange disk half sunk below the horizon. An unnatural coolness strokes her still exposed face, while the rest of her encased body feels warm and relaxed. The sun sets and the thread is wound across her chin, her mouth, her nose. Darkness is ultimately enacted by her final entombment within the thread which smells like the dusty attic of their new house.

She chews on the threads covering her mouth and they taste like paper but are as strong as wire. Everything is dark but she finds that she doesn't need to breathe here. The thread keeps her warm and she feels tired. As her body relaxes, she feels strangely at peace. She calls to sleep but it refuses to answer.

Now she is floating—downward—and the deeper she floats the darker it becomes inside her cocoon, even darker than the mere absence of light can explain. She somehow knows this darkness is the darkness of the inner earth and feels there is someone waiting for her at the end of her journey, someone who says he is a friend. She is afraid of him despite his steady reassurances. She sinks farther into the earth and the smell of dust and old paper become thick and choking.

At last, she sees a light, a light so bright it is blinding and she is now back in her bed, the morning sunlight feeling warm upon her face. Her mother is there, speaking excitedly, but Amanda cannot hear her. She watches her mother's mouth moving like when she is watching the TV with the sound turned off. Then Amanda looks and sees the empty jars on the shelves and understands her mother's concern.

She tries to get out of bed but cannot—the thick blankets too heavy and wrapped too tightly for her to move—and so she slips back into the welcome darkness of sleep.

14

June 28 • Wednesday Morning

1

Michael plodded downstairs, entered the kitchen and found Alan and Amanda sitting at the table. Amanda was eating Alpha Bits while his father had something that could best be described as flakes of tree bark mixed with rabbit pellets.

Michael removed a plastic cereal bowl from a bag on the counter. Boxes of plastic silverware lay nearby. After preparing some cereal for himself he sat down in one of the folding chairs but didn't begin eating immediately.

"Did you guys hear anything last night?" Michael inquired, looking first at his father. Alan was engrossed in a magazine—*PC Computing*—while eating, a habit Michael always found annoying.

"Hear what?" Alan replied as he turned another page but didn't look up.

This is a waste . . . he's not even going to believe me.

"Noises. They sounded like they were coming from under the house."

"Guess I didn't hear anything." Alan raised his eyes briefly to look at him but turned away almost immediately. He lifted the magazine and held it in front of him like one would hold a church psalm book; then he took another bite of cereal.

"Me neither—" Amanda began as if she was going to continue. Her mouth was open, a spoonful of cereal poised purposefully in front—then the spoon went in and the cereal disappeared. She turned and looked at him with an expression like the half-grin, barely held-in smile of someone waiting for the punch line of a joke.

"Well—*I* heard them," he said and turned away from Amanda to return his attention to his dad. "And it sounded like digging . . . or something." He took his first bite of cereal; it was already soft.

"Maybe it was mice," Amanda said and he could see just the hint of a smile in her eyes.

Then Alan said, "Or rats."

"Cool!" Amanda said and grinned.

"It could be the house itself, you know," Alan said. "Old houses—they have lots of strange noises. On the other hand, the place *has* been vacant for the last two years—it's possible we could have a rodent problem." Closing his magazine, he leaned back in his chair, then stood up and took his and Amanda's empty bowls to the sink.

"Mom sure wouldn't like that," Amanda added.

Michael decided to ignore his sister, even as he realized that what he'd predicted had come true—no one believed him. "I guess. But maybe," he began, but couldn't finish. Even though it was the expected reaction, it was still disappointing.

"You're absolutely right, Amanda," Alan said. "Mom would definitely not be a happy camper. So, Michael, what do you say—how about we take a look around that basement later on today, see if we can spot anything? Seems like we would have seen some evidence by now, though, if there actually were mice here." He turned around at the sink and leaned against the counter. Michael thought he looked puzzled, but then the look was gone. For a moment, Michael remembered the small dark shape he had seen in the basement.

"I'm helping too!" Amanda said and jumped up from the table. She put her hands on her hips and looked back and forth between Alan and Michael as if following the ball at a tennis match.

"All right, Amanda, you can help too. But you *aren't* keeping anything—got it?"

"Yeah." She gave Michael a hard stare. He stared back at her until she turned away.

"It wasn't mice . . . or rats," he said, and then to himself, too quietly for his father to hear, "it was something bigger." But Amanda heard him and looked at him with an inquisitive stare. He met her gaze once again then she looked away quickly, almost, he thought, as if she had seen something scary.

2

Michael and Amanda reached the basement before their father and turned on the first light they found which illuminated a four-foot spider strand hanging from the ceiling directly in front of them. Alan arrived shortly after and turned on two more lights. After a lengthy interval, during which Michael had the strangest feeling that his father had temporarily forgotten he wasn't alone, Alan turned to them with, what Michael judged, a rather uneasy smile on his face. Michael looked away and found his gaze drawn once again to the shadowy northwest corner.

"All right now, let's do this methodically. Michael, you check along there," Alan said, pointing to the right—the east wall, "and check along those other walls also. Up by the ceiling too. Amanda, you come with me . . . we'll check the other side."

Michael reluctantly shuffled toward his designated search area like an army private sentenced to latrine duty in the middle of summer. He didn't know why, but he was certain they weren't going to find anything.

"What we're looking for is any sort of sign—like chew marks or droppings," Alan said as Amanda giggled.

Within fifteen minutes, Amanda decided this wasn't going to be so much fun after all and went outside to play in the garden. Alan and Michael continued searching for another quarter of an hour, at the end of which they found exactly what Michael knew they would—nothing.

"Well, I don't know what to tell you Michael. No droppings, no sign of mice or rats. Maybe the noises you heard were upstairs, or maybe whatever's making the noises is living in the walls or floors . . ." Alan trailed off.

Michael, intrigued, carefully studied his father. He thought he had detected something in his voice, something almost like

What?

(uncertainty)

"No, I'm positive the noises came from down here," he said. He felt like a cancer patient explaining the specifics of his disease to a friend for the twentieth time. He immediately began to regret having brought the subject up. And yet . . .

And yet there had been just the slightest hint of something there—something Dad is holding back. Maybe he did hear the noises after all and just doesn't want to admit it? Or maybe he's seen something—something he doesn't know how to explain

(like shadows that weren't really shadows)

or maybe . . . it called his *name too?*

"Well, I've had enough for today," Alan said. "It was probably just old house noises or something anyway."

Yeah, Dad, sure. You go right ahead and believe that.

Alan began turning off the basement lights. Michael had already moved to the stairs and just as his father was reaching to extinguish the last bulb, they heard the doorbell ring.

3

"That's strange," Alan said, as he climbed the stairs from the basement. The ringing was incessant and so the closer Alan came to the door, the more irritated he became. Alan's irritation vanished though when he saw the size of the shadow cast by the person outside. At the same time, Sam arrived behind him. As he approached the door, the shadow quickly moved away.

Opening the door, Alan saw a white panel truck with the family's green Volvo resting on a tow dolly behind it. The blue lettering across the side of the truck read "Christianson." However, before he could see more, his view was suddenly obstructed by a wall of blue T-shirt. As he looked up, he made eye contact with the enormous man that had rung the bell. As

Alan stared, a white smile emerged from a tangle of wiry beard and overgrown mustache. The mover's teeth were so perfect and shiny white in contrast to his otherwise dark countenance that they actually seemed to light up his mustache and beard like a street lamp illuminating a circle in a dark parking lot.

"Howdy there. Mr. and Mrs. Sarasin? Christianson Moving. Name's Fred Kurtz," the man announced, extending a hairy hand which was attached to the end of a thick hairy arm. For a moment, Alan had the irrational thought that what he was looking at was one of the monstrous tree limbs of The Claw tree reaching out to grab him. Recovering from the brief interlude, he extended his own arm and graciously grabbed the man's enormous hand. Trying to shake the initially unresponsive arm, though, was like trying to curl a fifty-pound dumbbell.

"Yes, I'm Alan Sarasin and this is my wife, Samantha." Sam stepped forward and also shook the enormous mover's hand. "I didn't think you guys would be here so early."

"Well, we had her all packed up yesterday," the mover began, nodding his head toward the truck, "so all we had to do was drive on up here today and get to work. We left early this morning."

"You must have left *really* early."

"Yeah, that too." The man laughed and rubbed at the beard under his chin. "So, how're we going to do this?"

As he talked, the man's smile remained like a fixture on his countenance. It was, Alan thought, almost as if it were an external accessory—like a worn ornament or piece of jewelry.

"Well, I thought we'd use the front door—" Alan began.

"And I'll direct you where to put everything," Sam added.

"Suits me fine," Fred said. "We'll back up as close as we can, then lower the ramp the rest of the way. Then," he said, already walking toward the truck, "you just tell us where you want it and that's where we'll put it." Fred reached the truck and climbed into the driver's seat. After slamming the door, he started the engine.

Alan wondered why Fred hadn't left the truck running. As the mover had been getting in, Alan had caught a brief glimpse of another man sitting in the passenger seat. The contrast between the two was striking. While Fred appeared to be roughly on the order of six foot seven and somewhere between 300 and 350 pounds, the second man couldn't have been any more than five foot six or seven and weigh no more than 140. And while Fred had obviously been of American origin, the other man seemed to have been of foreign descent, possibly Asian.

Finally realizing that to back up the truck with the car still attached was going to present a problem, Fred got out and undid the straps on the tow dolly. Alan couldn't help but wince as he watched the big man struggle to squeeze his bulky frame into their car.

On the second try, Fred successfully started the Volvo and backed it expertly off the dolly. Once he'd parked it safely in the front yard, he returned to the truck. Gunning the engine he reversed the truck which quickly filled the yard with a white cloud of exhaust. Next, Fred turned the truck around in the road, backed it in and parked in their driveway at the best angle facing toward the front door that he could manage. The placement of the truck was seriously hampered though by a significant rise in the front lawn above the level of the driveway, thereby making it impossible to drive off of it more than a few feet.

As the two movers hopped out of the truck, Alan confirmed that the second man was definitely Asian. After they opened the truck's back and side doors the movers produced aluminum loading ramps from storage racks underneath the truck for each entranceway. Ironically, throughout the process, the smaller man seemed to have no trouble keeping up with his much larger companion.

Alan walked over to the front porch, climbed the steps and opened the two heavy oak doors, propping them open with rubber wedges.

For the next two hours, the movers, along with Alan and Michael carrying the smaller stuff, unloaded most of the truck's contents. As hard as they tried though, they were unable to keep up with the movers. At noon they stopped for lunch. Alan invited the movers inside but they declined, choosing instead to eat on the front porch. Alan and Michael were exhausted, while the movers seemed nearly as fresh as when they'd first arrived, although Alan thought the small man appeared at least a little tired. It was during the period when they were all working together, moving their belongings inside, that Fred informed Alan that his companion, Jung Chang, was Chinese and spoke little English.

"He makes for a pretty boring travel companion, let me tell you," Fred explained, while navigating the front steps carrying four table lamps at the same time: one in each hand and one under each armpit. "On the other hand, he sure is a good listener!" he said and laughed out loud as he continued transporting the lamps the rest of the way into the house.

It was a few minutes following this exchange that Jung noticed the medallion. Alan couldn't remember having put it in his pocket, but when he went to lift one of the smaller oriental rugs off the truck, the medallion accidentally fell out onto the aluminum truck bed with a resounding clatter. Jung, who was walking up the side ramp at the time, stopped and studied it until Alan hastily retrieved it. The instant it was out of view though, Jung continued working as if nothing had happened.

When they'd stopped for lunch at noon, they were down to the last and unfortunately largest pieces of furniture: the dining room set, a bed, the washer and dryer, and a big white Amana refrigerator.

Shortly after 12:30, Alan went back outside to help with the rest of the unloading while Michael remained indoors helping his mother unpack the boxes they'd already brought in. Alan walked onto the porch and sat down next to Fred on the cement porch wall. Mr. Chang was sitting by himself at the other end of the porch. Alan noticed that the Chinese man still had most of his lunch laid out in front of him—more or less untouched.

"I don't know, Mr. Sarasin. I think that Jung might be sick," Fred said, looking with concern toward the other end of the porch. "The guy looks pretty small, but he can usually pack it down with the best of 'em and today he's hardly touched his lunch."

For just a moment Alan thought for some strange reason that he smelled sawdust.

Fred then got up and stuffed the last of his lunch (the remains of a fourth sandwich) into the brown paper bag from which it had come and walked over to Jung.

"You all right? You sick?"

As Jung looked up, he put his hand flat on his stomach and rubbed; after that, he wiped his forehead in a back and forth motion. He then spoke a few words to Fred, but Alan couldn't understand him.

"Okay, why don't you go rest in the truck for a while, okay?" Fred said and pointed to the truck cab. Jung complied by putting the rest of his uneaten lunch away and then moving off slowly in the direction of the truck. Alan and Fred watched him as he struggled up into the cab and, leaving the door open, lay down on the front seat.

"Well, shoot, Mr. Sarasin, sorry about this," Fred said, now walking toward Alan all the while continuing to keep an eye on the truck. Fred stopped and stood directly in front of him with his hands on his hips before reaching up and scratching the back of his neck. His big smile had vanished.

"No, not at all, don't be," Alan said. "The man's obviously not feeling well—we'll just have to make do by ourselves. I'll help you move the rest."

By the way Fred looked at Alan, it was evident that the big man was sizing him up—and obviously finding him lacking.

"I really shouldn't let you, you know. It's against company policy."

"Sorry about your policy, but we'd like to have our stuff today, and I know you wouldn't want to have to make another trip. So why don't we just get to it? I won't tell if you won't? And Michael can help too."

Fred shrugged. "Okay. Your party."

4

Finally, they carried the last piece of furniture, an Ethan Allen china cabinet, into the house; Fred held one end while Alan, Sam and Michael struggled to support the other.

"You have to know how to move this stuff," Fred said.

Michael's arms felt like they were about to be pulled from his shoulders when, as they were approaching the porch steps, he heard a terrible retching sound coming from somewhere behind the truck. They stopped at the foot of the stairs and gently set the cabinet down. As Michael tried to shake his arms free of the memory of the weight they had just been holding, the sound repeated itself.

"What was that?" Sam asked.

"Jesus! Sounds like a cat trying to gargle a hairball," Fred said. Taking his cap off, he wiped the sweat from his forehead with the back of one enormous hand.

Michael looked inquiringly at his father. Alan met his stare but said nothing.

Alan walked toward the truck, stopping though after having gotten only about two-thirds of the way there. "I think," he said and turned back towards the others, "that Mr. Chang just spilled whatever lunch he *did* eat, onto our driveway."

Michael noted, with barely contained amusement, the pained expression that came across Fred's face, turning it into a mass of hair-covered wrinkles and rolls.

Walking up to and then past Alan, Fred stopped when he reached the back of the truck.

"Afraid you're right, Mr. Sarasin," he called while focusing his attention on the mess on the ground as if he were waiting for it to do something extraordinary. When Alan didn't immediately respond, Fred trudged back to the house so he wouldn't have to continue their dialogue at a distance. While looking back at the truck, he said, "I'm really sorry about this." Then he took his cap off and scratched his head; after which, he put the cap back on and turned around once again.

"It's all right," Alan said, making it clear however by the tone of his voice that it really *wasn't* all right.

Without another word, they went back to work. Working as a team, it took them only a couple more minutes to finish carrying the china cabinet into the house. Once inside, Sam offered Fred some lemonade, but he refused, saying they'd caused enough trouble already.

Michael went back outside and from the porch he could clearly see Mr. Chang slouched over in the passenger seat of the truck. Shortly thereafter, Fred came out and stood next to Michael.

"Yeah, I used to live up here in these parts," Fred announced.

Michael was by now straining to be polite but he sincerely wished the movers would leave so that he could go back inside and start unpacking—and what was even more important, check on the condition of his computer. He'd noticed that one of the boxes he thought his computer had been packed in appeared to have been damaged.

"Yep, my family used to live up here, back when the mine was going. That'd be my grandfather's time of course. Worked the ole' Sedgwick-Davey."

At the mention of the mine, Michael found himself listening with renewed interest. And then, without warning, the mover's voice suddenly . . . changed. It was just a slight change of tone and sound, and yet there was something more. It was as if . . .

as if he'd suddenly become a different person . . .

"You should check it out, boy. Check it out *real good*."

And then, just like that, he was gone—hurrying across the yard, on his way grabbing the tow dolly with one hand and then putting it up into the truck before closing the doors. Alan was coming out on the porch just as Fred was stepping up into the cab.

Fred rolled down his window and apologized once again before starting up the truck and moving it out of the driveway. As he drove past the front of the house, he waved through the open window of the cab. Alan waved back while Michael just stood and stared. After his father left the porch, he stood for a while in the front yard still lost in thought.

You should check it out, boy . . . check it out real good . . .

He continued to watch the moving truck as it left, his gaze following it as it rolled north and eventually disappeared into the woods beyond the top of the hill. As his gaze finished following the truck's path, he continued moving from left to right and found himself looking directly upon The Claw.

I was sick the first time I saw this house too, he reminded himself, his gaze transfixed on the tree.

He remained on the front lawn for a long time before climbing the porch steps for the last time that day. But as he closed the front doors behind him, he remembered the strange sounds he had heard earlier, the ones coming from underneath the house. Why he had suddenly thought of them in connection with people getting sick, he didn't know; but out there somewhere, just beyond his reach, he felt there was an answer which could explain the link. And with this also, the strange admonition of the mover—the phrase which the man had spoken as if he had mysteriously become someone else—stayed with him, as if it too were somehow connected.

You should check it out, boy . . . check it out real good . . .

In his mind, he stretched the limits of his imagination for an answer, a common denominator between the three seemingly disparate items—he stretched like a man on a swinging trapeze—but fell short.

15

June 29 • Thursday Night
Michael's Second Dream

In the dream he is outside, standing alone in the backyard. It is evening. He stares at the path leading into the woods and then he is walking on it. Ahead of him he hears voices, the sound of people chanting. He walks forward and the evening becomes blacker and the chanting gets louder. Within moments, it is pitch dark and with the darkness the air has become cold and so he hugs himself and walks faster. Above the trees ahead he can see an orange glow and smells smoke. Without transition he is abruptly there, at the edge of the Stone Circle. A fire burns in its center, flames rising well over a dozen feet into the air. The fire though makes no noise. Then the chanting stops and there is no one there—until the dancing orange light reveals the bodies in the trees. From every tree around the Stone Circle, bodies hang, held aloft by the branches they have been impaled upon. Black thorn-like branches protrude from chests, necks and heads like toothpicks through holiday gumdrops. The only sound is the blood raining upon the dead leaves of the forest floor.

As he watches, the great boulders of the Circle begin to bleed, the coursing blood starting as a small rivulet seeping from a deep pore or crack, then building into a steady, pulsing stream. He notices the palpitating rhythm of the boulder nearest him, like a granite heart pumping blood. The blood forms into pools and he realizes he is standing in one of them.

He cannot move even though he wants to. The liquid soaks through his shoes and into his socks, and the blood feels warm and he realizes he has stopped shivering. As the pools continue to grow they send tentacles of blood toward the center of the Circle and the base of the huge bonfire. Like spokes on a wheel, the blood flows from the rocks directly into the bonfire, turning the color of its flame from orange to ruby red whose light then paints the hanging bodies with a red so dark they appear nearly black. He is now walking farther into the Circle, his feet sinking into the blood-muddied ground. He approaches the silent fire but feels no heat and begins to shiver again. Rather than heat, it seems the fire is emanating waves of bitter, undulating cold. As he feels the warmth draining from his body, his shivering becomes uncontrollable. For relief, he plunges his hand into the flames but immediately snatches it back. The biting coldness burns and his aching hand turns black and shriveled with frostbite.

Without warning, the sound of the blood rain stops and in the trees he hears the bodies murmur.

Then he is within the fire itself. The cold is intense with a severity beyond description or endurance—like being plunged into the water of an ice-covered lake and the pain multiplied a thousand times. He screams but there is no sound as he watches the bodies in the trees fall from the branches like a gruesome autumn harvest, striking the ground with heavy, wet sounds. As the bodies collect on the ground, they begin to writhe and twist.

Back within the silent fire, he can no longer hear the murmuring voices and for this he is thankful. The bodies continue to fall, the only sound the thud as they repetitively strike the blood-soaked ground, like a dozen irregularly beating hearts heard simultaneously through a dozen stethoscopes. They fall by the hundreds and some of them land on the bleeding boulders. He winces at the sound of skulls cracking atop granite, the sound adding a staccato beat to that of the hearts.

The fallen bodies writhe on the ground, snaking and sliding their way across the sticky wet mud toward the fire and ultimately toward him. The first body quickly approaches the fire and its appearance is vividly illuminated by the red glow.

The body is blackened like his hand and slick with blood and mud. As the body snakes itself closer, it extends a blackened arm toward the pulsing fire. Then, as fingers which are now only stumps, reach without hesitation into the flame, Michael hears a scream and the body shrivels into an empty, black husk. With the shriveling of the body, he is subsequently infused with renewed energy and strength. As the other bodies approach the fire, the ritual is repeated again and again. And, like before, as each scream is uttered he feels yet another rush of energy while the fire burns ever brighter and higher.

Intoxicated with the power and strength of a hundred people, he feels strong enough to pick up one of the car-sized boulders and toss it like a basketball. Feeling he is about to explode with power, he searches for release. Then he realizes he is no longer standing in the fire—instead the fire has become *him—feeding itself from the power contained within him. Now when he moves, the fire moves with him. He walks to the nearest boulder and it instantly shatters at his touch. But as he continues to burn, the fire drains him, consuming the energy he has previously received from the dead. Time is running short and anxiety courses through him—an anxiety to* do something *with his power before it all drains away—but he doesn't know exactly what or how. The anxiety turns to panic as he begins to feel the energy draining from him faster and faster. However, he can do nothing but tolerate this strange sensation making him feel as if his own blood is running out of his veins and arteries and fanning out across the ground like that from the boulders. In frustration, he runs from the Circle and onto the path which leads back to the house. As he runs, burning through the forest, he sets trees and bushes on fire with green-colored flames. Within only seconds it seems, he reaches his house and realizes he is no longer burning. The mysterious energy is also gone—drained—from his body. Looking back at the burning forest he feels sadness at having caused such a disaster. Soon however his feeling of helplessness returns as the forest burns and the flames light the sky like the glow of a city. The flames make no smoke and burn rhythmically with colors that cycle among green, red and blue. The forest burns quickly, rapidly turning thousands of trees into ash. But then, as the flames fade and die, so too does the scene around him. Then, from within the darkness, a familiar voice speaks to him once again, though this time as if from a great distance . . .*

you should check it out, boy . . . check it out real good . . .

The voice keeps repeating the phrase over and over before it ultimately dissolves into the darkness, fading and evaporating like the dream itself.

16

June 30 • Friday

1

Michael woke with the dream of the Stone Circle and burning forest still seeming so real in his mind that for a moment he thought he could still feel his damp feet and smell burning trees. However, as he began to realize he was really awake and lying in bed, he became alarmed, thinking the house was on fire. Sitting up, he threw the blankets off and studied his feet, his legs, his arms. All appeared normal and clean. He sniffed the air but the smell of smoke had now gone.

I've never had dreams like the ones I've had in this house. What's going on here? The stress of the move? Or something else?

(you know exactly what it is)

Maybe it was something I ate or . . .

(oh please—stop pretending)

You're crazy.

(am I?)

Yes.

(doesn't change the facts though)

I know what you're thinking and it's ridiculous!

(how can you be sure?)

Because it's just too ridiculous.

(you're repeating yourself)

So?

(and I suppose those sounds you heard were just mice or . . . "old house sounds"?)

Who said anything about sounds?

(you're the one in denial)

Michael jumped out of bed and hurried over to his desk. As he sat down he couldn't help but notice the journal of Dr. Woulfe.

I'm not denying anything, just trying to figure out what's going on.

(you're denying the truth)

What you think isn't truth—it's fantasy.

(you'd feel better if you just admitted it)

You sound like a damn psychiatrist. Admitted what?

(the truth, of course)

Which is?

*(*you *need to say it, not me)*

Fine. You want me to say this house is haunted? Is that what you want? Does it make you happy? Will you leave me alone now?

(there—now don't you feel better?)

You're an asshole.

(you're talking to yourself)

I'm an asshole.

(now hug yourself and everything will be all right)

Screw you. Asshole.

2

With Alan, Sam and Amanda busy downstairs unpacking for the second day, Michael had time to examine the journal his father had found in the basement. Bringing it over from his desk, he laid it on the uncovered mattress of his bed and began flipping pages. He wasn't able to read most of the entries, other than an occasional word or two, as they were written in German. He could, though, decipher the years and most of the months which headed each entry. About halfway through the volume, he came upon an entry written in English. It was dated Friday—August 21, 1903.

Now that it has been determined, by forces not of my choosing, that I must leave my estate to reside in the United States, I should now choose to continue my writings and notes in what will have to be my new language of discourse, if for no better reason but for the practice.

To continue my work I will need a location with privacy—away from the prying eyes and superstitious dread of local inhabitants! I know that Dr. Grant has always praised the province they call Michigan—having hailed from there, and where, I believe, he still maintains a vacation residence.

My work must continue—there is no doubt of that. I am too close to stop now. So close that it is because of this proximity that I have been forced to abandon my home and flee to a foreign land. What a despicable irony is this! It saddens me for it to have come to this, but I would be much more saddened if required to quit my great work now. It must continue. And I shall indeed continue it.

Several pages later, Michael read about the details of Dr. Woulfe's trip to the United States, his selection of Boyne City, the purchase of this land and subsequent building of Woulfe House in the spring of 1904. Thereafter, the journal returned its focus to the doctor's "great work" which Michael had a difficult time understanding. In several locations, the text reverted to the doctor's native German. Part of his difficulty in gauging what the doctor had been working on he also had to admit stemmed from the simple fact that he knew nothing about the man. He knew he was a doctor, but a doctor of what? Also in this section, he found numerous indecipherable drawings made up of geometric shapes such as circles, squares, rectangles and triangles. At first, he thought they had something to do with astronomy or space science. Although he couldn't completely discount these ideas, he knew these assessments weren't completely accurate either, though for the life of him he could not clarify why.

He continued his reading, hoping to perhaps find more revelations in the doctor's journal. Toward the last quarter of the tome, the doctor once again resumed writing his notes in English. The first entry at this juncture, however, unfortunately left him with more questions than it answered. It was dated simply February, 1905:

If only to have the available notes of Philip and William Dam, they might answer so many questions that Jerod does not touch upon! Jerod mentions only dates of the consulted works—William, 1361 and Philip, 1347. Yes, my dear Philip, 1347, when the Black Death ravaged your dear old England; what a sad time that must have been for you! And again in 1361—such a price for failure! But I will not fail—I refuse to acknowledge its acceptance completely—its essence not even to be imagined. I'm so close! Perhaps it is the Kreis, but what then of its architecture? Shape, size, construction—at this time, I do not know—there is no more information!

As Michael read further, however, he discovered information spread amongst dozens of pages and in hastily scratched entries and diagrams that he slowly came to realize would forever change his outlook and beliefs of what he considered the rational world. As he arrived at this somewhat unconscious realization, still not fully understanding what it was the doctor had been trying to do, he was interrupted by a call from downstairs.

"Michael!"

It was his dad.

"Coming!" he said, then quickly reread the last passage which he had found, to try to convince himself once more of its validity. The entry, dated June, 1909 read:

The bonfire is built within the Kreis—a circle of small boulders set to create a ring of between six and ten feet in diameter. Each boulder of the Kreis must first be completely immersed in blood and then allowed to dry. I have found cow's blood to work

> *adequately for this purpose. The boulders must be precisely arranged so as to fit snugly against each of their neighbors thereby creating an unbroken ring. The unbrokenness of the ring, I know now, is of vital importance! The fuel for the fire itself should be hardwood logs, maple or oak, also precisely stacked so as to lean against each other at their tops thereby forming a cone with a base diameter as large as can be created within the Kreis itself. With the Kreis thus constructed as previously described, only then may the Gate be successfully established.*

He realized that the doctor was describing what he and Amanda had discovered in the center of the Stone Circle!

Gate? What does he mean by gate? A gateway to . . . what?

"Michael!" His father yelled again. Reluctantly, he closed the journal and stood up, looking for a suitable place to leave it. Suddenly, its possession mattered a great deal to him and therefore to leave it in the open seemed—unwise. He looked first at his desk but immediately discounted it—no locks. Then, spotting an old blue backpack, he carefully tucked the journal deep inside it much like a museum curator would reverently return a precious historical work to its display case. After he closed the zipper on the pack, he opened the door to his walk-in closet. The closet was big enough to have its own stairs, two of them about four feet in from the doorway, as well as a window which overlooked the driveway. Yesterday, he had begun filling this closet with boxes—the idea was to keep his room neat while he unpacked one box at a time.

He walked in and began climbing over the mounds of boxes, intent on reaching the farthest accesses of the closet. As he was stepping over one of the last boxes, he heard something break and, in response, swore under his breath.

Great! Now what the hell did I break? Isn't it enough the movers had to trash my computer?

When he finally arrived at the back of his closet, he ceremoniously stowed the backpack in the corner, sliding boxes against it to better conceal it. He turned around to renegotiate the obstacle course but just as he did a strange sensation began to ripple through his body, beginning inside his head, then traveling down to his feet—reminding him of the strange energy surge so manifest in his recent dream.

The Image, when it came, was like a daydream, floating into his mind as if he had suddenly become so tired he was unable to resist the warm embrace of sleep and, instead, welcomed it, and slipped into a dream state as . . .

he sees the basement, gray and full of shadows while somewhere behind him a light provides faint illumination of the white-washed wall in front of him and

. . . his awareness returned to him in his closet, peripherally, but lasting only long enough to feel himself fall heavily upon the same box that had previously produced the sound of something breaking and now he heard what he assumed was the same object shatter under his weight with a sound like crushing Styrofoam egg cartons . . .

he stares at the wall, recognizing it now as the north wall located at the east end of the basement by one of the corner rooms. He looks down at his hands and sees himself holding Dr. Woulfe's journal and then he is speaking but unable to comprehend his own words. As he begins to feel invigorated with renewed energy and power, it reminds him once again of his dream; and then he is walking into and through the wall in front of him as if it were nothing more than a white gossamer sheet of fog and

. . . as a single drip of saliva began a slow, elongated course from the corner of his mouth destined to land on the back of his right hand. He sat, focused exclusively on the Image, unable to sense any pain in his ankle which was presently folded beneath him even as its numbness slowly slid its way up his leg and . . .

he is somewhere underground and turns to look at the hole in the wall behind him. Seeing it, it makes him happy and waves of pleasure undulate orgasmically through his body until

. . . he absently pulled his ankle out from under him and stood up awkwardly . . .

the hole in the wall and the basement fade from view.

. . . and looked around once more inside his closet, feeling disoriented, wincing at the biting numbness in his leg.

What am I doing in here?

As he spotted the corner of his blue backpack partially hidden behind some boxes against the back wall, he rubbed his leg, wincing again at the tingling sensation that was rapidly climbing up past his knee.

He climbed back over the boxes. As he was clearing the last one, he heard his father, now in the hallway outside his bedroom door, call his name again. He successfully cleared the final hurdle and stumbled into his room where his father was standing in the doorway.

"So there you are! Didn't you hear me calling you?"

"I was just putting something away first."

"It takes you fifteen minutes to put something away in your closet?"

"No," Michael said and looked hard at his father, trying to determine if he was being sarcastic or perhaps thinking Michael was being secretive.

He decided his dad was kidding. The other alternative was too unthinkable. He thereby convinced himself with this argument that if he had indeed been daydreaming he would have at least remembered what it had been about.

"I was trying to find something."

"Oh, so now you were trying to find something and not put something away? Which is it?" Alan said, waiting for an answer somehow they both knew would not be coming. Alan stepped farther into the room, crossed his arms over his chest and leaned against the wall by the door. "Whenever you're ready, I could use your help downstairs."

His father stood a moment longer, looking at him, then abruptly turned and left and Michael followed him. As Michael descended the stairs, he thought again about the closet but this time it was the voice of his alter ego that began the conversation.

(So, if you think your dad was just kidding because you don't remember anything—why, pray tell, was your entire left leg numb from your foot up to your knee? Think something like that happens in only a minute or two?)

By the time he'd reached the bottom of the stairs, he had yet to come up with an adequate answer for himself.

What's happening to me? The nightmares are bad enough—now I'm blacking out in the middle of the day? Maybe this is how a brain tumor starts. Or maybe I'm just tired. I haven't had to do physical labor like this in a long time . . . so maybe it's just the fatigue . . . the stress of the move . . .

(stop lying to yourself)

And you—shut up! Our conversation is done. I've heard enough of your explanations for a while, thank you very much.

(okay, you're the boss; just don't say I didn't—)

Shut UP!

He attempted to reassure himself by citing again the possibility of fatigue as the culprit for his daydream, even while not thoroughly believing it. And so, for the first time since coming to their new house, he felt something more than simple worry, disappointment or depression.

Michael Sarasin was scared.

3

It was late afternoon when Michael and his parents finally quit working for the day. All the furniture was now arranged in its final location. Most of the boxes had been unpacked. Dishes had been put away, clothes hung up, and beds made.

"Can I ride into town and go to the library?" Michael asked as they were sitting at the kitchen table—Alan and Sam each with a can of Coors, Michael with a Cherry Coke. Amanda remained in her room upstairs, still arranging.

"Sure, why not? I guess you've earned it." Alan upended his beer and swallowed twice, hard. "Anything in particular you're planning on picking up?" He said as he wiped his mouth with the back of his hand.

"No, nothing really. Thought I'd see if I could find some more information on this house or its former owner. The first owner that is, I mean . . . Dr. Woulfe."

"A good project for you," Sam said.

"Sounds like a noble endeavor," Alan said and proceeded to drain the last of his beer. He stood up, took the empty can to the sink and rinsed it. "Just don't be gone too long, okay?"

"Okay," Michael said and left.

Upstairs, it was with trepidation that he went to retrieve his backpack and the journal he'd hidden there. While struggling to climb over the piles of boxes in his closet again, he resolved that, when he returned, he was going to find a better, or at least more accessible, hiding place for the journal.

He was downstairs in a matter of seconds and in a couple more was out the door, on his bike and pedaling hard, backpack and journal safely in his possession.

4

It took Michael nearly three-quarters of an hour to complete the ride into town. As he leaned his bike up against a huge maple on the opposite side of the street from the library, he realized that he was breathing heavily. His shirt felt like a hot, wet towel beneath his backpack. It was then that he noticed a group of neighborhood boys about his age playing a shirts and skins basketball game in the school playground on the same side of the street. He watched them with envy, wishing he could join them. But he knew he couldn't; he was just too different from other boys—different in the things he liked to do—the things he liked to talk about.

Then he recalled how that had started to change once—when Cindy came into his life. With her introduction into his world, he had made new friends and gone to parties. He instantly became more popular in school and started attending school sporting events for the first time in his life. But all that was changed now too.

Returning his attention to the playground, he noticed that one of the boys had become angry at what he claimed had been a foul committed against him by another. Without warning, he threw the basketball at the other boy. The ball hit the boy squarely in the chest and bounced away unnoticed as the rest of the boys quickly rushed in to restrain the two before things became nastier.

As he crossed the road to the library, Michael was shaking his head at the scene he'd just witnessed. He even smiled as he listened to the boys exchange insults ranging from the size of their sexual organs to the morality of their mothers. From the top of the library steps, he glanced behind him once more. By now, the boys had separated and it appeared the game was ready to continue.

Maybe I'm not missing so much after all.

Inside the library, he was disappointed when he discovered a woman he hadn't seen the last time he was there, presently seated behind the librarian's desk.

"Hi. Who are you?" He said and realized too late how rude he sounded. The woman immediately looked up from the papers spread out on the desk and fixed him with the stern glare of an experienced elementary teacher used to, but intolerant of, the impertinence of unruly children.

"I'm Mrs. Helen Burroway, if you so demand to know, young man," she said, her tone making it even more obvious that he had started out on Mrs. Burroway's bad side.

"Isn't Mr. Bentley here today?" he said, knowing but not caring that he was only making the situation worse. Mrs. Burroway didn't respond right away but continued looking at him with her menacing school-matronly gaze.

"No, Mr. Bentley is not," she said and paused. She studied him further, then continued. "He had a dentist appointment this morning and decided to make a day of it. Is there anything *I* can help you with? We have a wonderful selection of teen adventure in the young adult section over in the corner," she said and pointed behind him to the front corner of the building. He noticed that more than a dozen rings covered her fingers.

"Well . . . actually, what I'm looking for is a German/English dictionary."

"Oh," Mrs. Burroway said, raising an eyebrow. Then her eyes narrowed as she regarded him. She maintained her posture until he became uncomfortable and turned away. "You'll find that in the reference section," she said, finally breaking the silence. When he heard her step out from behind the desk, he turned back around. She was moving in the direction of the young adult section she had pointed to earlier before stopping abruptly at an island bookcase just outside of it. "You'll find the foreign dictionaries on the bottom shelf here," she said. Then, as if suddenly realizing she had been taken away from some matter which demanded her immediate attention, she rushed back to the desk.

After she left, Michael crouched down so he could get a better look at the indicated books. He quickly scanned the titles but after a first glance across the three dozen or so books present, didn't see what he was looking for. He started again, looking left to right, taking the time now on his second pass to carefully read each title. He stopped when he came to the "Langenscheidt Standard Dictionary." The gold print on the cover had faded considerably making the lettering on the book nearly illegible, which would probably explain why he'd missed it on his first pass. Removing the book from the shelf and holding it up to the glare of the fluorescent tubes over his head, he could barely make out "German-English" and "English-German" printed near the bottom of the spine in lettering so faded that it was little more than the indentation in the cover left behind by the printer. Pleased with his discovery, he picked up the small, yet impressively thick volume, and carried it over to the librarian's desk.

"Oh no, I'm sorry, you can't check that out—that's a reference book. We don't loan reference books—you'll have to look at it here."

"What? But—"

"I'm sorry, but that's the rule. All reference works *stay here.*" Mrs. Burroway dismissed him with her eyes.

"Fine," he replied and picked up the book. Taken aback, he trudged over to the single table and four chairs that resided in the general fiction area and sat down. He took his backpack off and, without quite meaning to, slammed it on top of the table. Out of the corner of his eye, he saw Mrs. Burroway flinch and cast a harsh glance his way. Deciding to ignore her, he unzipped his pack and carefully removed the antique journal. Shoving the backpack to the other end of the table, he placed the journal prominently in front of himself then slid it forward almost to the other side of the table. In front of this he carefully laid down the dictionary and the spiral notebook of his own journal. With his materials so arranged, he took a moment to cast a brief glance in the general direction of the librarian's desk and was pleased to catch Mrs. Burroway staring at him again. He turned back to his work, taking special satisfaction in ignoring her.

During the next three hours he translated, as best he could, many of the German entries in the journal. He started at the beginning with the first entry dated the same as the date which appeared on the cover. His translation was rough and full of questions, but, he hoped, he'd somehow managed to preserve the intent:

> *February 12, 1895*
> *Welcome to my journal. A journal you say? Yes my friend, whoever You happen to be. But this is not a journal for You, but for me. Its purpose is to serve as a record for a path(?) of research whose destination I cannot yet understand (or fathom?) which makes me lightheaded(?) upon thinking (speculation?). As I (think or fancy) myself a scholar (or teacher?) and even, perhaps, a scientist, I feel it my responsibility (duty?) to record my (experiments?) in this endeavor(?) either as (celebration? tribute?) to an eventual success or as discouragement (or deterrent?) to a failure whose consequences have already been proven (or shown?).*

As Michael read, he quickly forgot about the presence of Mrs. Burroway. In fact, he now felt like an archaeologist digging up an ancient tomb—or perhaps a paleontologist uncovering the fossilized skeleton of a previously unknown species of dinosaur. But along with his discovery, he knew, came responsibility. For the archaeologist and paleontologist, theirs was manifested in the form of the preservation, description and cataloging of their findings. But for Michael, his personal responsibility, as its truth began to bare its ugly, fanged head at him from out of the yellowed pages of Dr. Woulfe's journal, would instead be one of concealment if not outright destruction of the artifact itself.

In the journal, Michael eventually discovered answers to most of his questions, including the most important one, the one that he had had when he'd first stepped into the library three hours earlier. He knew, finally, the identity of the Great

Work the doctor spoke of, and why, upon the discovery of the nature of that work by his neighbors in his native Germany, they had seen fit to drive him from his home.

For it seems that Dr. Robert Benjamin Woulfe had been intent upon—through incantation, symbology, ritual and the research of notes dating back at least 600 years—establishing contact with the forces, spirits, and ghosts from the "Other Side." This "Other Side" was that realm of existence, postulated by religious orders the world over, which lay beyond death. But even more fascinating, and which as he read sent indescribable shivers across his back, was that Dr. Woulfe had also desired to *harness* such forces. And as near as Michael could tell, the doctor, through contact and the establishment of various control mechanisms, hoped to secure for himself one of these individual forces to act as his personal guide to lead him, upon his death, safely to this "Other Side."

Put simply, Dr. Woulfe hoped to secure for himself the passage of his soul beyond death, presumably to Heaven, through the making of his own reservations.

But how would he know that what he had contacted were representatives of Heaven . . . or of Hell?

Having collected his materials and gotten up to return the dictionary, Michael was once again cognizant of Mrs. Burroway's scrutinizing glare. Nevertheless, he ignored her, put the dictionary away, replaced the backpack on his shoulders and left.

Outside, the playground was now empty. Unlocking his bike, another question, one that would keep him puzzled throughout the entire ride back home, suddenly surfaced in his mind like one of those scenes from one of the B-rated horror flicks he sometimes watched. It was the scene, often repeated in one form or another, where some supposed-to-be-dead corpse is able, suddenly, violently, and miraculously to resurrect itself from out of the depths of the bathtub it supposedly had been drowned in, to snarl with a feral grin at the hapless hero. In Michael's scenario, his personal "corpse" that had in this instance surfaced, grinning and salivating from out of the pool of his mind, was the simple question:

Had Dr. Woulfe . . . succeeded?

17

1

"Well, well, look who finally decided to show up after all," Alan said when Michael arrived home. Michael looked at his watch—it was nearly 6:30. He realized he had become oblivious to the time while on his bicycle ride home because he was busy digesting the information he had gained at the library.

"Sorry, I got tied up at the library," he replied as he sat down on the side entrance stairs to take off his shoes. Alan remained at the top of the stairs, the light behind him projecting his image as a silhouette. Even without seeing him, Michael could still imagine the disapproving stare.

"I asked you not to spend too much time there; you knew it was getting late."

Michael turned around and saw his father with his arms crossed over his chest projecting the image of a castle guard barring entrance to his master's keep.

"I know. Guess I just lost track of time. Sorry."

"In that case I would think that you must have found something interesting."

As Michael stood up, he felt it best to focus his concentration on putting his shoes away in the cupboard built into the wall in order to hopefully avoid being drawn further into the confrontation.

"Well?" his father demanded. Michael reluctantly turned to look at him.

"Didn't find much, just some basic stuff."

"Is that so?"

He could hear the doubt in his father's voice as clearly as he could hear his own heart thudding in his chest. They stared at one another and his father's face, hidden by shadow, was for Michael unreadable. Michael now wondered if his father was going to remain in that position blocking the stairs until he received a satisfactory answer.

*He feels it too. He doesn't know what it is yet—hell—*I *don't even know what it is, but there's something . . . something here that's not right. And the fact he feels it too just confirms its presence that much more. Problem is, none of us knows how to deal with it, whatever it is. In the meantime, I become the whipping post. Again.*

"Well, at least you didn't miss supper," Alan said, pausing a moment longer, before turning and disappearing into the kitchen.

Michael hesitantly climbed the stairs as if he were ascending the gallows.

"We were just getting ready to sit down," Sam announced from the kitchen. "Burgers and macaroni and cheese."

Amanda and Alan were already seated at the table. Upon Michael's arrival, Amanda stared at him without blinking. Sam was carrying a pan to the table.

"No thanks. Guess I'm not very hungry. Think I'll just go up to my room for awhile—do some more unpacking maybe," he said and, without another glance, strode heavily up the two flights of stairs, his legs more out of shape than he'd thought, though he knew the cause in this case was more than simply the bicycle ride. As he left the kitchen, he heard his parents begin talking about him, but he ignored their conversation.

Upstairs in his room, he carefully removed the journal from his backpack. Then, inside his closet in a place where he'd previously found a moving box full of old school papers, he slid the book under the bottom of the stack. Despite his extended stay at the library, there was still a third of the journal he hadn't yet read. For now, though, he didn't think he could digest any more, not so much because of weariness but out of outright fear at what further diabolical secrets he might uncover. He reconsidered this as he wondered what could possibly be worse than what he had already uncovered. Then he remembered how, on the ride home, visions of human sacrifices had kept painting his mind a sanguine red—the Stone Circle serving as an evil backdrop for his terrified imaginings.

As he lay restlessly on his bed, exhausted, he debated whether or not to tell his father about his discovery. He stared at his closet door and for a moment found himself wishing that the door would suddenly open and someone would walk out and tell him what to do.

Maybe this Dr. Woulfe was just plain crazy—I don't have any information about what happened to him. Maybe he was carted off to some mental institution somewhere? Or what if he had succeeded, but only partially? Maybe something went wrong? Maybe whatever went wrong is still happening now, or been—awakened—again?

At this point, Michael thought almost anything was possible. It nevertheless all came down to the same thing. He needed more data. He resolved too, that while he continued his research, he would remain quiet. He couldn't be sure if his father would want to help, or if he would simply continue to deny that anything was wrong.

Confident with his decision, he fished through another box in his closet, finding a paperback sci-fi novel to read—*The End of Eternity*—by Isaac Asimov. Twenty minutes later, he felt his eyes beginning to droop. Turning out the bedside light, he crawled beneath the covers of his bed and instantly fell asleep.

2

Alan and Sam were tired. Three days of moving and unpacking had exhausted them. Although it was only a little past 9:30 they decided to call it an early night.

Not even attempting to get in his nightly reading, as soon as Sam had snuggled in, Alan turned off the light, climbed beneath the covers and within a quarter of an hour was fast asleep.

When he awakened, he looked at the bedside clock and at first couldn't believe it. He had been asleep for more than two hours, though it felt as if he had only drifted off a few minutes before. He was now lying awake in the silent darkness—and listening—when he thought he heard a sound above that of Sam's gentle breathing.

He tried to think, to recall the events of a dream, but could remember nothing which might explain the soft rasping sound. Then, just as he tried thinking of an alternate explanation, there was a sudden delicate tapping at their closed bedroom door.

Was that what I'd heard?

He didn't think so, but he continued listening, his breathing labored.

Slowly, the door swung open. It was so quiet that Alan thought he could actually hear the sound of someone breathing in the doorway. From out of the darkness, a faint but refreshingly familiar voice sent relief coursing through his body.

"Mommy?"

Amanda.

"Yes, honey, it's daddy. It's okay, I'm over here," he replied as he listened to the reassuring sound of Amanda's small feet as she padded across the bare wood floor to his bed.

"I heard a noise downstairs. Can I sleep with you?"

Alan's initial mental image of a small gray mouse digging in the dust of the basement suddenly morphed itself into that of a big shaggy rat the size of a tomcat—then again into that of a snarling, rabid wolf complete with foaming mouth and stinking, matted hair. Although normally not afraid of such things, he nevertheless found himself shivering involuntarily.

"Daddy?" Amanda asked again.

"Sure, honey, climb in."

He held the covers for her as she slid under next to him. After some initial shifting and turning, they finally lay comfortably on their sides, facing away from each other. Amanda seemed to drift off to sleep almost immediately while Sam had never heard her daughter get into the bed. Alan, however, felt content and yet anxious for their safety at the same time and remained awake, lying in the dark—eyes open—ears straining to catch the slightest squeak, scratch or rustle. After several minutes of silence, he closed his eyes and tried to sleep, but it proved elusive, his earlier fatigue seeming to have been satisfied, or at least corralled by the big bully of an awakened fear.

An hour passed, then two before he finally drifted off. Unknowingly, he held the medallion firmly in his hand, its gold metal warm against his palm. If he'd been awake, he might have felt the faint tingle as it suddenly began to vibrate.

Next to him, Amanda awakened. A few moments later, though, she fell back asleep . . . and dreamed.

18

Saturday Night
Amanda's Second Dream

In the dream, Amanda stands in the field next to The Claw Tree. It is late afternoon and the air is hot and still. She looks at the tree and sees the image of a face in its bark. The face is sexless and moves its mouth as if it is speaking but it makes no sound other than what she hears in her mind. The tree face tells her to "go underneath." She reaches out in the direction of the talking face but at the moment her trembling hand touches it, the face disappears and the tree shakes for a moment as if shivering.

Now she stands at the edge of the pond and stares into the brilliant clear water but is unable to see the discharge shaft of the spring. She wades into the pond and the water feels warm like a bath and is a pleasant relief from the hot, dry air.

She is wearing shorts and standing knee-deep in the water when she feels a gentle tug on her ankle. She looks down but sees nothing in the clear water which laps against her. Now however she is close enough to see the deep shaft in the center of the pond, and the water gets warmer the closer she moves toward it. She approaches the hole, and is standing at the edge of it when she feels another tug on her ankle, stronger this time which causes her to nearly fall. To keep her balance, she plants her right leg firmly in front of her. When she looks into the water again she sees only a cloud of silt which has been stirred up by her abrupt movement. Then she feels a gentle pulling on both legs; it is constant and strong, tugging her forward toward the hole. She is afraid and tries stepping backward, but the water holds her firmly and this time she does fall, landing on her bottom. Falling into the water, though, does not release the strong grip on her legs and she is dragged forward across the slippery mud toward the deep shaft. She reaches behind herself but is unable to find purchase in the muddy bottom. Her fingers dig furrows in the mud, clouding the water until it resembles chocolate milk. As she is pulled farther into the center of the pond, the water becomes deeper, immersing her body up to her neck and she realizes that she is being pulled down into the hole at the center. She wonders how much it will hurt to drown.

She is now underwater, sinking into the shaft. To her surprise, she no longer feels any fear as the sky above fades from view. She realizes she is able to breathe water like a fish and during her descent through the warm water, she continues looking above at the rapidly diminishing circle of brightness as it grows smaller and dimmer until gone as she floats downward into the blackness.

As the descent continues it feels as if her body is getting heavier—even somehow bigger. She feels as if she is growing, becoming an adult. She sinks into the darkness until her feet touch a stone bottom and at the instant of contact the water is gone and she finds herself standing alone in a dark cave. The air in the cave is cloying, saturated with cold moisture. She shivers and tries to hug herself to defend against the cold, while in a faint light whose origin she cannot see, she watches her breath congeal on the air into little white clouds which inexplicably drift away into the cave without dissipating. Water drips from the ceiling and walls, each drop echoing, making a sound like rain. But when she looks at the cave floor and although she can witness and hear the water dripping and running down the walls in snaking rivulets, she sees that the floor is dry and dusty. She continues watching the water drop from the ceiling—staring in fascination as it vaporizes an inch above the floor. She is now convinced that the rain is fake, a hoax perpetrated by someone or something of great power but limited knowledge and experience of the real world now somewhere far above her. She marvels at the depth of this revelation and then it is gone, replaced by a calm assurance.

The cave is suddenly gone and she stands on a hill covered with thick grass so green it seems almost to overwhelm her eyes with its color. From the base of this hill, the grass covers the gently rolling land to the horizon. Although she doesn't feel its effect, she notices how a breeze sends waves rippling across the green land. The hill she stands on is more than three times taller than any other hill she can see around her.

Next, a crowd of people encircles the base of her hill. They stand in reverent silence, faces upturned and staring. They surround her in a fat donut shape—thousands of motionless, staring people standing in rapt, waiting attention as she towers above them on her hill. She feels their expectation like a heavy hand on her shoulder.

She points toward the horizon and the people turn away from her and walk as if commanded in the direction to which she has pointed. As they walk, the land and people suddenly begin to change. The grass surrounding her hill turns gray like steel wool while the people turn black—their clothes, their skin, their hair. As the people walk forward and transform, they shed their clothes which subsequently fall to the ground in brittle, ragged pieces soon trampled into dust by the people behind them. In addition, their hair falls out in thick clumps and their skin glistens black like polished stone. They form a black column and march in an orderly fashion toward the horizon, ten to a row, turning the hills behind them into a visual black-gray wasteland.

She glances at her feet as the transformation spreads now through the grass up her hillside, also turning it from green to black like a consuming shadow. The darkness reaches her feet and seeps up her legs, turning them into shiny ebony. At the same time, she feels a burst of energy pour into her like a delicious flood and so she raises her arms above her, letting the blackness consume her.

She stands in front of the marching column, her body twice the height of any of the followers who march silently behind her. She leads them toward the horizon, the new feeling of power and strength charging her entire body, coursing through her veins like liquid electricity. As they continue their march toward what seems to be nowhere, the column at her back quickly catches up to her despite her effort to walk faster. Two of the marchers are now strutting beside her, inching their way ever closer to her side. Then they touch her, her thighs rubbing against their arms, creating a sound like glass rubbing against glass. Then they melt *into her, their bodies becoming a part of her body, subsequently amplifying the energy already possessed within her. The sudden introduction of this increased power makes her dizzy. The "merging" process continues two at a time, faster and faster.*

The marchers have now all disappeared, absorbed into her and once again her feeling of unnatural size returns. This time, though, it is more a feeling of enormous energy and power than that of physical stature.

Suddenly, she is back in the cave and walking forward along the passage until she enters a cavern as large as the modern-day domes built to enclose mammoth football arenas. The inside of the cavern glows with an eerie blue light and her feeling of strength and power is nearly overwhelming. She walks over to one of the walls and begins digging into the stone as if it were no more difficult than picking raw cotton, tearing out enormous chunks which she carelessly tosses behind her into a pile. Feeling the power flowing out of her body and into her hands and arms she digs ever more frantically at the rock, eventually creating a tunnel. Finally, her feeling of power fades and with it, her ability to dig and so she stops and listens. From the other side of the rock she hears the sound of digging as well. She backs out of her cave and waits for whatever it is that is on the other side. As the sound becomes louder, she is afraid. Somehow, she knows that what she has done is wrong. From somewhere behind her comes quiet laughter.

She runs—out of the cavern, through the cave, the light fading and the cavern disappearing as she runs faster and faster . . . the laughter continuing behind her, following her, reaching for her . . .

19

July 2 • Sunday

1

"I'm going outside," Amanda announced as she left the kitchen before anyone could respond.

Michael and Alan had both finished their breakfasts in silence. Amanda had come downstairs a short while after them and eaten hurriedly. Michael began to wonder if there was something bothering her. This thought made him uneasy and so he looked across the table at his father for some possible support.

Alan broke the silence first when he announced, "Guess I'll be working in the basement today. I was wondering if you could work on the library—most of the books are still boxed up. I think your mother is going to be working on the bedrooms and doing some more here in the kitchen."

Somewhere in the room a fly buzzed against a window and Michael muttered in agreement without even looking up from his empty bowl. Then his father asked if he was depressed about the damage done to his computer, assuring him they would eventually be reimbursed by the moving company. He tried to reassure his father by telling him he wasn't worried about it anymore as he watched him take his bowl to the sink. Alan turned around, briefly looked at him for a moment, and then left the kitchen. Instead of turning his attention to the library and its books, or even to his computer, Michael instead found himself worrying about Amanda again. In the brief moment she had sat with them, something about her behavior had bothered him. He couldn't pinpoint the source of his anxiety, yet the uncomfortable feeling persisted.

What the hell is going on in this place? Or is this what it's all about—we've moved into a house that just slowly drives us insane? Is that what happened to Dr. Woulfe?

Or . . . is it just . . . me?

This last thought sent a shiver throughout his body.

No. They feel it too. They're just too afraid to admit it—yet.

2

After Michael left the kitchen, he headed for the room designated to be the library, near the front of the house. It was a small room in comparison with most of the others, but with the addition of two large floor-to-ceiling bookcases, a leather couch and a library table, it promised one day to be a cozy place to curl up with a good read. Today, though, even though the bookcases were already in place, the books were unfortunately still packed in boxes and bags in a disorganized heap in the center of the floor.

As he unpacked the books, thoughts of Dr. Woulfe's journal never strayed far from his mind and so his thoughts continuously drifted in that direction. Sometimes it seemed as if he was suddenly awakening from a short nap after having spent periods daydreaming of the journal and possible explanations for what it meant. He was never quite sure how long these episodes lasted, but by lunch time, he discovered that he still hadn't opened all the boxes or put away a single book.

"I didn't think it was in the job description to read each one first," Sam interrupted, startling him as he was paging through a simulated red-leather edition of Fyodor Doesteovsky's *Crime and Punishment.* He remembered reading the book last fall and the twenty-four-page analysis he had written about it for school. His teacher was so impressed by his efforts that she had called his parents to tell them about it.

"Actually, I've already read it," he said and quickly closed the book as he studied the floor which revealed his lack of progress.

"Ready for some lunch?"

"Guess so." He stood up slowly, his knees momentarily not willing to cooperate.

Michael followed his mother to the kitchen. It seemed like it'd only been an hour since he'd started and so he was surprised to see by the kitchen clock that it was a quarter to one. Amanda and his father were sitting at the table, already eating the Spam burgers and Rice-a-Roni which Sam had prepared.

"Haven't seen you much all day, young lady," Sam said.

Michael slid a chair over to the table and the wooden legs squealed in protest as they were dragged across the linoleum. At the irritating sound, Amanda's head jerked up and her eyes darted around the room. When they stopped, she directed a scowl at her mother, then went back to eating.

"I was playing outside," she replied, and stuffed a forkful of rice in her mouth. Michael had never seen her so serious—her face drawn and sullen. She looked like a little girl who had been told she could never again play with her best friend.

When Michael remembered his earlier feeling of anxiety for his sister, he was genuinely concerned when he learned that she had been playing outside by herself all morning. It wasn't like her to play alone for long periods of time so he decided he'd try to talk privately with her later.

"Anything wrong?" Sam asked gently.

"No, not really . . . I don't know . . . I just had a bad dream last night."

Michael came to attention with a start that made his chair slide back with another screech. His fear had suddenly come alive like some long, thin worm, twisting its way out of his stomach and up into his throat. He thought he'd stopped breathing for several seconds. He swallowed hard, then took a deep breath. The snake around his throat temporarily loosened its grip but refused to let go.

"What . . . kind . . . of dreams?" Alan asked.

Michael felt his throat constrict again. As the realization of what he thought he was about to hear began to swell inside him like a rapidly expanding bubble that would soon break and splatter its revelation, his father confirmed his worst fear.

"I've been having some weird dreams too," Alan added.

Michael tried to will himself to regain control, to breathe normally, and slow his racing heart.

"You have?" Amanda inquired, and for the first time that day, Michael began to see some of the old Amanda—bright and smiling, full of youthful life.

Alan spoke again, shifting uncomfortably on his chair. "Yeah, some pretty strange stuff too," he said, glancing briefly at Sam before picking up his Spam burger for another bite. "Probably just from being in a new house and new town. Nothing to worry about."

"Yes, dear, your father is right," Sam said. "Nothing in a dream can hurt you."

Michael ignored his mother, sensing instead that his father was trying too hard to sound calm. He watched him take another large bite of his burger and chew it like a squirrel with a mouth stuffed full of nuts.

Okay, bud, time to lay your cards on the table.

"I've had some too," Michael added, but his throat was still constricted and the words came out too soft for anyone to hear him. He tried again and this time swallowed before speaking. "I've had some bad dreams too. I thought I was the only one though. Thought I was actually going crazy."

He saw his mother cast him a scathing glance, but he ignored it.

As he looked more carefully at his father he saw the fear reappear. Alan tried to mask it with a nervous smile. "There, you see, Michael's been having them too. Nothing to worry about."

But don't you even want to know what they were about? Don't you even care?

Alan went on, "It's okay, Amanda. Everyone has a bad dream once in a while. It's nothing to be worried about. They can be scary, I know, but you just have to remember that eventually you wake up and then it's all over. There's nothing in a dream that can hurt you, right?"

Don't be so sure.

"Yeah, I know. But I just don't like 'em," Amanda said, wrinkling her nose as if to accentuate her opinion.

Michael however was now looking anxiously at his father, waiting for him to go on.

Is that the best you can do? Is that all you're going to say? What are you so afraid of?

His mind was suddenly a swirl of questions and implications. Was something causing them to have these dreams? If so, what? And why? Did they mean something? Did they have something to do with the house? The cult?

While grappling with these questions, he found that a sudden serenity had settled upon him. Like a spring mist, it coated his body gently, slowly—all the while soothing away his fear and anxiety. At first though, it made him even more afraid—he thought something extraordinary must be happening to him—being done *to* him. A moment later, he relaxed and welcomed the calming warmth. At the same time, his throat began to loosen and his breathing once again returned to normal. As he tried to reflect on the questions he had previously been contemplating, he discovered, to his dismay, that he couldn't remember them. They were simply . . . gone. Erased.

Deleted.

This last thought bothered him for a moment until it, too, faded.

Guess it was nothing. Guess everything's going to be all right now. Maybe it was was *just the stress of moving and being tired.*

"Michael, are you all right? Michael? Michael?"

3

The afternoon proved little better, work-wise, for Michael. On the plus side, at least, he was no longer thinking about the dreams. He began the afternoon by hauling boxes up the four flights of stairs to the attic. His foray into this endeavor didn't last long though, for it was only minutes later when he'd stopped for his first break, wandered over to his bedroom, stretched out on his bed and within moments had Dr. Woulfe's journal in his hands once again.

He was stretched out comfortably, both the journal and notebook open in front of him, when the Image slid its way back into his mind, coming with the ease and familiarity of a lover sliding into the embrace of his beloved. The pleasant feeling lasted but a moment, though, as the Image that had now come stroking his mind with soft lover's caresses soon changed its mode of intrusion into the urgent groping of the merely lustful as it then roughly and wantonly seized control of his mind and . . .

he stands in the basement, in front of the wall by the room in the southeast corner, the white cement bulging at him, pulsing faintly like a dying heart and

. . . sweat now covered his body, even though he had never felt so cold . . .

a wall bubble—a fluid elasticity of the wall matter—forms in the shape of a large hand reaching out to him, not to grab, but in a pleading, wanting fashion, as the dying hand of an old woman stretches out to the world one last time before she slips into the darkness of the next and

. . . Michael could sense the sweat on his body but only vaguely, seeing nothing else now but the Image playing in his mind, its relentless demands overpowering his consciousness as does the rapist the body and will of its victim . . .

when he touches the hand it feels like a rubber glove filled with cold water and then it grabs and pulls him toward itself and the wall, and he is suddenly through the wall and being dragged into a dark underground passageway which he follows with the guidance of a dim light whose source he cannot see

. . . as Dr. Woulfe's journal slipped unnoticed to his bed, closing itself as he remained powerless, and subsequently unaware, immersed within the rapture of the Image, seeing nothing else now but the Image . . .

and he walks forward along the passage, the light becoming brighter the farther and deeper he goes and he feels an unknown presence behind him, someone he leads by the hand and he looks down at the hand and it is a small hand, a child's hand and then he is in a massive cavern and

. . . his father's intrusive shout abruptly cancelled the presence of the Image as if it had been a movie playing in his head that someone had suddenly turned off.

"Michael!"

He shook his head and sat up on the bed. Staring at the closed journal in front of him, he wondered why his clothes felt damp and sticky.

He had no recollection of the Image. Nevertheless, his mind felt blank and rested, as if he had been sleeping. Able to stand up at last, he stretched his arms above his head, then went downstairs in response to his father's summons.

4

That night, everyone turned in early—only Amanda insisting that she wasn't tired, adding that she was afraid of having more dreams. When he heard this, Michael sensed there had been something he had been planning to do—something which involved his sister—but right now he couldn't remember what it was.

From his room, Michael listened intently as his father and mother talked to her—trying to convince her that a dream could never hurt her, no matter how frightening it seemed. When Michael heard this, just for a moment, he felt there was something else—some thought or question or answer that, again, he had forgotten. As he struggled to remember, almost feeling the lost memory's efforts to break free, the memory only faded more and then was gone altogether. Instead of feeling frustrated, though, he only felt more tired.

Exhausted even further by this experience, he crawled into bed and was asleep within minutes.

5

According to his bedside clock, it was 2:32 AM and Alan was still lying in bed, awake and listening. He knew he was still awake and confirmed it by poking a finger into his side. He followed this test with a rigorous rubbing of both eyes, then once more lay still, his eyes now sore and hot as he focused his attention on the now unquiet darkness.

The sounds had begun softly, at first reminiscent of far-off digging or scratching. In time, these became louder, turning into some sort of moving whisper which seemed to start out in front of him, pass beneath and then behind him as all the while he lay in bed trying to convince himself it was only a dream while Sam slept on peacefully beside him.

Finding himself perspiring, Alan pushed off some of the blankets. When he stopped to listen again, the digging sounds had stopped.

And then the voices began.

No, they just sound *like voices. How could they be voices?*

He considered waking Sam, but quickly discounted the idea. She would either think he was crazy or would become frightened.

He was suddenly overwhelmed by an image of hundreds of graves lying in a field of black dirt underneath the house. In his vision he further imagined mummified Indian corpses wrapped in deer skins and buried in rows scattered randomly beneath their property. Then he saw the buried pelts begin to unravel as skeletal hands pushed against the time-ravaged skins, subsequently breaking holes in them. He saw them digging their way toward the surface—making a sound like that of an advancing mole army. And then he envisioned the hands, white shiny bones polished to a brilliant luster by the soft dirt, breaking through the surface of the ground—hundreds of them all at once—until a field of groping, clawing hands lay waving in the sunshine like some macabre crop.

He struggled to squeeze his eyes shut.

just like

(in your dream)

in that Poltergeist *movie. Maybe our house is buried on top of an old Indian graveyard and when we moved in, they were . . . stirred. Maybe it's their time, the time they have been waiting for, their time to rise up from the dead to terrify the living who have dared disturb their peaceful slumber.*

Then he thought about Amanda, her blonde hair just like that of the little girl in the movie.

(They're after Amanda. That's what they want. The spirits crave the innocent blood of a little girl in order to be able to sleep again.)

Stop it! Just stop it!

(You can't stop them, not until they get what they need, not until they have been satisfied, their appetites quenched by the young blood of the innocent.)

Alan forced himself up, being careful not to disturb Sam, hoping he was just sleeping and dreaming after all and that if he would only wake up it'd all be over. By now the sweat on his back had evaporated and he started to shiver. The sounds from downstairs had not stopped however and now sounded like murmuring—like voices speaking from underwater.

He held his breath.

It's just mice. Or rats. Right? That's all it is . . . right?

20

July 3 • Monday

1

Alan woke the next morning feeling strangely tired and worn. He couldn't recall being awake, though, anytime after drifting off once the voices had finally stopped. Sam had already gotten up, and he was alone in the bed.

On his way downstairs, he stopped briefly on the landing to stare at the world outside; the sky appeared gray and dull like the bottom of an old aluminum frying pan. When he reached the kitchen he found Sam pouring herself a bowl of cereal and Amanda seated at the table. There was no sign of Michael.

"Morning, dear," Sam said.

"Morning."

Alan walked over to the counter and opened the bread drawer. He removed a loaf of whole wheat, untied it and took out two slices.

"I think I'm going to go into town after breakfast and pick up some parts at the hardware store; see if I can fix that gazebo. Want to come?" he asked his daughter, then looked at Sam.

"I'd rather go into the field and see if I can catch some butterflies. I saw a big luna moth the other day—sure wish I could have caught him," Amanda said

"You go ahead dear, I still have lots of unpacking to do," Sam replied.

Alan thought his daughter had sounded strange—mechanical almost—as if reciting a script.

Alan put his bread in the toaster, pushed the lever down and turned back to the table.

"Did either of you . . . *hear* anything last night?"

He looked first toward Sam, then watched his daughter as she seemed to be taking longer to consider this question than he had anticipated. Unfortunately, there was no obvious expression on her face that he could read.

"Not me, why?" Sam said, now eating her cereal at the table. Amanda acted as if she had never heard his question.

"Nothing. Thought maybe I'd heard something. Probably just a dream. How about you, Amanda—any more dreams?"

"No," she said, in the same mechanical reply as before.

"That's good."

Alan caught his wife's glance, but neither of them it seemed, knew what else to say.

Alan proceeded to eat his breakfast in a hurry without really knowing why he felt rushed. Amanda poked at her Cheerios while he downed his two slices of toast which had been cooked to a point about four seconds shy of charcoal. Covering them with strawberry jam had made them barely edible. Amanda finished her cereal and was putting the bowl and spoon in the sink when Michael appeared.

As Alan took his last bite of toast he swallowed it with a grimace. "I'm going to town for a few things. Shouldn't be gone long. Need anything, Michael?"

Michael looked at him quizzically for several seconds and Alan wondered if he had even heard him. He had a strange look on his face as well, almost like . . .

. . . he was in a trance.

"No, Dad," Michael said.

As he scrutinized his son he wanted to say something, to ask him how he was, how he felt, something, anything—but for some inexplicable reason he couldn't. He knew he had to get into town and therefore his anxiety of wasting any more time kept him from saying more.

"Bye dear," he said and kissed Sam on the forehead as he left.

2

Alan drove the Volvo to town. The sky's earlier dull pallor had now brightened to the dusty tone of mausoleum granite. The overcast sky depressed him. As he thought about the voices from the night before, in the light of day, overcast or not, they didn't seem quite as frightening as they had in the dark. He tried relieving the tension by laughing at himself, but instead it came out sounding more like the cackling of a blood-lusting hyena . . . or of the insane. About three miles from town, he began an internal dialogue with himself.

So, were they really *voices, Alan? I mean, are you absolutely, beyond a doubt positive sure they were* human *voices talking to you from your basement? Because if that's the case, it only leaves us two choices: either your new house is haunted or you've flipped your gourd and frankly, neither one sounds like much of a choice in my book.*

Okay, smart-ass, so how do you explain the fact that both Michael and Amanda heard them too?

Heard what?

Voices!

Did they tell *you they heard voices? Or was it more like, Daddy I heard* something *downstairs?*

I don't know. I think Michael said he heard voices.

Okay, never mind, the point is, did they really hear voices or something that maybe just sounded *like voices?*

Well . . .

Okay then! Look, you're in an old house. Old houses make lots of noises. You're just not used to them yet. It could be water moaning in the pipes or something.

Water moaning?

Hey, it's just a thought. The point is, there're probably a hundred things that make strange noises in that place. You've only been moved in for a couple of days. Give it a chance. Everyone's a little on edge, what with the stress of moving and all.

Fine, you've made your point. Okay, the question then Mr. Smart Guy, is: what the hell do I do about it?

Easy. Next time you hear something—check it out—right? Get your lazy ass outta bed—go downstairs—and check it out. Nothing could be simpler.

Yeah, and that's just when you get it, like in one of those horror movies. The unsuspecting victim, showing heroism and courage totally alien to his character up to that point, is suddenly suffused with an undeniable curiosity. So he goes down into the deep, dark basement. He looks around, checks out every nook and cranny, finds nothing. And then, oh yeah, there's just this one little place he forgot to look and he thinks that after he checks it out everything'll be all right and he can go on back upstairs and snuggle-wuggle himself back into his nice warm bed. Except it's never all right, because when the misguided "hero" looks in this last dark corner that's when the monster jumps out and rips his head off in a spray of blood and guts.

Geez, bud, you gotta quit watching those movies. But come on now, is that stuff real? NO. Are there monsters, for God's sake, in your basement? NO. Pull yourself together, man! Remember, you're the father figure here, not the helpless bed wetter who thinks there's a monster living under his bed, and oh yeah, there's a big ugly troll hiding in the closet. Mommy, could you leave the light on, I'm scared . . .

Okay, okay, you're right. I should just check it out and next time that's exactly what I'll do, okay? Deal? Will that satisfy you?

Alan drove the rest of the way into town in blessed silence with the sky hanging above him like the bottom of a dead battleship.

3

When Alan finally arrived at his destination, Bernie's Hardware, he parked between a green and white BC Electric pickup and a slightly rusted silver-blue minivan with what looked to be a gunshot hole in its rear quarter panel. As he entered the store, a small brass bell announced his presence.

Alan cruised the aisles and had to admit to himself that he was impressed. The store was actually quite large and surprisingly well-stocked for a small town like Boyne City, especially when one considered it was one of three hardware stores in town. The only other customers he noticed in the place were a group of four, rough-looking locals.

He was in the nuts and bolts aisle when he happened to overhear their conversation in the next aisle. As he half-listened they seemed to be trying to quiet down. Their voices were still strong though and heavy enough so that he had no problem hearing them. At first, as a courtesy, he tried not to listen—but soon found himself doing everything he could to hear every word.

"How many did you say?" asked the first one whose voice sounded to Alan like that of a young man, perhaps no more than thirty. In the brief single glimpse he had had of them earlier, though, he was unable to remember the particulars as to what any of them had looked like.

"Two," a second one said. "Whatever it was got *two* of 'em. Ripped the shit right out of 'em too. Shit, old Scott said the ground was just soaked with blood. Tufts a hair and shit all over—but no bodies." This second voice was gruff and hoarse, like that of a longtime, heavy smoker.

"He didn't find nothing?" the first one inquired.

"I just told ya didn't I? Shit, Andy, I wonder about you sometimes, I really wonder," said the gruff-voiced one. Apparently, "shit" was his favorite word. "But what I wanna know is, what in the shit-hell coulda hauled off two a Scott's herd like that?"

"Coulda been a bear," said one of the others.

"Maybe a mountain lion," a fourth voice added.

"Yeah, maybe," Gruff-voice said. "Some a you probably's don't remember when we all had a problem like this before . . . Ed?"

"Yeah . . . I remember. But, Christ, that was back in fifty-five. Those folks gotta be long gone, no way they'd come back and start that business up again—would they?"

"I don't know. But I think we all best keep our ears to the ground real good from now on, know what I mean?" Gruff-voice said.

"Nothing wrong with that advice, I suppose," the one referred to as Ed said.

"Well, guys, I gotta get going. If I don't get that door fixed by this afternoon, Theresa's gonna have my hide."

"Aw shit, Andy. You pussy-whipped son-of-a-bitch; that woman's got you wrapped around her finger like a wet rag," Gruff-voice said, laughing. The sound of his voice was like gravel under the heel of a boot.

"Yeah maybe, but I'll take my Theresa long before I'd give your old wench a second glance. I wouldn't touch *that* beast with a ten-foot dick."

Gruff-voice started laughing again and this time it sounded like 15-grit gypsum paper scraping on a tin can. "Oh, that's a *good* one, dear boy—now's you just run along before I beat the living fuckshit outta your pussy-whipped hide. 'Bout the only thing you got that measures ten is your shit-for-brains IQ."

"Any day you wanna try, you old gas bag," Andy said, now laughing himself.

Alan was suddenly reminded of the movie *Grumpy Old Men.*

Hollywood ain't got nothing on you guys.

He heard the men leave the aisle and shuffle toward the front of the store; then he heard the jangle of the bell tied to the front door. Reaching the end of the aisle, he was surprised when he saw two of them standing at the front counter.

After Alan found what he'd come for, he moved up to the front of the store. One of the men, whom he knew instantly had to be Gruff-voice, was a huge glob of a man, in his fifties, his hair as much gray as brown. Underneath the unkempt hair hung a beaten face of pock-marked skin in rolls, weathered brown and wrinkled. Alan was immediately reminded of the dried apple-head dolls his mother used to make.

"So, Chuck, how's business?" Gruff-voice said to the young clerk running the cash register. He was buying a role of duct tape, several plastic pipe fittings and a container of chewing tobacco which he'd snatched from a rack near the register.

"Oh, you know how it is. Not bad, but going to get better when the summer people start rolling in and working on their houses and all," the clerk replied. "That's too bad there what happened to Scott."

"Yeah. But, shit, I just can't figure it, you know?"

"I hear you. We sure don't need any wild animals running around here scaring everybody. That'll be thirteen thirty-five."

Gruff-voice produced a billfold bulging with papers and currency. The billfold was attached to a chain prominently hooked to a loop on his jeans. He handed the clerk a ten, folded in fourths, along with four ones. The clerk returned his change.

"Thanks, Kirk."

"Yep. Later, Andy."

In his attention to Kirk, Alan had momentarily forgotten about the other man. So, he was surprised to see the one named Andy wasn't the young man he'd imagined him to be, but instead he appeared to be closer to 60 or even 70.

Just as Alan walked up behind him, Chuck was ringing up Andy's sale—several screws and a door hinge. Andy paid his bill, exchanged pleasantries with the clerk and left. When Alan dropped his own merchandise on the counter, a bolt rolled off onto the floor. As he bent over and picked it up, he noticed that the floor smelled like cow manure.

"You know those guys?" Alan asked Chuck, whose red name tag read: "My name is Charles Minter—How May I Help You?"

"Uh, yeah," Chuck said, slow and careful, like a pupil standing in front of the class reluctant to answer a teacher's question. His head bowed, he stared at what Alan had put on the counter as if it were the most interesting pile of hardware he had ever seen.

"What do you know about who they were talking about—this Scott—is he the one that lives out on Pleasant Valley?"

"That's him. Not too much. He lives way out, all the way to the end of the road. Has a farm. Cows and sheep. He comes in here quite a bit, 'specially in the summer. What do you want to know for?" the clerk asked looking up and eyeing Alan with suspicion. Alan had the impression that the clerk was a friend of the man and wasn't going to divulge anything further unless given a really good reason.

"Just curious. Name's Alan Sarasin. We just bought a house on Pleasant Valley," he said and began to extend his hand when the clerk turned away to check a bolt price on a list taped to the wall behind him. Alan lowered his hand.

"Really? You must mean Woulfe House," Chuck said, still looking intently at the price list, his voice trailing off as if his mind had drifted.

"That's the one. So what happened to his animals?"

The clerk turned around and began punching the cash register's keys. "Huh? Oh, you mean Scott's sheep. Yeah, well, nobody knows I guess."

"I thought I heard those guys say some of them were killed."

"Oh, they were killed all right. Two of them. Killed last night as a matter of fact," Chuck stammered, like someone trying to drive a stick shift for the first time, the car hitching and hiccupping. "Like I said, nobody knows what happened. They found a bunch of blood and all, but that was about it. No tracks, no noises, not much of nothing." Chuck looked at him again, his boyish face painted with an almost unnaturally serious expression. Then his voice changed, becoming deeper, slower. "What's really strange though is that *two* of them were gone. I mean, normally, if some wild animal's going to make a killing, it'll kill one animal and maybe drag it off—if something scares it that is. Otherwise, it'd just as soon sit right there and eat its fill and leave the rest for the scavengers. And then, if for some reason it killed more than one, it shoulda only took one and left the other. So, yeah, that's kinda strange—what kind of animal could have killed two full-grown sheep and been strong enough to drag both of them off—all without leaving a trace?" The clerk was staring now. Alan didn't think he was really looking at him though, and was suddenly reminded of the woman from the hotel.

What he taught wasn't the living . . . it was the dying . . .

"I see your point," Alan said and looked away. He found himself thinking again about the tree.

The Claw.

In his mind, he visualized the tree pulling itself out of the ground and then shifting along in the dark creating a sound like a wind soughing through a stand of white pine. Then he saw it stop and wait at the edge of a farmer's fenced-in pasture just before lunging forward like a supernatural jack-in-the-box only to grab two screaming sheep and crush them in its massive branches.

"I said, that'll be four sixty-five, sir."

"Oh, yeah, sorry."

Alan paid his bill, then left, the image of a sheep-snatching tree still vivid in his mind. Back inside his car, he laughed nervously to himself at the absurdity of the idea.

4

As they were climbing into bed that night, Alan mentioned the incident with their neighbor's sheep to Sam. He hadn't planned to or wanted to; it just came out of him in a sudden rush. Once begun though, he felt the need to tell the entire story and subsequently did so, leaving out nothing save for the vulgarities of the men's conversation.

Sam's initial response was to just lean over to the bedside table and turn out the lamp.

"So, what do you think?" Alan asked in the darkness, perplexed by his wife's lack of response.

"I don't know. What am I supposed to think?"

Alan sat up on his elbows and leaned closer to her.

"I thought you might be worried."

"Well, from now on we should probably keep the kids closer to the house. If there's a wild animal on the loose we shouldn't let them go running off too far by themselves."

"Right, *and—*"

"*And*, I'm sorry but I guess I'm just too exhausted to think or care about anything else right now."

"You're right, I'm sorry." He said as he laid his head back on his pillow. "It's been a long day. I shouldn't have brought it up."

"Good night," he said.

"Good night, dear."

5

In the hallway, Michael, who'd been lurking outside their room and had overheard their conversation, reflected for a moment about the death of two sheep—then crept back to his room.

What he didn't see though was Amanda, across the hall from him, her eyes shining in the blackness, her small body like a statue standing rigid in the dark shadow of her open bedroom door.

21

July 17 • Monday

1

At the end of June, Alan had arranged for a subscription to the local newspaper. In the weeks since, its delivery had been sporadic at best. So, when the story of Scott Farley's missing, and presumed dead, sheep made the local newspaper on two occasions, it happened coincidentally that these two occasions corresponded with missed deliveries on the part of their paper carrier.

The first of the two articles simply reported what had happened at the Farley's farm. This missed delivery occurred on the day Chester Hume, their newspaper carrier, had thrown the paper out the window of his pickup truck nearly a mile before reaching Woulfe house. If asked though, he would have claimed to have been unable to remember the incident. Despite missing this particular article, the story nevertheless would not have provided any additional information than what Alan had already overheard that day in the hardware store.

The second article—this time missed when Chester's '86 Chevy blew a front tire where Pleasant Valley showed itself from out of the woods to the north of the field containing The Tree—was a historical piece recounting several instances in the past when the local community had had similar problems with wild animals killing livestock. The primary focus of this article were the years 1954 and 1955 when there had been three separate cases of cattle killings, several missing sheep and a mutilated horse. Although local townsfolk had presumed a wild animal was responsible, none was ever seen or captured.

On Friday, July 7th, Alan had received a phone call from the head of the computer science department at Charlevoix Community College (affectionately referred to by the locals as C-cubed or CCC). Following the call, Alan attended his first interview for a teaching position on the tenth. He had been invited for a second interview today at 2 PM and was strongly optimistic he would be offered a position.

Samantha had started her job at BC Electric the day after the 4th of July holiday. Although things began slowly, the pace soon picked up. Within days she was able to feel relatively at home with familiar accounting tasks: balancing general ledger accounts, payroll, depreciation expenses, and working through a sales tax reporting problem complicated by the state's rate differential dependent on whether the account was residential or commercial.

Also, during the last two weeks, there'd been no mention of anyone having been afflicted by any more bad dreams. More noises, though, were still being heard in the middle of the night, but Sam had summarily discounted them simply as "old-house sounds."

Finally, and most significantly, Alan and Sam noticed, with genuine concern, the growing detachment of Michael and to a lesser extent, Amanda, from the family. Although their concern was mounting, they excused their lack of action with the rationale of a new home and new jobs.

But, they realized, they would have to deal with the matter soon.

2

"So, did anybody ever find out what happened to your neighbor's sheep?" asked Edward Swan, general manager of BC Electric, walking into Sam's office one day. He usually visited Sam's office at least two or three times a day, occasionally making her uncomfortable as the visits sometimes reminded her of what had transpired with her previous employer.

"Uh, no, I don't think so," she said, maintaining her attention on her computer. She was entering June revenue figures into a spreadsheet that tracked and compared the amounts from the last two years.

"You know, we had something like this happen before. It was a long time ago—back in the fifties I think," he continued and Sam was instantly reminded of someone's grandfather telling stories around a campfire. She stifled a yawn. "I was just a kid then of course, but I remember it because at the time it really stirred people up." By now he was sitting, legs crossed, in one of two orange chairs in front of her desk. Mr. Swan was what could best be described as a diminutive man, both in stature and, Sam thought, in personality. As such, she found his present posture disgusting and therefore attempted to avoid looking at him by keeping her attention fixed on her computer screen.

"Really?" she said, trying to sound interested. Concentrating on her work, she had actually heard only about half of what he had said.

Something about something happening back when he was a kid, I think.

For some inexplicable reason, the thought of wet dreams popped into her head and, despite her best efforts, she smiled.

Mistaking her smile as encouragement, Edward continued his tale with renewed enthusiasm. "Yeah, the sheriff even arranged groups of locals into hunting parties and they scoured the woods for days. My dad was in on some of it. For a while there, they were staying out all night. They didn't find anything of course—no tracks, no evidence of the animals that had been killed, nothing. I guess that's what got people so stirred up—it being something unknown—something they couldn't explain. And so they couldn't deal with it. Knowing it was done by a cougar or whatever would have set a lot of people's minds at rest, as funny as that sounds. They would have said, 'Oh, a cougar. That makes sense,' and then everything would have been all right."

Sam felt as if he were waiting for some sort of reaction from her. Her problem was compounded though by the fact that during his entire discourse she had listened to barely a word, having only the vaguest impression of it having something to do with wild animals.

. . . something they couldn't explain . . .

When she finally glanced over at him, he was smiling broadly—eagerly at her—like a puppy waiting for attention.

"Are there really wild animals around here?" she asked, hoping her question wouldn't betray the fact she hadn't been listening.

"Oh, yeah!" he said, his face now becoming, impossibly, even brighter, his smile wider. At that moment it took all of her willpower to keep from standing up and leaving the room, moving, getting out, going anywhere but *here*. "There've been bears . . . coyotes even . . . elk of course but none of them would ever really hurt you unless you got in the way of their mating or something . . . and mountain lions have been spotted on occasion."

"Wow," she offered dully.

He once again seemed to have misinterpreted the agitation in her reply and the tenseness of her body as concern and so he rushed on, "Nothing to be worried about of course; no one hardly ever sees anything like that . . . it's just that when you have an incident like this it makes people wonder, you know?"

She was beginning to feel nauseous, but forced a polite reply, "I suppose. Well, we're not too worried. We're keeping the kids close to the house of course and—"

"Good idea! You've got a lot of untamed wilderness out there by your place."

"We like it though," Sam said somewhat defensively and redirected her attention back to her spreadsheet. Sensing this signaled an end to the conversation, he stood up to leave.

"Well, guess I better let you get back to work. Everything going okay so far?"

She looked up from her computer screen and smiled, relieved at the possibility of finally being able to escape.

"Yes. Everything's fine. Your accounting practices are a little unusual, but I think I'm getting the hang of it."

"Good. See you then," he said and left.

Sam's relief wasn't complete however until she'd sat still for several moments in her chair and let her body adjust. As she went back to work, she tried to remember exactly what it was that Mr. Swan had been telling her, but was unsuccessful.

Soon after, her head was filled once again with the numbers—always black and white, exact, and defined—the aspect of her life she so dearly loved. Numbers that never lied, played games or put on false pretenses. Numbers that no matter their appearance, either handwritten, laser-printed or on a computer screen, could always be counted on to mean the same thing. And, although she was quickly able to forget about Edward Swan, she wasn't quite so successful with something he'd said, something that remained in her mind and refused, like a stain on a new white blouse, to go away.

. . . it had been something unknown . . . something they couldn't explain . . . something . . . it had been something . . . unknown . . . unexplainable . . .

3

Amanda stared at her brother sitting directly across from her at the kitchen table.

Dad had left for his job interview after putting together a lunch of sliced ham sandwiches and macaroni and cheese for them.

"You all right or what?" she asked, breaking the silence.

Michael stared at the sandwich in his hands.

"Or what."

"Fine, be a jerk." Amanda said, then stood up. "See if I give a rip."

Michael said nothing.

"I'm going outside. See if I can catch that luna moth."

Michael finally looked at her, his face devoid of expression. "Just remember to stick close to the house."

"It speaks."

"I mean it."

"*Okay*. I will! Geez, chill out. You've been acting pretty weird lately, you know? What's your deal, anyway?"

Michael, though, still seemed indifferent to her presence and had chosen to focus his attention instead on something behind her—as if he had forgotten her completely.

Amanda shrugged and went outside.

4

After Amanda left, Michael climbed the stairs to his room. He had nearly completed his reading of Dr. Woulfe's journal and was looking forward to its final pages, most of which, fortunately, were written in English. Safely in his room, he once again retrieved the journal from his backpack and lay down with it on his bed to continue his reading.

> **28 April 1921**
> With the contacts I have made thus far, I now believe it to be reasonably possible, certainly conceivable, that I may obtain some measure of guarantee of regular passage. To achieve this, I believe it can be accomplished to forge a bond with that with which I have made contact. A bond others will in time be able to benefit from. My theory maintains that one should be able to guarantee their passage through the formation of such a permanent bond, linking this side to theirs. The bond, once established, would then remain permanent, thereby allowing the forces of contact a glimpse into our side in exchange for future guidance to theirs.

Skipping ahead several pages of undecipherable German and elaborate diagrams, Michael then read the last entry in the notebook:

> **14 May 1921**
> I have now established a permanent Gate. The process has been exhausting but, I believe, immensely worthwhile. The passage is permanently viable and over the past three days I have traversed the locking and unlocking of it at will with no ill effects that I have been able to determine—and, I must add, with perfect security. A place of refuge, earthen lair

There was no more to the journal.

He looked more closely at the end of the book, searching for evidence to indicate that pages might have been removed, but found nothing.

Could there be another volume? That must be it—has to be! Somewhere there's got to be more of these notes. And I'm going to find them. I'm going to find them even if it means tearing this whole house apart.

Despite his concern, Michael nevertheless reluctantly closed Dr. Woulfe's journal. The look in his eyes at that moment, if Amanda or Alan had seen it, might have been more of a reason for a sleepless night than the threat of any nightmare.

22

July 18 • Tuesday

1

When Michael woke, the LED readout on his bedside clock informed him, in glowing red numerals like the slitted eyes of an alien creature, that it was 7:11 AM. Normally, this would have been his cue to throw his head back and sleep for at least two more hours, but not today. For today, he was instantly awake and eager to take action. Even going to sleep last night had been difficult; his racing mind refusing to let him rest. He not only felt it important that he get up; he *needed* to get up. There was something he had to do—something he had to do right *now*. Each passing second increased his sense of urgency that his time to complete this task was running short. He hadn't felt such anxiety since his final exam in Mrs. Hanscom's freshman typing class when the big black clock at the front of the room had sat ticking almost as loudly as the clacking of the twenty-four computer keyboards—each student knowing that only each word typed correctly during the allotted time interval counted as a point toward their final grade.

Throwing himself out of bed, his covers falling haphazardly in a heap on the floor, he paused to reflect once more on his self-appointed mission. He had resolved to find the next volume of Dr. Woulfe's journal.

But where should he start?

And then he remembered the specifics of the plan he had formulated last night while lying awake in sleepless agitation. A sense of renewed confidence surged throughout his body. He wanted to begin at the top of the house and work his way down because he thought that by starting at the top he was playing better odds. He recalled that the first journal had been found in the basement. Assuming the doctor had intended to keep his journals a secret, at least from the casual searcher, it seemed reasonable that he would put each volume in a different place. Therefore, if volume one had been placed in the basement, he thought it made sense that he might find the second in the attic.

On the other hand, maybe he put them all in the basement—just in different places?

Doubt began to creep in, his earlier resolve made during the dark of a sleepless night no longer seeming so certain when considered in the critical light of day.

Three minutes later, he was in the attic.

2

Lying in bed, Alan heard the attic door open. This was followed by the sound of soft footsteps treading up the wooden stairs. From the ceiling directly above his head, boards creaked and groaned.

It's another nightmare.

Except this time he *was* awake—he was sure of it. Then the sound of the footsteps stopped, then started again. It had to be Michael, he thought, the tread too heavy for Amanda.

Besides, what would Amanda be doing in the attic at this hour? Of course, then again, what would Michael?

He looked at his clock; it was seven-thirty.

Odd. What on earth could Michael be doing up there? Maybe we took a box of some of his stuff up there by mistake?

Satisfied with this answer, and hearing nothing more, he drifted back to sleep.

3

Michael tried—but failed—to climb the attic stairs quietly. The air was cold, almost like being underground. The attic was spacious; an eight-foot ceiling in the center sloped down at the walls to a line about two feet above the floor. Like the rest of the house, the attic sported a hardwood floor, although the boards here were neither sanded nor finished and so dark and aged as to appear almost black. In addition, Michael noticed large gaps in the floor which were packed full with dust and dirt. In the center of the open space the boxes Michael and Alan had brought up more than two weeks ago still sat unopened. The morning sun, shining in through one of the large multi-paned windows which had been built into each of the four walls, silhouetted the pile of boxes making them resemble the shadow of an Egyptian pyramid.

Michael's first inclination was that Dr. Woulfe may have hidden his notes under the floorboards. If so, he knew that under the present circumstances he might never find them as ripping up the floor was definitely not an option. Later, though, if he still hadn't found something, he might have to reconsider it. But for now, it was out of the question.

As he diligently reconnoitered the attic, he saw that it was spacious and empty but for the boxes. The only thing of interest he found was a large, homemade box fan in the window to the right of the stairs. The red-painted, four-winged fan blade was at least four feet in diameter and encased in a wood-framed box stapled over with wire mesh. A large electric motor mounted on a wooden platform beneath the fan was connected to the blade via a large V-belt. Michael remembered movies where the mere presence of such a machine would have been a guarantee that someone, at some future point, was destined to be chopped to bits by its whirring blades. He decided to refocus his attention on the walls.

The attic was dusty and smelled like the inside of an antique shop. The only other feature of note was a chimney which stood prominently next to the left side of the stairway. He looked again at the floor-level windows and decided to walk ahead to the one in front of him. Once there, he discovered that he was going to have to crouch down in order to see out. After wiping away the dust which covered one of the twelve window panes, he was amazed at how much he could see. From this vantage point, he discovered he was able to look out over the entire backyard, over the top of the barn and the carriage house. He could even see across most of the treetops of the surrounding woods. Looking out over the forest caused the memory of the Stone Circle to resurface briefly. Acting on reflex, he turned away and stood up.

Walking to the side of the attic opposite the fan, he looked out the window there. From this window he had a clear and all encompassing view of the field with the strange willow in the middle of it. At the sight of the gnarled tree, the sense of urgency he had previously felt upon awakening resurfaced. Waves of nauseous anxiety rippled up from his stomach towards his chest making it feel as if a hundred moths had suddenly been set free within the empty cage of his torso.

He still didn't know where to begin since he couldn't see any hiding places other than the already-discounted floor. He decided to check out the chimney. The square, red-brick column was covered with some sort of plaster or cement-like substance that was crumbling in several places and had left piles of white debris around the base. He first looked to where the chimney rose through the roof but saw nothing. Then he felt around the brick and walked around the entire column. Nothing.

Next, he took a slow walk, or more accurately a crawl, around the perimeter of the attic looking for anything out of the ordinary—a loose floorboard, a panel in the wall that could be removed—anything that suggested itself as having the slightest potential for concealing something as large as a notebook. When he came to the fan, he hesitated. Then, unplugging the motor, he searched the fan's housing. Again, nothing. Concluding his search of the attic's perimeter, he discovered that he'd returned to his starting point.

Discouraged, he shuffled to the head of the stairs, determined to continue his search throughout the rest of the house before considering anything so drastic as pulling up floorboards.

Once he was out of the attic and back in the hallway, he heard his father and sister downstairs in the kitchen. When he walked back into his room and glanced at his clock, he was surprised to see that it was nearly nine.

He felt disappointed. But his earlier anxiety, though temporarily having been dulled for the moment, had not gone away and urged him on. He had been so positive that he would find the doctor's notes in the attic. As he left his room and walked back into the hall, he realized that the second and first floors wouldn't hold much promise either—he couldn't go tearing into bedroom or living room walls any easier than he could take a crowbar to the attic floor.

So, back to the basement, I guess.

Resolute, he proceeded downstairs.

4

Michael found himself creeping down the stairway, almost feeling like a burglar in his own house but not knowing why. What he did feel certain about, though, was that he didn't want to be seen—or questioned about what he was doing. However, just as he reached the first floor, Alan spotted him.

"Hey there, early bird! So, what's got you up so early?" he called from the kitchen.

Michael fidgeted, wanting to make believe he hadn't heard his father and bolt into the basement. He'd almost done this when his mouth seemed to answer for him of its own accord.

"Nothing. Just looking around."

I know, I heard you up in the attic before eight. What were you looking for?"

As Michael turned to face his father, he found Alan staring at him strangely.

"Nothing," he said. Even though his father was communicating in the most friendly, good-morning-to-you manner, Michael still felt like the defendant on a witness stand. He was uncomfortable, and realizing it only made him more so. His hands felt wet and hot, and when he rubbed them on his jeans he saw his father note his behavior and frown.

The friendly wake-up manner now gone, Alan moved towards him and Michael nervously shifted his weight from one leg to the other.

At the same time a part of him thought that this might be the best time to let it all out; release the pressure and tell his father everything. Then, for some unknown reason, the words to an old Stetson cologne commercial plugged themselves into his head—easy for youuuuuu . . . Stetson . . . makes it easy . . . for you. Well, he definitely had no Stetson, and even if he took a bath in the stuff he still didn't think it would make a difference.

And then it got strange. A voice entered his head, not quite strong enough to obliterate the now endlessly repetitive ditty from the Stetson commercial which had temporarily taken over his mind, but still loud enough to be heard, and for now, that seemed to be all that mattered. The voice told him not to tell his father. Not to tell his father *anything*. Michael, like anyone else, had his own little "voice" in his head from time to time, and he always imagined it to be like the clichéd image of the devil on one shoulder and an angel on the other—but this one was different. Different in that he didn't recognize it. It, to be precise, felt *alien*—if that wasn't too strong of a feeling—too *outside* of him to be considered a real part of himself that he hadn't heard before. This voice felt more like telepathy, a true presence but one not of himself, that had somehow managed to weave a small hole into the back room of his consciousness in order to allow its message to be heard like a soft voice coming from the back row of a concert hall.

He decided to say nothing for the moment and as he reached this decision, his agitation miraculously evaporated. The voice, however, remained and to his surprise he actually welcomed it, perhaps because it had urged him to keep quiet about what he had been doing in the attic. It seemed strange to him though that the voice would want him to keep secret his search and although he experienced this concern regarding the voice—it nevertheless felt good to obey—somehow it felt *right*.

He needed more time to think things through, even while knowing that the moment was coming when he would ultimately be compelled to let the truth out—the truth about Dr. Woulfe, their house, the cult, the Stone Circle—everything he had gleaned from the doctor's journal—if not for his family's sake then at least for his own sanity. He'd kept it bottled up too long already and the mounting pressure, until a moment ago, had been almost unbearable. Now, at least, everything seemed okay. It felt better not to tell anyone, because now it seemed that everything was going to be all right. In time, the voice assured him, they'd all see.

"Nothing, huh," his father repeated. "Maybe it's time you and me had a little talk. What do you think, Michael?"

His immediate and intended answer was *I don't . . .* instead, he once again surprised himself. "Yeah, I guess so." The voice told him it would be all right—he could talk to his father—so long as he didn't tell him anything. Anything important.

Father and son moved toward the front of the house and entered the library. The now full bookcases dominated the wall across from the front bay window. Michael and his father sat down on opposite ends of a bluish-black leather couch against the other wall.

"Is everything all right? You've seemed preoccupied lately," his father began, starting what Michael already thought of as The Interrogation.

"Yeah, I'm okay," he said and relaxed—the voice was going to tell him what to say. He didn't need to worry.

"What about the sounds—the noises at night? Have you heard any more of them? Any more ideas what they might be?"

"You're the one who thinks they're rats or something, Dad."

"Yeah, well, lately, I'm not so sure. A while ago I could have sworn I'd heard something almost . . . almost like *voices*. Have you ever heard anything like that?"

Michael watched his father's eyes narrow and then opted to stare beyond him, out the bay window, seeking a distraction in a blue pickup truck that was driving by.

"No," he lied. The voice inside his head told him it was okay to lie every once in a while . . . about little things . . . little unimportant things.

"Hmm. Just my groggy imagination working overtime I guess. Haven't had any more of those dreams though. I still can't quite get over them—they were pretty strange. At least they seem to be over now. All the excitement of the move I guess."

Michael's heart seemed to stop. *Dreams*. Now the voice inside his head had gone silent. As he tried to focus on the dreams, his forehead began to hurt—sharp, hard pains almost like nails being hammered into his skull—as if something didn't *want* him to think about the dreams.

What else was this house capable of?

The sudden thought startled him as he realized that he had just attributed their house with being a living entity, an organism capable of conscious thought and perhaps evil design. Now he wondered, again, *What's going on here?* Then the voice returned and the pain in his head, along with thoughts and doubts about the house, vanished.

"Anything wrong? You looked kind of strange there for a moment."

Michael smiled. "No, nothing. Just thinking about something. Tired too probably—just not used to getting up so early."

Alan was looking at him strangely again, but Michael realized it didn't matter anymore.

"Yeah. Well . . . okay then. You know, if there's anything, anything at all that you want to talk about—"

By now he'd already tuned his father out. The voice told him it wasn't important for him to listen any longer.

". . . here if you need us."

"I know. I'm okay," he heard himself say.

"Well, all right then." Alan stood up. "I guess I'll be working in the backyard today—and the garden—if you need anything."

Michael stood up also. His father remained standing for awhile, not moving, just looking at him. Finally, he left in the direction of the kitchen.

The voice reassured him that he had done fine and not to worry about anything.

Leaving the library, Michael knew he needed to continue his search and went back downstairs into the basement.

5

Turning on lights along the way, Michael went into and then across the basement. Without knowing his destination—or its significance—he walked directly over to the wall that had been the focus of his Images—inside the small room in the northeast corner. He checked both the north and the east walls—floor to ceiling—but found nothing. When he rubbed at the powdery whitewash covering the walls, it floated down onto his feet and the floor in a snow-like cloud. On the wall where he'd rubbed, he wasn't surprised to find slight depressions that had been filled in with black paint. Confirming the existence of the markings, he felt no further desire to uncover them.

Next, he proceeded in a counter-clockwise direction on a perimeter search, ignoring the interior fieldstone. The floor was concrete except for the unique drainage system. He wondered again at the purpose of the drains until the voice returned and told him he needn't be concerned with them. After he'd squeezed past a huge green furnace, he came to a space underneath the basement stairs. His pulse quickened as he realized he needed a flashlight.

On the work-table in the central area of the basement, he found several boxes of tools and "basement stuff." Rummaging through the boxes, he found a big yellow lantern light—the same light Amanda had once played with as a pretend school bus. Thumbing the power button, he was relieved when the light flared to life. Back under the stairs, the big light quickly dissolved the shadows, revealing cobwebs that were as thick as the white thread used in a Halloween fun house. He wondered for a moment where the word cobweb had ever come from.

After all, cobs don't make them, spiders do.

As he worked his way deeper under the stairs, long, dust-caked strands of cobweb attached themselves to his shirt and hair. Under the last step of the stairway, he crouched down to get a closer look—but found nothing.

Turning off the light, he sat for awhile in the dark, deep in thought. This time though, he found that he wasn't as discouraged as he'd been in the attic. Instead, he tried to focus his concentration and to visualize where, if he had been Dr. Woulfe, he would have hidden his notes—besides of course the place where his father had found the first volume.

Maybe there aren't any more?

Then he heard something behind him and held his breath while trying to listen. Seconds passed but the sound was not repeated.

He stood up, turned on the lantern light and searched once again under each stair, around the rest of the outside walls, then along the inside wooden walls, even going so far as to pry loose some of the boards with his hands while tapping others with his fist. Nothing. He scanned the floor, looking for anything other than solid concrete—nothing. He pried up each of the circular drain grates and each time felt the cold air rise briskly into his face as he shined his flashlight into the revealed drain-pipe—and, again, nothing. He searched along the ceiling until his neck ached. Finally, he felt along the tops of pipes and was only rewarded with a shower of accumulated dust. When ultimately he sat down on the stairs, he knew now that he was truly discouraged.

Someone must have taken it. Maybe one of the former owners.

His thoughts returned to the attic. Although still not committed to trying to pull up floorboards, he nevertheless stood up and began to ascend the basement stairs. As he climbed, his stomach however began to protest, not quieting until he'd reached the second floor. So, instead of turning right toward the attic door, he turned left, to the bathroom. After he'd relieved himself, he returned to his room. He realized he was filthy and decided to take a bath. He grabbed a new set of clothes and returned to the bathroom. He filled the tub, then let himself slide into the warm water. He was out of ideas. As he soaked, without warning, the voice returned. The voice told him he had done well . . . and then explained where he needed to look next.

23

Amanda feels as if someone is watching her. She looks and sees the tree, its bark rough and black.

The Claw Tree. Did I really walk this far?

She glances back toward the house and it seems too far away, as if it is no longer real, almost like a dollhouse on display. She is puzzled by the extent of her progress and again senses someone watching her, so she swivels back to face the tree.

Then she hears a sound—a quiet, high-pitched, squeak. It reminds her of a girl from school—blonde-haired Marcy Bean—so small that the kids called her Bean Seed. Marcy's voice had sounded just like the voice she is hearing now . . . like someone stepping on a dog toy every time they talk.

The sound, she realizes, is coming from the tall grass about a dozen feet in front of her, located near the base of the tree. The grass is at least a foot deep, green and thick. The sound continues and she doesn't know whether it is insect or animal. Then its tiny voice seems to quiver or vibrate—almost as if it's laughing at her.

When she steps forward the sound stops. The silence seems unnatural though, somehow forced.

She waits and the sound begins again, this time though it's much softer. She wonders if perhaps it's now moving away from her. When she steps forward once again, this time the sound doesn't stop. Another step. Then another. The sound now seems to be coming from somewhere above her. When she looks up she is surprised to see one of the tree's massive branches hanging directly above her. However, something about the branch seems strange, almost as if it's . . .

(moving)

The laughing voice-sound continues and is soon joined by a second. She further scrutinizes the branch above her and then the other branches of the tree, looking for the source—some sort of rare cricket or a mouse perhaps—anything. Now it sounds like there are three of them and then a second later, half a dozen. With the presence of what feels like a multitude now, the sounds no longer seem like simple laughter but rather something else, something almost like . . .

(anguish)

pain.

"Stop it!" she yells up at the tree. Although on the surface the sounds irritate her, she is also strangely attracted to them and wants them to continue.

The sounds stop.

A sudden wind comes from behind her and sways the tree's heavy branches and the wood moans its protest. Behind the wind, as if at the end of a long exhale, comes a new sound, a voice . . . a . . .

(whisper)

a name

"Amanda"

24

Outside, dressed but still wet from his bath, Michael dashed across the driveway, barely noticing the startled look on his father's face, and then he was inside the carriage house, the side door screaming its protest at having been opened so quickly.

From inside, he heard the distant sound of his father shouting after him, but the sound was more like that of a radio playing somewhere far away and he ignored it.

As he stood in the gloom, waiting for his eyes to adjust, he at first didn't see it. However, after fumbling with the switch on the lantern light and getting the light to appear, he spotted a set of steep, narrow wooden stairs in the far corner of the room leading up into a dark hole in the ceiling. Wasting no time, he raced up the stairs into the second level.

Even with a single small window, it was dark, but only for a moment as the lantern's light obliterated the shadows. The same smell of dust he'd previously experienced in the attic assaulted him here, although on a grander scale. Mixed in with the dust were the smells of old dirt, rodent droppings, mildew and motor oil. His light played around the small cramped space and he discovered the floor was made of heavy wood planking several inches thick, cut rough and laid out unevenly. He then realized he was in what had once must have been a servant's quarters.

With barely a thought about it, he instantly knew where to look. In a corner diagonally opposite from the place where he had come up through the floor, he found a small cardboard box. Opening the box, he discovered—and quickly grabbed—

a cloth-covered object, roughly notebook-size. In another moment, he had uncovered a leather notebook with a label on the cover which read: "Tagebuch—Robert Woulfe" at the top and slightly below this: "Teil Zwei" (Volume Two).

He sat down and immediately opened the book. Using the illumination afforded by the lantern light, he began to read the notebook which smelled like old dried mushrooms. After half an hour, he turned off the light to conserve the battery and moved to a place where the small window let in enough light for him to read by.

Incredibly, most of the writings in the second volume were in English. The only places in the journal where German appeared, were as single words, many of which he fortunately already knew. There were also some small blocks of German set apart from the rest which he believed were the actual words or incantations used in the ceremonies and rituals of the cult. This volume of the doctor's journal was about twice as long as the first, stretching to 542 pages according to the neatly printed page numbers in the upper right-hand corner of each sheet. In addition, the entries were all dated. Turning to the last page, he found the final entry under the heading August 17, 1944.

Just about a week before he died.

Michael stayed within the second story of the carriage house until 6:30 that night. He returned in time for supper and although not hungry, he still felt obligated to put in an appearance. It turned out that the desire to turn over the next page of the doctor's journal burned with more strength than his body's desire for food. He did not participate in any of the dinner discussion and was relieved when it was finally over.

After supper, he went straight to his room. Behind his closed door, he sat at his desk and went back to reading. At 10 PM there was a soft knock on his door; it was his father.

"Mind if I come in for a minute?"

"Sure, Dad," he said, hastily closing the notebook. "I was just reading."

Alan stepped in, but remained near the door. He seemed to prefer to take a moment to study the doorframe before looking at him.

"So I see. Must be pretty interesting." His father made no move to come farther into the room.

"Just some old book I found in the carriage house," Michael said and wished for the return of the voice. He looked at his father, seeing that he was now staring at the notebook. He realized he was suddenly afraid of his father—afraid of what he might find out—of what he might do.

"Oh? What's the name of it?" Alan took three steps into the room.

Michael felt cornered. His first impulse was to lie. And then he astonished himself by doing just that, "It's a history book. About the Civil War." He opened the book, then, realizing his mistake, quickly shut it. Now he was staring intently down at it and at the same time feeling his father's eyes directed there also.

"I didn't know you were so interested in history," he said and took another step closer. Michael felt his fear transforming itself into something else—like a cornered animal, he actually found himself preparing to fight. And although he understood none of these feelings, he was not overwhelmed or even concerned by them. Instead, he felt reassured. Then he felt his fear begin to evaporate even though he couldn't sense the presence of the voice which had calmed him earlier. Yet, he truly did sense something—a presence that was very much similar, if not connected in some way, to that of the voice. Fortunately, it was sufficient enough to calm him and allow him to answer.

"Yeah, it's pretty interesting."

Alan turned and walked back to the door. Michael realized he had been holding his breath and let it out. With his father's retreat, the feeling of the presence had also gone.

"Don't stay up too late, okay? Your mother and I are turning in. See you in the morning." With his hand on the doorknob, he seemed to be waiting for a reply to what Michael thought had been a rhetorical question.

"Yep, see you tomorrow. Good night," he said and turned his attention back to the journal.

Alan left Michael's room at 10:15 PM. Four hours later—Michael was still reading.

25

Wednesday

1

The next morning, Sam woke up complaining of not feeling well. A few minutes after eight, she called in to work to let them know she would be staying home, then climbed back into bed. Instantly, upon hearing this, Alan thought back to the incident with the Chinese mover who had for no apparent reason become sick in their driveway. Although he desperately wanted to discount any theory linking the two illnesses together, he couldn't stop thinking about it.

With his mind preoccupied, he was not immediately concerned when Michael didn't show up for breakfast.

When eleven o'clock arrived, though, and Michael still hadn't come downstairs, Alan climbed the stairs to Michael's bedroom. Although disappointed, he wasn't really surprised to find Michael's door closed—the same as last night.

Michael never *used to close his door.*

He knocked. No answer. He knocked again—this time hard enough to rattle the door against the frame.

From the other side came a voice that at first he didn't recognize when it said, "What?" It was a voice that sounded sleepy, confused—almost like a hung-over drunkard being aroused against his will from a long slumber.

"Michael? Are you up yet?" He tried to turn the doorknob but discovered it was locked.

He's never locked his door before. Never.

"Michael, you okay? What's going on?"

He turned his head sideways, almost touching his ear to the door.

"Nothing—I'm okay—just tired. I'll be down soon."

Now that *sounds more like the Michael I know.*

Still, he had a feeling—sitting at the bottom of his stomach with the weight of a small stone—that something was wrong. He turned away from his son's door then hesitated.

Should he confront him? Demand to know what's troubling him?

He decided to leave him alone, at least for now.

Downstairs, he caught up with Sam who had now moved to what she referred to as the drawing room. He thought it ironic that they used it as their TV room; but based on her present condition, he knew better than to tease her about it.

"I'm worried about Michael," he said.

Sam was sitting near the bay window, having gotten out of bed only within the last half-hour. On the round oak table in front of her, she had spread out several gardening books and one of them was now open in front of her. A cup of coffee on a wooden coaster sat off to one side of the table, a thin column of steam rising lazily from inside the cup.

"What's he doing now?" she said as she aimlessly turned a page in what appeared to be a book about flowers. Alan sat down at the table directly opposite his wife.

"He's still up in his room. He's been there all day and he's got the door locked."

"Still depressed about the move?"

"I don't know. I think this is different. Last night, just before we went to bed, I stopped by his room. He was reading this old book and when I asked him what it was, he lied about it."

"What do you mean, he lied?"

"He said the book was about the Civil War."

"And you don't think it was?"

"No." Alan sensed Sam was about to turn her attention back to her book, ready perhaps to dismiss the entire incident.

"As I was leaving, I turned and saw him open it and it was a *written* book—a handwritten book I mean, like a notebook."

Sam stared at the floor for a moment before looking back up. "You're right, that doesn't sound like Michael." Having said this, she returned her attention to her book and began flipping pages once again.

"I know. So *now* do you understand my concern? And then this morning he won't even come out of his room and he's got the door locked."

Sam looked up again and grabbed her coffee. She took a small sip, put the cup back down and stared at a spot in the center of the table.

"You know," she said, "I think I saw him carrying something like that—something that could have been a notebook—out of the carriage house yesterday about the time he came inside for dinner." She glanced at him briefly, then returned to her book.

"Maybe it's that doctor's journal. But why would he lie about it? I'm the one who gave it to him in the first place."

"I wouldn't worry, Alan. At least he's showing an interest—an interest in the house—even if indirectly. If he can get interested in something, maybe it'll help him cope with his disappointment. And I know having his computer broken in the move has been especially hard on him."

"You're probably right." Alan paused and stared out the window. "It's just that he's so smart but he keeps too much bottled up inside. It's not healthy." He reached for one of her books. When he pulled it across the table, he saw it was about landscaping. On the cover was a picture of a garden, similar to what their backyard had probably once looked like—an overflowing greenness with a stone path weaving its way among a plethora of flowers, trees and shrubs. For a moment, he thought he had seen a face in the picture—the face of a man staring out from inside one of the bushes. He pulled the book closer and decided he had made a mistake.

"He just needs time Alan, that's all. Time to adjust. This is a big change for all of us. It's going to take a while to adapt and for Michael maybe it's going to take longer."

"I know, but I just worry about him. It's like I get the feeling he wants to talk to me, to tell me something, but in each instance at the last moment he seems to change his mind. I just wish he would communicate more, actually *talk* to me—to *us*—you know?"

He pushed the book back across the table and as he did so, Sam reached out and put her hand on top of his.

"Give him time, Alan, just give him time."

2

So they gave him time—all the rest of that day as it turned out. When, around 1 PM, Alan knocked on Michael's door for lunch, he again received a negative response. When supper came, their concerns had escalated. As before, Alan brought the subject up first. Sam, feeling better, was making dinner—cube steaks in a mushroom gravy sauce with mashed potatoes and peas. Alan was leaning against the counter by the stove.

"There's something wrong, Sam; we can't deny it any longer. He's not eating and he's been sitting up in that room all day with the door locked."

As he watched Sam stir the gravy and steaks he suddenly realized he was famished.

"So, what do we do about it?"

"We could try to talk to him—the both of us—ask him what the problem is."

Sam picked up a fork to test the potatoes.

"He might feel threatened, feel like we're ganging up on him."

When the fork went in easily, Sam turned on the burner for the peas.

"What's your suggestion then?" Alan asked, hearing the nuance of burgeoning desperation in his voice.

"I guess I don't have any." Sam turned off the burner for the potatoes and picked up a spatula.

"So, we go up together?"

There was a slight pause before she answered.

"We go up together."

"I'll lead the way," he said.

"Now?"

He was puzzled to see annoyance on his wife's face—the corner of her mouth turned up slightly, her eyes partially narrowed.

"Sure. Why not?"

Sam sighed and turned the burner under the peas from high back to low.

Together, they climbed the stairs to the second floor. Alan felt like a mourner in a funeral parlor walking the aisle to the front of the room to offer a last good-bye to a loved one. The problem was, this was exactly what he was afraid of. Michael had always been sort of distant from them. But, Alan thought, all teenagers went through such a stage, perhaps not always as severe as Michael's, but still it was "just a stage" as Sam had always referred to such things. But now, since the move, things seemed to have gotten worse. Alan was concerned they might be on the verge of losing him forever.

At the top of the stairs, Alan assumed the lead. He walked directly to Michael's door and with a single glance at Sam, knocked.

"Michael? It's almost supper time, how about coming downstairs and joining us?" They listened to the silence while looking with concern at one another.

Sam leaned closer to the door, "Michael? Are you in there?"

"Huh? Mom?"

Alan again thought Michael's voice sounded strange, certainly confused, even groggy—possibly slurred. In the next instant he had a vision of Michael at his desk, right arm bared with a piece of hospital tubing tied in a band below his shoulder. On the desk was a small box containing several bottles and next to the box a syringe, its plunger depressed. Michael sat at his desk with a faraway look on his face, head thrown back, a twisted smile on his face, answering them from the depths of a drug-induced stupor. However, as the vision faded, Alan was relieved, and then startled when the door was unlocked and thrown wide to reveal his son, hair slightly disheveled, but with eyes bright and clear, asking, "So, what are we having? I'm starved!"

26

July 20 & 21
Thursday and Friday

The words of the holy one, the true one, who has the key of David, who opens and no one shall shut, who shuts and no one opens.

- Revelation 3:7

1

The next day began much the same way with Michael not coming out of his room until nearly lunchtime.

Sam called in sick again and now Alan was beginning to worry about her as well. After yesterday afternoon and evening she had seemed fine but today she had awoken again feeling terrible. He had kidded her about morning sickness and gotten an angry glare in return.

For lunch, Alan cooked bratwurst, scalloped potatoes from a box and a can of creamed corn. While mixing the potatoes he misread the directions and put in two and a half cups of milk and one cup of water instead of the other way around. He tried to convince himself they'd probably taste better his way.

Amanda was first to the kitchen and sat down without a word. She had been playing outside by herself all morning and he had observed her near the claw tree on at least three different occasions. Michael and Sam arrived next.

"Glad you could join us for lunch, Michael," Alan said and caught a strange look from Sam. "Haven't seen much of you lately."

Michael made no reply. Standing at the counter, Alan took a long drink of coffee from a white mug with blue drawings of sailing yachts displayed on it.

"I thought it was lunch," Michael said. Alan sensed confusion in his son's voice and a vacuous frown rippled across Michael's face.

"It *is* lunch," Amanda said. "What's your *problem?*" It was the first thing she had said since sitting down.

"Oh," Michael said. He blinked with dull eyes and stared at his empty plate.

The food done, Alan set it on the table, having already set out plates and silverware. He sat down but jumped up again when he realized he had forgotten serving spoons. Just when he had sat down again, the phone rang.

"I'll get it," he said with a sigh, grabbing a single mouthful of corn before standing up.

He glanced at Sam on his way to the phone and she offered a weak smile in return. Before picking up the receiver, he swallowed and wiped his hands on his pants.

"Hello? Yes, this is Alan Sarasin."

Alan turned so that he could continue watching the table. Michael hadn't begun eating yet. Instead, he was sitting and staring at something that could only be the refrigerator door. Meanwhile, Amanda was wolfing down her potatoes. Sam, like her son, had yet to put anything on her plate and for a moment, he wasn't sure who looked worse—Sam or Michael. Then Michael appeared to wake up and began picking over his food as if it were something he didn't recognize. Alan continued listening to the voice on the phone—he had yet been given a chance to speak as he watched Michael finally take a small, hesitant bite.

"Really! That's great! Yes, I'll take it . . . sounds wonderful . . . Uh, yes, perhaps a little soon, but I can . . . Monday . . . yes . . . all right . . . I'll see you then . . . yes, thank you very much Dr. Stadler. And I look forward to working with you too. Okay, then . . . good-bye."

"Oh my God, you got the job!" Sam responded when Alan had hung up.

"I start on Monday," he said, unable to suppress the grinning happiness which had, for the moment, eclipsed his earlier worries about Michael and his wife. Staring at Sam, he was alarmed, though, when he saw her smile replaced by a look of deep concentration.

"What?" he almost demanded. She frowned at him for a second, before her smile returned.

"We should celebrate. And I know just how to do it." She got up from the table and walked out of the kitchen, her floor-length silk robe whispering across the linoleum. "I'll be right back."

She disappeared and he listened to her footfalls rise up the stairs.

"What'll you be teaching at the college?" Amanda asked.

Taken off guard, he nearly jumped at the question before turning around. He glanced briefly at Michael who was now staring at his food as if he were the only one in the room.

"I'll be teaching two classes in the fall—not sure what they'll be yet. In the meantime I'll be doing some administrative stuff—setting up PCs, tuning their network, stuff like that."

Alan watched with concern as Michael picked up a single potato slice with his fork and simply stared at it. Finally, he sniffed it before putting it in his mouth and chewing it slowly, as if he were afraid there could be something unpleasant hidden inside. Amanda, on the other hand, had nearly cleared her plate and drained her milk in one long swallow, leaving a visible white ring around her mouth. Alan found himself staring at it as he heard Sam once again on the stairs.

When Sam returned, she was carrying two brochures.

"Here's what we should do. I picked these up the other day. Mackinac Island," she said, pronouncing it Mack-an-naw as she practically threw the brochures into Alan's hands. He bent over and caught them like a pitcher catching a line-drive hit.

The first one featured a picture of a sleek hydrofoil. "Carson's Ferry Service" was printed at the top. The other contained pictures of The Grand Hotel, Arch Rock and information about Fort Michalemackinac, which was pictured on the brochure's cover. He glanced at them briefly before setting them down.

"Don't you think it'd be a little much—I mean, we've just moved into a new house and—"

"Actually, I think it would be *very good,*" Sam replied, " . . . for *all* of us."

He understood her implication. "You're right, it *would* be good," and picked up the brochures again.

"It's only about an hour drive from here. We could leave Saturday morning, say around eight, and make the nine o'clock boat. That should put us on the island by nine fifteen."

He realized then that she actually had been paying more attention than he'd originally thought to Michael's strange behavior. More than that, she had upstaged him by presenting a possible solution to the puzzling situation.

"Okay then. Let's do it!" He looked at his children to see if they shared his enthusiasm. He found instead Michael poking holes in his bratwurst with his fork while Amanda was staring out the kitchen window as if waiting for something.

2

Sam returned to work on Friday. During the day, Michael made less of an appearance at home than he had on the previous two days. Alan busied himself working in the basement—as much in an attempt to accomplish something as to keep from dwelling too much on what might be wrong with his son. Just before noon, though, he was forced to quit after he developed a severe headache. It was late afternoon and several aspirin later before he recovered.

3

After supper, Michael retreated to his room—his appearance at supper being his one and only that day. To appease Amanda's loud protests over being stuck alone with the supper dishes, they elected to use the dishwasher for the first time since moving in.

In most respects, the situation at dinner mirrored yesterday's lunch. Michael barely seemed to know where he was and only picked at his food, leaving most of it on his plate.

During dinner, Alan told Michael about his new job and their planned trip to Mackinac Island on Saturday. Michael seemed disinterested however, as if they were discussing someone else's family. Since there'd been no recognition, even when Alan told him about his new job, he suspected Michael's mind had never registered a single event from the previous day's lunch, or if he had, it was already forgotten. Even when Michael left the dinner table, Alan still wasn't sure whether Michael understood what their plans were for the following day.

All that night they left Michael alone in his room, the door closed and undoubtedly locked. Once, Alan crept up the stairs and stood outside his son's door for nearly ten minutes, listening. In the course of those ten minutes, though, he didn't hear a single sound. Whatever Michael was doing, he was doing it quietly.

27

July 22 • Early Saturday Morning

Michael is awake. He looks at his bedside clock radio—2:49 AM. He hears the voices again and this time he knows they are calling him. Lying awake, trying not to move, he listens. Despite their quiet softness, he knows the voices are calling him from the basement. He sits up but to his surprise finds that he is not afraid. The voices are asking for his help, pleading with him to do what only he can do. Although he doesn't know what the voices are asking of him, he feels compelled to obey.

Sliding out of bed to the floor, he stands still for a moment so as to ensure that the voices do not stop. They do not, but their tone changes, seemingly pleased that he is taking action. Still in the dark, he walks over to his door and unlocks it. He treads softly in the hallway before descending the stairs to the first floor, then finally into the basement where the naked cement sends ice-like waves into the bottoms of his feet. He manages to ignore the cold and although he doesn't realize it at the time, he has had no need to turn on any of the basement lights, and has easily negotiated his way across the basement floor, all the way toward the small room in the northeast corner—the room where the wall with the strange markings is.

He stands before the wall in the dark and is able to see through the poorly applied white wash to the markings below. Immediately, the lines and drawings begin to glow like tubes of blue neon. The glowing lines enable him to make out the overall structure of the drawing on the wall before him. Within the drawing, he can discern two concentric rectangles, the largest covering the entire wall from floor to ceiling; the smallest the size of a standard door. Within the border created by the two rectangles, symbols are inscribed. There are three symbols on each side, which are strange, and remind him of Egyptian hieroglyphics. At the top and center though is one he immediately recognizes—a pentagram. Other symbols on the wall reflect images suggestive of eyes and animals. Most are reflected in the form of varied squiggly lines while some are capped with small circles or other shapes such as triangles and ovals. One of the symbols, however, looks like a sword.

All of this observation takes place in an instant. And then the voices, silent throughout his walk into the basement, resume and he feels them inside his mind, speaking directly into his consciousness. Their sound is soft and soothing and so he relaxes and feels himself drifting toward sleep. With his tacit approval evidenced by his lack of resistance, he willingly opens himself up to them—allowing his mind to be taken over—allowing himself to become possessed. When he speaks next it is in a language no living linguist on earth would recognize.

"Waer Zipuguzu!
Hg Wg Lk Gk!
Luugurjur Ha Juk Lok!
Luugurjur Ha Kol Moja!
Luugurjur Ha Wsa Bwar Sa!
Waer Zipuguzu—Alar Daey!"

The strange sounds pour from his mouth effortlessly, as if they are his native tongue and with each exclamation, the blue heat of the sigils on the wall intensifies.

"Luugurjur Ha Juk Lok!
Luugurjur Ha Kol Moja!
Luugurjur Ha Wsa Bwar Sa!
Waer Zipuguzu—Alar Daey!"

Soon, the entire basement is awash in a brilliant blue glow that covers everything like a luminescent mold.

Upon repetition of the strange words, the glow at first seems to diminish, then to change color—the blue washing out to white before intensifying into an orange as deep and bright as the sun. Then the orange darkens into a red similar to the last glowing embers of a campfire. As the symbols on the wall complete their color change, Michael feels a strange trembling beneath his feet and sees a wavering in the lights.

He stops speaking but the voices are still within him and so he listens, though they are speaking in a language he doesn't understand. What he does understand though is the emotion permeating the tone of their strange language.

Pure and uninhibited . . . elation.

PART THREE

The Calling

And they marched up over the broad earth and surrounded the camp of the saints and the beloved city . . .

- Revelation 20:9

Prologue III

Boyne City
June 19, 1955 • Sunday, Early Morning

Scott Farley stood at the edge of the clearing for the second time that evening and wished he could have been anywhere but where he was right now. Beside him, and watching the now subdued activities around the fading fire in the center of the Stone Circle, were Sheriff Greg Kelly, acting deputy Jeff Wainwright and Boyne City mayor, Franklin Halstead. Behind these men were approximately sixty others—locals roused into action from their warm beds in the night by the sheriff and his deputies. The men had been granted temporary deputy status for the purpose of, as sheriff Kelly had put it, "To put an end, once and for all, to this sick satanic bullshit that has now cost us the dear life of one of our very own."

Although he had supposedly been referring to the death of George Montgomery, which at that time had yet to be confirmed, Scott knew otherwise. When first telling the sheriff and mayor about the events that had gone on in the clearing behind Ms. Woulfe's house, the sheriff did not seem overly concerned until Scott came to the part about Warren—the mayor's son—playing a prominent role in the cultists' ceremony. Action from that point on was speedy and significant.

Carl Hanscomb was the first to find a piece of George, a body part which would later be identified as a portion of George's right arm. At almost exactly the same time, Jeff

Wainwright tripped over a mostly intact leg. Viewing the grizzly discoveries, several of the men comprising the sheriff's posse became ill. One of these, Karl Witherstone, disgorged his stomach contents upon the shoes of Gerald Thompson, manager of Thompson's Grocery whose son, Kenny, had been a principal circulator of the initial cult rumors at the high school.

Scott had stood by numbly and watched the raid unfold in front of him. He didn't flinch even as the screams reached a crescendo punctuated by several gunshots that echoed behind him into the black woods like the barking of some monstrous, angry dog. The raid was over quickly and when it was done, Alfred Parsons and Henry Goldsmith were added to the list of dead headed by George Montgomery. Later, Warren would officially be listed as missing, while Sylvia Woulfe was presumed dead based on Deputy Jason Black's statement that he had shot her "a good many times" and Jeff Wainwright's description of her dead body. Scott, though, had seen something else, but chose to remain silent, for fear that if he were to describe what he'd seen it would have landed him in an asylum—a scenario very close to the truth.

Now, standing on the edge of the clearing, Scott didn't realize just how close he was to the exact spot where he, Raymond and George had sat crouched but a few short hours ago. He stared as they covered the bodies with white sheets which quickly stained red, creating, he thought, a more ghastly spectacle than if the bodies had been left uncovered.

Later, after the bodies had been removed, he was still standing at the edge of the clearing, motionless and staring at nothing. He remained in this nearly catatonic state and had to be led by a deputy from the clearing along the path which led back to Woulfe House. Along the way the deputy tried at first to make conversation but eventually gave up when Scott didn't respond. When they finally arrived back at the house, he was placed in the back of the deputy's police cruiser almost as if he were a criminal.

As the cruiser pulled out onto the road and headed back toward town, Scott broke out of his self-imposed paralysis. Sobbing uncontrollably, his trembling body was rocked by spasms. The deputy, watching him in his rearview mirror, pretended not to notice.

When Scott awoke several hours later in a white hospital room, it was without any recollection of how he had gotten there. He was alone but for his secret and like a cancer patient with an inoperable tumor, he knew it would be with him the rest of his life.

28

July 22 • Saturday

1

For the past two weeks, Michael's comprehension of his own actions and thoughts had been almost completely repressed. As they drove out of Boyne City, putting successive miles between themselves and Woulfe House, Michael's awareness gradually resurfaced from what up to now had been an impenetrable shroud of occluding, oppressive layers like a lost shipwreck revealed at the bottom of a suddenly dry lake bed. The process was slow and somewhat painful . . . but more wonderful than anything he had ever felt in his life. With each passing minute and mile, he began to feel more alive and in control of himself than he had in weeks. When he tried to think back over the events of the last two weeks, the feelings and images he received were strange; almost as if he were remembering a movie he had seen as opposed to events and places he had actually experienced.

As his awareness became his own once again, questions began to swirl in his mind like a whirlpool. And in the middle of this whirlpool was the large, black hole containing the truth of what *really* had happened during the last two weeks. But, to look there he worried, might be to risk plunging himself back within it—a descent he might not be fortunate enough to withdraw from a second time.

He felt caught. He knew that if he tried to think about, to pursue, to *understand* what it was that had happened to him, there was the risk that he might fall under its spell again. However, by not pursuing it, by not trying to understand it, he would never be able to know what really had happened. But he also realized that only by knowing, would he perhaps, be able to keep it from happening again.

In this way, the elation he'd first experienced, faded.

Something happened to me. Something that had to do with the house. And now that I'm not there, whatever it was, is losing its power over me. But . . . what have I done?

After the initial elation and awareness came fear. Something had indeed happened to him; something he didn't understand. To think that for at least the last two weeks, some force other than himself had been in complete control of his body—maybe even his mind—made him shudder. He could only wonder what he had done—or more specifically what had been done *to him*. He felt there had been a purpose involved. He had indeed accomplished *something* in the two-week interval, something of significant importance, but what it was, he had no idea.

Did I hurt anybody?

Concerned with this prospect, he looked wildly around the car for a moment, relieved that upon inspection of everyone present—Alan, Sam and Amanda—that all appeared okay.

But how did it happen? Was it something I did? Or something I allowed *to happen? Was it my fault?*

Regardless, he had no doubt about one thing—that whatever had caused him to blank out for the better part of two weeks wasn't the result of any mental disorder on his part. He sensed instead the unmistakable presence of something else, a presence as much outside of himself as the landscape he now observed flashing by the window next to him.

Was it the journal? Did I read something that provoked some sort of . . . possession of myself?

Two months ago, such an idea would have seemed preposterous and beyond consideration. Now however it seemed a perfectly valid alternative. When he next looked at his family riding silently in the car with him he thought of the movie *Invasion of the Body Snatchers.*

What if . . . what if they're possessed—right now—and they haven't been able to break out of it yet like I was able to? What if they're just . . . pretending?

He looked with concern at his mother and father seated in the front seat. Maybe it wasn't really his mother and father at all? Maybe when the one he thought was his father turned around, instead of his father's face, there would be some horrible lizard-like thing with yellow snake-eyes and a long, red tongue?

No. They're okay. Don't ask me how I know that, but I do. It was just me. And it's not going to happen again.

He surprised himself and was pleased with his resolve. Then he turned his thoughts back to the dreams.

They've got to be related to this somehow. What caused them? Or were they the start of it?

Try as he might, he couldn't think of any way they could be related to his possession—and yet somehow felt they were. Again, he concentrated on external factors—it must have been something *outside* of him that caused or influenced the dreams.

Possession. That's what happened to me—something possessed me. But what? And why? And if it could do it to me, and has a strong connection with the house, what's going to keep it from doing the same thing to my parents—or, even worse, Amanda? And if the dreams are some sort of start to the whole thing—Dad and Amanda said they've had dreams too. Maybe it gets into your head through your dreams when you're sleeping, when you're the most vulnerable? Then, once inside, it grows, like some sort of tumor or something until it's eventually big enough and strong enough to take over completely.

Unable to find the answers to these questions, he gave up. Then, for the first time, he realized he was holding a paperback novel, *Hyperion*, by Dan Simmons. Furthermore, the book was open (page 234) as if he had been reading it. He had no idea what the book was about but did remember buying it some time before the move. Closing the book, he sighed and stared out the window at a passing farm where the rusted tower of an old windmill stood like a protective sentinel over a homestead that had, apparently, long ago forgotten it.

2

Alan had been able to get everyone on the road before 8 AM. As he drove, Amanda and Sam chatted pleasantly—and endlessly it seemed—about the trip, the house, the garden, and Amanda's always-favorite subject—insects. Meanwhile, Michael once again appeared to be lost in his own private world. Alan watched him closely in the rearview mirror, checking him every couple of minutes, searching for clues as to how he might be able to break through his son's shell.

In truth, he had little confidence in Sam's plan. Michael already seemed to have for the time being drifted away from them. And, although it seemed perhaps unnatural, Alan felt it probably wasn't. Michael would soon be sixteen and Alan remembered what it had been like for him when he was that age—the pressures from peers to fit in, to be cool, to be one of the gang—the pressures from one's own body—the constant siren song you could never seem to keep out of your mind for long. Then, add to this mix the move, the new house and town, and the anticipation of a new school, and he thought he understood what was making Michael act the way he was. And so, to think some weekend getaway vacation was going to solve everything seemed at best, wishful thinking. Perhaps, to a certain extent, it might help him forget the move and the house temporarily, and for that alone maybe it was worth it. But, as far as providing any kind of permanent solution, Alan was convinced there would be none. All that Michael really needed, he believed, was time.

Which is all any of us ever need, isn't it? Time. Time to do the things we think have to be done. And in the end of course—none of us ever has enough.

As Alan continued watching his son, the impossible suddenly became possible. For, as he glanced in the rearview mirror yet again, he saw what appeared to be the beginning of a transformation. As he watched in growing amazement, the word that kept coming to mind was *awakening,* for what he was observing reminded him of the movie *Awakenings* in which Robin Williams played a doctor dealing with patients afflicted with the "sleeping sickness" epidemic of the 1920's. As he watched, though, he remained cautious in his hope. For even in the movie, the return to awareness had, in the end, been only temporary, and yet he knew he wasn't going to be able to remain unaffected by what he was witnessing.

At first, Michael blinked his eyes and looked around him several times, as if suddenly realizing where he was—or as if he were coming awake after having been asleep. Once, Michael even seemed to look at him but the contact was brief, Michael turning away after only a glance. Nevertheless, it seemed his son's whole manner had changed in an instant. Most of it was physical, from a sudden brightness in his eyes to the way he now held his head and body. It was also evident in the way he was sitting—where before he had sat with almost a statue-like stillness, he had now become more animated—a glance here, a brush of his hair there. He suddenly seemed *alive* again. Then too, his eyes now possessed an unmistakable *awareness* wholly unlike the listless faraway gaze that had been the norm for the last several days. And yet even beyond all this, there was more. It wasn't only the physical looks and actions, there seemed to be an entirely new aura surrounding his son—where before he had projected a negative indifference, there now seemed to emanate a positive optimism. It was nothing he could specifically see, but swore he could feel.

No matter. Wherever his son had previously been, it seemed he had now, miraculously, returned. And although as wonderful as it was to watch, it was also frightening.

"There're no cars allowed on the island," Alan began. "To get around, we'll either have to walk or rent bicycles. So I thought we'd rent bikes in the afternoon. And I think we all know who's going to be riding rings around the rest of us." He waited to see if his gambit would provoke any reaction.

It didn't work though. As Amanda and Sam continued talking about butterflies, future picnics in the gazebo and what kinds of flowers and plants they should put in the garden, Michael remained quiet.

But I know he's definitely changed somehow, changed for the better.

From elation to fear to frustration—Alan's emotions unknowingly had followed a course similar to his son's.

"So, how's the research going into the late, great Dr. Woulfe?" he asked during a pause in Sam and Amanda's discussion which currently centered on what kinds of perennials to plant in order to attract the most butterflies and hummingbirds. At first he feared he would be ignored again as Michael had now returned to his reading. But after a moment, Michael replied.

"Okay," Michael said after which he looked up from his book, closed it and put it beside him.

Alan decided to let things rest for the time being, but still felt better. In just that one word response, he had detected more emotion and warmth from his son than he had observed in several days.

Yes, he's definitely coming out of it—whatever it is—or was. Maybe he has no more of an idea of what was wrong than I do. Is that even possible? And if so, wouldn't that mean? . . .

29

July 23 • Sunday

1

They checked out of the Brentwood Hotel on Mackinac Island Sunday morning, reaching the docks in time to catch the 11:25 boat to the mainland. During the ride, Amanda was especially quiet, as if saddened at having to leave. Samantha however smiled, content to bask in the success of her plan while Alan busied himself taking pictures of the Mackinac bridge, a task he had neglected when they'd first arrived on the island.

Throughout the weekend, Michael had felt more like his normal self than at any other time since his family's move to Boyne City. He actively participated with his family in all their activities while they toured the famous fort, took a horse and buggy ride, and rented bicycles for their own personal tour of the island. Michael, for the moment, felt free.

The drive home remained quiet. Several times Sam attempted to start conversations with Amanda but in each instance Amanda quickly lost interest after only a few brief exchanges. The silence seemed to grow less penetrable and more palpable the closer they came to Boyne City. By the time they finally pulled into their driveway, the silence had seemed to become a blanket, smothering the sound of the engine, muffling the rolling tires. The moment at which the blanket of silence seemed to become absolute was interrupted when Michael noticed their unexpected visitor.

"It's him!" Michael exclaimed.

The man was standing conspicuously in the middle of their driveway, his arms hanging limply at his sides in an easy, relaxed posture—as if he were waiting for them. Michael immediately recognized the canvas coat, long hair and, most notably, the blazing green eyes.

Alan stopped the Cherokee with so much force that their bodies were pulled tight against their seat belts. Then, as Michael threw open his door and leaped out, the stranger bolted into the backyard. As Michael took off in pursuit he heard a voice yell after him (his father?), but before he could stop to acknowledge it he was in the woods, chasing after the stranger along the path to the Stone Circle. Similar to the reaction he'd had in the center of town the night they'd arrived in Boyne City, his body had taken over without waiting for his mind to consider the alternatives—or consequences. As to what he would do if he actually caught the man, or worse yet, the man turned on him, he hadn't taken the time to consider and so brushed such thoughts away almost as soon as they raised themselves.

As he ran, he thought he could hear his pursuing father's shouts behind him but only peripherally. He knew he was getting himself into even more trouble by ignoring them—yet he found the urge of the chase more powerful than the threat of any parental reprisal.

As he ran, an anger, which had previously lain dormant, was awakened within him—fueling both his pursuit and his resolve. He wanted and needed to know who this man was and why he kept following them. He wondered too, though he had no idea why, if perhaps the stranger might know something that could aid him in explaining or at least understanding his two week lapse of awareness. Logic told him that in some way his "episode" was linked to the house. The stranger also seemed somehow connected with the house. A long shot yes, but right now long was better than none.

Michael continued pursuing the man despite being unable to see him, relying exclusively on the sounds of his footfalls and the occasional snap of a twig or branch. Although he was aware the stranger was following the trail leading to the Stone Circle, the sudden appearance of the clearing nevertheless startled him. He entered the stone ring and stopped.

There was no sign of the stranger.

He struggled to listen, but could discern little over the heavy sounds of his breathing and heartbeat. Looking around the clearing, he could see nothing to indicate in which direction the stranger might have gone. He fell to his knees as his chest burned from the unanticipated exertion of the chase which had been in violent contrast to his previous one-hour ride in the car. As he fought to regain control of his body, he briefly entertained the idea that he might actually be having a heart attack. He sat for several minutes—waiting for the pressure to subside and his breathing to return to a normal rhythm.

When he heard an unexpected sound in the woods to his left he turned quickly in that direction. What he saw next he couldn't believe. As he tried to comprehend the impossible sight, his heart seemed to pause for several seconds before thankfully deciding to beat once again. Then he heard something behind him; the sound of someone half-walking, half-running. He froze and waited, no longer sure of anything and having no idea what to expect next.

His father came stumbling into view and lurched his way over to him. Once he reached him, Alan stopped and slouched against one of the large boulders to compose himself, then bent over. His breath came in rasps and wheezes, like an engine sputtering on its last drop of fuel.

Michael thought again of heart attacks then said, talking as much to himself perhaps as to his father, "I lost him. Again."

"You . . . shouldn't . . . have . . . run . . . after him . . . like that," his father wheezed. "That was . . . stupid."

Michael did not respond though, lost once again in the thought of the impossible event he had just witnessed—unable to comprehend its reality—and if real, unable to fathom its significance.

2

Alan, as was to have been expected, insisted on calling the police. While he was getting ready to call, Michael, Sam and Amanda remained with him in the kitchen. Sam and Amanda were sitting at the table as Michael was watching the events transpire from the doorway connecting the kitchen and dining rooms. For once, Michael realized he and his mother were actually in agreement on something—calling the police would be a waste of time. Alan would have none of their objections though and paced the kitchen like a restless mother cat that has just had its litter taken from it. Michael thought again about, as he now liked to refer to it, his lapse—wondering if perhaps something similar was now happening to his father. Finally, Alan went over to the phone, picked it up and dialed.

Hanging up after a lengthy and, at times, heated discussion, he turned his attention to Sam.

"You were right. They're not going to do a thing. They say it's just a local character, a guy named Harvey Olds who lives in the woods around here. They said he's totally harmless and we've got nothing to worry about. They're not even going to send a car."

Michael noted the way his father's words were rushed, his father's continually darting eyes, his arms crossing over his chest, then uncrossing . . .

"I told you they wouldn't do anything," Sam said. "Not that I'm especially happy about it."

Alan opened his mouth, then quickly closed it and looked down at the floor.

"You have to remember, we're not in the big city anymore, Alan. Not everyone who looks or acts a little different is a hold-up man or a serial killer. Things are more laid back here."

"I know. But still . . . I mean, if nothing else, the guy was trespassing, right?" Alan looked first to Sam, then to Michael for support.

An uneasy silence prevailed throughout the room.

Then, it was as if everyone started to move at once and just as abruptly stopped as the sound of the doorbell moaned in what could best be described as a woeful tone that seemed to have a difficult time traveling through the suddenly thick air emanating from the front hallway.

3

When the doorbell chimed a second time, Sam left the kitchen and moved into the front hallway. Michael heard her open the door to the vestibule and then the front door. The rest of them waited in anticipation; then all looked at each other quizzically as they heard her surprised exclamation.

"Dad!?"

"Yeah, that's me. Mind if I come in?"

Alan immediately left the kitchen and Michael started to follow, but then stopped when he saw Amanda had remained seated, staring at her placemat.

"You coming, or what?"

When Amanda stood up she did so without meeting his gaze. They all reached the hallway just in time to see their grandfather stride in dressed in a gray top hat with a red feather in the band, a white business shirt, no tie, and blue pinstripe slacks. He was holding a black leather suitcase barely larger than a briefcase.

"Grandpa?" Amanda asked hesitantly as Richard Knapp strode in ahead of Sam who was closing the door behind them.

"None other, young lady! Hi, Michael, Alan," he said, shaking first Alan's hand, then Michael's. He put the suitcase down and took off his hat.

"Dad, what ever are you *doing* here?" Sam asked.

Richard turned around to face her and said, "Well, my dear, that's pretty easy—I think—and I know this will probably come as sort of a shock to you, but to put it as simply as I can . . . I've left her." He looked briefly at Michael and Alan, flashing each of them a nervous smile. When he dropped his hat on top of his suitcase, it slipped to the floor.

"You've *what?*"

Richard turned back to Sam and put his hands on her shoulders.

"I've left her . . . your mother. For good."

Michael thought his mother didn't know whether to laugh or cry. As she hugged her father, she ended up doing some of both.

30

Naples, Florida
July 24 • Monday

"Okay class, let's review what we've learned today. The time for the moon to complete one revolution around the earth is called what?"

Mr. Roger Williams paced the floor in front of the summer makeup session of his senior high school physics class, waiting for a response. Mr. Williams was a relatively small man, 5 foot 5, and nearly bald. He was 43 years old. At present, he was marching in front of his classroom like a sergeant coldly reviewing his troops in preparation for a battle in which the casualties were expected to be heavy.

"The sidereal period."

"Correct, Emily. Now, who can explain, with some degree of detail, the two different types of tides we just talked about? Yes, Loren?"

"There's a body tide, which is the stretching of the moon 'cause of gravity—and the ocean tide, which is the moon's effect on the earth."

"Yes! Excellent answer and precisely correct. Now, then, can anyone explain what Roche's Limit is?"

To get an "A" in one of Mr. Williams' classes was about as likely as Mr. Williams suddenly growing a new head of hair. It was no secret around South Florida High that his students despised him—and it wasn't only the academically-challenged students—the view was shared universally throughout the campus. It was a fact, that over the course of Mr. Williams' tenure that more than one student had graduated from SFH with a near-perfect 4.00 average having received their only less than perfect mark in one of Mr. Williams' classes. And his senior physics class in particular had a reputation for being one of the hardest.

Also prominent in the discourse among the students concerning Mr. Williams (who they called Roager the Ogre, but never to his face or anywhere even close to his presence) was the notion that he was gay, since he was not, nor had ever been, married. Although Mr. Williams possessed full knowledge of his reputation as a fierce and impossible task master (a persona he took great pleasure in projecting and maintaining) he was however unaware of this other view of himself. If he had, he probably wouldn't have cared very much, even though it wasn't true. The truth, however, was that Mr. Williams had a special attraction to teenage girls. And although one might well find it hard to believe that in contemporary society such a pedophile could manage to keep his dark secret hidden, he had indeed done so in fact, relatively successfully. For Mr. Williams had been able to exercise an iron restraint in this area that had failed him only twice in nearly 20 years of teaching most of the same children he secretly coveted. He had only had momentary lapses of control in 1981 and 1986. Luckily, in both cases, the touching and fondling was never reported by his victims who had been too scared, or simply shrugged the episodes off as accidents. To be able to continue to maintain the secrecy of his sexual proclivities and still satisfy the full extent of his desires, he traveled frequently to the cities of Miami, Hialeah, Hollywood and Ft. Lauderdale where he picked up mostly runaways. Tragedy always surrounded these rendezvous of course, as in each instance when he was through, he indiscriminately dumped their bodies in the Everglades, counting on the alligators to destroy the evidence. To date, as far as he knew, none of the bodies had ever been found—or missed.

"Well anyone? I do recall I went over this today; please correct me if I'm mistaken," Mr. Williams said, his ceaseless pacing across the tile floor the only sound in the room. When he finally stopped moving, his students, most of them with heads bowed or focused in other directions, suddenly looked up and stared.

"Uh . . . doesn't it have something to do with the distance between two bodies whose gravitational fields interact in a way whereby the bigger affects the smaller?" came a timid reply from the back of the room—Emily again.

But Mr. Williams seemed not to have heard her as he stood motionless before them, like a dog that has suddenly heard the invisible sound of his master's whistle and is trying to get a bead on its direction. To his students it seemed as if he had momentarily slipped into some sort of trance as he stared vacuously toward a point on the back wall.

"Mr. Williams?" said Patty Wolanchek from the front row, who cared not so much for the impossible "A" but was committed to settle for anything that would allow her to graduate at the end of summer. There was however no response to her query.

"Mr. Williams, are you all right?" asked Loren, sitting two chairs behind Patty.

"What's wrong with him?" whispered Patty to her friend Gale, sitting next to her. Gale was about to reply when Mr. Williams seemed to come back to the discussion, to return as it were from wherever it was he had been. His response, though, unfortunately did nothing to alleviate the confusion brewing among his students.

"I have to leave now," he announced without looking at them. The buzzing in the classroom increased immediately.

Puzzled looks spread quickly around the room. Whispered snippets of conversation included: *What did he say? What's his problem, man? Jesus, I don't think I can take this shit any more. Did he say he was leaving? Hey, does that mean we get to leave early? What about the test, we're supposed to review for the test today . . .*

"Yes, I'm afraid that's what I must do. It's time," Mr. Williams said and when he said this he seemed to no longer be talking to his students but rather to someone they couldn't see standing next to him. Then his eyes focused again on that faraway, unseen spot somewhere in the distance that had seized his attention the moment before.

And then—he left. Without a single glance backward, without taking his briefcase which lay open on the oak desk at the front of the room—or even his sport coat which was draped casually over the back of his desk chair, and without another word to his students who could do nothing more than stare dumbly after him as they had no idea how to deal with such an unexpected turn of events—Mr. Roger Williams walked out of his classroom.

None of his students would ever see him again.

31

"Why did you leave Grandma?" Amanda asked Richard the next morning while they were sitting outside in the gazebo. Richard had come upon Amanda after finishing his morning walk; the first of what he promised her was going to be his new morning ritual.

He smiled at his granddaughter sitting opposite him in the gazebo, then glanced into the woods. The sun was already hot but the cool air coming from the shady recesses of the trees felt refreshing after his exercise. Tomorrow, he thought, he would have to try out the path that led into the forest. He had noticed it at the same time Amanda had startled him in the yard with what appeared to be the onset of a youthful interrogation.

"Well—" he began slowly but didn't have time to continue as Amanda supplied her own answer to what he had been carefully trying to word.

"Is it because she's so mean?"

He tried not to laugh at her serious tone but found he couldn't hold it in. He laughed at his granddaughter's perceptiveness and was genuinely relieved at not having to come up with his own reply. When she didn't continue the dialogue, though, he abruptly stopped and noticed that her eyes were even more reflecting of her serious tone, almost cold—the eyes of someone considerably older. He therefore decided that under the circumstances she deserved nothing less than the truth and that perhaps now was the time to take the first steps towards honoring the agreement he had made with himself during his long drive north.

"Yes, I guess it was because she was so . . . mean," he said.

"But why would she be mean to *you?*" Amanda's gaze remained intense, her voice serious. For some inexplicable reason, Richard chose this particular moment to look back into the woods. He also realized there was something in Amanda's voice he hadn't heard before, something that was almost like an underlying current . . . or even a presence not altogether her own. Then he laughed at himself in his mind at the thought and turned his attention back to her question.

"That, I don't know any more than I know why she's so . . . mean, to your mother. Fact is, she's mean to a lot of people—your mother, me, the people who work at our house, the people she works with at her company." He was pleasantly surprised at how easy it was to finally be able to talk about such things—easier than he had ever imagined it could be; so much so in fact that it made him regret having waited so long. "I guess it started about the time her own mother died—your great grandmother. This was before you were born. Your grandma took it pretty hard even though she didn't let it show to anyone. But I could see it, she couldn't hide it from everyone; and when she realized I could see how much she hurt, it made her react in an even more negative manner towards me. It sounds strange I know, but that's what happened." He stopped for a moment and looked down at his hands, then back into the woods. Amanda remained motionless. "Soon after, when her father died, she, being his only child, inherited his company. From that point on, she poured her whole soul into her work—her passion, her caring . . . everything. She left room in her life for nothing else . . . nothing that is except perhaps your uncle Kevin, but that's another story. She always seemed able to make room for him. But anyway, after that point, there wasn't much left of the woman I married."

Amanda maintained her quiet demeanor while her grandfather's eyes remained focused on the woods and the path which led into shaded darkness.

"Kevin was always her favorite. In your grandmother's eyes *he* could do no wrong—but only because he'd made himself a carbon copy of her." He paused again, now looking away from the woods and back in Amanda's direction who continued to demonstrate a degree of fascination at a level well beyond her years. Looking back to the woods once again he realized he didn't even know his granddaughter's age—nine, ten? "But I know her animosity was because of something Kevin had done to her, something very bad, when they were kids." He returned his attention to Amanda once more and this time forced a smile. Amanda remained impassive.

"What did Uncle Kevin do that was so bad?" she asked, her small brow knitted in little waves of worry.

(worry . . . or anger?)

"Well . . . it's pretty hard to explain . . . you'll have to wait until you're a little older," he said, wondering if he had already said too much and so he tried to mask his concern with another smile. Amanda remained silent a moment longer and the appearance of a sudden, previously unseen hardness in her eyes reminded him uncomfortably of Augustine.

"That's okay. And you know what, grandpa?" she said, the seriousness in her eyes and face as well as that in her voice miraculously having been wiped away and replaced by the exuberance of youth.

"What, sweetheart?"

"You can stay with us as long as you want," she added with a smile.

"And I think I'll do just that, dear."

Richard, when he noticed his granddaughter's smile, thought it was one of the most beautiful things he had ever seen, and yet . . . there seemed to be just a trace of mischievousness in it as well.

He remained quiet for another moment and then suddenly broke out in laughter, laughing as much at her comment as to relieve his own tension.

Amanda grinned, got up, and sat down next to him. He put his arm around her shoulders and pulled her against him. He realized that he could have sat that way forever, hugging his granddaughter, the smell of her newly washed hair teasing his nose with the smell of fresh-cut apples.

I'm finally home, he thought.

But to have seen his granddaughter's smile at that moment would have brought an entirely different thought to mind.

32

July 25 • Tuesday

1

With his parents gone and his grandfather busily engaged in keeping Amanda occupied, Michael thought again about returning to the town library. He wondered what else he might be able to find out about their house and the local history, and decided it was time to ride his bike back into town. He left his room to find his grandfather to tell him where he was going.

In the past three days, Richard had, to everyone's delight, become a regular part of the family—almost as if he had always been with them. He was easy to talk to and always willing to listen. He never interrupted and never ignored him, which made Michael wonder what he might think about his ideas and the events that had been happening at the house. Then he felt concerned that his grandfather, in time, might also dream.

He found Richard and Amanda walking along the path leading out of the woods and caught up with them inside the gazebo. As he entered, they both looked up. They were breathing heavily and his grandfather's forehead glistened with a wet sheen as he was talking with Amanda about the possibilities living in the country had to offer. As Michael politely waited for a break in their conversation, he reflected again on the list of negatives he had started to compile in his journal on their way from Farmington Hills—the list now seeming insignificant in light of what he was afraid the future held for them now.

He remained standing as he waited, leaning against the entranceway, listening past his sister and grandfather's conversation to the remote echoes of birds in the forest behind them.

"Where'd you guys go?" he was able to ask finally, afraid to hear the answer he already knew.

"I took Grandpa out to see the Stone Circle," Amanda said and cast a glare at him, as if challenging him.

"An interesting place," Richard said. "I wonder what it was used for?" Richard continued as he looked sideways at him, squinting slightly.

Michael ignored the question. "I thought I'd go into town to the library."

"Oh, what for?"

His grandfather's question sounded neither suspicious nor threatening—as Michael had anticipated. Instead, he thought his grandfather actually sounded interested.

Nevertheless, he hesitated. Should he lie or tell the truth? He'd read once that police interrogators used similar hesitations to ascertain when someone was lying. While staring at the crude patch of plywood his father had used to cover the hole in the gazebo floor, he made up his mind.

"I'm going to see if I can find some more information on the history of our house and the town."

"Sounds interesting," Richard said.

It was something new, and actually refreshing, to have an adult taking an interest in his activities. He liked it, but at the same time it made him a little uneasy.

"When you come back you'll have to share what you found. Does your research include this Stone Circle place?"

"Actually, I already know a little bit about it. Can I wait and tell you about it when I get back though?" He started moving out of the gazebo, afraid where further questions might lead. He desperately wanted to tell his grandfather what he knew and even some of what he suspected—but he felt now wasn't the time. And, for reasons he couldn't explain, he felt averse to talking about it in front of Amanda.

"It's a deal. Have fun."

"I'll try not to be gone long—couple of hours." He was by now halfway down the steps.

His grandfather returned his attention to Amanda and they began discussing what they wanted to do next—go on an insect hunting safari, or go back inside the house. As he left them, he heard Amanda tell Richard that she wanted to go bug collecting . . . and that there was something she wanted to show him.

Michael literally ran back into the house, went up to his room, grabbed his backpack and ran back downstairs. Seconds later, he was outside, on his bike and racing down the driveway. As he turned onto the road toward town, he looked back and spotted his grandfather and sister already on their way into the field. Again, he was glad Richard had come to stay with them if for no other reason than he felt there might be safety in numbers against whatever the future might hold for them. And, he thought, it also made him happy to see his sister finally having fun with someone who took the time to play with her.

His good mood lasted only a few seconds more, though, as he realized he was now passing the part of the field where The Tree stood alone reaching out from the ground like the dead, arthritic claw of some enormous monster. The sight of it caused him to refocus once again on his objective.

He gave the tree another glance though and despite his best efforts, found himself imagining again what kind of beast it would be if the tree actually were the claw of some monstrous buried creature. This in turn caused him to wonder what would have been the tragic result if just such a beast had been loosed upon the world. As he reached the top of the hill where the road began its meandering course through the forest, he hoped never to find out.

2

Michael made excellent time to the library—20.4 mph average speed according to his bike cyclometer. This time, though, no one was playing basketball on the courts across the street; no one was arguing the calls with personal insults. As he mounted the library steps, he looked back and noticed that there were no cars parked nearby. Overall, things seemed strangely quiet, as if it were a Sunday morning instead of a Tuesday afternoon.

He entered the library and was relieved to find Tedric seated in his normal place behind his desk. Until that moment he hadn't considered what he would do if it had been Mrs. Burroway again. As Michael approached, the librarian looked up from his work to welcome him.

"Well, hello there Michael. How ya doing?"

Michael saw that Tedric was busy putting labels on microfilm jackets. He looked but was unable to determine the subject matter. He wiped at the sweat on his forehead and face and dried his hands on his pants. If his mother had seen him, she would have been furious—which is exactly why he did it.

"Okay, I guess," he said, still trying to catch his breath. He forced himself to talk slowly. "Do you have any more information on our house? I'd like to find out some more about the previous owners."

"Actually, I do," Tedric said and Michael noticed how his smile reminded him of a child proud to show off his favorite toy. Tedric carefully put the microfilm labels down and adjusted his glasses, which had slid down his nose. "After you'd expressed so much interest in these matters, I've been going through some things I ran across right here in the library and finding out quite a bit, actually. It seems that house of yours has gone through a lot of owners over the years. I was surprised myself when I started putting it all together. It also seems that many of these people haven't had the best of luck while living there, either."

"Oh? What happened?"

Michael found himself interested and yet afraid at the same time. He thought of the peculiar phrase Tedric had used—*gone through a lot of owners*—as if the house were a living entity capable of consuming its tenants.

"Probably the most famous, and tragic case, involved the Wilsons. Here, let me show you." Tedric opened his desk drawer and pulled out a file folder filled with what looked like a thick stack of old newspaper clippings. Michael looked for a label but didn't see one. "Here it is, 1957. I stumbled across this the other day and brought it up—figured you'd be along soon." He smiled again, but didn't show Michael the article right away. "Anyway, it seems one of the Wilson daughters hanged herself."

"Wow. How old was she?" Michael asked and continued trying to see over the top of the folder, even rocking up on the tips of his toes. Tedric however didn't seem to notice.

"Sixteen. It was a pretty big news item for a long time after it happened. Shocked a lot of people. One night she just up and hanged herself from that big willow out in the field by your house."

Shivers were now running up and down Michael's spine like a pack of ants racing between the nape of his neck and the backs of his knees. The strange tree was certainly a curiosity, but now, knowing someone had actually used it to kill themselves . . .

No wonder the thing gives everybody the creeps . . .

"Did . . . did they know why she did it?"

"Well, she'd been having trouble in school, even got herself kicked out for a while. But then she seemed to get it together, even went back to class and was getting good grades again. Shortly thereafter though, she found she was with child and I guess she didn't know how to handle it. And remember now," he continued, looking directly at Michael over the top of the file folder, "this was 1957; folks wasn't as understanding or acceptin' as they seem to be now 'bout such things. Back then, it would have been a big scandal, enough to ruin a family—so she didn't tell them. Her folks, I mean."

Tedric looked back at his folder again and continued flipping through articles. Michael felt scared, sick and excited all at the same time. Even stranger, he felt a loss, as if he had actually known the dead girl—a girl who had lived and died before he had even been born. Regardless, he could identify with her plight, her need for understanding in a society not yet prepared to give it. He listened to the rest of what Tedric had to tell him concerning the Wilson family only peripherally, unable to get the dead girl out of his mind. He even tried imagining what she might have looked like—wondering if she had been pretty. He imagined she might have looked like Lisa Vanderwall, a girl he remembered from his freshman class in

Farmington Hills who had been killed in a horse-riding accident at her grandparents' farm in Vermont. Lisa had been a plain-looking girl—thin, average height, long brown hair and brown eyes. Plain, but pretty in her own unique way.

And then the image changed. As Michael began to admire the portrait he'd formed inside his mind, Lisa's face suddenly faded and was replaced by that of a dog—a dog recently hit by a car and dragging its hind quarters behind it as it traveled along the gravel shoulder of a road while making a painful whimpering sound. It was always the sound he remembered most—that sound full of pain, anguish, and suffering—the memory of which sent shards of nauseous agony slicing into the center of his mind. But then he blinked and just as quickly as it had appeared, the memory faded.

"Now, after the Wilsons, there was a young artist fellow, name of Marcus LaSalle. Fairly successful too . . . that is, until he bought your house."

"Let me guess," Michael interrupted, putting his hands on his hips, "He killed himself in the attic or something."

"Oh no, nothing like that. He just became . . . obsessed."

Michael slowly let his arms down.

"With that tree, the same one the Wilson girl hanged herself from. Story goes he started painting it and pretty soon couldn't paint nothing else. He tried to sell the pictures, but could find no buyers. The bank eventually foreclosed on him."

Michael's legs felt tired and he wanted to sit down, but he didn't want to miss anything Tedric was telling him.

"Now, the next thing doesn't occur until the seventies," Tedric said, as he pulled yet another news article from his folder. Michael thought this time the librarian might hand him the paper, but again he didn't. "Here we go—1977. John and Sarah Young moved in with their son Jeremy. Shortly after they moved in, the boy, only six years old, disappears. They find him six days later—'apparent animal attack' the police report said. Next, we move ahead to 1980 when a guy by the name of Cecil George buys the place." Tedric pulled out another newspaper clipping and this time Michael could see part of an ad for the Boyne City Greenhouse on the back. "Nine months later, Mr. George mysteriously disappears and to this day no one knows what happened to him."

Michael redirected his attention from the ad to Tedric and noticed that the librarian's face now seemed to be hanging. Tedric let out a long sigh.

"That's quite a history," Michael said. "Makes one sort of wonder though, doesn't it?"

"Sure. And that ain't all of it. There're still some gaps here. Give me a little more time and I'll probably be able to fill them in for you as well. Right from the time that little Michelle Wilson hanged 'erself, folks around here have been calling that place cursed and haunted," Tedric said, shifting his eyes away as if embarrassed.

Tedric looked back at him again, perhaps waiting for some sort of reaction. Michael realized he was getting a feeling about Tedric much like the one he had had about his grandfather that morning—that this was someone he liked, someone he could trust—someone that took him seriously—someone he could call a friend.

"Anyway, after Cecil George disappeared, the place sat empty near ten years as best I recall. Family didn't know what to do, you know? Just kept hoping he'd show up someday. 'Course he never did and eventually they had to give up and that's when they sold it to the Hawkins—the folks you bought it from. Now, far as I know they didn't have no problems, but then again I never knew 'em personally. There were folks around here that talked about noises and such, but I never paid much mind to that kind of talk."

"Noises?" Michael felt suddenly cold. "What do you mean? Noises like what?"

"Oh . . . well . . . I don't know. Like I's told you, I never paid much mind to that sort of talk, but I think they meant stuff like ghost-noises you know, things going bump in the night, that sort of thing. Like I said, a lot of people think the house is just plain haunted. No telling though if there's any truth to the stories even if you believe in that kind of stuff."

"Oh." Michael began to shiver and again it felt like that same ant army scurrying up and down his spine. A haunted house?

Let's just hope that's really all it is.

(ALL it is?)

If there's one thing I've learned about life, it's that no matter how bad it looks, you never, ever say that it can't get any worse, because the second you do, that's when it usually does. There's always *worse.*

3

Her grandfather stayed with her for several hours, searching the fields and visiting The Tree. After having seen the tree and shortly thereafter complaining of a headache, Richard went back to the house to make himself a late lunch. Amanda however remained in the fields and continued her insect collecting excursion.

After the clear morning, the sun had since slipped behind a wall of gray clouds moving in from the west and it now looked like it was going to rain soon.

Traveling all the while in the general direction of the tree, she kept her eyes focused on the ground, scouring it for any faint movement that would signify the existence of a bug. However, the graying light made it difficult for her to spot much in the tall grass and as the cloud cover raced across the sky, a wind made itself an undeniable presence and the threat of a rainstorm became more imminent.

Amanda continued her search, suddenly intent on reaching the tree again. She tried telling herself this was simply because it was at the tree that she hoped to find the elusive luna moth, though all the while knowing this wasn't the real reason. However, when she tried thinking about her true intentions it was like something she had once known but had temporarily forgotten. And it wasn't so much a reason as a need—a need as real and physical as eating or breathing—a need which was insistent and almost painful.

She looked ahead at her destination and stopped when she noticed the edge of a small water pool about ten feet in front of her. It was the very same pool she had seen in her dream. But it wasn't the pool that had caused her to stop—it was the man. He was standing about two hundred feet away, looking directly at her. She immediately recognized him as the man she and the rest of her family had seen earlier in their driveway, the man her brother said had been stalking them.

Harvey Olds remained steadfast in the tall grass, unmoving, almost as if he were another part of the landscape, as natural as a tree or a stone. He stared at her, his face and eyes unreadable at such a distance, but Amanda nevertheless felt the presence of his stare as if it were a living thing reaching out for her. Then she became afraid—not of the stranger—but of the tree and she wondered what it was that had possessed her to come so close to it; then she realized she was staring directly at it and in the next instant things changed.

Although he was still as far away as before, when she turned back to the man, his presence now somehow felt closer.

She sensed he'd somehow moved. But she decided that she wasn't going to wait to see what he would do next; instead, she turned and bolted for the house.

4

Amanda ran as fast as she could but it wasn't fast enough to escape the rain. She'd made it only halfway to the house when it started. When the rain came, it did not do so slowly or hesitantly; as if guilty for having to do what it must, but came all at once with full, pounding force.

She felt like she was now running faster than she had ever run before in her life. She was almost to the house before realizing her grandfather was standing on the front porch. She disregarded his presence and ran past him to the side entrance, slamming the door behind her. She was as soaked as if she had been dunked in a pool. She stopped only long enough to take off her shoes before bolting up the stairs to her room, where, once she felt safely locked inside, she hesitated only a moment before finding the courage to look back toward the tree from the vantage point of her second-story bedroom window. The landscape surrounding the tree, however, was open and empty for as far as she could see.

33

1

"I'm home!"

Michael, in his room upstairs, heard his mother's announcement but for the moment was distracted, then startled to see Dr. Woulfe's journal in front of him on the bed without any recollection of his having taken the book out. This caused him to pause and reflect on his earlier possession and he was suddenly afraid that it might be happening again. Then his head seemed to clear and he remembered getting the journal out after he'd come home from the library. This time at least, his fugue had been of his own making. Since learning of the deaths and one disappearance connected with their home, his thoughts had been more or less in turmoil. His agitation further intensified when, after coming home after the long and exhausting bike ride in the rain, he had learned of Amanda's encounter with Harvey Olds. Although his grandfather said that he hadn't seen the stranger himself, Michael had no reason to doubt his sister's story. This second appearance of the stranger in so short a time made him even more anxious to discover Harvey's connection to the overall scheme of things. He was positive that Harvey was connected in some way—either to their house, or to the events that had occurred there in the past. He also felt things were beginning to escalate—unfortunately without him having gained any new information which might be helpful.

2

Later that evening, Michael spoke with Amanda in his bedroom—he sitting at his desk, Amanda lying on the bed. Below them came the familiar kitchen sounds of clashing pans and running water; their mother cooking a late dinner.

"Have you been having any more dreams?" he asked slowly, beginning their conversation. He knew the dreams had scared her. But they were also important to his quest and at this point, he needed all the information he could get. When nothing makes sense, he thought, one has to grab at whatever one can in the hopes of finding some possible thread that might eventually tie it all together.

"No, not for a while. I sure hope *those* are done."

She's different somehow. More serious. Older, or . . .

(like she's hiding something)

He was disappointed. The dreams had indeed been scary, but they were also part of what was going on, maybe one of the most important parts.

(yeah, and what if they were an integral part of your possession? you said it yourself—what if the dreams are the start to the whole thing? and now you want them back?)

No. They didn't cause my possession. Don't ask me how I know that now, but I don't think that's the case. The dreams are more like . . . messages or something.

(messages . . . from whom?)

"Can you tell me about them—about your dreams, that is—tell me what happened in them?"

Amanda seemed almost happy to respond and told him about becoming a butterfly, flying over the tree and field . . . and about the people impaled on the ground. She also recounted her dream as leader of the plastic-like black people. She finished by telling him how, toward the end of the dream, she had felt superhuman strength, as if she could do anything she wanted.

For several moments, Michael sat staring but not really seeing his sister. Her revelation caused him to remember his own dream and the similarity of the bonding of people into himself and the resulting feeling of strength.

But what's the connection?

Then, speaking quietly, almost as if he were talking to himself, he said, “I just wish I knew what all this *means*.”

Downstairs, the sound of the side door opening and closing brought him back to the present. Dad was home. This was confirmed when they heard the sound of two shoes dropping heavily to the floor.

“So, what do you think Dad’s going to do?” Amanda said.

“What do you . . . oh, about Harvey? I don’t know.”

They listened as their mother welcomed their father home. Although muffled, the words of their conversation were nevertheless understandable.

“I’m going to my room,” Amanda suddenly announced, catching him off-guard.

A few minutes later, he had forgotten all about his sister—the conversation below had suddenly become much more interesting.

3

Alan walked to the refrigerator and retrieved a beer. He grabbed another and offered it silently to Richard who declined it by shaking his head.

“So,” Richard began, “has Sam told you about our little incident?”

Alan felt the refreshing coldness of the beer can in his hand gently climb its way up his arm. He pulled out a chair at the kitchen table and sat down while Richard remained standing near the counter. Alan looked over at his wife who was frying hamburger in a skillet and seemed oblivious to the conversation.

“I feel like it’s my fault—” Richard began. Alan saw Richard’s jaw quiver and now felt another kind of coldness seep out from his chest, up to his neck and back down into his legs.

“Don’t Dad—this was nothing to do with you,” Sam said as she turned away from the stove to face them.

“Maybe. Still, if perhaps I had been watching her closer—”

“Something happened to Amanda?” Alan interrupted.

"She thinks she saw that man again," Sam said and turned back to the stove.

"Harvey Olds?"

"She said she saw him standing in the field next to that awful-looking tree."

Alan turned his attention toward Sam as she vigorously stirred a pan of something thick and red. A picture from one of his dreams came into his mind and though he tried, he couldn't get it out—it was the girl—hanging gray and dead from one of the tree's thick, finger-like branches, her fragile body swinging back and forth in front of a full moon. But in his mind this time, her face was no longer a stranger's but instead was Amanda's—his beloved daughter hanging lifeless from the tree and then speaking . . . *what he taught wasn't the living . . . it was the dying . . .*

"What was she doing all the way out there by herself?" He stopped and realized he needed to soften his tone. "She's okay though, right?"

"Yes. Dad was on the porch when she came running back to the house. He said he didn't even see him. I wonder if he was even there at all."

"To be honest, it had started to rain pretty hard," Richard said. "I could have easily missed him—it was a long ways away—" he said, his voice obviously still heavy with guilt. Alan, to his surprise, found himself feeling sorry for him.

The silence in the kitchen stretched on for several seconds.

"Well, now that I've heard your good news, I've got some of my own to share," Alan said sarcastically.

"I can hardly wait," Sam said as she poured a box of spaghetti noodles into a large pot of boiling water.

"Remember that report about our neighbor having two of his sheep killed?"

"Yeah?" Sam said and pushed the spaghetti down into the water.

"Well, now one of his *cows* is missing. This time, the story even made the local paper. I read about it at work."

"It probably wandered off through a hole in the fence. It's probably out in our back woods somewhere right now. Maybe the guy's just a lousy farmer," Sam said.

"No, it didn't wander off. The authorities are quite certain the cow was killed." Alan paused before going on, wondering if he even *should* go on. "They eventually found its head—but that's *all* they found."

Richard wrinkled his face in disgust and walked past Alan to the cupboards where he began retrieving dishes.

"What?" Sam exclaimed. "Jesus, don't let the kids hear *that.*" She turned away from the stove to look at him for a moment before walking over to the pantry. She came back with a can of mushrooms.

"I think maybe I'll have that beer now, after all," Richard said and stepped toward the refrigerator.

"What *I really* want to know is—what in the world's *going on* around here?" Alan continued as he took a long, hard swallow of his beer and found that, like his son had discovered earlier, he was waiting for an answer that was not going to come.

4

Everyone turned in early that night after watching half of *Jurassic Park* on video for the sixth time. Michael was having a hard time drifting off—which wasn't unusual. Since they had moved into Woulfe House, his sleeping patterns had been anything but regular. Over the last week it seemed to have been improving somewhat, but now, here he was again, wide awake.

The story he had overheard about the butchered cow had now become just another part of the puzzle he was trying, albeit so far unsuccessfully, to put together. Each night he attempted to rearrange the pieces into some sort of arrangement that he hoped would combine to make sense—but each night he failed to make even two of the many pieces he had so far collected fit together. So, as he lay in bed this time, he tried to think of something that could perhaps explain this latest piece—the cow's strange death. At first, he envisioned a hairy ogre coming out of the woods. Next, he saw a man he imagined to be Dr. Woulfe tying the cow up in the basement of the house. Then he saw him bring forth and employ a large knife to eviscerate the animal, thereby allowing the cow's blood to spill across the floor in a splashing flood that quickly surged to a depth of four inches because all the floor drains were plugged.

Finally, though, the one image that, once it appeared, kept repeating itself over and over again in his mind—was that of six robed and hooded figures marching out of the woods into the Stone Circle. There, in the center of the Circle, was a cow. The robed figures approached the lone cow, stopped and then two of them picked up an enormous saw like the kind lumberjacks had once used. The robed figures then sawed off the living head of the cow and afterwards, the six of them carried the body away like pallbearers with an enormous coffin.

Several hours later, Michael eventually managed to push the strange images aside and drifted into an uneasy sleep . . . and dreamed.

5

Sam was awakened by strange sounds coming from the basement. Beside her, Alan was breathing slowly and heavily. She lay still as she listened and thought about Harvey Olds, wondering if perhaps he had now taken the final step by breaking into their home. For the moment at least, she decided there was no immediate need to wake Alan. As she pondered what to do next, she heard soft footsteps on the stairs but then they faded and seemed to move away from her, going downstairs.

She sat up feeling scared, yet something continued to prevent her from awakening Alan. As she dragged herself out of bed she swayed slightly as the last traces of sleep ran begrudgingly out of her body. The wood floor beneath her bare feet felt cold.

In the hallway, she stopped to listen again and this time was sure she heard what sounded like people talking somewhere downstairs, possibly in the basement. She hesitated again and considered for the last time, before beginning her descent, whether or not to wake Alan. Then, despite not having reached a decision, her feet seemed to take off of their own accord and she found herself stepping slowly and quietly down the stairs. Halfway down, a board groaned in protest at her weight and she froze, holding her breath—listening to see if her presence might have been detected. But the voices from the basement—she was sure they were coming from the basement now—continued. She tried as best she could to hear what they were saying, but couldn't.

Her feet took off again and it was like she were watching someone else as she descended the stairs to the first floor and then turned toward the steps which led down into the basement.

The voices stopped and then she heard movement—a faint rustling sound like a piece of plastic being dragged over the floor. She couldn't help but think about bodies being dragged and then, for the first time, wondered if she was actually awake or merely in the middle of an extremely lucid dream.

On the landing to the basement she stopped when she noticed a blue light glowing beneath her. As she wondered about the source of the light, the shuffling sound began again. Then the glow faded and disappeared. After she'd safely negotiated the rest of her descent, at the foot of the stairs she turned on the first light she could find, instantly bathing her surroundings in a yellow harshness.

In the northeast corner was a little girl standing near the wall. The girl turned towards her, and blinked at Sam from under the glare of the light.

"Amanda?"

6

Amanda blinked her eyes rapidly in the darkness. She couldn't remember if she had fallen asleep and been awakened, or if she had been lying awake the whole time.

She knew that a Voice had called her by name. But she wasn't sure if she'd physically heard it—or whether the voice had originated only inside her head. She sat up and listened, not sure if she was awake or dreaming. To her surprise, she wasn't frightened, even when the Voice called her again, this time speaking her name unmistakably—quietly—but in a tone replete with command. It was a voice, she felt, which could not be denied nor ignored. As she rose from her bed and stood up, she listened. And this time, when the Voice talked to her, she walked over to her bedroom door and opened it. Treading obediently into the hallway, she paused to stop again. The Voice was quiet but nevertheless insistent, as she moved toward the stairs and began to descend.

She didn't turn on any lights and didn't stop until she'd arrived in the basement, where she noticed a glow on the wall in the corner. The glow was a shade of blue like the waters of the Caribbean she had seen in pictures. The glow traced an outline on the wall roughly the size and shape of a doorway. Then the Voice returned.

"Yes, I must," Amanda said in response to the Voice's question. Then she asked, "Do I have to go now?"

"*The time is at hand,*" the Voice replied and it sounded to Amanda like it was going to say more, but it didn't. She realized that the Voice had left and felt a dull sadness at its departure. As she stood, wondering where the voice had gone or even if she had heard it at all, the blue outline of the door slowly began to fade and soon disappeared completely.

It seemed as if she had been standing in the dark for hours when an unexpected light came on. After the darkness, the light seemed like the sun. As she blinked her eyes in an attempt to counteract the painful brilliance, she no longer remembered the Voice or even why she was now in the basement, but what she did know was that her mom was there and this knowledge comforted her.

As her mother led her back upstairs to her bed, she decided she must have been dreaming after all.

7

"What's going on? I thought I heard voices," Alan said when Sam climbed back into bed.

"Just Amanda. She was sleepwalking. I found her in the basement. Sleepwalking and . . . talking to herself."

"That's strange," Alan said, his voice muffled and tired. He was already drifting back to sleep.

"Yes. Strange indeed," she whispered.

She tried to remember the voices she thought she'd heard, the ones that had awakened her. Although the memory was already fading, she thought though that there had been more than one. Even though she couldn't picture Amanda playacting out a conversation between imaginary people, in thinking about it further, she determined that's what it must have been. She continued to lay awake in an attempt to bring some sense of order to the night's events, but the more she tried remembering the particulars of the voice sounds, the fuzzier their memory became. Finally, she gave up, and welcomed the unthinking comfort of sleep.

34

July 27 • Thursday Night
Michael's Third Dream

In the dream, Michael stands at the edge of the Stone Circle and watches the cultists standing in their own circle surrounding a great bonfire. All the cultists but one are dressed in black robes. The solitary figure, small like a child, is dressed in white. The figure in white stands apart from the others and when one of the cultists approaches the lone figure and removes its hood, he recognizes Amanda. He thinks he should do something but instead watches helplessly as his sister walks directly into the burning inferno. He is afraid to look and turns away. But when he turns back, he sees Amanda standing almost regally in the center of the engulfing flames. She then walks out the other side of the fire, unharmed. She extends her arm and points directly at him. Simultaneously, all of the cultists turn to see where she is pointing while her eyes begin to glow like emerald lasers. Out of the darkness, a man, his face a black shadow, appears behind Amanda and puts his hand on her shoulder. The shadow-man laughs and the sound rustles the tree leaves.

Michael is now running through the tangled wilds of the forest while behind him a hundred cultists crash recklessly through the brush like a pack of animals in pursuit of prey. Wild raspberry bushes claw and tear mercilessly at his body as he rips through their groping branches. His pursuers, as they close the gap, scream like wild beasts and then he is suddenly falling, an unseen yawning black chasm having opened before him. He lands hard, hearing bones crack and splinter, and yet feels no pain. Then he feels hands underneath him, softly lifting him up, and he is once again able to stand when a voice whispers in his ear "Go!" He runs again, this time out of the darkness and along the path which leads back to the house.

As he nears his house, he no longer hears his pursuers and so he slows, walking almost casually into his backyard in the twilight. To his surprise, his sister is there to meet him—still dressed in her white robe. Her hood is now back in place, her face hidden in shadow like the man's from the Circle. He is afraid to look directly into his sister's face, but knows in time he will. Then, even though he doesn't want to, he finds himself willing himself to see it, but where her face should be, there is in its place only a dark, almost surreal shadow. He stands still, saying nothing while Amanda waits at the corner of the house, holding something in her right hand, an object that looks long and has a handle. On the far end of the object, something gleams like silver and he wonders if it might be a hammer. To get a closer look he walks forward and sees that the object in her hand is a bloody hand ax and at his sister's feet is Ghost, the family cat, its four severed legs and tail stacked in a bloody pile in the grass. As he watches, the cat manages a single, barely audible cry and then dies.

When he looks back to his sister's face he sees a white smile gleaming out at him from the hooded shadow. Then she tells him in a deep, booming voice, "Welcome home . . . brother Michael." She reaches up with the hand that isn't wielding the ax—and pulls back her hood. Before he is forced to look he turns and runs. He runs to the other side of the house, then into the field towards the Tree, all the while racing through grass which is brown and dead. When he finally looks behind him he sees not one but what appear to be several dozen Amandas scurrying after him. All of the Amandas are white-robed and hooded and each carries a hand ax.

He runs for the Tree and at first it seems as if he is getting no closer. Then he is falling against it and his face and hands come away wet, a wetness that feels like warm, sticky syrup and he realizes the tree is covered with blood and its branches filled with cut-up cats. As he regains his footing, he watches in fear as the Amanda creatures form a ring surrounding him and the tree. He screams defiantly at them but they do not respond. Then something touches his shoulder and as he whirls around, he sees the toe of a shoe. When he looks up, he sees hanging above him the body of the mysterious stranger. Shaken, Michael falls to the ground and, while lying on his back, watches as the dead man's purple, grotesquely swollen face cracks into a broad grin, its laughter cackling forth like a demon's. Then he senses more than sees the Amanda-things as they rush him. In an instant, they cover him in a stinging, biting mass before he escapes by drifting into a comforting darkness painted by the echoing laughter of the hanged man.

35

Tulia, Texas
July 31 • Monday

Maria Cedellia sat at her kitchen table in the mobile home she shared with her three children—Emily, Anna and Carlos—and thought about her life. She thought about what her parents would think if they could see her now. Then she wondered if her parents were both still alive—she had neither seen nor had contact with them in more than seven years. And then, she thought about her husband Jim, who had been gone for nearly two years now, saying at the time he left that he had finally had enough of her "funny religion." This last observation caused her to once again reflect on how, throughout their rocky marriage, their conversations always seemed to go.

"What the hell you doing giving away more of my hard-earned money again to those religious crazies?" he would say. He always called them "those religious crazies" or sometimes "freaks" or "nuts." She figured such epithets were as much as her old Jim's imagination could handle on a good day, where a good day meant any day where he actually came home after work instead of spending all night and a fair portion of the next morning at Tilly's Tavern in downtown Tulia, a small town located on the north-south road that linked Amarillo with Lubbock. The eight-unit mobile home park they lived in was only four miles north of Tulia.

"You wouldn't understand, Jim," she would reply, which in turn always made him even angrier.

"Yeah, you always say that. Why don't you try explaining it to me for once then, huh? Hell knows why I even let you go to their meetings," he would say and follow this with another enormous swallow from one of the 40-oz. beers he preferred to drink.

"*You* don't let me do anything. I go because *I* want to go, and don't you ever even *think* about stopping me because you can't."

"Jesus, you're one mouthy bitch, you know that? I don't even know why I put up with your mouthy crap."

"Yeah, well you sure have some nerve. You sit there and complain about a couple of bucks I give to the Society while just about every other night you're down at Tilly's pissing away more in one night than I give them in a month."

And, more often than not, the conclusion of such arguments resulted in Jim storming out of the house anyway to head for Tilly's. He rarely hit her and she had always thanked God for that. And so it happened that one night, two years and a month ago now, he had left and never come back. There had been some hard times for a while after that but fortunately her friends in the Society had been there to help her and the kids until she could find a job. And, in one of life's little ironies, she had eventually found herself a job at none other than the infamous Tilly's. She usually worked five days a week, three to midnight, with Mondays and Tuesdays off. She couldn't afford a babysitter, so she normally left Emily in charge of Carlos, 7 and Anna, 5.

"Emily, do we have any sour cream?" she asked her oldest daughter who would turn 14 a week from tomorrow. For her birthday, Maria hoped to buy her the music box they had seen in Sullivan's three months ago. Emily had been wanting the box ever since that day, even though she knew they couldn't afford it.

"I think so, I think there's half a container left in the fridge," Emily said.

"How does stroganoff sound tonight?"

"All right! My favorite!" The smile Maria witnessed on her daughter's face helped to confirm her decision to go ahead and purchase the music box for her birthday, no matter the cost.

"I want pizza," Carlos interjected. He said the same thing nearly every night. And, just like every other night, they ignored him.

"Yeah, pizza!" Anna chimed in.

"All right you two, maybe tomorrow. We'll see. I made pretty good tips last week with the rodeo boys in town." She of course failed to mention one young man in particular, a dark-skinned ranch hand who had taken a special interest in her last Saturday night. Afterwards, as they'd agreed, he paid her $60. It hadn't been her first time.

Maria took a pound of hamburger out of the freezer and placed it in a large skillet on the stove. From a cupboard she retrieved egg noodles and a can of store-brand cream of mushroom soup.

Their dinner requests deferred, Carlos and Anna were now otherwise occupied watching television on the 13-inch color set Maria had found in the trash one day and had a neighbor fix for them. While Carlos and Anna sat on the floor and watched TV, Emily remained curled up nearby on the couch reading a book. Since it was summer, Emily found the time to read a book nearly every day.

There's hope for that girl, Maria thought, as she observed Emily in the living room. *I can take comfort in that. I just wish I could get her out of this rathole town in the middle of nowhere to someplace where she can make something of herself.*

Maria's "other" tip money went into a coffee can the children didn't know about, one which she kept well hidden. Some day she hoped, the money would allow her to fulfill a dream and move to Wisconsin where her brother worked as a civil engineer, even though she hadn't had any contact with him in over four years. She currently had just over five hundred dollars in the can.

And then it happened.

Thoughts of Emily, of the money, of her brother and of the move to Wisconsin—instantly vanished—swept from her mind as easily as a broom sweeps a floor. Immediately, other thoughts came forth to take their place—an image of a place she had to go to, a place where she had never been before, and of people she had to meet—thoughts that would allow no argument—or delay.

"Mom, do you think we could go to Plainview tomorrow? I need to take some books back," Emily said, as she entered the kitchen.

Maria stood in front of the stove, a spatula in her hand, while in the frying pan, the hamburger burned. Maria nevertheless continued looking straight ahead, seemingly transfixed on something Emily could not discern.

Emily rushed past her mother to the stove, screaming, "Mom! It's burning!" As she grabbed at the spatula in her mother's hand, it fell and clattered to the floor. Emily snatched it up, not bothering to clean it before turning the meat over. Maria allowed herself to be pushed aside, not reacting, instead continuing to stare straight ahead, oblivious to the smoke that now hung in the air in a cloud as thick as the cigarette haze at Tilly's.

"Mom, what's wrong? Are you all right?" Emily asked, her voice already shaking as she grabbed her mother by the shoulders. She led her mother to the kitchen table and sat her down in one of the metal folding chairs they'd been forced to purchase at the new Wal-Mart in Amarillo after Jim had smashed all the wooden ones one night in a drunken rage. Still, Maria didn't react, but simply allowed herself to be led over to the table like a child and then seated. As she sat, she appeared to be staring right through a faded picture of Elvis on the wall in front of her.

"Mom! Can you hear me, what's going on?" Emily cried. Months of playing mother to her sister and brother had made a strong girl out of Emily, but she wasn't prepared to deal with something like this.

Maria stood up and as she did, her chair fell over, neatly folding itself together on the way down, crashing into a bag of empty aluminum cans destined for the recycling center. As the bag toppled over in a loud clatter of metal on the linoleum floor, Maria didn't even flinch. Emily worried that the noise might have been loud enough to bring Carlos and Anna away from the TV.

"I have to go now," Maria said, her eyes still seeming to be staring off into nothing. To Emily it sounded as if her mother had spoken from a trance.

"*Go?* Where do you have to go, Mom?" Emily asked, her voice quaking, now on the edge of hysteria, the tears beginning to flow unchecked down her cheeks.

"I have to go *now*," Maria repeated, like a pull-string doll that can only say one thing.

Maria moved toward the door and picked up her purse without stopping to look at it.

"I have to go now," she repeated.

Emily began crying. "Mom . . . Mom! . . . please! Where are you going . . . what's *wrong?*" She choked on the words as her entire body began to shake.

As Maria's hand latched onto the doorknob, Emily clawed frantically at her arm, trying to restrain her. Maria didn't seem to notice though and her strength proved to be too much for her daughter. She opened the door and the two of them stepped out into darkness. Behind them, Carlos and Anna were now crying.

Maria, with Emily by her side, marched for their car, a 1978 Chevrolet Impala with one hundred and eighty thousand miles on it. At this time of night the single streetlight outside their trailer cast an orange glow on the gray car making it look like a slab of old meat. When Maria reached the car door, all the while pulling Emily behind her, Emily refused to let go and continued pleading with her mother for what she somehow knew would be the last time.

"No Mom . . . please don't go . . . *please don't go!"*

When Maria climbed into the car, she closed the door firmly behind her, forcing Emily to let go in order to save her arm from being crushed. As the old engine roared to life, it drowned out Emily's sobs. As her mother drove away without another word or even a single look back, Emily fell to her knees in the orange dirt and sobbed, rocking back and forth while repeating over and over ". . . please don't go . . . please don't go . . ."

From the open door of the trailer, Carlos and Anna's wailing mixed with the distant, answering yowls of desert coyotes, creating an almost surrealistic chorus of sound . . . like some sort of Calling.

36

Monday Night
Amanda's Third Dream

In the dream, Amanda runs down a narrow path through the woods, chasing the strange man, hearing him crashing and stumbling ahead of her. She runs for what seems like a long time but surprisingly doesn't tire. Then, when she no longer is able to hear the man, she spots a clearing ahead—the Stone Circle. She reaches the Circle but this time it is the fort from Mackinac Island that awaits her and there is no longer any sign of the man. Even though the sun is high above her, the fort looks dark as if it's exuding shadow, its windows black pits. Behind her, a door slams.

Then she finds herself inside one of the buildings inside the fort. She recognizes the building as a jail and is soon transfixed by a gaping hole in the floor from which a faint glow is emanating from an unseen light source located somewhere in the underground cell. As she approaches the hole she hears a gentle humming like a large electric motor running in another room.

Without warning she is down inside the holding cell comprised of rough block walls and a dirt floor. When she steps forward and pushes on the wall in front of her it swings silently inward, revealing a hand-dug dirt tunnel stretching forward into blackness. An echoing laugh floats out of the darkness accompanied by the smell of woody, fungal decay.

She enters the tunnel cautiously and instantly senses that the air is colder even than in the cell—and wet. It is dark, but she is still able to see clearly. Ahead, a faint blue glow encourages her to continue forward. When she reaches the glow's source she finds a small fire burning in the center of a large cavern, a fire comprised exclusively of flames, sitting alone on the smooth stone floor. She sees no fuel source for the fire and the flames make no sound, waving silently like wind-blown flags viewed through a strong pair of binoculars. To compound the mystery, she notices that the base of the fire floats several inches above the floor.

She doesn't remember moving but is suddenly standing at the edge of the strange fire. The flames produce neither heat nor cold but seem to grow taller and brighter in response to her presence. The fire is now as tall as she is. When she reaches her hand toward the flames, an instant before contact, the fire vanishes and she is surrounded by blackness. She looks up and sees a starlight-speckled dome above her. From the faint light, she is able to discern that she is standing near the center of what must be the Stone Circle. Animal sounds, weird and indescribable, surround her but seem more like the murmuring of a crowd of children hidden within the black forest.

The fire returns again, startling her, appearing this time in the center of the fire pit inside the Stone Circle. She notices that the fire burns with the same blue flame as before. As she watches, the flames begin to coalesce, bundling and compacting themselves together, forming the shape of something familiar. As the shape becomes more solid and distinct she realizes it is somehow forming itself into the shape of a man. When the process is complete, the "man" steps out of the blue fire in a body made of blue flame. With ghost-like appendages the man beckons to her. She is simultaneously afraid of and yet drawn to this strange man-fire and as she steps backward . . .

. . . she is back in the cavern where the blue fire now towers above her with a height more than twice her own. As she reaches her hand inside the flames, she feels an electric tingle, a tingle which makes her feel warm and good. When she senses a presence behind her she quickly withdraws her

hand. As she stares more intently into the flames they turn darker, becoming almost black until they are able to reflect the scene behind her much like a reflection when seen in a dark pool of water.

A man stands behind her and in the fire-reflection he looks dark and enormous. He calls to her and she hears his voice, not with her ears but from inside her head. As he talks to her, she listens to his smooth voice and her body quivers with a strange sense of pleasure. Before he even touches her she senses his presence immediately behind her. At the moment of contact, her body floods with a surge of tremendous strength. She gasps with the pleasure of it, then stretches a hand toward the cavern wall. Before her outstretched arm the rock cracks and explodes with a sound like an exploding cannon.

Behind her, the man-fire laughs.

37

August 1 • Tuesday

1

As Michael rode his bike to the library, he kept glancing behind him as if expecting to see someone. The fear wasn't something new; since their trip to the island it had been growing inside him, expanding with each passing day. The problem was—he couldn't identify what it was he was afraid of—which was at least half of what made it so frightening. Today, it was the fear that someone might be chasing him. Tomorrow, it might be a shadow. It was, though, he decided, a fear of impending disaster. It was a fear based on the anticipation of an unknown, an unknown he knew might exist only in his mind. This last idea was the most frightening of course—that it could be another stage of his degeneration which had begun with the episode of the forgotten two weeks. He argued with himself about it daily and the fundamental problem was that neither explanation was any better than the other—either he was going crazy—or something bad was going to happen to them very soon.

As Pleasant Valley Road entered the woods, his thoughts returned to the dreams. Were they more than simple slide shows of his subconscious imagination?

Or, are they related in some way to the other events connected with our move and the house? And why do I keep seeing Amanda in them? And what was she doing in the basement the other night when Mom found her "sleepwalking?"

He felt he possessed the capacity to comprehend the connection between the dreams and the house but to this point the specific link had eluded him, like a memory that has been misplaced—the ghost of its presence remaining like the tingly feeling of static electricity that hangs in the air after a summer thunderstorm. But more than that, it felt like there was something out there he wasn't *supposed* to remember, as if some force were barricading the synapses in his brain, sending the probing strands of his consciousness to dead-ends in order to protect the real answer.

Coming out of the woods, he pedaled hard across the flats leading into town. As always, he was timing his ride and noticed, that as he passed the Boyne City city limit sign, he was more than a minute under his best time.

As he entered town he passed a house where two kids were playing near a pile of used red bricks. The boys appeared to be about Amanda's age. As he blew past them, the taller of the two lifted a broken brick into the air, cocking his arm as if he were going to throw it at him. Michael continued looking straight ahead and passed them without incident. However, one of the boys, he didn't know which but supposed it was the one who had been holding the brick, shouted after him, "I can ride faster than you!"

He rode the next four blocks to the library without incident and without seeing anybody else. When he arrived in front of the library and stopped the timer on his cyclometer, he noted with satisfaction that he had beaten his previous best time by nearly two minutes. Breathing hard, he climbed the steps to the library doors.

2

"Tedric—I need your help," Michael said breathlessly, relieved to find Tedric alone.

"Well, Michael! How can I help?" Tedric was sitting behind his desk with a large stack of what appeared to be new hardcover books. Michael noted *Rose Madder*, by Stephen King, on top.

"Well . . . I don't know quite where to start." He had originally intended to tell the librarian everything that had transpired with himself, his family, and the house—now he found he wasn't so sure.

What if he just laughs? What if after I leave he makes a call to my parents and tells them he thinks I need professional help?

"I guess . . . I guess I'm just scared," he began, surprised at the unanticipated vacillation he heard in his voice—and the honest answer he had provided. When he looked down at the floor, his attention was momentarily diverted when he saw a penny so dirty it was nearly black.

See a penny pick it up, all day long you'll have good luck. See a penny leave it lay, bad luck'll follow you 'round all day.

He looked up from the penny back to Tedric.

"Scared? Of what?"

"I don't know really . . . our house I think."

Tedric looked at him like he had just said he could fly.

Here it comes, The Look . . . next question, will it be followed by, The Laugh?

"How could you be scared of a house?"

"Well—you know there's all the stuff that's happened there—the Wilson girl hanging herself, the death of that little boy, and that guy who disappeared. And you know about the Woulfes and about the cult."

"But that's all in the past. It's nothing to be worrying about now . . . is it?"

When Michael looked at him, he realized Tedric could see the answer in his eyes even without him saying it.

"That's what I'm not so sure about. I haven't told you all that's happened since we moved in."

"What *has* happened?" Tedric said, lowering his voice. The librarian's eyes focused on him—not like someone about to laugh or someone only being nice to humor him—but as a concerned friend, someone who wanted to help. Nevertheless, Michael grew uncomfortable under the intensity of Tedric's gaze and shifted his weight, wishing he could sit down.

"Well . . . noises, I guess you'd say. And sometimes . . . they sound like voices. We've been hearing them in the middle of the night . . . and I do mean *we*, it's not just me but all of us, though my parents keep saying it's old-house noises or mice—"

Tedric placed his elbows on his desk and folded his hands in front of his face.

"Well, maybe they are—house sounds—you know?"

"Yeah, maybe . . . but I don't think so. Did you hear about our neighbor, Scott Farley?"

"No, I don't—"

"About his sheep disappearing and now a whole cow?" Tedric still maintained a blank expression and Michael wondered how someone so immersed in local happenings could have missed such relatively big news. "With the cow, all they found was the head and a bunch of blood," he said and without waiting for a response rushed on, fearing that to stop might mark the end of his resolve and he needed to get it all out, "And then there're the dreams—"

"Dreams?" Tedric lowered his hands.

"Yeah, really weird ones, complex, like nothing I've ever had before. I think they might have something to do with it."

"Have to do with what?"

He sensed the beginning of a growing exasperation in Tedric's voice and knew he would have to give him more.

"I don't know . . . everything I guess. Sometimes I feel like I have the answer, like it's right on the tip of my tongue, but then as soon as I try and grab it or at least see it, there's nothing there. It's like it's something I used to know but have forgotten. And I think the dreams might be part of the answer, a sort of missing link, but I don't know what or how they connect to anything. I just don't know what to do anymore. And I think that something bad is going to happen to us."

Michael looked at the floor again and found himself focusing once again on the penny as he waited for Tedric.

"I don't know Michael, I think maybe you're just upset from the move. You're still adjusting to a new house, a new town—a new life. Maybe it's going to take more time?"

"Great, now you sound like my parents."

Tedric sighed, then said, "What do you want me to do?"

Michael couldn't mistake the sincerity of the librarian's question and forced himself to look at him.

"I want to do more research on our house, the town, Dr. Woulfe, anything that could in any way be connected to our house or the people that have lived there."

"Well, if it'll ease your mind, I can do the research for you in my files and let you know if I find anything out. Deal?"

"Um . . . yeah. That would be great. You don't mind?" He stared incredulously at the librarian, waiting for him to dissolve like the image from one of his dreams.

"Not at all, I'll just be doing my job, and I'll be glad to do it. And while we're at it—" he said and he pulled out the file he had shown him previously, "why don't you go and make copies of these? And then . . . go on home. I promise, I'll let you know the second I discover anything you might be interested in."

Michael took the file and smiled at the librarian. On impulse he shot out his hand and the librarian grabbed it with a grin.

"All right . . . and thanks Tedric."

Michael made the copies and although he tried, Tedric wouldn't allow him to pay for them. When he left the library, he was in better spirits than he had been in several days. He felt exceptionally fortunate to have met Tedric. If they had still been in the city, he might have been suspicious of such good-naturedness, but here he found himself accepting it as graciously as it had been given. He had perhaps finally found a positive to living in a small town to help offset his long list of negatives. With a smile, Michael said good-bye and left.

His good feeling lasted only until he saw who was waiting for him outside. Instantly, everything dissolved into a seething rage.

Across the street, against one of the large maples, stood Harvey Olds.

He was looking at Michael and smiling.

3

At first, all Michael could do was stare. He had never seen him this close—and for this long—before. At this distance, he could see that Harvey Olds was a short man, only a couple of inches taller than Michael's own 5' 5", but considerably heavier, at least 200 lbs., maybe more. The man's brown, disheveled hair hung like a shaggy horse's tail down his back, contrasting with the bare white dome prominent above his forehead. He wore dirty jeans, the knees worn white with quarter-sized holes in them. On top of a white T-shirt that was surprisingly clean, he wore, despite the warm weather, the olive army coat Michael remembered from having seen him before. And then there were his eyes—burning like green emeralds which seemed to possess the power to penetrate his skull and read his thoughts.

Throughout Michael's inspection of him, Harvey hadn't moved. He simply stood next to his bike, a department store ten-speed, its color faded nearly beyond recognition. His smile remained fixed, as if it were a mask.

Michael didn't even bother looking for traffic before bolting across the street. He hoped by this maneuver to surprise and thereby finally confront the man who had been stalking him in town, at his house and in his dreams. As he ran, he noticed that Harvey Olds' smile didn't disappear—instead—it broadened. As Michael reached a point halfway across the street, Harvey suddenly threw himself on his bike and rocketed down the road and around a corner. Michael stopped at the spot where Harvey had been standing but a moment before. Then he turned, ran back across the road, and grabbed his own bike which he'd parked near the library entrance. As he attempted to begin pursuit, he nearly fell off when his hands slipped off the metal—he had forgotten to undo his bike lock. Conscious of time slipping away, he fumbled for several moments with the big Kryptonite lock before finally releasing it. He hopped on his bike and set off like an Olympic sprinter, determined once and for all to put an end to *this* mystery.

From Drummond Avenue in front of the library, he made a sharp turn onto Lake Street and was surprised to see Harvey only a block ahead of him—he thought he would have been farther ahead by now, judging by previous experiences. Michael pushed harder, standing above his seat and smashing his pedals down like someone stepping on cockroaches that have startled them into an uncontrollable fury.

Harvey headed south. After two more blocks, Michael had narrowed the gap to less than a hundred feet. But when Harvey looked behind him and saw the proximity of his pursuer, he put on a burst of speed and pulled away before making a right turn onto Pine Street. Nearly two blocks ahead he slowed his bike and Michael once again narrowed the distance. As he caught up with him this time, he realized the stranger was playing with him, leading him on, not wanting to lose him as he no doubt could have easily done. Knowing he was not intended to overcome his nemesis, Michael wondered exactly where the man was going—and for what purpose.

As they flew through the quiet residential streets, taking corners with complete disregard for personal safety, startling youngsters on their own bikes and at one point temporarily delaying a three-person Frisbee toss, Michael wondered if they were traveling in circles.

Heading south again, Michael observed they were speeding out of town along a narrow road he had never seen before that snaked through thick woods and seemed largely unused. Then, just before they'd come to a place where it looked like the trees were about to give way to open fields, Harvey turned off, disappearing into dense greenness.

Well, this looks like the end—either of the mystery—or maybe of me.

For the first time since the chase had begun he finally had the time to allow himself to feel fear.

He slowed and where the stranger had disappeared, he discovered a narrow overgrown road leading into the dense woods that at one time could have been an old driveway. Ahead of him, about 200 feet as best he could estimate, Harvey Olds had stopped and now stood leaning on his bicycle, waiting for him.

As he closed the gap to less than a semi-trailer's length, he noticed that Harvey didn't appear to be tired. With the apparent certainty of finally catching up with this mysterious man and confronting him, Michael wondered what he was going to say to him.

Slowing to a stop less than a dozen feet from him, he decided to let go the reins of his fear and let it charge forth under the snarling guise of anger. But the stranger disrupted his plan by speaking first, addressing him like an old friend.

"Hello, Michael," he said, his voice quiet, sincere—even somewhat sophisticated and reminiscent of the character Dr. Hannibal Lecter—the psychiatrist serial killer, Hannibal the Cannibal, from the movie *Silence of the Lambs*.

"How do you know my name?" Michael demanded, continuing to inch his way closer, now being only a few feet away. He remained atop his bike, though, straddling the top tube with one foot still on a pedal.

"Oh, I know a lot of things—you'd be surprised," Harvey said and smiled.

The man had perfect teeth.

"Why have you been spying on my family?"

"Spying?" He laughed, closing his eyes and throwing his head back. "Oh no, my dear young man, I assure you that what I have been doing is not spying."

"Well, whatever you want to call it, it's all the same to us and we'd like you to stop." Michael was amazed at the control he heard in his voice.

However, Harvey's jovial attitude instantly evaporated as his entire face suddenly seemed to wrinkle and fold in upon itself in a menacing glare of anger. "It's because of your own ignorance that I must watch you! You have no idea of the danger you're in . . . well beyond your pathetic level of comprehension *boy*," he spat, sounding like a teacher berating his best student for falling short of a predetermined, and impossible, level of perfection.

"Don't be so sure. I may know more than you think." Michael's leg was growing tired and numb from keeping his foot on the pedal and so he stepped off and planted both feet firmly on the ground in a wide, what he hoped would appear to be defiant, stance. "So if you're so smart and all-knowing—amaze me with your wisdom."

Harvey remained where he'd been standing and stared at him more closely—evaluating him. Michael's heart began to race as he wondered if perhaps some of the answers he'd been seeking were right here before him, in the possession of this dirty, strange man. Somewhere off to his left a crow let out a single, somehow apprehensive, caw.

"I think I should talk to your father instead," he replied.

Michael didn't believe him. Actually, he felt as if Harvey were playing with him again and the idea made him angrier.

"Why? He doesn't know anything. *I'm* the one you need to talk to. I know about our house, about Dr. Woulfe and his daughter Sylvia. I also know about the suicide, the animal attack on the little boy, and the man that disappeared." Suddenly, he wasn't sure how much more he should reveal. Then he worried that he had already said too much and the thought caused a web of icy tendrils to spread itself out across his back. At the same time, he heard something shuffling across the ground behind him, rustling the leaves, moving toward him.

"So . . . you *have* been doing your homework. Congratulations. But those little tidbits are but a fraction of a whole greater than your pitiful child's comprehension is capable of grasping."

"I know who *you* are."

Harvey moved his head ever so slightly, smiling in condescension. "I doubt that."

"Your name is Harvey—"

He burst into laughter. "Yes, yes," he began, trying unsuccessfully to get his laughter under control. His eyes turned red and moist with the effort, "Harvey Olds . . . yes . . . I guess that's what I told them, isn't it?" he said, then stopped laughing as suddenly as if someone had turned off a switch on the back of his head. *"But that's not my real name. Do you know my real name, mister young Sherlock Holmes?"* he said and to Michael the timbre of his voice sounded like the hissing of a huge snake from some animated Disney feature. Around him, the woods seemed too quiet, as if in bated anticipation of Harvey's promised revelation. It was as if the world had come to a stop, waiting for him to reach understanding.

He was at a loss when suddenly it became clear to him, though how exactly, he didn't know. "No, you can't be . . . there's no way."

"*Yes,*" he hissed again. "There is a way—and I will tell you—if your impertinence will allow. My name . . . *is Cecil George.*"

With the stranger's remarkable pronouncement, the world seemed to have been regenerated. The crow suddenly cawed three times in rapid succession, the rustling sound behind him came again, this time moving away to his right, and the wind fluttered the leaves on a nearby maple making a sound like muffled clapping.

"Impossible," he said, though he could already sense the presence of truth in it.

"Not at all, my young friend. It all started in 1980, the year I bought Woulfe House. Do you know about the fire?"

Michael said nothing.

"I didn't think so. There was a fire in the house—in the kitchen—in the fall of 1980. It marked my first . . . contact."

"Contact with what?" Michael asked immediately, at the same time fearing and yet desperate for the answer.

And that's when Harvey changed.

"I . . . I guess I don't really know for sure," he began and at that instant, his voice . . . altered. No longer was it the smooth confident arrogance of the informed, but had transformed into the confused whimpering of a lost child. The transformation led Michael to again question the man's credibility and sanity, reminding him that he had no idea who he was dealing with—crazed loner—or . . .

What?

"A force, spirit . . . I'm not sure exactly what you'd call it . . . but it nearly drove me insane," he said and then his voice became more serene, comfortably informative, and Michael felt as if he could just as easily have been listening to his father explaining how to configure a master-slave setup in a dual hard disk computer. "I thought I could handle it, could communicate with it—but I was wrong—and it nearly cost me my life. As it was, it took nearly ten years of it—that's how long it took me to . . . get back. In 1990, I returned to Boyne City. I monitored the Hawkins, much as I've been monitoring you and your family, Michael. I felt it was my obligation—to protect them, and now you, as best I could. But for whatever reason, the Hawkins at least . . . remained untouched. But now

. . . now it's worse. I can't tell you how I know, but I can feel it again, Michael. Your family is in grave danger. Something has awakened it, whatever it is, again . . . awakened it in a way I never did—or could. You have to get out. You have to get your family out—you're all in terrible danger."

Yes . . . I've felt it . . .

"But . . . I don't understand . . . what is this . . . this force? *What's the danger?*" Michael pleaded, and now he knew the fear was really there, like a fresh coat of paint covering each of his words, making them slide and slip against each other as they tumbled out of his mouth. The crow he had heard earlier had started up again and this time was joined by a second.

"I don't really know for sure . . . but it's extremely powerful," Harvey said, his voice having returned to its previous smooth sincerity. "In trying to communicate with it, my mind was nearly destroyed. And, as a result, I wandered around aimlessly for ten years, not knowing who I was, where my family was—where I belonged. Then in time I started to get snatches of it back. Just a little at a time though—like half-remembered dreams. I would from time to time see people and places that somehow seemed familiar but I lacked the ability to distinguish who or what they were."

Just like me . . . just like those two weeks I can't remember . . .

"But what's the *danger?* Does it have something to do with Amanda? Tell me!" Michael said, feeling momentarily ashamed of his eagerness, but quickly brushing the shame aside—his thirst for answers, regardless of the source, more consuming. There were at least three crows in the woods now, cawing incessantly. He felt as though they were screaming at him.

This time it was the pleading, child's voice that answered.

"I don't . . . I don't know . . . I think I better go. I've told you all I can for now. Please believe me, you've got to believe me—you've got to convince your parents that there's evil . . . *unspeakable evil* . . . in that house." He took up his bike and put his foot on one of the pedals. "You have to get out now—before it's too late," he said, his eyes wild and sparkling like chips of black-green obsidian. In the next instant, Harvey remounted his bike and began pedaling, traveling deeper into the woods.

Michael looked at Harvey *(Cecil?)* and reminded himself once again what the man was—a stranger—a stranger who might actually be crazier and more dangerous than anything they'd come across in their house so far. But, at the same time, he felt there was somehow a certain truth in what Harvey had said. If all that he'd shared with Michael was not the complete truth, at least a major portion of what he had said was true. There were just too many similarities in Harvey's revelations to what had been happening to him and his family to be able to discount it completely—it felt too *right* to be entirely a lie.

But then, as he watched the man ride away, Michael's hostility quickly returned as he realized that although Harvey had spoken much, he had said little. Most of Michael's questions still remained unanswered.

"But how?" he yelled after him, trying to make his voice carry over the shrieks of the screaming crows. "They're not going to believe me—I have no proof, nothing to show them! How can I convince them? How do I even know *you're* telling me the truth?"

"You'll find out in time," Michael thought he heard him say but wasn't sure where the words had come from, their sound seeming too clear to have been spoken by the rapidly departing man. Then Michael heard him shout, "I know it's hard, Michael, but you've got to believe me—your lives depend on it—I can't emphasize that enough. I'm sorry, but I've got to go!"

It seemed as if there was an entire flock of crows in the woods now, yet the incredible noise felt somehow artificial due to their continued invisibility.

"Wait!"

He called after him, but Harvey Olds—a.k.a. Cecil George—was already far away, cycling ever deeper into the woods. For just a moment, Michael considered following him, then decided against it, somehow knowing that in this instance a second chase wouldn't be as successful. And there was still the memory of the event he had seen transpire at the Stone Circle. Anyway, he thought, he needed some time to think about what Harvey, or Cecil, had said—to see if it really made sense or if it was just the mad ravings of a homeless lunatic.

A month ago the answer would have been simple. Now—he wasn't so sure.

Behind him, the crows continued to scream.

38

1

As Michael rode home he couldn't help thinking more about what Harvey Olds (he still had trouble thinking of him as Cecil George, no matter if he believed that part of his story or not) had told him. Part of him wanted to believe every word—about strange forces and the danger his family was in as long as they stayed in Woulfe House. It clarified everything so easily—maybe too easily. Meanwhile, another part of him tried to convince him that, quite simply, Harvey Olds was a lunatic—nuttier than a barrel of walnuts. And finally, there was still a third part of him which thought that what Harvey Olds was trying to tell him was not only the truth but only a prelude to something more terrible—that to attempt to know the entirety of it all would demand a willingness to risk one's sanity as Harvey claimed to have had happen to him. As he considered all three possibilities, a fourth presented itself—that there might be a little bit of truth in all three theories—that some of what Harvey had said was true, that he was at least partially crazy, and that some of the things he had said were only the tips of a flotilla of icebergs.

Then he remembered the "awakening" Harvey had mentioned.

But what exactly had been awakened—and how?

He didn't know for sure, but felt strongly that he was somehow responsible. He thought about Dr. Woulfe's journals and wondered if the answer lay there—that it was the journals that had started everything—that by reading them he had somehow set into motion something terrible . . . and perhaps even unstoppable. However, he realized this wasn't the first time he had thought about the journals in this way. But an essential question still remained—what to do about all that had recently transpired? He could neither prove nor disprove anything. It seemed a veritable Catch-22—he would have to wait until whatever it was that was going to happen, happened (or at least began to happen) before he could try figuring out how anything fit together. There were still too many disconnected pieces. There were the dreams, the journals, the noises from the basement, the recent animal attacks, Harvey Olds and the things he had said, his own two-week fugue, the things that had happened to past residents of Woulfe House, the activities of the cult, and the "feelings" he had experienced during episodes such as his first exploration of the basement, the discovery of the floor drains and finally, the visit to the Stone Circle. Add to this conundrum some of the other "little" things that on the surface may or may not mean anything such as the strange comments of their neighbor, Scott Farley, or the comment the moving man had made, or even the one mover's sudden sickness.

Then he remembered what he had seen at the Stone Circle the day he had chased Harvey out of their driveway. He hadn't told his father or anyone else about what he'd witnessed and still wasn't sure he believed what he'd seen with his own eyes. As he had stood in the Circle, trying to determine where Harvey had gone, he heard a twig snap and turned in an effort to discover its source. Between two boulders, he saw Harvey standing just beyond the Circle in where the thickest part of the forest began. And then he was gone—vanished—as if he had simply dropped into a hole or been instantly teleported.

How did it all fit together? Did it fit together? Or, was he just trying to read too much into too many things that, in reality, had nothing to do with each other?

When he was halfway home, riding considerably slower than he had on the trip into town, he heard the sound of a siren, faint and shrill, behind him. He continued riding, trying to forget his questions and theories and fears, if only for the moment. Periodically, he glanced behind himself, remembering how he had felt on the ride out, but was unable to see anything due to the sharp curves and the trees growing along the roadway like soldiers standing along an esplanade. As he approached the top of the last hill before his house, a white sheriff's car sped past him with lights and siren blazing, startling him with its sudden loudness. He momentarily ran off the road, losing precious momentum near the top of his long climb.

When he emerged from the woods at the top of the hill, he was breathing hard. In the distance, he saw his house but no sign of the police car. As he coasted down into the flatlands, the white sheriff's car returned, this time lightless and silent, from the opposite direction. As Michael passed alongside The Tree in the field to his left, the sheriff's car pulled into their driveway. Immediately, Michael slammed the gear lever of his ten-speed forward and took off in a sprint. He took the corner into the driveway dangerously fast and was forced to come to a skidding stop in front of the side door. The police officer had already gone inside.

2

When he entered the house, Michael heard the police officer talking.

"No, we're pretty sure it was an animal attack."

Michael entered the kitchen where his mother, father, Richard, Amanda and the officer had gathered.

"Cleaned out the whole chest cavity and—"

"Please . . . is a full description necessary?" Sam said, turning to look at her son. Michael quickly recognized the look of exasperation, having seen it many times before. He was thankful he wasn't the cause of it this time.

The police officer's eyes swept from Sam to Amanda standing next to her, chewing on one of her fingernails as if it were a stubborn piece of beef jerky.

"No . . . I guess not," the officer said.

"Michael," Alan began. "This is Sheriff Bruce Kelly."

The man was large, but not fat. He had taken off his hat and was spinning it in hands that ended in thick, short fingers. Although there was no apparent bald spot on his pate, his hair was thin, most of the strands cemented together with sweat. In addition, his uniform was wrinkled, though Michael suspected it had more than likely been perfectly ironed and crisp when the day had begun. At his belt, the sheriff wore a big automatic with two spare clips.

To Michael, the sheriff's face seemed unnaturally long, as if it had been taken by the forehead and chin and stretched. Despite the length of it, his face appeared almost childlike—the evidence of beard stubble nearly undetectable. He had heard enough of the sheriff's deep, powerful voice, though, to know that this more than compensated for any boyishness portrayed by his looks.

"Our neighbor, Mr. Scott Farley, was killed last night," Alan said quietly. "The sheriff thinks it was a wild animal."

Michael felt his heart flutter. He remembered the boy Tedric had told him about—how they had found him six days after his disappearance—and how his cause of death had been listed as "apparent animal attack."

"The sheriff was wondering if we had seen or heard anything in the area that would suggest the presence of such an animal," Richard said from the corner where he stood leaning against the refrigerator.

"Oh," he said. Michael felt dizzy and sick. The sheriff looked at him oddly, as if sensing his distress and, having taken quick note of it, dismissed him. The sheriff turned his attention to Michael's father.

Michael fought for control as he surveyed the room. Sam and Amanda were in front of the kitchen sink—his mother defiant and defensive, Amanda bored, her fingernail for the time being forgotten. Alan was leaning by the stove, opposite Richard. As Michael looked about the kitchen, it seemed as if everyone were moving although they were standing still. Meanwhile, the sheriff had repositioned himself to stand between Richard and Alan in the archway which led to the formal dining room; opposite Sam and Amanda.

"So, *do* any of you remember hearing anything strange last night, or during any other night the past couple of weeks?" the sheriff said and stopped spinning his hat. "You probably know that, prior to Mr. Farley's death, several of his farm animals were killed?"

"Yes, we heard about the sheep," Alan answered.

"And the cow?"

"Yes."

At first, Michael thought the sheriff was going to say something else but then he seemed to change his mind. The look he turned upon his father, though, made Michael think the sheriff hadn't necessarily believed him.

"We believe the deaths of Mr. Farley's farm animals were also due to animal attacks. We also believe that this same animal was probably responsible for the mur . . . death of Mr. Farley."

"You almost said murder," Michael blurted.

The sheriff snapped his head around and Michael was reminded of a predator responding to the sound of a small animal—locating its prey and preparing for the attack should the situation appear favorable.

"A slip of the tongue. I assure you this was only an animal attack. Mr. Farley, living out on his farm alone, probably got careless, maybe left a door open, something like that," the sheriff said, then turned away, dismissing him again. "So, *have* any of you heard anything that might have sounded like some sort of an animal . . . or even anything else . . . anything strange?"

No one spoke. As the sheriff regarded each of them in turn, they all shook their heads, then looked at one another. Michael didn't believe the sheriff's slip, and was convinced it could only mean the subject of murder was very much on the sheriff's mind. The idea made him nervous—not only that there could be a murderer about, but that their local sheriff, the individual sworn to protect them, seemed to be concealing something. He decided he didn't care much for Sheriff Bruce Kelly. And he trusted him even less.

"No, I guess not," Alan said.

Then Michael remembered the noises from their basement. But, if his father wasn't going to bring them up, he decided there would be no reason for him to either. As he continued thinking about the noises, an image of his uncle's ranch and its killing room came rushing into his mind like an unexpected blow. The sudden image was intense and painful. For the second or two that it lasted, it blocked out all else and was the only thing he could see—the room before him and everyone in it being replaced by the vision of the bloodied killing room. He tried to fight it, drawing energy from a part of his mind that up to that moment he felt had never been exercised before—and ultimately succeeded in dispelling the image. Though the image had essentially cleared, it left behind a kind of afterglow—as if a shadow of itself had been indelibly burned onto the picture tube of his mind.

Michael was elated—he had finally fought against something, something important—and won.

As he refocused his attention on the situation in the kitchen, he realized no one was talking and wondered how much of the conversation he had missed.

"But how can you be certain it was an animal attack?" he heard himself ask out loud.

Sheriff Kelly instantly swiveled around in a way that made Michael think of someone looking behind himself to see what he had stepped on while already knowing he was not going to like it. "We know our job son, and when I say it was an animal attack, believe me, it was an animal attack."

"What about Harvey Olds?" he asked, this time locking eyes with the sheriff and refusing to let him dismiss him again. Based on the response to his eye contact, he thought the question had thrown the sheriff off balance.

"What about him?" the sheriff said with enough ice in his voice that Michael half expected to see his breath condense in the air.

"I mean, how do you know it wasn't him? He's been wandering around on our property and who knows where else. Maybe *he* did it," Michael said, relishing the strength he felt his voice projected, then added, "I would think he'd at least be a suspect."

"Maybe you haven't been following too closely—son—I said the death was an animal attack . . . do . . . you . . . understand?" the sheriff said, overstating the last words like someone talking to a mentally-challenged child while directing a feigned smile that sent a coldness into Michael's body like a sharp, frozen stick. But Michael didn't break eye contact until the sheriff did.

"Well, if you do think of anything, please be sure and contact the sheriff's office. We've got a state wildlife expert coming in, but he won't be here until tomorrow morning. In the meantime, we'd like to get some sort of an idea of what we're up against here."

"Sure thing, Sheriff," Alan said. Michael sensed uncertainty in his father's voice.

"Well, sorry to have bothered you. I'll be getting on my way then," the sheriff said.

Michael followed him to the door. The sheriff opened it and was about to step out when he turned and leaned in close, like a teenager turning back to give his date her first kiss. At first, that was exactly what Michael thought the man was going to do. For a few nauseous seconds he was nearly overpowered by the smell of strong cologne and musty cigars.

"Now, I don't want you to be giving me any trouble—you hear me son?" the sheriff whispered hotly in his ear. "You mess with me and I'll squash you like a goddamned bug on the sidewalk. Am I making myself clear?" The sheriff pulled back then, as if waiting for a reaction—some flippant remark he could act upon with the heavy fists of his authority.

But Michael could think of only one thing to say, "What are you afraid of, Sheriff?"

Sheriff Kelly glared at him and he could sense the sheriff quickly considering and rejecting several possible replies. Finally, he turned without saying anything more and strutted to his car. As he got in and closed the door, Michael made eye contact with him once again and the look he saw at that moment was unmistakable—it was the look of pure hatred.

The sheriff leaned out his open window.

"Here's some free advice for you, son. And you'd do well to heed it—might save you a heap a trouble later on."

Michael almost stopped breathing. As he sensed a sudden change in the sheriff's manner, he was instantly reminded of Fred, the big moving man who had uttered his own bit of personal advice prior to his departure. He also felt as if he had been transported back into a dream and feared what might be lurking around the next, dark corner. And so, when the sheriff was about to offer his personal insight, Michael listened intently, as if he were listening to a whisper rendered outside the realm of a reality that consisted of his standing outside and listening to the words of his local sheriff.

"Don't be messing in things you don't understand."

And then, from somewhere else (inside his head?) came . . .

. . . your sister already knows . . .

Then, before Michael could reply, the sheriff started his car and was gone in a rumble of crunching gravel and roaring engine. The sound of the sheriff's voice, though, lingered on.

. . . your sister already knows . . . already knows . . . your SISTER . . .

39

August 2 • Wednesday

1

The next morning at breakfast, Michael found his grandfather alone in the kitchen.

They exchanged the usual pleasantries and then Richard asked, “What do you know about this place—this house I mean?”

“Like what?” Michael replied, as he turned his back to his grandfather and retrieved milk from the refrigerator. Pouring the milk over his cereal, some of it splashed onto the counter. He wiped it up with the dishrag from the sink and as he carried his bowl back to the table, Richard elaborated.

“Well, I heard you say you’ve been doing some research at the library and I was wondering if you’d come up with anything.”

“Well . . . yeah, I guess I have,” he said and sat down opposite his grandfather. Not for the first time, he felt himself in a position in which he had to decide how much of the truth he wanted to reveal. He was hesitant because he was afraid he wouldn’t be believed—like when he’d attempted to explain to his father the noises he had heard in the basement. Then a sudden suspicion invaded his thoughts—that maybe his grandfather was working for his parents, probing for information to report back to them. Almost immediately, though, he knew the idea was ridiculous.

"So what kinds of things have you found out?" Richard prodded.

Michael was conscious of his grandfather's stare. He was going to have to tell him something—but how much? To be honest, a part of him felt relieved. He felt the time had come, despite the risk of any possible personal consequences, to share at least some of what he knew and for that he was thankful. The burden had become increasingly heavy, for although he had confided in Tedric, it wasn't the same. Tedric was an outsider, someone not personally connected to them and the house. Richard, though, was his grandfather, and at the moment, living under the same roof. Therefore, whatever was going to happen, would happen to all of them, Richard included. Because of this, Michael thought he at least deserved the chance—the chance to know the house's history, to know about the noises in the basement, to know about the dreams—and to make his own determination.

Another aspect of the significant difference between Tedric and Richard—and this was what made him hesitate most of all—was that Tedric, in his capacity as an outsider, would have only as much influence upon him as Michael himself would allow. Richard, though, as a relative, could easily initiate action against him—either directly or by talking to his parents. He could readily imagine how such an exchange might go . . .

Sam, I think Michael may need help . . . some professional help.

Or maybe . . .

Sam? Do you know the fantastic story Michael just told me? No? Well, you're not going to believe this, but he just said . . .

And yet if Richard *did* believe him, if he took him seriously, Michael would have a powerful ally. And although he hadn't quite given up on his father, he was afraid that by the time he convinced him of the veracity of his beliefs it would be too late.

Too late for what?

He took another bite of cereal and as he did so several pieces of it fell onto the table. For a moment, he stared at the food hopefully, as if like the psychic who reads tea leaves for clues he might glean some possible guidance in whatever cosmic pattern the brown shapes had made on the tabletop.

"I . . . I think there's something wrong with this place," he began as he picked up the fallen cereal. He put them back in his bowl, then took another bite as he waited for the ridicule he anticipated would follow.

The ridicule, though, never came. And as he contemplated the basis of the silence, he knew somehow that it would *never* come. More than this, he realized he had made the right decision. Initially, the thought shocked him—he wasn't used to being able to make such determinations so quickly. And yet with these sudden and powerful realizations, there also came a certain serenity. For before his eyes appeared to be a friend willing to listen—and possibly—even willing to help. In the space of a couple seconds he felt positive of this, though he couldn't explain why. But whatever it was that was coming—and above all else he knew for certain *something* was coming—the possibility that perhaps he wouldn't have to face it alone suddenly seemed a comforting reality.

"Something wrong? What do you mean?" Richard asked and Michael was unable to detect any lessening of the seriousness in his grandfather's tone or in the look of concern in his large, caring eyes.

As he paused to consider how best to proceed, he realized now was one of the first times since moving into Woulfe House that he had actually felt happy and even, if only just a little bit, secure. Under the present circumstances, his grandfather's sincerity had moved him like no amount of his father's wheedling, consternation or angry prodding could ever have.

He took a deep breath.

"For one thing, I've learned that bad things have happened to the people who lived here before us."

"What kind of bad things? How bad were they?" Richard said, his eyes dark and serious.

"Some of them . . . some of them were really bad," he continued and took another bite of his cereal, which was now soggy and flavorless.

Now it was no longer a personal concern that made him hesitate, but more concern for the potential impact it would have on his grandfather if he were privy to the information he was about to relate, as if by possessing such knowledge, Michael would place him in more danger than he was already.

"It's okay, I promise I won't make fun of you," his grandfather said, misinterpreting Michael's hesitation.

Michael tried to smile, but failed. "Well . . . I guess I'll start with the most recent history first. We bought the house from the Hawkinses and as far as we know—"

"*We?*"

"Well . . . Tedric and I. Tedric is the librarian downtown."

"Sorry. Please continue, I didn't mean to interrupt," Richard said and Michael noticed his grandfather hadn't taken another bite of his toast which now lay cool and uninviting since Michael's revelations had begun. Michael's gaze remained transfixed on the untouched toast as he began again.

"So anyway, as far as we know, nothing happened to the Hawkinses," he said. "Before them, the owner was a man by the name of Cecil George. Cecil bought the house in the fall of 1980. A few months later though, he disappeared. His family didn't give up hope for his return though, and the house remained vacant for eight years until they realized it was unlikely that he would return and finally parted with it, selling it to the Hawkinses." Michael paused a moment to look up from the toast and was pleased to see that his grandfather was still listening, still interested. "And now comes the good part, which I'm not exactly sure what to make of yet—but—you know that weird guy we keep seeing?" As he said this, he shifted in his chair, glancing quickly at his grandfather before returning his gaze to his hands, the table, and finally the untouched toast again.

"The homeless guy you told me about? Harry—"

"*Harvey*. Harvey Olds. Well . . . I talked to him yesterday and—"

"Michael, you didn't! Are you sure that was a good idea? From what I've heard that might have been a very dangerous thing to do."

As he sensed his grandfather leaning forward across the table with concern, Michael forced himself to look at him.

"I know. And if Dad found out, he'd probably ground me, but I *had* to. Anyway, I met him outside the library. And when I talked to him he told me his real name wasn't Harvey Olds . . . it's Cecil George."

He paused, not daring to break eye contact, waiting to see how Richard would react.

"Interesting," Richard said, narrowing his eyes. "Either he is indeed crazy, or this is some kind of scam to get his house back. Or, I suppose . . . it could be both."

Michael looked past his grandfather to the kitchen window and thought he could almost hear his grandfather thinking, considering, evaluating.

"Yes," Michael said. "He could be lying—or even crazy—I guess there's no way to know for sure. But he feels we should get out of the house . . . and the sooner the better."

Richard leaned back in his chair.

"Get out? Seems a bit extreme. Of course, if he is indeed this long lost owner, or even if he *isn't*, that may be his plan, to try and scare us out."

"He says we're in danger. He says this house is like—haunted—or something."

"Haunted?" Richard said mockingly, throwing his head forward—mocking not Michael but Harvey. "Is that the best he could come up with? Did he perchance happen to say who the ghosts were?"

The sudden shift in the dialogue made Michael hesitate again. But as he regarded his grandfather's face, and saw the care and seriousness reflected in his eyes, he knew it would be all right to continue. So far at least, Richard had listened to everything he had to say with an open mind, questioning only the validity of the information as Michael himself had, but never questioning *him*.

"Sorta. He said it was this *force*. And he also said that when he tried to fight it, back in 1980, it nearly drove him insane and that's why he disappeared. He says it took him ten years to get his memory back."

"Sounds a little too convenient to me. What do you think?"

He had no choice but to answer honestly. "I don't know yet."

After this exchange, neither of them spoke for several moments.

"Well, it sounds to me like it confirms at least one theory that you've been considering—that the guy is crazy—whether he's this former owner or not."

"Maybe," Michael said immediately, but his grandfather frowned.

"You're not convinced?"

For the first time, there was a hint of doubt in Richard's voice—doubt directed at Michael.

"Well, I guess I'm not. It's just that he didn't *sound* crazy. What he was saying actually made a certain amount of sense. I can't really explain it though. Repeating what he said now, I find myself agreeing more with you, but when I was *there*, when I was listening to *him* tell it . . . I had this feeling . . . that he wasn't crazy at all. And yes, I know I'm no expert, but I really felt there was something . . . I don't know . . . *right* about what he was telling me. I even felt . . . a goodness about him. Like when you're talking to a priest, you feel a goodness about him because you know he's good—you trust him—and no matter what he says you're going to believe him because of who he is. Now, it's true I don't . . . or for that matter nobody probably, really knows who this guy is. He calls himself Harvey Olds but tells me he's Cecil George, a guy who disappeared fifteen years ago. But then again, and this just occurred to me, if he isn't Cecil George, how then would he even know who Cecil George *was?*"

As Richard leaned back in his chair again, he folded his hands on top of his head.

"Interesting points, Michael. But still, just like you said, a lot of what you feel is just that—it's *feeling*. And I'm not saying you're wrong. We all like to think we *know* people." Richard leaned forward again, as if ready to impart a secret. "But did you ever notice, like when they catch one of those serial killers, like that Jeffrey Dahmer—he was the one in where was it, Milwaukee? Anyway, he was the one who killed the people and ate parts of them and stored them in his freezer. God, that was awful. But anyway, whenever they had the news coverage on and they were interviewing his neighbors, people who supposedly *knew* him—they all had pretty much the same thing to say—and it seems to be the same with just about all of these really sick weirdoes, 'Oh, he was such a nice man. I just can't believe it. He was always so nice and normal; we never suspected anything.' You know what I'm saying?"

"Yeah, I guess so. Nobody ever seems to know, but still—" Michael said, but his grandfather didn't let him finish. There was suddenly an intensity in his grandfather's eyes that Michael had never seen before.

"You know, the more I've been around, the more I genuinely believe there's this dark, hideous animal within all of us, Michael. Most of us—we manage to keep it locked up—closed away in a dark, but never entirely forgotten, corner of our mind somewhere—where we think we can keep it under control. It remains in its cage and though it may snarl and rage against us from time to time, most of us know that we dare not let it out. Because we know if we do let it out, then our control will be gone, and a beast that wild and savage might not be able to be caught again before it could do some real damage. And then there're others, thankfully they're in the minority, but they'll always be there, that no matter what laws we pass, no matter what penalties we impose—the ones like Jeffrey Dahmer—who will open the gate. Some of them will even do it gleefully, thrilling at the prospect of the adventure to come, hardly able to wait to see what the beast is going to do. And then there're others who do it hesitantly, thinking they have the capability to try it out on some sort of trial basis. But, unfortunately, there's no thirty-day money-back guarantee because once you let that animal loose, *it* becomes the one in control. Then the beast takes over and the person becomes the physiological manifestation of the beast—its appetite becomes the individual's appetite, its rage their rage, its violence and cold-heartedness becomes his or her own. And that's why you never see it coming—because I think everyone already possesses this presence in his or her psychological makeup. Everyone has a personal beast kept prisoner in its own cage within a little corner of his or her own mind and sadly we can't predict who those individuals are that are going to open the door—even though some of them do so hesitantly, slowly—while others willingly throw it wide, ripping the cage door off its hinges, never to be closed again."

Michael was transfixed by his grandfather's insights, unable to add anything, while all the while knowing there was more to his grandfather's analogy of cages and beasts than just the topic at hand. Furthermore, he knew that if his mother had had the opportunity to hear her father's story, she would have seen the truth in it as well—however, in reference to a different person altogether than Harvey Olds.

"That's a pretty interesting theory," he said finally, not quite knowing how to correctly respond to what he knew must have been a great emotional outpouring for his grandfather. But he knew he would never be able to comfort him meaningfully, that his grandfather's peace and reconciliation would ultimately have to come from within. In a similar way, he knew it would only be himself, and only remotely his grandfather's assistance, that he could rely on to deal with whatever was coming.

For the moment, Richard remained quiet, no longer looking at him, seeming fascinated with something on the floor.

"Well, we might as well go on," Michael said.

Richard seemed to recover and looked up.

"So what else happened? A disappearance, that's not so bad, is it?"

"No . . . but I'm only just getting started," Michael said, hesitating for only a second this time before plunging ahead, "Before Cecil, there was the Young family. They bought the house in 1974. They had a little boy—Jeremy Young—and two years later they had a daughter. One year after the daughter was born, in 1977 I think, Jeremy Young disappeared."

"*Another* disappearance? Did he run away from home? How old was he?"

"He was six years old at the time . . . and no, he didn't run away. In fact, it was just that many days, six, after he disappeared . . . that they eventually found his body."

Michael at first thought his grandfather hadn't heard him. He had turned away, as if thinking of something else. Then Richard suddenly turned back, blurting out, "Dead? How?"

"Animal attack."

Now Richard seemed distant, and Michael wondered if maybe he had finally quit believing him.

"Really. You're not trying to put one over on me now, are you?" His grandfather's eyes, having lost their previous intensity, were dark once again.

"Absolutely not. And I have copies of the newspaper articles to prove it," Michael shot back, perhaps more vehemently than he'd intended.

"I don't doubt it," Richard said, sounding apologetic. "That's pretty interesting. Makes you begin to wonder about your neighbor."

"Exactly. First it was a couple of his sheep, then a cow . . . then him."

"I get the impression, though, that that's not what you think. But it could after all still be just that, right, an animal? A stray cougar getting a little rambunctious now and then could have come along every couple of years, especially up here. I hear there're even coyotes around."

Michael found himself staring at his grandfather's toast again.

"Yeah, you're probably right—besides, I don't have any better ideas. But there's still lots more to tell. Before the Young's there was an elderly couple and as far as we know nothing happened to them other than they died of old age. They lived in the house beginning in 1962, and in 1971 the man, Ernest Crowley, died. Two years later, his wife passed away at a nursing home. When their kids inherited the house, they sold it to the Young's."

"I never would have guessed that so many people had been through here."

"Yeah, I was quite surprised myself when I started doing the research. Anyway, before the Crowley's, there was an artist . . . I can't remember his first name . . . but his last name was LaSalle. He was doing pretty well, selling his work and getting a lot of recognition . . . that is, until he bought the house. After that all he could paint was one thing . . . The Tree."

"You mean—"

"Right, that strange tree in the field," Michael said, nodding his head in the direction of the field. "The bank eventually foreclosed on him. And then—"

"You mean there's *still* more?"

"Just two more."

"Oh, is that all? And you've got all this memorized?"

"Well . . . yeah. It's not that much really, and I've been working on it for quite a while." Michael actually felt himself blushing at his grandfather's unsolicited praise, thankful again that he had made the decision to confide in him.

"All right, go on then. By the sounds of it, we haven't even gotten to the best of it yet, am I right?" Richard leaned back in his chair and crossed his arms.

"Right. So anyway, now we go back to the 1950's and the Wilson family—"

"Please, don't make it sound like so long ago," Richard said with a grin. Despite his best efforts to contain himself, Michael smiled.

"Sorry, but . . . Michelle Wilson, the sixteen-year-old daughter of parents Larry and Lisa Wilson . . . committed suicide in 1957."

"My God. How did she do it?" The grin was gone now.

"Hanged herself. Like to guess where?"

"Well . . . there's the basement . . . or one of the bedrooms—" Richard's face suddenly lit up with understanding.

"That's right," Michael coaxed.

"Oh come on, you can't be serious . . . The Tree?"

"The Tree."

There was a pause, interrupted when Richard noted, "That raises an interesting point, Michael. Did the artist know about the suicide?"

Michael looked down again at his cereal bowl where the brown pieces had now swollen themselves into what looked like egg-like nodules ready to hatch forth something grotesque.

"I don't know. I never really thought about the connection. If I had to guess, I would say probably not, since according to Tedric that was the only way people were able to unload the house—by selling it to outsiders—people who didn't know its history."

"That's possible. However, this artist fellow might just have been macabre enough to perhaps find it . . . amusing in some way. And that could be why he painted the tree, only it unfortunately grew into an obsession for him . . . his own particular breed of beast let out to play."

"I suppose."

Silence again. Richard waited patiently as Michael steeled himself to relate the final bit of history that needed telling—the final and perhaps most important part.

"Well, anyway, so now that you've heard about everyone else, that leaves only the founding fathers, so to speak. Although in this case, more like founding father and daughter—the Woulfes."

But Michael never got the chance to go on because, in the brief silence preceding the continuation of his tale, a child's scream shattered the air so loudly it sounded like a bomb going off. For a second, he and his grandfather did nothing but stare into each other's eyes. And then they were up, simultaneously flinging their kitchen chairs aside and racing for the stairs.

Outside, they ran toward the backyard, and were about to round the corner of the house, when Amanda screamed again.

2

When they arrived in the backyard, they found Amanda on the ground, knees drawn up to her chest, face buried against her legs. Great, wracking sobs were making her entire body quiver and shake. A short distance from where she sat was Ghost's head staring at them sightlessly from a patch of bloody grass. Michael performed a quick search of the grounds, but could find no sign of the rest of the cat's body or of the perpetrator of the heinous murder. Richard sank to his knees next to his granddaughter and hugged her tightly. He attempted to soothe her cries with softly whispered words of "It's going to be all right" and "There now, it's okay . . . it's okay."

Amanda pulled her face away and spoke.

"Sacrifice?"

Michael tried to assure himself that he hadn't heard his sister's question correctly. He examined the grounds once more, searching for tracks or other evidence as to what had killed his sister's cat. Somewhere in the woods behind them a crow cawed loudly as if mocking them.

Sacrifice?

Michael turned and as he did, met his grandfather's stare.

Richard lifted, then carried Amanda inside the house. At first, Michael followed behind them, then turned in the direction of the carriage house.

He hardly noticed the door as it made its customary screech of protest. Inside, he grabbed a shovel, then made his way back to where Ghost's head lay. At first, he couldn't find it and experienced a sudden fear that someone—or something—had taken it. But then he spotted it, several yards away, and moved to where he was standing over it. Its vacant eyes stared up at him like two glass marbles in which he imagined he could see his own reflection. If death had a face, he thought, this was it.

Gently scooping up the head with the shovel, he walked through the garden and onto the path leading into the woods.

Who did this? Or rather . . . what did this? Was it the same thing that killed their neighbor? Or was it Harvey Olds, playing a joke on them, beginning his campaign of trying to scare them out of their house?

As he walked along the path he examined the head more closely.

Not cut . . . torn . . . ripped off. So if a crazy man did it, would he have ripped the cat's head off . . . or cut it off?

After pondering this thought he answered himself with two additional questions.

But doesn't it depend on whether the man in question is a homeless vagrant? Do homeless vagrants have ready access to knives?

Unfortunately, answers to these last questions were too unpleasant to contemplate and so he returned his attention to his task. By now he had walked a significant distance into the woods, perhaps as far as a quarter of a mile. He realized he had the feeling again, the one he and Amanda had had when they set off for the Stone Circle, that the woods seemed unnaturally quiet. Except for the single crow he had heard earlier, the woods had remained silent all throughout his walk. At the same time, he felt an awareness of anticipated sound, like the feeling one gets walking into an empty sports stadium. But he also thought he sensed the presence of an observer lurking somewhere within the dark recesses of the trees.

Sacrifice.

About twenty feet off the trail to his right he saw a small, cleared space. Taking a deep breath, he walked off the path.

When he reached the small clearing he let out an involuntary groan of relief as he put the shovel down. He let the head roll softly to the ground, thankful when the small furry ball came to rest face down. He dug the burial hole as quickly as he could, finding the soil more difficult to work than expected. He was sweating profusely by the time he was done. After wiping the perspiration off his face with a corner of his T-shirt, he searched for something to mark the grave with. Finding nothing, he broke up several sticks and placed four of them vertically into the newly turned ground, creating a box around the burial plot. Using two more sticks, he made a cross on top of the small mound.

He remained at the site, staring at the mound of fresh earth for several minutes. As he looked at the grave and the inadequate sticks which marked its location, the thoughts and ideas as to what it all could mean—and Amanda's

(sacrifice)

question—tried to invade his mind but each time he managed to push them away. For the moment at least, the reasons, the whys, and the hows would have to be ignored.

Having regained his composure, he turned back toward the path and home but knew, somewhere deep within himself, that the inevitable "later" was coming sooner than he liked. Reaching the path, he wondered if what he had been dreading for so long, that feeling of an impending something, of a danger coming to all of them . . . had now finally arrived and that one dead and mutilated cat was its announcement to the guests that the party was officially underway.

3

Back inside the house, Michael met his grandfather coming down the stairs.

"She's better," Richard said. Michael saw a strange, haunted look in his grandfather's eyes, one which he couldn't readily interpret. "She's up in her room now—going to lie down for awhile."

His grandfather suddenly looked older.

"Later—perhaps after supper—we'll talk some more—okay?" Richard said and then moved past him toward the library. He seemed, Michael thought, almost a different person.

"Okay. And Grandpa?"

"Yes?"

"I'm glad you're here," he said. Richard returned a weary smile, then turned and continued on his way.

40

1

"So how *would* he know anything about this guy disappearing?" Sam asked that evening when Richard told her and Alan what Michael had discovered about the history of their house. It was after dinner and they were in the library. Sam and Alan were sitting on the leather couch while Richard paced back and forth in front of them. Richard felt like a high school principal, or a psychologist.

"He says he has the newspaper articles to prove all of it. Also, the local librarian, a gentleman by the name of Tedric, has been helping him gather information."

"So what do *you* think we should do?" Sam asked, directing the question at her father—it seeming not to matter that her last inquiry had been ignored. It was Alan, though, who answered. He looked alternately between Sam and Richard.

"Well, there's no sense making any rash decisions. We're certainly not going to pack up and leave just because some homeless guy living in the woods claims he's this missing former owner, and we're all in danger. Who knows, even if he *is* this guy, it could just be some plot to try and get the house."

"Absolutely," Sam said, leaning forward on the couch, as if about to stand up. "This whole thing is ridiculous. We don't know anything about this guy and I'm certainly not going to live my life based on the advice of some loony."

"I certainly would've expected no less," Richard continued calmly, trying he hoped, to diffuse the tension he felt building in the room. "But, as that guy on the radio says, you need to hear the rest of the story."

Whereupon, Richard reiterated the full account, almost exactly to the word as Michael had done that morning, telling them of the death of Jeremy Young, about the Crowley's and the financial decline of the young artist. And, as he related each of these events, Sam and Alan sat listening, for the most part passively, trying to digest it all . . . until he came to the part about the suicide of Michelle Wilson.

"Did you say suicide?" Alan asked, almost demanding confirmation.

Richard was surprised at the sudden intensity of his interest. But when he turned to look more closely at him, what he saw in his son-in-law's eyes wasn't a look of authority—but of something a lot like fear.

"Do you know . . . how?" Alan continued, in a softer tone, his eyes never drifting from an intense probe of Richard's face.

"Hanged herself . . . from one of the branches of that tree out there in the field."

Alan continued staring, as if he hadn't understood.

When Michael entered the room everyone turned to acknowledge his presence, everyone that is, except Alan, whose gaze, like that of a child who has suddenly heard the end of an upsetting ghost story, remained transfixed on Richard.

And yet Richard was somehow positive . . . that Alan wasn't even seeing him.

2

Michael placed himself directly in front of his father until he turned toward him. Behind them, Michael heard the sound of the TV being turned on, followed by the snap and hum of the VCR; Amanda was starting a movie before going to bed.

"That's impossible. I . . . I dreamed about her . . . I *saw* her . . . *in my dream,*" Alan said.

"What?" Michael asked, thinking maybe it hadn't been such a good idea after all to step into the middle of their conversation. Now that he had though, he wondered if he was about to be reprimanded for it. But then his father's words began to sink in—*I dreamed about her*—and though the words were sinking in slowly, it was nevertheless with the impact of a saw-toothed dagger twisting and tearing. Alan repeated himself.

No one said anything or moved as they waited for him to go on. "It was the first . . . the first of the *weird* dreams I had, right after we moved in. I was standing by the tree and there was this person there, a teenage girl, and she was swinging on a rope from the tree. I thought it was just a nightmare," he said, trailing off as if having lost his train of thought.

Still, no one said anything. Michael could sense Richard looking at him as he in turn watched his parents. While Alan stared into the antique reproduction globe mounted on a stand in the corner, Michael searched his father's face, not really looking to see what was there, but thinking instead about what his father had said—and what it might mean.

The dreams do *mean something! So is that what they are—visions of the past—like some sort of psychic echo? And if so, how was his family picking them up . . . and why? Did that mean that these echoes, or whatever they were, were in the house somehow—maybe a part of it—existing as some latent force of memory, a force able to be tapped into by the subconscious? Or maybe it's something totally different—maybe the mysterious "force" Harvey was trying to warn us about?*

He felt on the edge of an intuitive leap, almost as if he were tottering on the shore of a lake containing some great revelation. But just when he reached out to grab it . . . it pulled away. And so he continued to stretch, trying to will it back to him. His frustration at his inability to bridge the gap was immediate and painful. In desperation, his head filled with other possibilities, other explanations. But ultimately he was forced to acknowledge that the truth had gotten away, gliding slowly and surely, a black, barely distinguishable shape sinking back into the impenetrable subconscious soup of his mind.

"What are you talking about, Alan?" Sam asked. Her forehead was furrowed, her eyes deep and impenetrable. Then, as if realizing her mistake and being embarrassed by it, the furrows disappeared and she blinked. "It was just a coincidence. That tree . . . it's rather unusual as we all know . . . to have a dream about it; well, it only seems natural you'd dream about such things in connection with it. And the idea of people hanging themselves from trees—being hanged from trees—dates back centuries at least. Therefore, it certainly doesn't seem unreasonable that you would have had a dream about someone being hanged from a tree."

Michael considered his mother's argument, but only briefly; perhaps he might even have agreed it was indeed possible, if not for the almost imperceptible tremor he had sensed in her voice when she had explained it. A tremor, he thought, that made him certain she no more believed her explanation than he did.

"Yes, but I dreamed the victim was a teenage girl," Alan said.

Michael reflected more closely on what was happening—something had happened to his father, something strange that he was unable to explain—and no one was listening. No one believed him. He felt little satisfaction in the turning of the tables, though.

"Are you *sure?* Could you describe her?"

"Well, I . . . it was dark . . . night in the dream. I don't really remember seeing her face . . . other than her eyes maybe."

"There, you see? Perfectly explainable without some mysterious *haunting force*."

Michael stared intently at his mother, seeing in her face and eyes what she probably couldn't admit even to herself—that she really didn't know—that none of them really knew.

Regardless, something was beginning to happen—perhaps the impending something he feared.

But what is it? And where is it going to end?

"Enough about dreams," Sam continued. "What *does* seem real is that we have some sort of wild animal running around. And until we hear that this thing has been hunted down and caught or killed, everyone is to stay indoors unless we all go out together. And certainly no more forays into the back woods," she said and looked directly at Michael.

He knew what she was implying—but was surprised to find he no longer cared.

"I agree," Alan said.

"Well," Michael began. "I guess it's probably time then to tell you about the Woulfes."

His mother misunderstood. "Wolves?"

"No, not the animal kind," Richard explained before Michael could reply, "the people kind. The man who built this house—his name was Dr. Woulfe," he said and turned back toward Michael.

"Oh," Sam said, then smiled as if it were a joke. But as she surveyed the room she quickly realized that no one else was smiling.

3

"Really, the story isn't so much about Dr. Woulfe the father, but more about Dr. Woulfe, the daughter. Although Robert Woulfe started it all, it was his daughter who really got things going," Michael began. They had now reconvened in the library after a short break during which Richard had tucked Amanda into bed. Alan now sat on the couch; Richard stood near the bookcases. This time, though, Sam wasn't present, having elected instead to take a bath. Michael wasn't sure if it was because she didn't want to hear any more or whether she was afraid to, or both.

Michael was the one pacing the floor now.

"How so?" Alan asked.

As he continued telling the story, he was conscious of himself taking on the monotonous drone of a museum tour guide.

"Dr. Robert Benjamin Woulfe was born in Germany in 1870 and came to the United States, directly to Boyne City, in 1903. Three years later, in 1906, he built this house. In 1918, he married a local woman, Marion Albany, and two years later they had a daughter, Sylvia. Marion died shortly after the birth and Dr. Woulfe died in 1944. In 1948, the daughter, Sylvia, the sole heir, after having left, came back after several years to the house and, in 1952, started the cult."

"The cult?" Alan asked.

Michael saw his father glance over at Richard, but Richard didn't provide the knowing smile Alan was probably looking for—the smile which would have meant *it's okay, he's just kidding, it was only a joke.*

"Okay . . . so this Sylvia started a cult," Alan said and turned his attention back to Michael. "What exactly are we talking about here?"

"Well . . . I'm not really sure," he said, suddenly no longer as willing to share the information he had gained.

Is he going to believe me? What if he laughs? What if . . .

"It had a pretty good following actually," Michael continued. "It just didn't last long. By 1955 it was over."

Standing near the bookcases, Richard seemed to be preoccupied more with the books than with Michael's tale. Abruptly, he turned, and spoke for the first time. "What happened?" He walked over to a chair by the globe and sat down.

"One night the locals raided one of their meetings. During the confrontation at the Stone Circle, Sylvia . . . some deputized locals . . . and a boy, the mayor's son—were killed."

"Wow," Alan said. Then his eyebrows lowered and his chin seemed to push his lower lip up. "Wait a minute here . . . that Stone Circle? You mean—"

"Yes," Michael said and stopped pacing. He turned to his father. "The Stone Circle is the place where they had their meetings—and was where the raid occurred. Following the raid though, despite an extensive search, Sylvia Woulfe's body was never found."

"Then how did they know she was dead?" Richard asked. Michael looked sideways at him—Richard was hunched forward in his chair, his elbow on his knee as if ready to rise again.

"Well, there were some who believed she *didn't* die—that she escaped. But one of the deputies said he saw her shot several times. His statement was in the newspapers."

"So then, what is this all supposed to mean?" Alan asked.

At first, Michael didn't answer, primarily because he didn't *have* an answer. Not a complete answer anyway. He had ideas, even theories—but what would his father think of them? He was confident his grandfather would give them an honest listen, but with his father present he decided it best, at least for now, to just tell the truth. And so he simply replied, "I don't know."

At first, Alan looked disgusted, but then his face fell and he just looked tired. "Well, that's a nice ghost story, but I don't know if it has much to do with us. There is one question I guess it does answer though."

Michael waited for his father to continue.

"Why we got this house so cheap," Alan said and stood up.

Gee, figure that one out on your own, Dad?

He suddenly wanted to scream at his father, but he knew there was more in his father's mind—he could see it in his eyes—and hear it in his voice, something he was concealing.

But why won't you talk about it? Why can't you just admit there's something going on—even if we don't have the slightest clue what it is yet? How can you sit there and be so blind? You even dreamed of the Wilson girl—and yet you still think there's nothing weird going on?

But although Michael raged against his father in his mind, his mouth remained closed since he knew speaking would accomplish nothing. In fact, it would probably make his father that much more close-minded.

Alan yawned and added, "Guess I'll head on up to bed. I'd recommend the same for you two as well," he said and glanced at both of them in turn.

Michael felt his father's gaze linger longer on him but was unable to meet his eyes, afraid of what he might say.

"Good night, Alan," Richard said and when Alan had left the room, Richard turned to Michael. Michael wondered what he was thinking, fearing that he may have turned against him, that he no longer believed him, that he was on his parents' side now. But Richard stood up, smiled as he said good night, gave him a reassuring pat on the shoulder, and left without another word.

Despite his earlier anger, Michael felt relieved. He had told his mother and father most of what he had learned and although they hadn't seemingly thought all that much about it, nevertheless, they hadn't laughed or made fun of him.

He knew his grandfather had sensed there was more to tell—and he was especially glad now that he hadn't been pressured to go on.

After turning off the downstairs lights, he headed for bed and as he climbed the stairs, he again found himself feeling good that his grandfather had come to stay with them. But as he neared his bedroom, his feelings of happiness quickly faded, replaced by a sudden fear; for he found himself hoping for the first time in a long time—that he wouldn't dream.

4

It's my dream—I dreamed of her, swinging from The Tree!

Alan lay in bed unable to sleep. Samantha had already dozed off more than an hour ago. Although he thought he had done a good job appearing unmoved by all that his son had revealed, he couldn't lie to himself. What bothered him most was the dream. For the last hour, he had been lying awake thinking about it. And as he began to remember each detail with ever more clarity, he soon found himself becoming more afraid and more thoroughly terrified perhaps, than ever before in his life. In the course of the last hour everything had come tumbling down on him at once. Everything that Michael had found out—all of it was *true.* There was indeed something "going on" at their house, something perhaps very terrible. The noises, the dreams, the animal attacks, a disappearance, a suicide, the death of Ghost and even some sort of satanic cult . . . all of it had happened here, right *here* . . . in *their* house! Suddenly, the idea of their house having been built atop an Indian graveyard no longer seemed quite so ridiculous. Then, for the first time in weeks, the haunting words of the hotel clerk returned—*what he taught wasn't the living . . . it was the dying.*

But what, in God's name, did it mean?

He didn't like any of the answers he came up with—for they were answers that would require him to believe in things that, so far in his life, he had always relegated to the world of the preposterous and superstitious. They were ideas that a well-educated adult was supposed to recognize as the simple beliefs of the less-informed, and unscientific in their basis.

He fingered the medallion in the darkness—he had taken to sleeping with it nearly every night now—and tried to trace its symbols with his finger. Finally, he was able to sleep and as he slept, he dreamed.

41

Wednesday Night
Alan's Second Dream

In the dream he stands in the dark next to the misshapen willow. The wind howls and it starts to rain. Thunder crashes and lightning explodes around him like the world's largest disco light gone out of control. He is cold and wet, and hugs himself for comfort. He stands next to the tree for cover but its bare upper branches provide none. The wind causes the enormous branches to creak and nearby he hears something hit the ground with a soft plop. During the next lightning flash he looks up and sees hundreds of small hanging globes that look like fruit. He feels along the ground for the one that he heard fall, and eventually finds it. It is wet and soft when he picks it up and is about the size of a baseball. When a lightning bolt strikes the ground, sending out a fountain of sparks not far away, the brilliant flash provides a single camera-flash glimpse of the object in his hand—it is the head of Ghost. Then the head starts to move—turning itself in his hand—and hisses wetly at him over the shrieking of the wind. He throws it down in disgust but doesn't hear it hit the ground.

The lightning intensifies, scaring him; then abruptly stops. The rain stops also and the wind is silent. As he listens, he hears only The Tree's wet, dripping branches. From out of the quiet two voices call softly to him. Immediately, he recognizes the sound of his long-dead parents. He walks away from the tree but doesn't go more than a few feet when he hears them call out again, this time from above. He looks up and a silent lightning flash reveals his mother's and father's bodies. Their skin, he notices, is black and gray, their clothes tattered rags of burned cloth revealing gaping holes in their flesh through which he can see ribs and vertebrae—the bones gray and blackened and smoking.

The next lightning flash, silent like the one before it, sets the entire sky on fire, allowing him a longer view. He recognizes his childhood nightmare about the day his parents were fatally electrocuted, his father trapped on the fuse box, his mother likewise forever bonded to him in melting, burning flesh when she had unsuccessfully tried to pull him away. Both begin to speak at the same time that the wind returns and he barely hears them above the howling.

"Come to us Alan . . . help us . . . let us go."

He turns from them and runs through the black night . . . and into a cathedral. Inside, he feels a fundamental change in the dream, more a stylistic change, as if he were watching a movie where a different director has produced each half. The magnificent church is lit by thousands of burning candles and the ceiling towers hundreds of feet above his head. He approaches a massive gold altar where he kneels and pulls forth the gold medallion which feels heavy and warm in his hand. As he lifts the medallion above his head as an offering, it instantly bursts into a light so intense that it causes him to shut his eyes against the sudden brilliance.

When he is able to open his eyes again, he sees standing before him the stranger, Harvey Olds, dressed in white priest's robes. Harvey stands at the altar and as he lifts his arms toward him, Alan begins to float above the floor. The medallion light is gone and when he feels a warm weight around his neck he realizes he is now wearing the medallion. He floats up to the ceiling of the cathedral but instead of stopping he continues through the stone and outside into bright daylight, above their home on Pleasant Valley Road. He looks around but there is no evidence of the cathedral. He continues to rise higher, now thousands of feet into the air. Below him, on the ground, he notices that he can now see the shape and design of the medallion as defined by a subtle shade difference between the grass and tree color. The medallion shape forms a circle at least two miles in diameter with their house at its center. Even the smallest details of the medallion's distinct design are visible on the ground below him, though almost so subtle as to be invisible.

And then he feels a strange sensation, as if some outside force is trying to pull him out of the dream, a force that doesn't want him to see any more. The force ultimately wins and in the next instant he finds himself back on the ground again, standing in the field on the opposite side of the road in front of the house.

He senses another stylistic shift in the dream and sees that their house is now painted black with blue trim. When he starts to cross the road he is nearly run down by a screaming woman in a cherry-red Buick. Her car seems to move in slow motion as it first spins and then enters the ditch and flips over. He runs toward the car, but has covered barely half the distance when it explodes like a scene from a Hollywood action-adventure movie. Over the crescendo of the explosion and fire, he hears a woman's scream but the voice he hears is Sam's, the sound of the scream exploding outward, ensconced on the expanding surface of the fireball. As the scream reaches him, it hits him like a punch and seems to coat him, the heat baking it onto the surface of his skin like a layer of paint.

He leaves the road and walks back toward the house and the dream-style shifts once again. The house is no longer black but now appears in the original form and color in which they'd bought it. This time Harvey Olds is standing on the front porch, dressed in a butler's suit. Harvey plays doorman, smiling warmly at him, and waves his arm in a welcoming gesture, inviting Alan into his own home.

42

August 3 • Thursday

1

During their entire ride into town Michael noticed that his sister had said nothing. Such a feat had been unheard of before . . .

(what?)

Before we moved into Woulfe House.

Richard was driving them to the library in his Jaguar, and for Michael his driving style was reminiscent of his mother's—fast. Once in the library, Michael was disappointed to learn that Tedric had no new information for him. So he and his grandfather decided to do their own research by looking through Tedric's archives of the local newspaper while Amanda was content to stay upstairs with Tedric.

Richard followed closely behind Michael down into the darkness of the library's basement. At the bottom of the stairs, he located the light switch and turned it on. Michael was again confronted by the similarity of the layout of the library's basement to that of the basement in their house. In each case, an outside door opened onto a landing with one set of stairs leading up to the first level and the other down into the basement. And both were filled with shadows that seemed to move whenever you weren't looking directly at them.

"So where, or rather, *when* do you want to start looking, Michael?"

"Well, I thought we should start around the time Dr. Woulfe came to Boyne City—1903." He turned to Richard. "How about if I take the odd years and you take the even?"

"Works for me." Richard grinned.

They walked farther into the room, trying to take it all in. One of the first things they noticed was that wherever they looked, they were faced with shelves, cabinets and stacked boxes of printed materials of every size and description. On the floor in front of one shelf was a box of *Saturday Evening Posts*, two bags of *Time* magazines, and a beer box overflowing with paperback romances.

"But what exactly are we looking for?"

"I don't know. Whatever looks like it could have something to do with our house or the cult. Anything, I guess, that looks interesting."

"Afraid that doesn't narrow it down for me much."

Michael said nothing as he walked over to a set of three-foot wide gray metal shelves—the kind usually found in garages and work rooms.

"The newspapers are in these big books here, arranged by year. They're pretty old, so we have to be careful," he said as he waved his arm up and down the rack. The books were newspaper-page size with blue hardcovers, arranged in stacks of ten to twenty books each but neither the spines of the books nor the shelves were labeled.

Richard approached one of the shelves. "Does the librarian let just anyone come down here and look at these?" He wiped the dust off the cover of the top one in an attempt to read the year stamped in small gold letters on its face.

"Actually, no. Tedric's kind of . . . my friend I guess. He lets me come down here by myself. Normally, people tell him what they're looking for and he just gets it for them."

"That's pretty nice of him," Richard said. He bent down to get a closer look at the books on the bottom shelf.

"Tedric actually helped get me started on my research with his files. In them I found out quite a bit—most of that stuff I already told you about," Michael said, then added, "But I think there's more."

"What more?"

"I don't know . . . it's just a feeling I have," he said and turned what he hoped was a sheepish look toward his grandfather. When Richard didn't smile, he continued. "Maybe something that ties some of these things together. And I don't think it's going to be easy to find."

"Well, we better get started then," Richard replied as he brushed the dust off a book on the second shelf. "Looks like this pile starts with 1935."

Michael smiled at his grandfather's enthusiasm and in relief that the questions were, at least for the moment, over. "Yeah. I think the ones we want are on the bottom."

Richard looked down and rubbed his hands together to get the dust off. On the bottom shelf, they found the books that started with the year 1900. Not only were the books dusty, but smelled strongly of mildew. Michael pulled out the 1900 volume and handed it to Richard, then took the 1901 for himself and went over to the folding table in the middle of the room. As they started flipping the pages of their respective books, the paper seemed to release an even stronger mildewy aroma. They continued their work in silence, scanning headlines, only occasionally stopping to read part of an article aloud to one another. It was a slow, tedious process.

"Hey, listen to this!" Michael suddenly exclaimed more than an hour later. He was in the 1921 book. "I don't know what it means, but it definitely sounds interesting. It says that on July eight there was a mining accident at the copper mine here in Boyne City."

He read the article to Richard.

***Boyne City Eagle*—Friday July 8, 1921**
Mine Tunnel Collapses—Nine Men Missing
BOYNE CITY, MI—A mine collapse at the Sedgwick-Davey Copper mine in Boyne City has left nine mine workers missing and presumed dead. A spokesman for the mining company, Mr. Craig Larkin, said the miners were working in a new portion of the mine following a vein when the tunnel behind them collapsed. Currently, work crews are attempting to clear the tunnel. Missing at this time are: Clarence Agerson, Ernie Touroo, Kenneth Henning, Merton

Brock, Roger Walton, Joseph Kalkofen, John Rowe, Andrew Sides and Matthew Mapleson.

Matthew Mapleson. Wasn't there a kid in my biology class last year with a name something like that? Matthew Maples? Marples? Marbles?

"But that's only the start, because when you flip ahead here to July eleventh, listen to this."

***Boyne City Eagle*—Monday July 11, 1921**
Tunnel Reopened—Men Still Missing
BOYNE CITY, MI—Officials of the Sedgwick-Davey Copper Mine in Boyne City have reopened the tunnel thought to have caused the death of nine missing miners believed to have been working in the mine at the time of the collapse. However, no bodies have been found, nor any evidence of the missing miner's whereabouts. A search of the mine continues.

"Pretty strange, don't you think?"

And then he remembered—the words floating into his mind as if someone were whispering them in his ear—the words of the moving man—the words he had uttered just before leaving, stating them in a way so strange that at the moment they were spoken they seemed to have been uttered by a completely different person.

You should check it out, boy. Check it out real good.

Michael realized his grandfather had been talking while he had been distracted by the memory.

"What did you say?"

"I *said*, that yes, it is strange. Seems to me like they would have found them. I wonder if maybe something shifted or got closed off in some way that left them trapped in a part of the mine no one could see?"

"Could be. I'm going to keep looking; see if I can find anything more about it."

That's right boy, you check it out. Check it out real good.

Michael continued scanning the papers for the year 1921, finding and reading more than a dozen articles concerned with the unexplained disappearance of the miners. But the miners were never found. Several articles proposed theories as to the events surrounding the men's disappearance, but each proved to amount to nothing more than speculation. About two weeks after the accident, the mining company took the position that the miners had walked off the job—that there hadn't been an accident at all.

"How about 1922? Anything there?" Michael said.

"Couple of articles, nothing more than what we've found already. More theories and one marking the one-year anniversary."

They continued scanning, finding nothing until 1928, when Richard found another article about the copper mine, this time detailing its closing. Richard read the article aloud.

> ***Boyne City Eagle*—Tuesday July 10, 1928**
> **Copper Mine to Close**
> BOYNE CITY, MI—Mr. Franklin Sedgwick, general manager and partner in the Sedgwick-Davey Copper Mine, has formally announced the permanent closing of the mine. When asked why the mine was closing, Mr. Sedgwick complained about the unreliability of the work force and a deteriorating supply of producing veins. Workers were told the mine would close permanently on Friday, July 13.
>
> Since the beginning of the year, the mining company has had a recurrent problem with miners walking off the job, apparently without giving notice or reason. None of the departing workers could ever be questioned though as each left town immediately after quitting. Mine officials have remained baffled at this aberrant behavior, saying they know of no outstanding worker complaints or safety issues to warrant such behavior on the part of the miners. The extraordinary turnover rate of the employees, according to Mr. Sedgwick, is one of the primary reasons for the closing of the mine. Mr. Sedgwick said his company has four other mines, all of them located in the Michigan Upper Peninsula that would benefit more from his time and resources.

When Richard finished, Michael said, "Now that's even stranger. People just walking off the job for no apparent reason. Maybe it proves that the company may have been right after all about those other men. Still seems strange though. There's gotta be more to it than just what that article says. I mean, there must have been some sort of reason why they couldn't get anyone to work."

Richard looked pensive.

"I wonder if Tedric knows anything about this," Michael said as he closed the book.

"Why don't you ask him? I don't know about you, but I'm getting tired of looking through these books—we've been at it almost an hour and a half." He looked at his watch and yawned. "Amanda's probably ready to leave too."

"Yeah, guess I am too for that matter."

Okay, Fred. So I checked it out. Now, if only you were here to tell me what it means.

And even though this is what he thought, he would bet that if Fred the moving man had been around to hear his question—he wouldn't have been able to provide any better answers than Michael could.

They put the books away, then slowly climbed the stairs.

2

Upstairs, they found Tedric helping a teenage girl check out three books and a magazine. The girl was wearing a tight white shirt and cutoff jeans. Michael was able to tear his eyes away from this pleasant distraction long enough to see there were two other people present as well—an older man who looked to be about Richard's age, though his hair was completely white, and a tall, middle-aged woman who wore her brown hair pulled back in a single long braid that reached nearly to her waist. Her orange blouse actually made his eyes hurt. The white-haired man and the woman with the braid were busy scanning the stacks in the general fiction area. Then he spotted Amanda in the young adult section, though not before Richard had already started on his way over to her.

Michael waited patiently for Tedric to help the girl, wondering how old she was and if he might see her in school when it started in the fall. A moment later, though, she was gone without even having given him a glance.

"Now then, Michael, what can I help you with?"

For a fraction of a second he forgot what he was going to ask; then it was back and with greater urgency. "Tedric, what do you know about the Sedgwick-Davey Copper Mine?"

"Oh, quite a bit you might say. There're a lot of stories surrounding that old mine, both back when it was open and after they closed it in . . . let's see, was it twenty-eight or twenty-nine? I never could remember—"

"1928."

"Right, just before the Depression."

"We found several articles on it downstairs," he said. "What do you know about the nine miners who disappeared?"

"You mean the ones from the cave-in?"

Michael nodded.

"Well, yes, that was a hot topic back then. The mining company claimed the guys just walked off, even went so far as to suggest that they caused the cave-in themselves, to make everybody think they were dead. Of course, the company never offered any explanation as to what benefit this would have been for the miners, but that's what they said just the same."

"What do *you* think?"

"Well, I don't rightly know. All I know is what I read . . . and what my mother told me."

Tedric hesitated. He looked away, but when he looked back, he must have noted the intensity of Michael's interest, because he continued to relate his tale, albeit reluctantly.

"My mother said there was something weird about the mine, that they'd gone and accidentally connected into some other set of tunnels and that the mining company covered it all up—pun intended I suppose—'cause they couldn't explain it. And there were other folks my mother knew that said the *company* itself caused the cave-in to seal it up . . . get rid of the witnesses. Truth is, the families of all those men that disappeared didn't disappear with them. There were some mighty sad wives and children they left behind. I don't see how nine men, all a them with wives and kids and all, would just up and walk out on 'em together."

Michael thought about this for a moment, agreeing without feeling the need to say so.

Another set of tunnels? What did that mean?

"How about later, when they closed it?"

"Well now, that was something else different entirely. Those men *did* walk off, there weren't no question about that—they walked off, took their families with them, and moved away. I don't think there was a one a them that stayed around. When they quit, they quit good and everybody knew it."

"But *why?* Why did they quit?"

"No one knows for sure, not even the men that worked there, if you can believe that. Soon after, the rumors started that the place was haunted—that there were Tommy Knockers—the ghosts of those nine missing men—hauntin' the place and dropping rocks on the miners while they were working. Don't know if that had anything to do with 'em walking off or not, but that's what went around town after they closed it. And there's people here in town to this day that'll swear it's the truth."

"Haunted, huh?" Something about this seemed familiar, but for the time being he couldn't place it.

(yeah, you know, haunted . . . like your house)

Somehow . . . I don't think so. In fact . . . I think our house has something a whole lot worse wrong with it.

"Oh, and this you might be interested in, Michael, 'cause it's got to do with your cult, Dr. Woulfe's cult I mean."

Tedric smiled then quickly averted his eyes.

"What's that?"

"Well, when they closed the mine, they sealed it all up of course. Put boards across the entrance and all, sealed it up real tight—or so they thought. Well then, a little while after that, sometime in the mid-thirties I guess it was, this Dr. Woulfe and some locals were caught trespassing—caught right inside the mine. Come to find out they were holding secret meetings in there. Some of the local kids caught 'em at it. After that, they closed the place up even tighter. But that still wasn't the end of it. In fact, I think I still got the article on this one . . . let me get it, okay?"

Tedric walked out from behind his desk and headed in the direction of the stairs. As Michael waited for him to return, Richard came back with Amanda.

"How much longer you plan on staying, Michael?"

From the wall clock over Richard's shoulder he could see it was nearly noon.

"We probably ought to be getting back to the house and checking in on your dad."

"And I'm hungry," Amanda said to no one in particular.

"I don't know, Tedric's getting me some stuff and I think I'd like to do some more research yet—do some reading on cults, find out if there were any others like the Woulfes'."

Richard paused for a moment to think about this, looking at Michael. Michael, however, couldn't help but continue glancing behind him at the stairs, anxiously waiting for Tedric to come back.

"Okay. How about if I go on and take Amanda home now? Then, when you're ready to leave, give me a call and I'll come back and pick you up."

"You don't mind?"

"Nope. Not a problem at all. So, okay then . . . we'll see you a little later." Richard and Amanda turned toward the front door. When they left, the door slammed loudly behind them. A minute later, Tedric returned from the basement.

"I found it!"

When Tedric reached the top of the stairs, he was breathing hard.

"Here, read this," Tedric said as he hurried over to him and handed Michael a newspaper clipping dated August 3, 1980. Michael took a quick glance, but there was nothing to identify from which paper the clipping had come from.

> BOYNE CITY, MI—James Wilfred Lawson was killed today in a freak accident involving an abandoned copper mine in this small resort community. Apparently, the boy, 12, was killed when he fell down a ventilation hole into one of the mine tunnels of the Sedgwick-Davey Copper Mine, closed since 1928.
>
> James Lawson and two friends, Jeffrey Hawthorne and Brian Christiansen, all of Boyne City, were playing the game Dungeons and Dragons, a fantasy role-playing game that has players making up imaginary characters and then role-playing these

> characters on adventures. Apparently, the boys had decided to take the game a step further and had begun playing the game for real in the once-sealed confines of the abandoned copper mine.

"Something about this seems to be related," he said quietly, wanting to have said it only to himself and was surprised when he realized he had spoken the words aloud.

He had that same feeling again—the feeling that he was on the verge of making an important connection. But just like before—it slipped away before he could grab it.

And then there was the thing that the moving man had said—or had he really said it at all? As he thought about it now, it seemed more like something that had come out of one of his dreams.

You should check it out, boy. Check it out realllll goooood.

"Related? To what?" Tedric asked.

"I'm not sure," he said slowly, thoughtfully, drifting slowly back into the present. "But something seems to tie in here. I know it sounds crazy, but something about this mine and the disappearance of those miners has to do with our house."

"Are you sure?"

He could sense the doubt in the librarian's voice—and something else as well.

(he thinks you're crazy, loony tunes, one suit short of a full deck—)

All right—I get the picture.

(no you don't—don't you remember? you're still fumbling with the pieces—)

"No," Michael answered, "it's just based on . . . a feeling." This time when he looked at Tedric, the librarian was staring at him in much the same way his mother looked at him when he'd done something she didn't understand and that she usually didn't like.

3

"I have a couple of books on cults," Tedric said a few minutes later. "Have a seat and I'll bring them out to you."

"Okay," Michael said, and walked toward the study table. He felt like a student and Tedric his teacher. "You sure have been a big help, Tedric. I really appreciate it."

"No thanks necessary, Michael. Just part of my job."

Michael quickly reached the study table. It was the only one in the upstairs part of the library and was the same one he had used to do his translations the day Mrs. Burroway had refused to lend him the German-English dictionary. The table was made of solid oak and marked with decades worth of gouges and scratched patterns. As soon as he sat down, Tedric returned with two small books.

"These two are pretty old, but they still might help you. 'Fraid it's the best I could do."

He took the books. The first was entitled *Cult Society in America*; the other, *Alternative Religions*.

"They'll do fine. Thanks," he said and settled down to read.

He found *Cult Society in America* the most interesting since, among other things, it contained pictures. The photographs were mostly of cult activities prominent throughout the United States, but also included were line drawings showing some of the different symbology used by the various cults. He studied these closely, but saw nothing that looked familiar to anything he'd seen in Dr. Woulfe's journals.

As he continued reading, he learned that most cults were really fringe religions, many of them based on the standard Christian Bible only differing from other mainstream religions in their sometimes idiosyncratic interpretations of certain scriptures. Then he turned his attention to the section on the more dangerous, largely satanic cults. Many of these groups were rumored to have engaged in everything from sexual improprieties (including the sexual abuse of children) to human sacrifice.

As he delved further into the two books, he lost consciousness of his surroundings—and of time. Within what seemed to be only the passage of minutes, several hours elapsed.

In his reading, he learned about the Process Church of the Final Judgment, located near Los Angeles; Our Lady of Endor

Coven; the Ophite Cultus Satanis, founded in the late 1940s by Herbert Sloane in relatively nearby Columbus, Ohio; the Church of Satanic Brotherhood, an offshoot of the much larger Church of Satan (even recognized by the U.S. military as a valid religious preference); and the Brotherhood of the Ram in California.

But while he read and found nearly all of the information interesting, none of it seemed relevant to what Dr. Woulfe and his daughter's group were purported to have been doing. While many of the cults practiced demon calling, when it came to the specific reasoning for such Callings, the answers were either nonexistent, vague or unrelated.

He was still flipping pages when he became aware of the time and was about to quit, when he stopped to read the caption under a photograph of a religious gathering in New Mexico. He had passed by the photograph several times already, but this particular time it caught his attention. He read the caption for the first time: "A rare look into a secret cult meeting. Pictured is a meeting of the Society of the Guided Path with founder, Matthew Morenson directing his followers. May 21, 1952." But what had especially caught his eye was not so much the photograph but the name—Matthew Morenson. Somehow, it seemed familiar. Not only familiar, he decided, but as if it were accompanied by a voice

(make sure you check it out, boy—check it out real good)

inside his head telling him to pay special attention—telling him that something here was important.

But from where? Had he been a local resident? No, that sounds almost right, but I don't think that's it. What then? Something about the name—

He decided to ask Tedric about it. Maybe he might know who the figure in the picture was, assuming of course the link he felt existed was indeed real. He took the book over to the librarian's desk. Ironically, it seemed to Michael, Tedric was reading.

"Matthew Morenson. Hmm. I don't right recall. Sounds familiar though to me too."

"Wait a minute . . . I've got an idea."

Michael returned to the basement and retrieved the newspaper book for the year 1921. As he was carrying it back upstairs, he began awkwardly paging through it so that by the time he reached Tedric's desk he had found the article about the cave-in. He laid the book down on the desk and ran his finger slowly across the words in the article until he came to the names of the nine missing miners. He read the list again and stopped when he came to the last name . . . Matthew Mapleson.

Matthew Mapleson . . . Matthew Morenson. Did it mean anything?

He felt there was something here, though at present there didn't appear to be any legitimate reason to believe the two names might be related.

Or the same.

"Look at this, Tedric. These are the names of the nine missing miners. Look at the last one."

Michael held up the huge book over Tedric's desk.

"Yeah? So?"

"The names—don't you see the names? Look how close they are."

He tried to point and hold the book at the same time but couldn't. Tedric stared at the page again and this time Michael could tell he was studying it.

"Now wait a minute . . . you trying to tell me, you think that fella in the picture might be Matthew Mapleson?"

"That's exactly what I'm wondering. Problem is, how do I find out for sure? There wouldn't happen to be some way you could get a picture of Mr. Mapleson, is there?"

He closed the heavy book and set it on the floor. As he stood up he thought he saw something move out of the corner of his eye.

"Actually, I just might. I know that his son still lives around here. He might have a picture of his father. I could find out for you."

"Really? That would be great!"

After Michael took the newspaper book back downstairs, he returned to the study table and collected his notes. He slung his pack across one shoulder and brought the two books over to Tedric's desk.

"Leaving?"

"Yeah, there's somebody I've gotta see. I'm hoping he might know something about this stuff. I'll see you later, okay?" he said, already on his way towards the stairs and the front door. At the top of the stairs, he turned around. "And you'll let me know the second you find out anything more about Mr. Mapleson?"

Tedric smiled. "You can count on me, Michael."

43

1

This would be the first time Michael actually *wanted* to see Harvey Olds. Michael was downtown, walking fast, intending to traverse every street in town until he found him. As it turned out, he didn't have far to go—he found Harvey in the first place he looked—the park.

"I have to talk to you," Michael announced without preamble when he found Harvey sitting on the ground with his back against a large maple.

"About what?" Harvey said around a mouthful of sandwich. Michael wondered if the sandwich had been stolen—or maybe even picked out of the trash.

"What do you know about the Sedgwick-Davey Copper Mine?"

"Nothing more than anyone else," he said, and took another bite.

Unlike their first meeting, this time Michael felt in control of the situation. As Harvey lifted up his sandwich again, Michael thought he saw his hands tremble. For once he wasn't afraid of him. In fact, he thought Harvey looked like nothing more than a small-time big-city street punk who occasionally made extra money by snitching on his friends to the police. As Michael waited before asking his next question, Harvey's eyes seemed to look everywhere but directly at him, darting and shifting along with jerky, nervous movements of his head.

"What about the cave-in, in 1921, when those nine miners disappeared? Know anything about that?"

"Never heard of it," he said, not looking at Michael, concentrating instead on his sandwich, and then on some kids riding by on bikes.

Michael believed him only partially and while it gave him a certain degree of satisfaction to know that maybe some of his knowledge exceeded Harvey Olds'

(Cecil Georges'?)

it was also a concern to think that although he now had more parts of the puzzle to work with, he still seemed to have less of it put together than Harvey did—or at least claimed he did. Michael was determined, though, to find out just how complete a picture Harvey had.

"What if I told you I think those nine miners didn't vanish, but rather left town to start cults in other parts of the country? What would you say to that?"

Harvey looked up at him for the first time, his mouth frozen in mid-chew, his cheeks bulging. Despite his comical appearance, Harvey's eyes held a look Michael could only interpret as something as close to terror as he had ever seen.

"Tedric, the librarian, is confirming it right now."

"It's time we talk," he said suddenly, in the strong, controlling voice Michael remembered from the first day they had talked. He realized that whatever control over the situation he may have previously had, it was gone now.

"I thought I already said that."

"No, I mean we have to *talk.* But not here . . . it's not safe." Harvey's gaze probed every direction in the park. Michael felt like he was in a spy movie.

"You'll have to follow me," Harvey said and stood up. Brushing crumbs from his dirty clothes, he wrapped the last half of his sandwich in a Subway wrapper and stuffed the bundle into one of his coat pockets. Michael wrinkled his nose as he imagined what else might be in that filthy pocket.

"Where're you going?"

"To where I live."

"I can't—I don't have my bike with me—my grandfather dropped—"

"Get on the back of mine, I can carry you."

Michael looked dubiously at Harvey's bike lying on the ground nearby. Harvey then picked it up and, straddling it, held out a hand.

Michael knew what his father would say in this instance—could in fact actually hear his very words inside his head as he took the proffered hand and got on the seat—*What!? Are you absolutely out of your mind? What did he do, zap you with an intelligence reducer? I just can't believe you'd do something so totally irresponsible—*

But he paid the voice no mind. It was clear to him now (though he knew he couldn't have adequately explained it to anyone else in order to make them believe it) that they, meaning him and his family, were all involved in something they hadn't bargained for—something far more all-encompassing than simply the idea of a haunted house. Whatever it was, it now appeared to be something that had spread its tentacles over not only an entire town, but perhaps even across a country as well. Though Tedric hadn't yet come up with the proof of what was implied by the photograph, Michael had no doubt he inevitably would. Still, the overwhelming question remained—what did it all mean? And then beyond this—what should or could he do about it? Suddenly, the possibility that their lives could really be at stake in the grand scheme of it all didn't seem quite so far-fetched—if it ever had.

For a brief moment, Michael wondered if the homeless man was strong enough to ride and control the bike while at the same time carrying the both of them. He needn't have worried.

2

Michael was again impressed at the strength exhibited by Harvey Olds. Harvey wasn't even breathing hard as he carried Michael on his bike for what amounted to a nearly four-mile ride out of town.

They traveled out on Pleasant Valley Road, and at the three-way stop where Michael usually continued to go straight, Harvey turned left onto a dirt road Michael had barely noticed before. The road was rough and it was obvious that no one—no one besides Harvey Olds apparently—lived on it. They followed the two-track defile that was little more than a parallel set of ruts (some of them as deep as a foot or more) for about a quarter of a mile before stopping. When he was finally able to get off the bike, Michael noticed a barely perceptible path leading through the tall grass into the woods. Harvey walked his bike in front of him down the path and Michael followed closely behind.

"Is this . . . where you live?"

"Yes. Not much farther now."

As they walked deeper into the woods, Michael began to imagine things. Things like Harvey suddenly turning against him and doing whatever he wanted—the "whatever" creating all sorts of disturbing pictures inside his head, most of them involving his demise. But he remained steadfast. He had told his grandfather he felt there was something right about Harvey, perhaps even something a little good, and now was his best chance to prove his theory—even if it meant risking his life.

They followed the path as it twisted and meandered through the grass and into the woods. The path wasn't very well-defined and at times there seemed to be hints of other pathways crossing and re-crossing the one they were following. Then he realized it was probably a deliberate ploy by Harvey to keep the curious away—taking different routes each time in order to prevent creating a trail that could be easily followed.

Michael marveled again at their apparent mutual trust for each other, deciding the stakes were too important for other trivialities. The continued exertion required by walking, combined with the thought of this new-found trust, made him sweat. As he wiped his forehead with the back of his hand he wondered just how much farther they were going—and what might lie in store for him at the end of the trail.

After what seemed to take nearly an hour, but in fact was no more than fifteen minutes, they came to a small clearing in the middle of a thick stand of white pines. Here the ground was a springy carpet of brown pine needles that felt almost like air beneath his feet. In the clearing on one side was a crudely assembled—fort. It was the only word he could think of to describe it. A fort that looked like the type kids usually constructed of branches and bark. A fire pit smoldered outside the doorway of the structure, which appeared to be makeshift and temporary. Whatever else he might be, Michael thought, Mr. Harvey Olds was a cautious man.

As Harvey wheeled his bike into the clearing, propping it against the side of his residence, Michael couldn't help but ask the obvious again, "You live here?"

"Yes. Not much compared to your place, is it?"

"No. But . . . how do you survive? What about winter?"

"I manage."

He noted Harvey had calmed down considerably since their meeting in the park. His movements appeared more sure and calculated; his voice now sounded strong and controlled.

"So, you go first—what do you know about the mine?" Michael asked. He remained at the edge of the clearing, the return of his earlier anxiety holding him back.

Harvey however didn't answer. Instead, he busied himself tidying things around his home—pulling the uneaten half of his sandwich out of his pocket and putting it in a dirty, gray Styrofoam cooler, then stirring up the ashes of his fire and dropping kindling on it to get the flames going again.

Looking at the fire made Michael feel hotter and he was at a loss imagining how Harvey could still be wearing his thick coat—especially after the long, strenuous ride.

As Harvey continued to straighten and tidy, Michael wondered if he hadn't heard his question or was just ignoring him. He decided in favor of the latter but wondered why. His anxiety was struggling to return but he managed to brush it away for the moment. Harvey now seemed to be moving even faster and reminded Michael of a scurrying mouse, darting from corner to corner, stopping every couple of seconds to sniff the air for danger before darting off again. Based on his movements, Michael saw that Harvey's calmness had disappeared and his agitation seemed not only to have returned, but had intensified. Despite this, Michael's impatience grew, knowing his grandfather would by now be worrying about him. But Michael wanted answers. Any answers.

"Well? Why did you have to bring me all the way out here? Why not talk in the park?"

Michael wasn't prepared for the intensity of Harvey's reaction. From his location near his lean-to, Harvey whirled about while at the same time seeming to fly at him across the small clearing in one quick, ferocious movement.

"Because! It's not *safe!* You understand *nothing!*" Harvey barked at him with enough vehemence to force Michael to take a step backward.

But this time Michael was determined not to let himself be pushed around, whatever the consequences, so he stepped forward—first one step—then two.

"I understand nothing—what about you? If you're so damn smart what do you know about the copper mine? Can you answer me that?"

But Harvey just stood there looking at him—perhaps trying to measure the depth of his concern. When he answered, his voice had again become calm and controlled.

"All right—maybe I didn't know that—you're right," he said, almost as if he were about to apologize. Then he became agitated again, bursting out in an angry gush, "But I know a lot of other things, things *you* wouldn't believe," he said, stopping again suddenly as if bewildered.

Michael found himself also beginning to feel bewildered. Harvey's constant sudden and intense changes of voice and mannerisms were getting difficult to follow—and almost impossible to understand.

Is this how a crazy person behaves? Is that what I'm seeing and hearing—the ravings of a homeless lunatic?

He knew this was what he *wanted* to believe because once again he could feel the truth in Harvey's words . . . whereas the truths of a crazy person could easily be ignored.

When Harvey continued, his voice had changed again—now it was the soft murmuring tone of someone talking to himself. "And . . . and I don't know what has triggered it . . . something has triggered it . . . I don't know what that something is either," he said, then in a louder voice, "But what I *do* know is what's going to happen," then added, this time in a voice so quiet that Michael almost didn't hear him, "I was shown that much at least."

But Michael wasn't about to let him get away with partial revelations—not this time.

"What do you mean, *shown?*"

"A vision . . . a vision given me by Teufel," Harvey said, staring, his green eyes boring into Michael. And yet Michael had the distinct feeling that Harvey wasn't even seeing him.

"Who's Teufel?"

Harvey's eyes refocused.

"Teufel is the name of the Power—of the force I told you about before. Teufel is . . . Evil. Only one step away from the devil himself."

(and you still think he's not crazy?)

"You mean . . . like a demon or something?"

"Yes, that's exactly what I mean, but more powerful. The demons are actually disciples of Teufel. He controls them . . . directs them."

Were they really talking about demons? Was this for real or just another bad dream?

"Okay, so . . . what exactly did this Teufel show you?"

Harvey's eyes began to wander again. He turned, then shuffled over toward his fire.

"I can't tell you."

"What?" Michael took a step forward. "Come on! What kind of game are you playing here? You stand there and try to tell me about forces and demons and visions of evil, talking as if you want to help me, to make me understand, then all of a sudden it's some big secret. I don't think you really know—"

Without warning, Harvey whirled around to face him, the quick intensity of his action enough to stop Michael from completing his sentence.

"What do you know about Woulfe's cult?" Harvey asked, stabbing Michael with eyes like beams of white hot energy.

Michael struggled to find an answer, even as he realized he had allowed Harvey to regain control of the conversation again. Michael felt like a beginning chess player being toyed with by the grand master.

"They were trying to reach the Other Side, trying to reach this . . . Teufel I guess—" Michael said. He felt as if he were being tested and cursed himself for sounding so unsure.

"And?" Harvey said, demanding he continue.

"And what?" Michael replied helplessly.

"That's only part of it," Harvey said, walking up to him, staring him down, their noses only inches away from each other. "Dr. Woulfe had perfected the process for establishing Gates, pathways between this world and the world beyond death. But, do . . . you . . . know . . . *why?*"

"No, I don't know . . . to allow cult members to talk to their dead relatives or—"

"Not hardly," Harvey said, backing up, the sound of disappointment in his voice mixed with a cold sarcasm. But his stabbing gaze never wavered from Michael's face. "No, the cultists were after that which all men have craved—and been denied—since time's beginning. *Immortality,"* he said, almost hissing the last word.

"You can't be serious," Michael said, as he tried to match Harvey's sarcasm with some of his own. Then he decided to use what was left of his sudden and increasingly fleeting confidence to plunge forward, "How, by selling their souls to the devil?"

Harvey smiled.

"You're more right than you know."

The sight of Harvey's smile made him forget how irate he had been only a moment ago and—amazingly—he felt goose bumps ripple up and down his arms. He noticed that Harvey seemed to have relaxed once again. Then, before Michael could manage a reply, Harvey continued, explaining the cult's activities in a dull voice like the one Michael remembered his elementary math teacher using when explaining long division.

"The ceremony was entitled The Calling," Harvey began. "Those individuals wishing to join the cult, called pre-initiates or The Unbonded, had to go through The Calling in order to become a full member of the cult. Full members were called *Mitsglied*—The Bonded. And The Calling ceremony itself was just what it sounds like, the calling of a demon." Harvey turned and walked back to his fire. From a position behind it, he turned to face him. "First, a Gate would be fashioned using a huge bonfire. Once established, a demon would be Called into the Gate. The pre-initiate would then attempt to . . . *bond* with the demon, a sort of possession if you will."

"You mean to say then that all the members of the cult were . . . possessed . . . by demons?"

"That's exactly what I mean, though a possession of a sort you've probably never heard of before."

But Michael for the moment had tuned him out. For upon hearing the word possession, there was only one thing that came to mind—his forgotten two weeks.

Is that what happened to me? But I didn't go into any bonfire—except in my dreams—and I certainly don't remember calling forth any demon.

"But why? It doesn't make any sense. Why would anyone allow such a thing?"

Harvey continued to stare into his fire.

"I already told you—immortality. It wasn't a possession like what you've seen in the movies. This was a *mutual* possession—a sort of cohabitation if you prefer. The human host retained most of the control over its demon-possessor in a mutually-shared, and *mutually-aware*, environment. It was believed that by becoming Bonded, such demons—they called them *daemons*—would at the time of the member's bodily death, be able to act as a guide for the member's soul in its journey to the other side. It was thought that without such a guide, the soul would be forever lost, unable to find its way, left to the whims of chance."

Harvey lifted his gaze from the fire to Michael.

"Unbelievable. But what did the de- . . . *daemons* have to gain from all this?"

Harvey looked unsure for a moment, as if trying to decide how best to continue. The hesitation made Michael think that perhaps he had hit on another of the areas where Harvey was not going to be forthcoming.

"Once a month, during the dark of the moon . . . the cultists would meet. At that time, they would give themselves over to their demon-possessor . . . and allow them to feed."

Michael found himself thinking about animal and human sacrifices and began to shiver. Then he thought of his neighbor, killed "by apparent animal attack" and the little boy, Jeremy Young and Ghost's death . . . and wondered. Before he could ask a question, though, Harvey went on.

"There were also *Damons*, which were higher level demons. Once bonded, members could, at a later time, attempt to bond with a Damon. It was believed that this provided an even surer guarantee of passage," Harvey said. He had now picked up a long stick and was poking at his fire. "But only six members were allowed to be bonded with Damons at one time. These six members subsequently formed a higher rank of membership within the cult called the *Rat*, or council. Their leader, Sylvia, was called the *Ratsmitglied*, or councilor. There was also a secondary leader, called the *Sekunde*—"

"Whoa, whoa, hang on here, you're losing me. Did I miss something? Mind telling me again, exactly how you know all this?"

Harvey put his stick down before answering, leaving the hot end propped on the edge of the fire pit.

"I've had fourteen years to research it."

"Come on, Harvey, I may be young but I'm not stupid. This stuff you're telling me isn't in some encyclopedia on cultism in a library somewhere. Believe me, I've looked."

"You're right, it isn't," Harvey said, smiling his small knowing smile again.

Then realization struck. "No . . . you didn't—"

"For all your obvious ignorance, you seem to catch on rather quickly," Harvey said and smiled even broader—a sickish, hungry smile. "Dr. Woulfe's journals that you so *conveniently* found—"

Michael had never gotten far into his reading of the second volume. Nevertheless, he tried contemplating the implications of Harvey's claim to have planted both journals. Suddenly, his mind refused to take any more—it was too much—demon possession, feedings, gates to hell.

"But why, why me? Why are you telling me all this?" he demanded, not caring whether Harvey heard the quaver in his voice or not.

"Because you asked!" Harvey almost shouted back at him. Then he continued more quietly, "And to save your family. You're the only one who can convince them. They're in *danger*. Something has awakened Teufel." Then Harvey's eyes widened with a sudden, terrible realization. "My . . . you didn't—"

"Didn't *what?*" Michael cried, exasperated.

"The tunnels . . . that's *got* to be it . . . *you opened the tunnels!*" Harvey said, his voice booming through the forest, startling several crows nearby which took immediate flight with a loud cawing of protest.

"What tunnels? I don't even know what you're talking about!" Michael said, trying to calm himself even as he felt a sense of truth in what Harvey had said . . . and now felt two, previously and seemingly disparate sections of the puzzle that had become his life . . . suddenly come together in a perfect, interlocking match.

But Harvey said nothing and chose instead to watch Michael as if he were able to follow the connections taking place inside his head. And when finally he did respond to his question, it was delivered in the soft, gentle voice of an understanding friend.

"The tunnels under your house . . . you opened them."

"But how could I have?" Michael began, not bothering to even question the existence of such an underground network but simply accepting it as fact . . . and from that fact, building implications upon it like bricks of a house placed on top of a foundation—implications he would deal with later. "But . . . how could I have opened them? I don't even know where they are . . . what they are."

"But you did . . . you *must* have, it's the only explanation. And if you don't remember, then it must mean—"

"What? *What* does it mean?"

And then Harvey said the last—and the worst—thing Michael would have expected.

"Amanda," he uttered, as if the name explained everything. To Michael, though, it only sent a cold dagger of dread through his already pounding heart.

"What about her?" he said, the question coming out barely above a whisper.

"Has she been acting . . . strange in any way?"

"I don't know. We've all been having bad dreams . . . but . . . my mom found her sleepwalking in the basement once."

Harvey seemed to move like a blur, coming from behind the fire to grab Michael by the shoulders and hold him with a strength that felt capable of crushing his shoulder blades like cheap cardboard, "She's in terrible danger, Michael. Terrible, terrible danger—you've got to believe me. You need to get them all out of that house *at once!*"

"But *why?*" he pleaded, and in the next instant, changed the tone of his voice to a demand even as Harvey still held him, "What's going to happen to Amanda?"

Harvey let him go, walked a few steps away and then turned around. This time though, he didn't look at him as he answered.

"I . . . I can't tell you—"

"Come on, Harvey, not again! That's not going to be good enough this time. *What's going to happen to Amanda?*"

Suddenly, though, Michael realized that he had lost him—and as much as he tried to hang onto it, his anger evaporated.

Harvey paced, his eyes studying the ground while his hands and arms seemed to have taken on minds of their own, rhythmically performing strange jerks and gyrations as he mumbled to himself.

"The force, it's there, felt and taken, insidious snake of the mind, wrapping itself, constricting—" he began, and looked once at Michael—allowing Michael to see the wild look in eyes that no longer registered his presence, eyes that darted feverishly, seemingly in every direction at once as he spoke. And as the meaningless jumble poured out of Harvey's mouth, he seemed equally oblivious to the saliva that dribbled from each corner and the stream of tears that poured freely from each eye, ". . . no longer can I feel its sick cold heart, it now feasts on my eyes so that I cannot see, cannot see what it wishes to keep hidden!"

Michael backed slowly out of the clearing, though it was obvious that Harvey was far beyond trying to detain him. And then, for the first time since his having met Harvey in the park, Michael was genuinely, thoroughly afraid.

So when he had stepped about a dozen feet out of the clearing and back into the woods, he didn't hesitate but turned and ran. Behind him, he could hear the insane shouts and yells that followed him and although he felt they were not necessarily aimed at him, they still had an effect like small electric spikes sent hurtling and stinging into his backside, prodding him forward ever faster and faster, all the way home.

44

Atlanta, Georgia
August 4 • Friday

1

Georgia Highway Patrol officer Ken Baxter never saw the knife, only felt it for the brief moment when it made its sudden and fatal plunge into the left side of his chest. The knife, expertly targeted between the 3rd and 4th ribs, slid up and to the side, quickly finding the center of the pumping mass of his heart—and stilling it forever with a single, violent intrusion.

Officer Baxter's dying eyes stared momentarily into the weathered face of his killer, then saw nothing more even before his body had completed its fall onto the gravel shoulder of Interstate 75 just north of Atlanta, Georgia.

The attack had been savage and unexpected from the man Officer Baxter had pulled over for traveling 72 on the 55-mph posted section of the interstate. Under other circumstances, he might even have been amused to realize that the speed of the particular offender he had stopped coincided precisely with his age—if only he had lived long enough to find out.

2

Larry Johnston looked at the growing pool of blood from the officer lying dead at his feet. Then he stared at the double-edged 11-inch dagger grasped in his hand. But although his eyes gazed upon these things, his mind was unaware of them. He was conscious instead of the relative significance of the objects—his mind merely registering the fact that an obstacle had presented itself—and been quickly and easily eliminated.

Then Larry, with a swift and strong kick, sent the police officer's body tumbling off the shoulder of the interstate down a steep embankment to lie obscured from view in the long grass at the bottom.

Larry didn't even take the time to clean the swiftly congealing blood on his knife before thrusting it back into its leather scabbard hidden beneath his sweater. He returned to his station wagon, having already forgotten the officer, and pulled away in a spew of gravel and dust. As he drove, the flashing lights of the officer's cruiser danced across his rearview mirror for a few moments before disappearing at almost the same rate as the sun completed its appearance in this particular part of the world, signifying the end of yet another day.

Continuing north, Larry didn't notice nor care as the speedometer needle crept its way back across its dial to stop, twitching spasmodically, in the blank area between the 70 and 75 at the center of his dashboard.

As he drove, now crossing the border into Tennessee, a sudden smile crossed his mouth and then just as suddenly was gone.

45

August 5 • Saturday Morning

1

Michael sat up in bed, having been awakened by the sound of agitated voices coming from outside his bedroom door. Someone was crying and he wondered if he was once again dreaming. The clock told him it was 7:47 AM.

"There, there, honey, it's all right . . . it's all right," he heard his father say. Then he realized it was Amanda his father was comforting and wondered what had happened and thought again about Ghost.

Maybe she had a bad dream about Ghost?

But then another voice spoke.

Or, maybe, just maybe, it was Teufel, eh boy? How about that? Seems a bit more likely to me, don't you think? Face it, deep down you know what Harvey said is right and this proves it again—as if you didn't have enough to convince you already. Teufel is after Amanda and with each passing moment he's getting closer. Question is, how long are you going to wait before you do something? Until it's too late? Think you can live with that?

After he jumped out of bed and opened his door, the first thing he saw was the blood. It had run down Amanda's bare legs in small thin streaks, and at first he tried to tell himself they were only strands of yarn she'd taped to her legs as part of some costume. The illusion only lasted a second, however.

Amanda was standing in the middle of the hallway, her head resting on her dad's shoulder. Alan was sitting on his knees directly in front of her. Richard and Sam were also standing in the hallway; Sam behind Alan and Richard just outside the doorway of the guest bedroom.

"What happened?" Michael asked. He looked at Richard, but it was his father who answered.

"I don't know. She just started yelling and when I got up I found her out here like this." Amanda had by now stopped crying but continued to sniffle and her small body was still shaking.

Then Sam moved, walking past them heading toward the bathroom at the end of the hall. She went in and they heard the sound of water running. She came back shortly thereafter carrying a damp washcloth.

"Come on, honey, let's clean you up," she said and knelt down beside Amanda. As Amanda unclasped herself from Alan and attempted to stand erect, she was still shaking. Sam cleaned the blood off her thin legs, in the process revealing several long, shallow scratches. Michael thought they looked like wavy lines drawn with a red pen and even tried to tell himself that that was all they were.

Amanda was wearing a single sock with a ruffled top and two small blue hearts stitched about an inch below the ruffle. As Michael stared, he noticed a bright red spot on the white cotton that could have been another heart but he knew it wasn't.

"She was probably sleepwalking again and got tangled up in something down in the basement," Sam said. Then she asked Amanda, "Where's your other sock honey?"

"I don't know," Amanda replied, sounding lost.

Based on her response, Michael thought that she sounded much too devoid of energy for a young girl used to performing cartwheels in the grass or squealing with delight upon the discovery of a new butterfly.

"Probably lost it in the basement. Don't worry. We'll find it," Sam said in an attempt to reassure her.

Michael however didn't think Amanda had been sleepwalking.

Well, there you go, Michael. Proof positive, as they say. Wouldn't you agree? You don't honestly think those scratches came from some sort of sleepwalking episode now do you? Let's be real now.

Michael walked over to Amanda, bent over and examined her legs. The scratches stretched from mid-thigh to ankle on both legs. There were two on her right leg, three on the left. He tried to think of some other explanation but couldn't.

Claw marks.

"Amanda, were you down in the basement again?" Alan asked softly.

Still fighting back sniffles Amanda tried to reply. "I . . . I don't think so. I don't remember."

"It's okay. You're going to be okay now, all right?" Sam said.

Sam finished cleaning the wounds and the lines now looked pink. Things having calmed down, Alan led Amanda back to her room where she lay down. After a few soothing words of comfort he gently closed her door and returned to the hallway. For several seconds everyone stood there looking at one another, unsure of what to do next, confused and perhaps even afraid but trying not to show it. Michael was conscious of his grandfather staring at him but didn't turn to avoid confirming it.

"You think she was sleepwalking again?" Alan asked Sam.

Sam turned to face him. "And I suppose you've got a better explanation? Maybe ghosts in the night who go around scratching up little girls' legs?"

"No, of course not. It's just—"

"It's just *what?*"

Michael could see the fire in his mother's eyes—a fire she probably thought was anger—but to him looked more like fear.

"I don't know!" Alan said, exasperated.

Silence followed, filling several awkward seconds.

Alan continued, "What if this has something to do with those animal attacks? Maybe we should let the police know—"

"Oh *please,*" Sam interrupted. "Are you trying to say some wild animal big enough to kill a man would come into our house without making a sound, cut a couple of scratches on Amanda's legs and then leave?"

"I think we should report it . . . let them be the ones to decide."

"Fine. Then *you* call them and *you* explain it."

Sam cast a brief glance at Michael, then turned and headed back to the bathroom, closing the door with enough force so as to be considered a slam. A second later, they heard the sound of running water again.

Without a word, Alan headed downstairs. For a second, Michael was glad—until he remembered the sheriff's admonition. He turned his attention to his grandfather.

"What is it, Michael?"

"Nothing."

Michael looked away. His grandfather moved out of the doorway to stand in front of him.

"Come on now, you know me better than that by now. And I know you know something about what happened here. This is, after all, your sister—"

"You think I don't know that?" he shot back, much louder and angrier than he had intended.

Richard continued, speaking even more quietly now, "Yes, of course you do. And I'm sorry. I guess we're all a little on edge after what happened—"

Michael stepped back, then turned away and stared at the floor.

"After I left the library yesterday I went to see Harvey Olds," he began, talking, he hoped, quietly enough so that his mother wouldn't hear. He paused for a moment, expecting a reaction—what kind he didn't know—but Richard only stood patiently, waiting for him to continue. Michael moved closer. "I wanted to ask him about the copper mine and the missing miners, but he said he didn't know anything about them. But then he talked about the cult. He told me what they used to do—it's too much to tell you about now—but then he went on to tell me something else. This force, or whatever it is he claims to be that is a part of this house, he actually gave it a name—Teufel. Then he said I must have somehow or other opened up some sort of tunnels underneath our house and by doing so, I've in turn awakened this Teufel. I still have no idea what he was talking about. But he was adamant that Teufel was an imminent danger to Amanda and that we needed to get her out of the house as soon as possible."

Richard said nothing and Michael wondered if he was trying to find the words to let him down easy—appropriate words to express his disbelief about what Michael had just told him.

"I don't know, Michael, this is getting pretty far out. Do you believe him?"

"It's not that simple. I really don't know how to make you understand—*I* don't even understand it myself—but somehow I think there's more at work here than either of us realize and I think Harvey knows more about it than anyone. *He said Amanda was in danger—and look at what just happened.*"

For a while, Richard just stood there looking at him.

"Do *you* think Amanda is in real danger?"

Michael looked at him—stared at him without blinking, hoping somehow to be able to will his convictions to flow to his grandfather via the power of his stare alone.

"Yes."

2

Sheriff Kelly arrived an hour and a half later. He met with the entire family in the kitchen and examined Amanda's legs. In the end, he pronounced there was nothing to worry about. When asked if anything new had come to light regarding the animal attacks at their neighbor's farm, he said there was no new information.

During his visit, the sheriff seemed to make a conscious point of ignoring Michael. A few minutes later, he left.

3

"Michael? Can I talk to you a minute?" Alan asked.

Michael was by the door in the kitchen, listening to make sure he could hear the sound of the sheriff driving away from the house and returning to town.

His father didn't wait for an answer but instead simply marched toward the library, expecting Michael to follow. And so he did—but not without first casting a backward glance at his grandfather.

Richard merely shrugged.

When Michael reached the library, at first Alan said nothing—he just stood looking out the large bay window for several moments. Then his father turned and faced him with the most serious expression of helplessness Michael had ever seen.

"Michael, what's going on?"

"What do you mean?"

"I mean, what in the world is going on here, in this house . . . in this town? I know you've been doing research at the library. You told me something about some of the former owners . . . and about their bad . . . experiences. Do you think something like that may be happening to us?"

"Well—" he began and was about to deny having any such ideas when a picture of Harvey Olds suddenly flashed into his mind—Harvey Olds with a wild look of insanity in his eyes telling him they were all in danger—Amanda most of all. If ever he had a chance to try and convince his father that something real—something strange and very likely beyond their control was happening to them—this was the perfect opportunity.

"I think Amanda is in danger."

Without hesitation, his father asked, "What sort of danger?"

Michael couldn't believe it. Could there be hope after all?

Michael moved farther into the room, stopped for a moment, then continued to the couch and sat down. Alan remained standing in front of the window.

"Well . . . about that I'm not really sure. It has something to do with the cult, the cult Sylvia Woulfe started," he said and paused, anticipating a response. But Alan only looked at him, waiting for him to go on. "This cult . . . they were trying to contact forces from the other side . . . demons. Anyway,

Harvey thinks that somehow these demons may have been awakened again by . . . our moving in here. He also thinks they could be especially dangerous to Amanda."

He waited for the explosion of disbelief and anger as his father realized what he had done.

"Did you say Harvey? You mean that creepy homeless guy . . . the same one who claims to be this guy who used to own our house?"

Yep, here it comes, right on schedule, I can already hear him—Are you crazy? Do you have any idea what you've done? and on and on and—

"Yeah—" Michael began, again recognizing the beginning of doubt in his father's voice, sensing already that he had tried . . . and failed again. But instead of despair, he felt anger as he wondered how much longer it was going to take—and more importantly—how much time Amanda had left.

"When exactly did you talk to him?"

"I met him outside the library two days ago," Michael said and hoped his father could sense the subtle, angry defiant tone in his voice.

Alan looked as if he were about to pursue this angle, then appeared to change his mind and turned back to the window.

Well, well—miracles do happen.

"I don't know, Michael. You almost had me going there for a minute."

"But—"

Alan turned around again, holding up a hand to stop him.

"I know what you're going to say, Michael, but *come on!* How can you trust this guy? Let's look at this logically, shall we? For one thing, how can we even believe *anything* this guy has to say? He lives out in the woods for God's sake. Nuttier than a fruitcake."

Michael could feel his anger building now. He shouted at his father in his mind—wishing he had the courage to actually say the words aloud.

You were the one that asked me! And all I did was try to tell you! If you don't like what I've got to say—why ask in the first place?

But what angered him most was that he could sense fear in his father's voice. Not only fear, he thought, but helplessness as well. He realized his father wasn't angry because of what he had done, or even because of what he had said—his father was angry because he was *afraid.*

Then Michael thought again about Amanda—seeing once again the red lines on her legs—and how he had tried so hard to convince himself that they were merely pieces of yarn or marks left by a red pen.

"You know the old abandoned copper mine—the Sedgwick-Davey Copper Mine?"

His father nodded.

"Well, in 1921, nine miners disappeared. At first it was reported they were killed in a cave-in, then later that they'd just walked off."

"So what does this have to do with anything?"

"Well, I'm not *real* sure, but what I do know is this: those nine miners didn't disappear. They went off to live in other states, scattering themselves across the country . . . and started up individual cults of their own."

Now his father looked genuinely interested.

"I don't see the connection."

Now, he knew, came the tricky part. But he had gone this far; there was no turning back. "Actually, I think they were *sent* out. Sent by this Teufel—that's the name of the thing Harvey says is behind all this—the head demon I guess you'd call him. Apparently, there're some sort of tunnels under our house. Based on my research, I think they might even lead all the way to the copper mine back in town. I think what happened is these miners were working in the mine on a new mine shaft when they broke into these tunnels and—"

"And . . . this super demon took over their minds and sent them out into the world as his disciples or something?" Alan said, the patronizing tone in his voice as clear as if he were holding up a neon sign. "Okay, so let me get this straight. We've got a haunted house, a tunnel network underneath it, zombie-miners—and all of them are after Amanda. Is that about right? Is that what you want me to believe?"

"Yeah, that's basically it—except for the part about the haunted house."

"Oh, sorry." Alan crossed his arms. "I don't know, Michael. Actually, I probably could've handled a haunted house, but this, this is just . . . well, I don't know exactly *what* this is. So, since you seem to have it all figured out, why Amanda?"

"That part I don't know yet. You don't believe me though do you?"

Alan looked out the window, as if pausing to consider his answer, before turning back around. Then he stepped closer to the couch.

"Well . . . I can't lie to you, Michael, but no, I don't believe you. Not entirely. Can you blame me?"

"I knew it—" Michael said and started to rise. He was getting ready to leave, when his father put his hands out to stop him and so he sat back down. He found himself staring at the floor, examining the pattern in the dark red Oriental rug. Then he imagined the rug pattern was a maze—and he and Amanda were lost in it—alone again against the world.

"Now wait just a second. What did you expect, Michael? I'm supposed to swallow this cult and demon story? What proof do you have?"

He thought about this for a moment, but didn't look up. "What about the journals? Dr. Woulfe's journals?"

"What do they prove? Any psycho can write down anything he wants. Just because it's in writing doesn't mean it's true."

When Michael felt his father leaning closer to him, he looked up.

"What about the dreams, then?" he said, knowing with this query he had scored a point—however minimal.

"What about them?" Alan said, carefully.

His father had indeed been leaning towards him—but now he straightened up.

"Have you ever had dreams like that before? *Ever?*"

"No, can't say that I have, but what does that mean anyway? Dreams aren't reality."

Michael looked away again and this time found himself staring out the window past his father—wondering what the future held for them. He saw a blue jay land on the wall of the porch. Something startled it though, and it took off. For a moment he wished he could be that blue jay, able to fly away from any problem or out of any situation in which he didn't feel comfortable.

Then he remembered the dog. He tried to will the memory away, but it wouldn't be denied this time. He remembered how he had found the animal, hurt and suffering, one of its legs mangled by the car that had hit it. And he couldn't forget the sound—that pitiful whimpering sound filled with incalculable pain—and how he had felt so sorry for the animal. He had tried to help it, to give it comfort, but was rejected. But most of all, he remembered what he'd done next—how his sorrow had turned to anger from the rejection and how the creature's whimpering had driven him to fury. He shut his mind to the specifics of the memory, but carried the anger back with him to the present.

"The dreams are a part of it I think, part of this . . . awakening. It could be it's them trying to reach us, trying to reach us through our dreams." He stared at his father, but he appeared to remain unmoved—arms crossed again, eyes dark and serious and so he continued. "How do you explain your dream about the Wilson girl's suicide? And what about the sounds in the basement? The voices? And do you *really* believe Amanda was just sleepwalking?"

"Well . . . I don't know, but I'm sure there's—"

Just then, they heard footsteps on the stairs.

"Okay, so just suppose, just *suppose* that all of this stuff you're telling me is true. So then what? What are we supposed to do about it?"

Michael gave his father a hard stare and saw frustration, apprehension—fear on his face.

"Leave. We have to get out of here—and the sooner the better."

"Just like that? Just pick up and leave a house we've been in scarcely two months?"

Michael again gazed at the floor and used the time to try to think of some element of hope that might put a check on his growing despair.

"There's no other way," he said, so quietly he wondered if his father had even heard him. But it didn't matter. The conversation was over.

Sam walked into the library. “Hey guys, what’s going on? Sounds like a pretty heavy discussion. Mind if I join you?”

“Not at all,” his father said. “We were pretty much done anyhow. Right, Michael?”

But before Michael could answer, the phone rang.

“I’ll get it!” Richard said from the parlor.

Without another word, Michael left the library.

4

“So, what did you think of our good sheriff, Mr. Kelly?” Michael asked Richard sometime later.

They were in Michael’s bedroom where Richard had come after answering the phone. The call had been from Tedric, confirming he was going to meet with the son of the missing miner, Matthew Morenson. The son’s name was Jack. Tedric would talk to him tomorrow morning at his house in town. The news, though, did little to boost Michael’s spirits. He was only now realizing how exhausting the conversation with his father had been.

“I gather you and him don’t get along too well. Want to tell me about it?”

“Sure, why not,” Michael said and sat down on his bed. Richard walked over to the desk, turned the chair around and sat down also. “He’s hiding something,” Michael finished.

(like your father?)

“Perhaps, but then again, he may not have a choice. If your neighbor *was* murdered he might not be able to tell you because of the investigation.”

“Maybe. But I think it’s more than that—call it another feeling.”

“But what else could there be?”

Michael didn’t answer right away and instead delayed his response, swinging his legs forward and back while looking out his bedroom window to the woods beyond. The sky was overcast and gray.

“I don’t know; like I said, it’s just another of my dumb feelings.”

"Don't put yourself down so hard, Michael. There's nothing wrong with having hunches; good cops will tell you that's usually what solves cases."

"Thanks," he said and smiled, but it was a fake smile, like the plastic Dracula teeth Amanda had worn last Halloween.

"Hey, no problem kiddo," he said and stood up. He walked over to where Michael was and put his hand on his shoulder. "You going to be all right?"

Michael stared up into his grandfather's eyes and immediately felt better. He looked past him out the window again, where his gaze found the single black window of the carriage house staring back at him like the eye of a Cyclops. "Yeah, just scared I guess. Something's going to happen, I know it is . . . I just want to be prepared for it . . . and I also want to protect my sister."

"And I believe you."

"You do?" he said, unable to hide the surprise in his voice. He craned his neck to look again into his grandfather's eyes for assurance of his honesty.

"Yes. And I don't know if everything is quite as bad as what you're probably thinking, but I do believe you're on the trail of *something*—we just don't know where it's going to lead us yet. Facts are accumulating, there's no question about that—the dreams are real and all of you have had them. The cult was also real. Amanda's cat is dead and your neighbor is dead and there's no denying the scratches on Amanda's legs. There's Harvey's explanation of course, his Teufel, demon of the underworld or whatever he's supposed to be—and then there's the truth. Regardless, we're going to have to wait it out as they say. I don't see what other choice we have, at least right now."

Michael, moved by his grandfather's words, felt some of his despair replaced by a fragile hope.

"I sure don't know what I'd be doing if you weren't here. My dad doesn't want to acknowledge what's happening at all. He'll listen, but doesn't want to believe any of it."

"I think he knows Michael, at least in his heart, that something is going on—something not so easily explicable as old house sounds or some other such *practical* explanation. And I don't think he's ever going to forget that dream he had.

But he's also the father and feels he has an obligation to act the part of the strong one—the unifying glue for keeping his family together."

"Maybe you're right."

Richard walked around to stand in front of him.

"Remember, he's supposed to be the one in charge, the leader, strong and courageous, the family's anchor of stability. He has to be hard-nosed—he wouldn't be doing his job if he wasn't. And your mom—she's got a lot going on in her life right now, the move, a new job, even her relationship with *her* mother—she feels she doesn't have room on her plate for anything else, and I don't think you can blame her."

"No, I guess I don't," he said after a pause and looked once again at Richard. "You sure have a way of making someone feel better," he said and couldn't help but smile.

"No problem. I guess maybe that's *my* job. We all have our jobs to do: son, daughter, father, mother, brother—and I'm the grandpa. Whatever happens, I'm going to be here," he said and grinned.

"I hope you never leave," Michael said seriously. "You're the only one that listens to me."

"Give them a chance, Michael, okay? Just give them a chance."

Richard moved toward the door.

"I'll try. But they need to give *me* a chance too."

Richard nodded and left. Michael remained sitting on his bed. It was nearly noon and he looked outside again at the gray-black sky which promised another summer thunderstorm. More clouds were moving in and, as he watched, they turned the sky darker and the day into a preternatural evening. Then, almost as if in answer to his unspoken thought, a far-off rumble rattled the old windows of his bedroom like an invisible spirit, knocking at the glass to be let in.

Except, according to Harvey at least, I've already opened the door.

46

1

At the dinner table the conversation was as light as the rain falling outside in a gentle sustained patter that promised its continued presence for the entire night. The storm had moved in earlier that afternoon and the rain and lightning had been intense at times, only calming some within the last hour. Through the leaded-glass windows of the dining room the sky appeared completely black, though it was only a few minutes past six in the evening.

Serving dishes heaping with chicken in wine sauce, mashed potatoes, mixed vegetables, and a basket of dinner rolls occupied the center of the table and during the meal had been passed with little comment.

Preoccupied, Amanda picked at her food without enthusiasm—looking at no one and saying nothing. Michael watched her with a sense of helplessness, wondering if she too, like himself before, was now imprisoned within a world of another's making.

He wanted to stand up and yell at the top of his lungs for someone—anyone—*to do something!* But he didn't, and wondered instead what task had been set aside for Amanda to fulfill—and how he might be able to stop it.

He had been wrestling with the question all afternoon, in the end it only making him more frustrated and angry. He welcomed the anger though, pulling it deep within himself much as a smoker will the first drag on a cigarette after a long abstinence. It was an anger being generated from two sources:

frustration at his parent's refusal bordering on denial to acknowledge the presence of the danger they all were in—and hatred at whatever force, be it Teufel or something else, that was the antagonist behind it all. And so he drew his rage inward, hanging fast to it, letting it build its explosive potential—to what end though, he didn't know.

"So," Richard began, "I'm a little late in saying this I know—but I hope you don't think that by my unannounced visit I was barging in on you all—although I guess that's exactly what I did. What I mean though, is I hope I'm not going to be a bother to you if I stay here for a little while until I can figure out exactly what it is I want to do," he said, as he took a second helping of mashed potatoes.

"Why don't you just live *here*, Grandpa, we've got lots of room!" Amanda said, oblivious to her father's wince, her mother's sudden look of surprise—or Michael's profound astonishment.

Michael studied his sister and was surprised to no longer see any discernible trace of her previous detachment. It was as if while he hadn't been looking, someone had replaced the mannequin sitting at the table with his real sister once again.

Or is this just more of the act? More of the performance to reassure us everything is supposed to be all right?

Or is it just . . . me? Is Dad right, and all of this is just my own paranoia getting carried away, building conspiracies from a 40-year-old history and a couple of unfortunate animal attacks?

Everyone but Michael laughed at Amanda's remark for he too wished much the same thing—that his grandfather would stay with them forever. But by remaining with them would he then be placing himself in the same danger as the rest of them? Or maybe—even more? After all, if Teufel were trying to make some sort of connection with them, it might not like a new player coming in, in the middle of the game. On the other hand, maybe it didn't care. Maybe it was so focused on Amanda—or so sure of itself—that it felt confident in its ability and wouldn't see any of their actions as a serious threat to it anyhow?

"We'll see, honey, we'll see," Richard said.

"He can stay here as long as he wants," Sam said, smiling at her father before turning to Amanda. "But eventually, he's going to want to live in his own place again, so he can have his own things in his own house."

"Oh," Amanda said and it was immediately obvious to Michael that she had relapsed once more into the quiet melancholy that had become her personality since Ghost's death. He worried too that she may not realize the danger she was in. At the same time, he determined that for him to warn her might do nothing but frighten her unnecessarily.

"This is a wonderful place you have here, though, Samantha," Richard said. "I really mean it."

"Thank you. We like it too, don't we?" Sam said and turned to Alan for confirmation. She frowned however when he didn't immediately respond and an uneasy silence followed.

Michael found himself once again focusing his attention on the time he couldn't remember—the two-week period before the family had gone to Mackinac Island. He also thought about what Harvey had told him about him being responsible for having opened some sort of tunnels beneath their house. And then he made a connection when he realized that the noises—the sound of voices, or whatever the source of the noise had been from the basement—had been quiet ever since.

Was it because I did what they wanted? But what did I really *do? By opening some tunnels, does that now mean these creatures are loose? That Teufel's loose?*

Michael thought some more about this and the "animal attacks" blamed for the death of their neighbor, their neighbor's farm animals, and Amanda's cat.

But the sheep were killed before that, weren't they? So whatever it was must have been free before. So by opening the tunnels, have I only increased this freedom? Throwing the gates wide—like grandpa said about some people letting free their dark inner selves. But what is it exactly that I have let loose? And can it ever be contained again?

Outside, the rain was falling heavier while inside, none of them—including Michael—noticed.

2

The trees stood in a motionless, almost fearful, silence as if attuned to the far-off ravages of an approaching firestorm. Their leaves hung limp on their branches, soaked and burdened by the pouring rain that continued to beat them.

At the edge of the forest, an animal waited. Blending into the cloak of darkness provided by the underbrush it made no noise nor did it move. The animal simply crouched among the thick undergrowth of young maples and oaks, studying the field which comprised the cow pasture located behind Scott Farley's farm. The animal waited—oblivious to the rain soaking into its brown-black fur and collecting to run off in heavy drops onto the dank ground. The animal, its attention fixed upon the shapes moving ponderously inside the fenced field, remained quiet and motionless, oblivious as well to a small maple limb that dipped repetitively from each strike of a raindrop to brush the pointed top of the animal's erect ear. If one could have observed the animal in its current state, one might have mistaken it for dead—or perhaps even a stuffed taxidermist's trophy.

A disturbance near one of the farm buildings focused the animal's attention. Although other forest creatures—red squirrels, rabbits, chipmunks and birds—hadn't noticed the disturbance, the animal sensed it immediately.

When the disturbance occurred again, the animal moved its head, quickly and confidently, so fast and precise as to have been almost imperceptible. This second disturbance allowed the observing animal the opportunity to target the source of the sound as precisely as radar—placing the location several hundred yards directly in front of it—inside one of the barns.

However, the source of the disturbance was still unknown to the animal, yet too far away for the presence of any distinguishing odors to betray its origin, but the animal was able to identify the source nonetheless, as it was able to employ senses beyond those of its other, more primitive, forest-mates.

Behind the animal, five other identical creatures also waited, blending equally into the blackness. Although they had noted the disturbance within the barn also, they didn't move, waiting instead upon the silent command of their leader.

3

Inside the barn, Scott Farley's only son, Bo, sat at a small desk. He had just slid his chair back and it was this sound, heard above the rain, the cows and the sheep, that the animals at the edge of the woods had heard—and targeted.

Bo was thinking of leaving for home at the same instant that in a house a mile up the road to the north, Michael Sarasin was thinking about tunnels.

Thoughts of leaving, however, soon turned into thoughts of how long it would take him to sell his father's farm so he would be able to return to his own life in town—and, more importantly, buy the Bayliner power boat he'd already picked out. He decided he would start by trying to sell the livestock at the next Wednesday livestock auction in town.

Satisfied with this decision, Bo decided to call it a night. Too tired to bring in the herd though, he decided he'd just leave the doors open on the two barns, confident that if the animals wanted to come inside they could do so of their own accord, which most of them had already done. Bo stood up, stretched his back, twisting from side to side, and walked toward the door.

4

The animals waiting in the woods, if described, might best be likened to some sort of mythological werewolves, or perhaps beasts that were a cross between a bear and a wolf. While the strange animals possessed the bulk and thick hide of the bear, they had the distinct faces and legs of a wolf. Their mouths, however, were more closely akin to a shark than to any land-dwelling creature; triangular-shaped razor-edged teeth filling two distinct rows on each jaw. And, though the animals were big, which might suggest a sluggish or lumbering gait, they were as fast as any other creature that dwelled on the American continent. Likewise, their savagery had no equal, save one, within the natural world to which they had temporarily been granted access.

While the lead animal waited, covertly watching and listening as the human moved about inside its barn, a red squirrel made the fatal mistake of running past its head. A single, lightning-quick movement of the animal's left front leg terminated the squirrel's life in a silent instant. Just as quickly, the rodent was swept off its feet and devoured in a single swallow.

At last, the animal started to move. Although not needed, the now-moderate pattering of the rain hid any sound the animal might have made as it inched forward out of the woods. Behind it, the other animals followed closely in formation.

The lead animal paused momentarily at the wooden fence enclosing the cow pasture, then noiselessly jumped over it. Landing safely on the other side, it waited to sense if its presence had been detected. It hadn't. The leader's five followers then duplicated the action and quickly joined it, now inside the cow pasture, forming a single pack. Together, they moved silently toward a group of three large cows who seemed oblivious to the rain—and to the unnatural intrusion.

Without any indication of audible communication prior to attacking, the six animals neatly divided themselves into three equal groups. Each group then moved upon its respective prey, stalking it with precision by calculating distance and attack speed, angle of jump and target area.

One of the cows lifted its head from the wet grass it had been chewing and gazed into the darkness. Seeing nothing, however, it flared its nostrils and returned to its feeding.

When the attack came, it was without sound: no exclamations of blood lusty shrieks or bursts of snarling rage. Instead, the only recognizable sound was the light patter of the rain on the wet ground mixed with the barely perceptible charge of twenty-four padded feet.

Moving in unison, the animals struck in perfect simultaneity. Their double rows of teeth sunk deeply into the large, bulbous protrusions that comprised the meat of the cows' necks—at once removing the animals' capacity for making noise—and for living. The dripping chunks of neck meat, held firmly within the great jaws of the strange animals, were quickly devoured as easily and completely as was the red squirrel which had proceeded them.

As the animals continued feasting on their reward, Richard Knapp, in a house a mile to the north, ripped into one last chicken leg.

5

In downtown Boyne City, a man was traveling down Main Street in a 1984 Chevy station wagon sporting Georgia license plates. Directly behind him, another car followed—driven by a woman from Texas who had left three young children at home. And while the two people from different parts of the country didn't know each other—each had come for the same purpose.

And so, as Larry Johnston of Georgia and Maria Cedellia of Texas arrived in Boyne City that day, they didn't know nor did they care that already nearly thirty others had arrived before them. They also cared little that many more would arrive after them, including a high school teacher, Mr. Roger Williams of Florida who, at the time, was less than an hour's drive away.

6

Sheriff Bruce Kelly sat in his parked police cruiser next to the hardware store on Main Street and watched the influx of new arrivals. He noted, without professional interest, that almost all of the arriving vehicles had come from out of state. As he watched, he made silent eye contact with many of the drivers though they didn't acknowledge each other in any other way—that is, until the arrival of Larry Johnston.

As Larry and the sheriff regarded each other, the sheriff smiled slightly and the older man left the procession, turning his station wagon onto the side street and parking it near the sheriff's cruiser. Larry stepped out of his car just as Maria Cedellia's Texas Impala glided past. Larry watched Maria's car for a moment, then walked around to the passenger side of the police car, opened the door and got in.

From within the car, both men watched silently as the cars passed in front of them in the darkness and rain. At the same time as the strange influx of arrivals was occurring, a similar, though less noticeable, parallel exodus of long-time residents was also in progress.

The sheriff turned to get a closer look at the man from Georgia. Although they stared knowingly into each other's eyes despite having never met, they said nothing. And as they turned away from each other to look out once again at the rain, the sheriff was able to see the reflection of his own half-grin on the glass of the windshield.

"The farm is ready," the sheriff said.

"Excellent," Larry replied. Several seconds of silence ensued and then, without another word, Larry opened the car door and went out again into the rain.

As the sheriff watched the man walk away, he couldn't help but grin once more.

7

When Bo Farley snapped the light switch in his dead father's barn to its OFF position, he had only enough time to wonder whether the shuffling sound he'd heard at the same time had been caused by the switch or something else. It was the last thought he would ever have.

A dark shape, masked by the blackness inside the barn, suddenly leaped and struck. Bo Farley's severed head hit the ground a full second before the rest of his body. And in less time than it took the Sarasins to clear the remains of their supper from their dining room table, all that remained of Bo Farley were a few spatters of red stickiness and a single glistening fingernail perched atop the corner of a hay bale. Before the following dawn, the fingernail would be casually disregarded by the barn's new inhabitants as a discarded beetle carapace.

The animals had only been gone less than half an hour when the first four cars arrived at the farm. By midnight, roughly five hours later, the number of new tenants had swollen to forty-six.

47

Amanda lay in bed, listening to the Voice. She no longer feared it, but welcomed it and missed it when it left her each night. On this particular night though, she noticed that the Voice sounded different—anxious, but anxious in a good way—excited, maybe even happy. She was glad and hoped that she was part of the reason.

The Voice told her she had done well, and that she had ensured the success of The Calling. But then it cautioned her. It said there was still much to do before The Coming and spoke of a gate. She started to envision the fancy wrought-iron one at Walkens Park, but the Voice immediately got angry and so she swept the image from her mind—one of many tricks the Voice had taught her.

Then the Voice began to speak about Michael. It said he could present a problem and that if this were to occur, something might have to be done about him. When the Voice started to tell her what might have to happen to her brother it so terrified her that she *filtered* the Voice—a trick she had taught herself. She was confident that the Voice didn't know about her special trick as she knew it would cause her trouble if she were to reveal it. By filtering the Voice she was able to listen to a conversation with two minds. One mind listened in order to be able to maintain the flow of the conversation while simultaneously blocking the undesirable thoughts from reaching her other mind, where her awareness resided. She was proud of herself for having acquired this skill, but at the same time knew it would be extremely dangerous for her to be found out. For the most part, she had only used it previously with her family, where it worked well. To this point, she had never tried to use it on the Voice before.

Now it was time to stop filtering and listen to her instructions. During the Voice's discourse, she became scared a couple of times but in each instance successfully resisted the urge to filter again. She realized that she'd been listening for a long time but knew she didn't have to worry about remembering—several nights ago the Voice had taught her a trick for that technique as well.

When it was finally time for the Voice to leave she wasn't sad.

I'm ready, she spoke-thought to the Voice.

Yes, it is time. We must prepare for the Coming. And we must let nothing interfere.

Yes, Amanda replied. *Nothing interfere.*

48

August 6 • Sunday

1

"Michael? Mind if I come in?" Richard asked.

When Michael turned from his desk he saw Richard standing in his bedroom doorway. It was morning, but Michael hadn't yet joined the family for breakfast.

"Sure, come in," he said, then turned back to finish the sentence he was writing before closing his journal. "I was just trying out some of my ideas. Things can take on a different perspective when they're written down as opposed to when all you're doing is thinking about them."

Richard stepped into the room.

"Is there a problem you'd like to talk about? You seemed pretty agitated last night at dinner," Richard said and sat down on the edge of Michael's still unmade bed.

When Michael turned his desk chair around he detected concern reflected in the softness of his grandfather's eyes. But then he reminded himself how his grandfather's presence in their home might in some way affect the future course of events.

As if I really have any idea what those events are going to be.

"I'm worried about Amanda. She's not been acting like herself and I'm thinking it has to do with some of the things Harvey said."

"Like what?" Richard prodded gently.

"Well . . . that she's in danger," he said and paused. Should he go on?

He's the only one I've got. If I don't tell him, who am *I going to tell?*

"Just before you arrived . . . I think I did something."

Richard sat forward and waited for him to continue. Michael tried to relax and, much to his relief, found that he could.

"The two weeks before we went to Mackinac Island is a complete blank for me—I can't remember a single thing from that entire time period."

"Nothing?"

"Absolutely nothing."

"What do you think happened? Did you have an accident? . . ."

The warm concern he felt emanating from his grandfather left him unable to answer, so he asked a question instead. "Do you believe in ghosts . . . spirits?"

Richard pushed himself farther back on the bed. He seemed to be pondering something as he looked past Michael and out the window. "Hmm. Not the kind of question I was expecting," he said and turned back to Michael. "But, I'll tell you what I think. The way I see it is this. Just in the past fifty years or so we've learned an awful lot about a great many things. And it seems that every time we come to an age where we think we can't possibly go any further, it seems we always do. I remember a quote I read by the director of the US Patent Office, a quote I've come to recognize more and more, with each passing day of my life, as a fallacy. He said: 'Everything that *can* be invented *has* been invented.' He said that in the year 1899."

Richard paused and his gaze strayed to the window again before returning his attention to Michael.

"So, I guess what I'm trying to say, in a convoluted sort of way perhaps, is that although we've come a long way in terms of technology and the sciences, I think there's more out there yet to be learned. Perhaps a lot more. I like to imagine it as a whole sky full of big balloons of knowledge," he said and waved his hands above his head while looking at the ceiling as if he could actually envision what he was imagining. "And every once in a while somebody somewhere comes up with the pin that pops one and inside they discover this whole treasure trove of new knowledge. So, in getting back to your question about ghosts, I don't think anyone really knows for sure. I think, however, that the possibility is valid simply because we know absolutely nothing about the world that exists beyond death or even, as some believe, other planes of consciousness. So, I think there're an awful lot of balloons out there yet, and some of them are still a long ways out of reach. Eventually, we'll get to some more of them. And if and when we finally do discover the truth, it's going to be more amazing and wonderful than anything anyone has ever imagined."

Michael was overwhelmed. He hadn't expected such a long, philosophical answer—or one that gave him so much hope—a hope that his grandfather would be the one to understand and perhaps even capable of helping him in a plan he was currently formalizing in his mind.

"I think I was possessed," Michael said, and paused for a reaction to his abrupt pronouncement. Just like before though, Richard didn't smile or laugh or smirk but simply sat quietly and attentively—waiting for him to go on.

"Those two weeks I was . . . out, I think someone—or something—was controlling me. Remember when I told you Harvey said I was responsible for the opening of some sort of tunnels underneath our house? Well, I think he may have been right, and it was this Teufel that used me as his tool to do just that."

"Have you found these tunnels?" Richard asked.

"No. I keep looking—again this morning—but I still can't find anything."

Before continuing, Richard stared down momentarily at the bed. This time when he spoke, Michael had the impression he was doing so reluctantly.

"There could be another explanation. Some kind of medical explanation. I'm no doctor, so I can't tell you for sure.

But maybe there's some sort of problem with the house. You've heard about radon, right?"

"Yeah, sure. But what does—"

"Well, maybe there's some sort of similar problem—not radon per se—but something like it—maybe even something that affects younger people more. Something that might have built up enough of a concentration to cause some sort of amnesiac reaction. You said yourself that when you left, it was sort of 'lifted,' in a slow, gradual sort of way. And then when you came back, maybe you'd somehow developed an immunity or tolerance for the effect, while Amanda, however, being younger and in a weakened state caused by the stress due to her cat's death, has now become . . . infected."

For the next few moments Michael didn't say anything. He looked away, toward his closet door, pausing to consider his grandfather's theory.

"Yeah, I guess it could be something like that but—"

"I want to believe you, Michael, I really do, but I don't think we can close ourselves off to other possibilities."

Michael suddenly became angry. Though ashamed to direct it toward the one person he thought he could count on the most, he nevertheless couldn't repress it.

"I've considered other possibilities too. As much as everyone thinks I *want* to believe this ghost or cult story or whatever the heck it is—I don't! I don't want to believe it any more than any of you . . . mainly 'cause it scares the crap out of me. But I think it's the truth . . . and so I think that what Harvey Olds has been telling me is also the truth." He clasped his hands together in his lap in order to stop their sudden trembling—but not so quick that his grandfather didn't notice.

Downstairs, the phone rang. Immediately, Michael found himself becoming even more tense as both waited for the phone to be answered. A moment later there came a shout from his father.

"Michael! It's for you!"

Michael glanced at Richard, then stood. But as he left his room he stopped for a moment in the doorway and turned to face his grandfather once more.

"And I also think it's time to *do something*. And if you or anyone else doesn't want to help me, then I'll do it myself," he said, and left.

2

Michael took the phone from his father in the kitchen. It was Tedric.

"Michael, I have some good news for you, I think."

Michael's breathing slowed.

Was this going to be it? The first part of some sort of proof?

"What have you found?" he tried to say—and succeeded—though the words came out in a whisper.

"I have a photograph of Michael Morenson. And I also have your book here. I think you'll find that Mr. Morenson and Mr. Mapleson bear quite a remarkable resemblance to one another. In fact, you could probably even say they might be twins."

Michael had been holding the telephone receiver so close and hard against the side of his head that his ear had begun to ache. He relaxed his grip and took a deep breath.

"You're sure?"

"Quite positive. Tell you what, I'll be at the library this afternoon doing some work. The library will be officially closed, but if you want to stop by, I'll let you in."

"Uh . . . yeah. Yeah, I might just do that."

"Michael, are you all right?"

"Uh . . . yes. Yes, Tedric, I am. In fact, I don't think I've felt quite this good in a long time."

"Well," Tedric said and paused, "I should be at the library around one thirty and if you stop by any time before five, I should still be there."

"Thanks, Tedric. You have no idea how much this means to me."

"It was no problem, Michael. No problem at all. Well, gotta go. Guess I'll see you this afternoon then?"

"You can count on it."

Michael said good-bye and hung up the phone. When he looked up, he was surprised to see Richard standing behind him. There was no sign of his father, however.

"What did he have to say?" Richard inquired.

Michael told him.

3

"So, what do you think?" Michael asked his grandfather a few hours later as they sat in the drawing room. Richard was sitting in one of two chairs at the table looking through a *Smithsonian* magazine—one of about half a dozen piled in the table's center.

"Well, I think we need to stop by the library this afternoon and see that photograph. Then . . . if it checks out like Tedric says it does, well . . . then I think we better go have a look at that mine."

It took Michael several seconds to digest what Richard had just said . . . and its implications.

"You mean you believe me?"

"Let's just say, based on the new information, I think some more investigation is in order. I don't know what we'll find—most likely nothing—but it seems the next logical step is to go into that mine and see what there is to be seen . . . I guess you might say it *feels* like the next step," Richard said and grinned.

Michael felt himself grinning right along with him.

"*And—*," Richard continued, "especially in view of the nature of this next step, I think that for now we handle this exclusively on our own—you agree?"

"Absolutely," Michael said without hesitation. "When do you want to go?"

"How does tonight sound?"

4

The rain started again after eleven, but by 12:30 it had stopped. By two o'clock, the clouds had disappeared and the sun was shining. As the temperature soared to 85, the clinging wetness made the air thick and cloying.

Sam found her father sitting in the gazebo in the backyard and wondered how he could stand to be outside in the near steam room-like conditions. She approached through the garden, entered the gazebo and sat down on the bench opposite him. For several minutes they said nothing, enjoying the peaceful serenity of their surroundings, as well as their own quiet company.

Sam couldn't remember the last time she had felt so at peace with her father and was more thankful than she had previously realized up to this point that he had come to stay with them.

"Why'd you leave?" Sam asked.

Richard looked down at his feet and breathed a heavy sigh. When he finally looked up, he turned his head to stare into the garden, deliberately avoiding her eyes. "I just couldn't go on living that kind of life anymore, Samantha. You were right, Sam. You were *always* right."

He turned away again and stared into the woods.

"It wasn't always this way you know. When I first married her she was the sweetest, most loving woman you ever could have seen. Hard to believe, I know. But it's just as hard for me to believe that she has turned into what she is now. For so long I refused to see it. I just kept looking back at the past—seeing her as she used to be. I kept telling myself that one day she would stop being this person she'd become, that she would just stop it all and once again be the woman with whom I first fell in love. But unfortunately, that never happened. And every year it got worse and became more difficult for me to keep the dream alive—the fantasy of what she once was but would never be again. And so finally I decided—life's just too short—I have a daughter who needs me, two wonderful grandchildren I hardly even know . . . it was time to end the charade."

By now Sam's eyes were filled with tears, tears of happiness mostly, knowing her father had been . . . what? Reborn. No longer was he that same cowed man she had seen on so many occasions during visits to the house—a house in which she knew her father lived literally and figuratively in a separate wing from her mother—and had for many years. Here again, for the first time in a very long time, was the father she had once known and always loved.

"Dad? . . ."

Richard lowered his head and stared at his shoes.

"Yes?" he said quietly as he lifted his face to look at her again. When he saw her tears, at first he started to turn away, but then stood and walked over to her. She rose to meet him and they embraced fiercely. As they hugged, Sam tried to keep from crying; tried to be as strong as her father, but failed. After several minutes, they let go of each other and sat down on the bench. Sam clasped her father's hand.

"It's not all your fault, you know. I never gave you the credit you deserved. I saw how you seemed so . . . so subservient to her and I . . . I—"

"Despised me?"

She didn't answer right away and in the silence, she realized he had already supplied the answer. She wiped her eyes with the back of her hand.

"I guess I did. And for that I'm sorry—I'm *really, truly* sorry."

"You have nothing to be sorry about, my dear. It is I who should be asking forgiveness of you. I did nothing for far, far too long. For this I have despised *myself* for a very long time."

Richard put his arm around her and pulled her close.

"I'm sorry, Sam."

"You don't have to be. Not now. It's all behind us now and all we have to do is go on from here."

"Yes, that we certainly can do," Richard said and hesitated before continuing. "I would like to live here, Sam. Not in the same house with you, dear, don't get me wrong. What I mean is, over the years, I've been able to put a little aside. Your mother doesn't know about it. It's in a separate account, in my name. It's enough for me to start fresh."

Sam looked at him with a mixture of hope and confusion.

"The money your mother gave me, I saved some of it. Well, maybe more than some of it, a lot of it actually. With it, I plan to start a new life, up here, in this area. I'd like to be close to you. Close to my grandchildren. You're the only family I have. If you think that would work?"

Sam was suddenly so happy, she started to cry again.

"Of course that would work," she exclaimed, smiling broadly. "That would be wonderful! That would be fantastic!"

Sam hugged her father again and then, holding hands, they talked, over the course of the next hour or more, about houses and land and the kids and the local area, but more than anything they talked about their future. A future where her children would know their grandfather as a man of strength and caring, of hope and affection, of kindness and compassion and would, she was certain, in time, come to love him forever as completely and dearly as she did.

5

Michael and Richard reached the library a few minutes past three in the afternoon. Michael had to knock twice before Tedric heard them.

"I've got it up at my desk," he said when he saw them. Michael wouldn't have thought the old man capable of the excitement he heard in his voice if he hadn't been there to hear it for himself. It made him feel good that he could bring such youthful enthusiasm back into someone's life, even if only for a little while—that is, until he remembered what he was there to confirm.

They followed Tedric up the stairs to his desk. All the lights in the library were off but for a single lamp on the desk. As a result, the stacks of books, hidden in shadow, made Michael feel like a trespasser.

"Here it is," Tedric announced. When he'd reached his desk he turned and handed Michael a book. Michael recognized it as the one containing the picture of "A rare look into a cult meeting." The book was open with the photograph Tedric had obtained from Mr. Morenson's son lying between the open pages.

Michael looked first at the photograph—then at the picture in the book. It was definitely the same person in both pictures. Immediately, he felt a complex thrill of excitement—and dread, as this signified the first of his theories to be proven true. And though he felt a certain vindication, he also realized a new level of fear. For if this aspect of his hypothesis were true—it made the other parts that much more likely to be true as well.

Unable to think of anything to say under the circumstances, he handed the book to his grandfather. After Richard had studied the picture and photograph for several seconds, he put the book down on the desk. When he looked up, his face was long and serious.

"It's enough for me," he proclaimed. Richard looked at Tedric and then turned to Michael. "I think we know what to do next."

"So what *are* you going to do?" Tedric asked. Michael and Richard looked briefly at the librarian—then at each other. Michael could see the caution being recommended in his grandfather's eyes, but he decided the librarian deserved at least some sort of explanation for all the help he had given them.

Tedric continued, "This has something to do with your house, doesn't it? About that strange stuff you said was happening."

"Yes, it does," Michael answered. "We're . . . we're going to go into the copper mine."

"Yer gonna break into the old mine?" Tedric said, so excited that he momentarily slipped into the dialect he usually tried so hard to conceal. "What for?"

"We're not entirely sure," Richard answered.

"You're in some sort of trouble, aren't you, Michael? I can read it in your eyes. Let me help you, I could—"

"No!" Michael said vehemently and immediately wished he could retract the harshness with which he had answered. "You've already helped us enough, Tedric, and I'm extremely grateful but . . . we've got to do the rest on our own. It . . . it could be dangerous."

For a moment Tedric looked hurt; then the excitement came back into his eyes but this time it was an excitement mixed with something else.

"Something strange is going on around here," he said. "And I don't know if this has anything to do with what you guys are doing or what." It took Michael a second to realize the librarian had changed the subject, and another to comprehend what he'd said.

"What do you mean by strange?" Michael asked.

"It's too . . . quiet. And I know how dumb that probably sounds, but it's the only way I can describe it. People I've known all my life are suddenly gone. I called up Keith McDonald this morning—a good friend of mine—and he wasn't home. He's *always* home. So then I called his neighbor, who I also know, and nobody answered there either."

"Are these church-going folks, perhaps? Maybe they were at church?" Richard asked.

"No. And that ain't all of it. When I was driving in today I passed David Richardson. He and his wife were in their car and it looked like they had it all packed up. When I drove by them, I waved but David just looked at me like he didn't know who I was. Thing is, David hates to drive. And I mean that. I don't even think he has a license. It wasn't more than a week ago I remember him telling me he hadn't driven in over a year and he said if he never drove anywhere again it would be too soon."

"Are you sure about this?" Michael asked. It was the only thing he could think of to say at the moment as his mind reeled with disturbing possibilities. How did this new occurrence fit in with the rest of the puzzle? With miners that had started up branch cults in other parts of the country? With strange noises coming from under their house? With the dreams they had been having? With all the things Harvey Olds had said about Teufel and demons and bondings and gates—

Do people in town know something we don't? Maybe they already know what's going to happen? Or is there something more? Something like what happened to me during those two weeks I can't remember? Some sort of mass hallucination . . . or possession.

(Teufel getting rid of the witnesses)

"Of course I'm sure. Something's definitely going on."

Michael wondered then if maybe they had quit having the dreams because they had begun living one instead—a nightmare that was only going to get stranger—and more deadly as it progressed.

"Well, we've taken up enough of your time, Mr. Bentley; we better be leaving now," Richard said and prodded Michael toward the doorway. Michael didn't understand why his grandfather wanted them to leave so suddenly, but he was too busy pondering the questions and implications of what Tedric had just told them to care.

6

After Michael and Richard left, Tedric looked toward the closed door they had gone through and thought about what he should do next. As he sat at his desk, his thoughts echoed those of Michael's declaration of action to his grandfather and he reached a decision. As soon as he was done with his work, he would drive over to the police station. There, he resolved, he would talk to the sheriff himself and see if he could get some answers.

49

By the time Michael and his grandfather finally slipped out of the house, it was after eleven. Richard's silver Jaguar was as quiet as the cat it was named after as he drove it stealthily out of the driveway. They drove for almost a mile before turning on the headlights.

In town, they parked on James Street, as near to the mine entrance as they dared. Only one other car was parked on the street at this hour, a red, older-model Toyota. All the houses on the street were as dark as if they'd been abandoned which caused Michael to remember what Tedric had said about people leaving town.

Just past the Toyota, Michael sensed the presence of the dark hulk of the shed, and momentarily remembered the night he had chased Harvey and how he thought the shed had whispered to him. It seemed like years ago now.

To get to the mine, they first had to cross an open, overgrown lot. They crossed the lot without incident and shortly thereafter, reached the base of Avalanche Mountain. Avalanche Mountain wasn't really a mountain at all but rather a large, steep hill. A sandy path, probably worn by the local kids, guided them up the face to the top. It was a slow climb, but with the moon only days from full, it was possible for it to be successfully negotiated without the risk of using flashlights. By the time they arrived at the boarded-up entrance to the mine, it was midnight.

Within the knapsacks they had brought along, they had flashlights, a hand ax, two hacksaws, a pair of tin snips, a small cross-cut saw, a hammer, a crow bar, some rope, chalk, and a pair of bolt cutters. Once they climbed over the chain-link fence which guarded the mine, it required only the crow bar to pry away several boards at the mine entrance in order to create a hole large enough for them to slip through.

Once inside, Michael couldn't believe how dark it was. Never before had he been in such complete and utter blackness. It lasted for only a moment though as Richard turned on a flashlight. He handed the light to Michael then brought out a second, which he switched on for himself. Immediately, they projected their lights around the floor, walls, ceiling and down the length of the mine tunnel in front of them.

Michael had been expecting something bigger and was surprised to discover the tunnel was only roughly eight feet wide and about seven feet tall. In addition, the air was wet and musty and he was able to pick out several large clumps of fungus and mushrooms growing on the floor in a shallow depression to his right.

Without a word, they began walking. The main corridor was a straight and level path that went for several hundred feet whereupon it opened into a small cavern which presented them with four options: two passages continuing ahead at a slight incline, a third leading off at an angle to their right, roughly level with the main corridor, and finally, a fourth jutting off at a ninety degree angle to their left and sloping steeply downward.

They considered their options briefly in silence before Michael walked forward and chose the level corridor leading off to the right. They followed the corridor for a long time, ignoring countless small side passages that led off it at random intervals. Several times they startled large colonies of rats that scurried away from their lights into cracks or side passages. For a moment, Michael wondered what the rats ate in such an environment before deciding he really didn't want to know.

A moment later they arrived at a strange-looking room that disoriented them at first. It was a cavern, roughly twenty feet in height, sloping away from them at a steep upward angle. Large columns of rock about four feet thick had been left at periodic intervals for support. The cavern, several hundred feet wide, went on for an indeterminate distance. It was as if they had opened a door onto a huge room tilted at a 45-degree angle.

"Looks like they hit a vein here," Richard observed. It was the first thing either of them had said since entering the mine. Michael thought the cavern looked like a large crack that had split the rock for hundreds of feet upward. While the floor of the cavern sloped sharply upward, the rock columns had been constructed vertically.

"Might as well go back the other way; I don't think we'll find anything up there," Michael said and turned to go. Richard followed without comment. On the way back, they took time to briefly explore several side passages, finding one which led to a room containing a small table. In the room, they found several wooden swords, most of them broken. They surmised they had stumbled upon one of the places used by the boys back in the 80s who had played Dungeons and Dragons—an activity which had come to a tragic end with the death of one of them when he had fallen down a ventilation shaft. Michael wondered how—or if—they had ever recovered the boy's body. Then he thought about the rats again and shivered in the cool air of the tunnel.

Back once again at the main junction they next followed the downward-leading shaft, but after traveling only a short ways, found it flooded with polluted greenish water.

In the junction again, this time Michael chose one of the passageways that led to the right and sloped upward. They followed this tunnel for what seemed hours, being sure at each intersection to mark their choice of direction with the chalk they had brought.

"So, how do you think this mine is related to what's happening at the house?" Richard said as they passed under a vertical shaft about a foot in diameter. Shining their lights up at it, they were unable to see an end to it.

"I'm not sure. Harvey thinks there're tunnels everywhere, including under our house—the ones I told you he thinks I opened."

"Did you?"

"I told you, I don't know. I don't remember anything about opening any tunnels and since my talk with Harvey I've looked in the basement lots of times and never found anything.

If there were any tunnel entrance down there, I thought I would have found it by now. Besides, you'd think I'd remember something like that, don't you?"

"One would hope, unless you've been . . . prevented from remembering it."

Michael hadn't wanted to consider this possibility. The mention of it made him shiver again, and the mine suddenly felt even colder than it had a moment ago. In response, he pulled his coat tighter and crossed his arms against the wet chill.

"What I still don't understand is how the miners were involved. Why send them out?" Michael asked.

"To further his power, his reach, perhaps?"

"Maybe, but why? If the gateways were here—"

"Ah, but maybe that was the whole point?"

Michael stopped and looked quizzically at his grandfather, Richard's face a chiseled multitude of gray and black shadows.

"What do you mean?"

"By sending out these—disciples if you will—they could construct other gateways wherever they settled," Richard said.

"Yeah, but I still don't see why. He could possess more people, but why would he want to? What I don't understand about this whole thing is, what were these demons, or whatever they were, getting out of it? Harvey said the cultists would let their possessors 'free' once a month during the dark of the moon, but to me that doesn't seem like it was enough."

Richard pointed his flashlight at a sharp outcropping of rock at roughly knee level.

"I think the answer to that one is obvious—," Richard said, trailing off, to give Michael time to come up with the answer himself. He had it almost immediately.

Souls.

It felt—almost right—but not quite.

"Yeah, maybe you're right, but somehow it still doesn't . . . I guess it seems too, I don't know, *complex* somehow. It's an awful lot of trouble to go to, to snare a few human souls. I'd think there would have been easier ways."

"Perhaps. But I don't really see much else to go on right now."

"And besides, if this was the way for the devil, or this Teufel, to recruit souls for hell, why aren't there more of these cults all over the world? Why just half a dozen or so? If this was just a way of gathering souls, it seems this process should have been going on for hundreds—maybe thousands of years."

"Maybe. But remember what I said this morning. We're always finding new things, new knowledge, inventing new machines. So maybe the devil isn't so smart either and this is something new, something he just figured out how to do in the recent past. Maybe the miners were only a pilot project? And maybe this could be what your Harvey Olds was hinting at was coming—and why we have to stop it now, before it explodes out of control."

Michael said nothing as he considered this idea. As they walked, he noticed that their feet made strange echoes in the tunnel, making it sound as if they were an army instead of just two people. He concluded that he liked his grandfather's idea—but he felt a nagging sensation that something was still missing. He stared ahead into the tunnel.

"Not bad, but I don't know, I still think there's something we're not getting, something we're not seeing."

They walked on in silence until they arrived at a section of the mine that appeared to be the last area to have been worked. Here they found two old drills and several dozen drill bits as well as piles of broken ore that had never been removed, some of it solid chunks of green-encrusted copper. Richard hoisted a piece the size of a football.

"Bet you could make a lot of pennies out of this," he said.

Michael smiled, sat down against the wall and looked at his watch, surprised to see it was nearly four a.m. He started to close his eyes but the darkness instantly brought to the forefront of his consciousness visions that had, so far, only been dancing in the background. He quickly opened his eyes again.

He began to doubt himself. They were in an abandoned copper mine at four o'clock in the morning, talking about cult miners and demons. Had he been overreacting to everything? Was his grandfather just humoring him, or were they both crazy?

Then he remembered the scratches on Amanda's legs, her blank stare at the dinner table, the death of Ghost and their neighbor. He also remembered the sheriff's warning and the moving man's advice. At the same time, he couldn't forget the sound of voices in the night, and passages in a journal that talked of reaching a place which existed, as best he could determine, somewhere beyond earthly death.

As he gazed at his surroundings once again, a small fleck of white caught his attention. Immediately, and without knowing how, he knew what it was, but refused to acknowledge it. From his present vantage point near the floor, the object appeared little bigger than a postage stamp resting in a pile of rubble near a side passage.

"In fact, you would have thought they would have reopened this mine during the Second World War. If it was true what the owner had said and the primary reason for closing it was because of a lack of good help, then it seems it would have been worthwhile opening it again and extracting the copper for the war effort."

Michael barely heard his grandfather's words though. When he tried standing he discovered that his legs were too weak and his arms felt as if he had just finished lifting heavy weights. Finally, he was able to stand but with the change of angle, the spot had disappeared. He dragged himself slowly toward the pile of rocks and when he got there he stopped. The fear that had now assumed control of his insides felt like a gnawing parasite, chewing away at him, consuming him from within. Ignoring the pain for the moment, he bent down and began pulling the rocks away. He tried to convince himself that it hadn't really been what he thought it was and felt an unanticipated laugh rise within himself that he knew he dare not let out. He lifted another rock and then another, his dread escalating with each removed stone. At last he could see the object of his search and knew he could no longer pretend to deny the truth. The fear inside him now was like some bloated living thing, grown fat with what it had consumed, all the while having expanded within him like an alien fetus. After he lifted away one last rock that felt as heavy as the fear which lay inside him, the object was revealed in its entirety. The rocks, it seemed, had been piled in such a way that the object had been invisible but for a single point close to the floor. He wondered briefly who, or what, had piled the rocks. His mouth felt dry and hot as he reached down with a trembling hand and pulled the object free.

It was a small, white sock.

Suddenly, he felt it move in his hand. Whether the movement was real or imagined, he nevertheless gasped and dropped the sock as if it had bitten him.

"What is it?" his grandfather said with alarm from the other side of the cavern. Richard rushed over to where Michael was standing and when he arrived they both stood and stared at the sock on the floor as if neither recognized it. The sock, they both could see, had a ruffled top—like the kind a girl would wear.

Near the top, below the ruffle, were two blue hearts.

Michael was suddenly overwhelmed and his knees buckled and he would have dropped to the floor if his grandfather hadn't caught him.

Images exploded into his mind as if driven there by some form of cerebral injection. At first, he tried stopping them, until he realized what they were and watched as he saw himself walking into the basement, then speaking in a language he didn't understand. He watched in fascination and horror as the Image wall in front of him dissolved to reveal a dark, dirt passage.

As the Image faded, not allowing him sufficient time to view what lay in the tunnel that had opened beyond their basement wall, his imagination took over, producing a picture nearly as vivid as the Image itself. In the picture, he could see Amanda in a trance-like state, responding to voices calling out to her from the basement. Watching her, his attention was drawn to her eyes—sightless and glazed—as she approached the wall. He observed, helpless and in fear, as she stood, immobile, while the wall in front of her slowly dissolved and revealed a wild, hungry-looking beast which immediately beckoned to her. At first, she declined its invitation but as she turned to walk away, the beast reached out and wrapped two hairy-clawed hands around her legs and began dragging her backward into the tunnel. She tried to resist, kicking and pistoning her legs—and eventually the claw hands slipped, leaving red furrows down her legs where she'd pulled free—but not before the beast was able to pull off one of her white socks and take it back into the tunnel with him.

"Michael! Michael, what is it?" his grandfather was shouting at him, shaking him. After he returned to the present despite great difficulty, at first he was unsure as to where he was. Then he looked up into his grandfather's worried eyes and realization slammed into him like a fist closing and squeezing around his heart.

"We have to get back to the house."

"But—"

"I just remembered how I opened the tunnel in the basement. And I also know why you can't see it. I *did* do it!" He grabbed desperately at his grandfather, trying to pull him along. "*Amanda's in danger, we have to get back to the house . . . we have to get back before it's too late! It's Amanda . . . Teufel is after Amanda!*"

PART FOUR

The Gate

Then I saw an angel coming down from heaven, holding in his hand the key of the bottomless pit and a great chain. And he seized the dragon, that ancient serpent, who is the Devil and Satan, and bound him for a thousand years, and threw him into the pit and shut it and sealed it over him, that he should deceive the nations no more, till the thousand years were ended. After that he must be loosed for a little while.

- Revelation 20:1-3

Prologue IV

Boyne City
June 18, 1955 • Saturday

Sylvia Woulfe was dying. The first bullet had struck her in the shoulder; the second had grazed her left side and broken a rib; the third had gone directly into her chest. Her black robe, soaked with blood, clung to her like some groping thing. She felt cold, as if the air was devouring the heat from her body, sucking the warmth from her like a vampire.

She finally reached the hidden tunnel entrance and managed to slip inside unnoticed. The tunnel resembled a black tomb . . . until she saw the light. It was a blue light and she knew its source and let it guide her. Each time she faltered, the light came closer, warming and beckoning.

She walked for what seemed hours before arriving at a small, dead-end cavern perhaps fifteen or twenty feet in diameter. When the last of her strength had drained, she fell to the dirt floor and closed her eyes. On the ground, she smelled musky dirt and blood and something else—like the odor of an animal long dead. Breathing heavily, she pulled herself into a fetal position for warmth, keeping her eyes closed, even as she sensed the approach of the light. The light's caress upon the exposed skin of her face and arms was colder than anything she had ever felt before and she wanted to cry out; yet the overpowering cold had paralyzed her muscles. She tried to move her legs but the robe, now frozen stiff like a steel suit, restrained her. For a moment her skin burned with the severity of the coldness and then she felt nothing. Still, the intensity of the cold increased as the light grew nearer and brighter, now only able to be sensed through her permanently-frozen eyelids. There was a sudden, intense pain again but only for a moment; then it was gone, replaced by an excruciating feeling of exhaustion.

She felt herself slipping away—from the light, out of the tunnel, down into a bottomless darkness.

It was a darkness however that welcomed her, comforted her, warmed her. And . . . in time . . . it became her.

50

August 6 & 7
Sunday Night and Monday

1

Amanda's eyes opened upon a state of semi-darkness. The moon, visible outside her window, shone into her bedroom, bathing it in a milky luster. She listened intently as the Voice called to her. The sound was reassuring as it had been before, but this time it was especially firm, and she knew she needed to obey it at once. As she slipped out of bed, her pillow fell to the floor but she ignored it. Obediently, she crossed her room and opened her bedroom door. The Voice urged her onward and there was no question as to her obeying—its power promising pain in consequence for disobedience.

She padded down the stairs without noise.

From the top of the basement steps, the blue glow was now clearly visible and she descended without hesitation towards the light. From the opposite wall the tunnel gaped—its throat a blackness noticeably darker than the surrounding shadows. It was the perimeter of the tunnel's entranceway that was producing the glowing blue light—the light accentuating the symbols displayed between the two rectangles which formed the border of the tunnel's doorway.

Amanda began to experience a sense of doubt. Something was wrong. The doorway into the tunnel now frightened her.

She knew there was something in there, lurking in the blackness, something . . . bad.

Sensing this, the Voice purred reassurance.

Amanda marveled almost to the point of reverence at the beauty of the blue lights . . . and the hue calmed her and allowed her fear to fade and then disappear. No longer did the black maw of the tunnel disturb her—but instead welcomed her forward. She took several steps closer and as she did the blue intensified into an even more wondrous and calming display.

Lost in the beauty of the blue glow, Amanda stepped, devoid of fear, into the tunnel.

2

When Michael and his grandfather reached the mine entrance they hurriedly pushed themselves through the hole they had made previously. During the egress, Michael felt something sharp gouge his arm but didn't stop to acknowledge the pain. Then he almost lost his balance twice as he raced down the steep hillside on the way back to the car. At the bottom, waiting for his grandfather to catch up, he wondered what would happen if they were already too late.

When Richard reached the car several minutes later, gasping for breath, Michael felt ashamed for having been so inconsiderate. The feeling was quickly pushed aside, though, by a panic that was consuming him more and more with each passing minute.

"A little fast on your feet, aren't you?" Richard said between gasps. "You realize that you're not going to get there any faster if I have a coronary."

Michael could think of nothing to say at the moment, being too apprehensive about Amanda. Before unlocking the doors, Richard opened the trunk to stow their gear. As soon as they got in Richard brought the car to life. No longer any need for stealth, they roared away from the curb and accelerated rapidly through and out of town.

"I'm sure she's going to be all right, Michael," Richard said in an attempt to reassure his grandson as they turned onto

Pleasant Valley Road. In seconds, Richard had the car up to 75. The all-LED readout on the dash bathed the inside of the car in a greenish glow that suddenly made Michael feel nauseous. To avoid its glare he turned aside and looked out the side window at the nearly full moon. He could still see the dash lights reflected in the glass, though, and closed his eyes, seeking relief as the car glided over the rises and dips in the road like a spaceship.

"He's after her, I know it—*I can feel it*—we've got to hurry."

"All right, I believe you. I saw the sock too. I'm going as fast as I can."

Michael wondered briefly what would happen to them, and more importantly to Amanda, if they hit a deer—a real possibility given they were on a deserted country road going 75 miles per hour at just past 5 AM on a Monday morning.

They reached Woulfe House at 5:11 AM and Michael jumped out of the car before Richard had even come to a complete stop. Michael threw open the side door of their house and bolted up the stairs, ignoring the loud pounding sound his shoes made on the bare oaken steps. He paused only long enough to throw on the light switch that turned on the hallway light at the top of the stairs. The light immediately revealed that the door to Amanda's room was standing ajar. He rushed in just as Alan was opening the door from the master bedroom.

"Michael! What on earth's going on here?" he demanded, but Michael ignored him. He ran past his father and down the stairs, taking them three at a time. He was vaguely aware of shouting coming from behind him but ignored it and never slowed his pace.

Richard had only gotten as far as the landing when Michael came flying back down, nearly colliding with him. Richard, without a word, turned and followed.

Richard, Alan and finally Sam, who had by now joined the group, caught up with him in the basement.

"Alan . . . what's—" Sam began but Michael didn't let his mother finish.

"We're too late! *Damn it*, we're too late!" He tried looking everywhere at once and when he finally turned toward his family, he couldn't hold back the tears.

"Michael? Michael, what's wrong?" Sam pleaded. "Oh my God, look at your arm!"

He could already sense his mother's panic—a panic he knew would reach its peak fury once she realized what had happened to Amanda. When he glanced down at his arm he remembered the scratch he had suffered coming out of the mine. It now seemed like a lifetime ago. The blood had run in wild streaks from his wrist to his elbow, and reminded him of the scratches he'd seen on Amanda's legs. A flood of despair threatened to engulf him.

"Where's Amanda, Michael? Do you know where Amanda is?" his father asked, almost pleading.

Michael slowly looked up from his arm and stared at his father. It was several long seconds before he could make his mouth move.

"She's gone . . . we're too late . . . Amanda's gone and it's all my fault," he announced, stating it simply and tiredly as the last, desperately clinging doubts were finally cast aside, replaced by the terror of what he knew now lay ahead.

As he gazed into each of their confused and worried faces, seeing the tears forming in his mother's eyes, he realized the horrible dreams they had all been having had been nothing but a glimpse into future events that even he had not been wholly ready to accept. But now he knew that the real nightmare—for all of them—had actually begun.

As he turned away, his mother suddenly screamed.

3

The kitchen clock read 5:47 after they had completed their search of the house . . . and to their dismay found nothing. Michael was pacing the room like a hungry African zoo cat being taunted by visitors, while Sam was leaning against the counter, alternately chewing the nails on her left hand, then those on her right. She had managed to calm down after her first bout of hysteria—which had lasted several minutes. To

Michael, her outbursts had been expected—her current silence was not—and frightened him even more as he knew it was only the calm before the storm they were now inextricably locked into.

Richard, who seemed to have managed to remain the calmest, sat at the kitchen table listening to the one-sided telephone conversation being conducted between Alan and the police.

"It's my fault," Michael said again, "I shouldn't have left her. I knew she was in danger and I didn't do anything." He continued his pacing, studying the floor in front of him.

"What are you talking about, Michael?" his mother asked. "Do you know what's happened? Do you know where Amanda *is?*" She still hadn't comprehended the true nature of their situation—she was not yet ready to believe. The one unmistakable fact that she had no trouble understanding, though, was that her daughter was gone. "Was . . . was it the animal, Michael?" she said and began crying again.

Seeing his mother's tears instantly brought back the memory of the only other time he had ever seen her like this—when he and Amanda had been found in the woods at Yellowstone. That time, though, her initial cries had been tears of happiness—soon to be replaced by an almost uncontrollable anger directed exclusively at him. It was also an anger, he thought, that had remained present, more or less, ever since that day. And so he found himself anticipating its return and was surprised that it hadn't yet appeared.

Michael stifled a laugh before answering her question. "You could say that . . . an animal called Teufel."

His mother looked like she was about to say something, then stopped when they heard Alan replace the phone receiver.

"They say there's nothing they can do—twenty-four hours and—"

"What!?" Sam exploded. Her eyes were red and watery. Alan rushed to her side and tried to put his arm around her but she pushed him away.

"Amanda's *missing!* She's *gone!* And nobody has any idea where she is. Nobody, that is, except my son. And the only story *he* can come up with sounds like something out of some tabloid rag. And now you're telling me we have to sit around and wait twenty-four hours? *Bull SHIT!*"

"I know, honey, I know, but that's what they said. Twenty-four hours before they can do anything. However, they did say that we could come in later and fill out a missing person's report."

"But . . . how can they? For God's sake, Alan, she's just a child!"

"That's not right," Richard began. "The twenty-four-hour provision should only apply to adults."

"I tried to tell them—"

"*Who* did you tell?" Sam demanded.

"The night dispatcher. She was the only one there. She said they only have one car out and they couldn't let him come all the way out here . . . for . . . a runaway."

"A *runaway?* She's not a runaway—my daughter's been *kidnapped!*"

Richard stood up, backed away from the table and pushed his chair in as if he were about to leave, but then he turned and faced Michael.

"You might as well tell them, Michael. Tell them the *whole* story this time. It looks like we've got the time." Richard motioned for Sam and Alan to take seats at the table.

Sam moved reluctantly toward the proffered seat, then whirled on Michael. He could see the fire in her eyes and knew that what he'd been expecting had finally arrived.

"*You* did this! You *knew* this was going to happen, didn't you?"

Richard spoke, thereby saving him from replying.

"Samantha, please. Listen to what he has to say first."

Sam looked like she was about to say more when she looked from Richard to Michael, then back to Richard again. Finally, she sat down and crossed her arms. Alan sat down next to her. Richard took his original seat and turned his attention to Michael, who discontinued his pacing and, sighing heavily, took the only chair left at the end of the table.

"Well," he began, feeling like he was in a bad detective movie—then wishing that that was all it was. "This is what we know so far . . ."

4

As Michael began his tale, starting from the beginning, Alan patiently listened. And although he had heard most of it before, he had never listened as attentively as he did now for he realized no longer could it be so summarily dismissed. As could be expected in the second telling, Michael's words took on new meaning for him as he struggled to grasp the awful truth that everything his son had been telling him was not only true, but also had everything to do with the disappearance of his daughter. His own share of the blame in Amanda's disappearance did not sit lightly upon him as the sound of Michael's voice carried them through the rest of the morning.

51

1

Michael kept talking until nearly 7 AM. During this time, he told his family everything—not only about his research and what Harvey Olds had said, but also disclosing his own theories and ideas, especially those concerning the mine and the missing miners leaving to start up cults elsewhere across the country. When he came to the part about finding Amanda's sock, Sam broke down and cried uncontrollably on Alan's shoulder while Alan just sat and listened as if in shock. Richard simply looked pensive.

At quarter to eight, Richard volunteered to drive them to the police station. The ride was tensive and quiet, and Michael thought his parents appeared to be stunned. He knew each of them were still trying to come to a personal understanding of what constituted the truth and that even with Amanda's absence as proof, it wouldn't happen for them all at once. He only hoped they could ultimately unite in time to help save her. And he was sure she could be saved—that she was only being held. What specific role Amanda was to play in the unfolding course of events, he still wasn't sure about, though during his retelling of what he did know, he had begun to form some semblance of an idea. And if his idea were correct, then they did have time—but only a little. He could only hope it would be enough.

2

The police station was a small, relatively inconspicuous one-story building constructed of dark brown brick situated on the edge of a residential area in town. When they arrived, it was so quiet around the building that Michael wondered if they were in the right place. A single white police car parked near the back, though, dispelled his concern. Once inside, they discovered to their dismay that they would have to wait until the regular day staff arrived at 8 AM.

The sheriff agreed to see them personally, although it wasn't until 8:09 when they were finally invited into his office. Michael wondered if the delay had been intentional—and decided it probably was.

The interior of the sheriff's office was small and cluttered with papers and files. There were only two chairs and Alan had to remove a large stack of files from one of them before he and Sam could sit down. Richard stood in the corner while Michael positioned himself behind his parents in front of the closed door. Sheriff Kelly was sitting behind his desk, a gas-station-brand insulated mug full of coffee steaming beside him. Michael was surprised that the sheriff didn't have his legs propped up on the corner of the desk—it seemed to be the only missing detail in this drama.

"So, what's this I hear about a missing daughter?"

"Well—," Sam began, then looked at Alan before continuing, "she's . . . disappeared."

"Disappeared?"

Michael thought the expression on the sheriff's face looked like someone upon whom a joke had been relayed but either didn't get it or was waiting to hear if there was more to follow.

As the sheriff waited for the conversation to continue, he took a noisy sip of his coffee after which he continued to hold the mug which had "Blarney Castle" printed on its side in bright yellow letters.

"We found her bedroom empty around five this morning," Sam said. "She was just . . . gone."

"Did you look for her?" the sheriff asked, in a tone which infuriated Michael who looked over at Richard and could tell by the frown on his face that he felt the same way.

"Look?" Sam answered.

"Yeah, you know, *look* for her. Look around the house—the attic, basement, closets."

The sheriff took another sip of his coffee.

"Of *course* we did! That's the *first thing* we did!" Sam said, her voice trembling with anger.

"I see. And did you search outside? The woods? Your barn?"

"Well . . . not exactly," Sam said.

"I see," the sheriff said, making plain to them in the way that he'd said it, that he felt they were wasting his valuable time. "You performed a barely adequate search, and yet you're convinced she's missing and I'm supposed to immediately launch a full-scale search and rescue operation. Is that the picture?" He slammed his coffee mug down as an exclamation point and redirected his attention to paging through several stacks of papers and reports on his desk, as if the papers had suddenly taken on greater importance.

"Now, wait just a second here!" Alan exclaimed, raising his voice. "We're not talking about some disgruntled teenager here—Amanda's just a little girl! She wouldn't go and hide herself at five o'clock in the morning simply because she had nothing else better to do!"

The sheriff paused in his paper shuffling, his irritation now almost imperceptible. When next he spoke, he did so slowly and quietly, as if trying to calm an irate child, "I understand that, Mr. Sarasin. But the standard procedure is twenty-four hours—"

"*Fuck* your twenty-four hours . . !" Alan cried and stood up, shoving his chair back hard. Fortunately, Michael managed to grab it before it went over.

The sheriff acted at first as if he hadn't noticed, but then he too stood up, still holding one of the reports he had been looking at. "Okay, I think I've had about enough of this," he said and walked to the door, shoving by Michael as if he wasn't there. He opened the door and stood beside it, waiting for them to leave. He didn't even bother to look at them as he continued, "And if you haven't filled out the missing persons form, please be sure to do so before leaving. Then go home. If she doesn't show up before, we'll begin looking for her tomorrow."

"Tomor—" Sam began but wasn't allowed to finish.

"*Good day*," Sheriff Bruce Kelly said curtly.

When they had filed out, Sam turned to speak again, but the sheriff shut the door in her face. She hesitated only a moment before opening it. From behind her, Michael could see the sheriff was already sitting back down at his desk. Nor did he seem surprised that his closed door had been ignored—just angry. Michael held his breath.

"All right, *Mr. Sheriff.* You go ahead and sit on your big fat ass until tomorrow. And when we find her—if there's so much as a scratch on her—*I'm going to rip your god-damned balls off!*"

Michael waited for the explosion he felt sure would follow. Behind him, no one made a sound as they waited to see what the sheriff would do. But when the sheriff finally spoke, it was softly, barely above a whisper, as if someone were in church discussing the weather while waiting for the sermon to begin—except as he spoke, his words became harsher and sharper—replete with an authority that would accept nothing less than total obedience.

"Spoken with eloquence, Mrs. Sarasin. And now I'm going to tell *you* something—and this time you *will* listen. We will wait twenty-four hours. At the end of that time, if your daughter has not been found, we will launch a complete and thorough search. And finally—and this is the most important part, Mrs. Sarasin—if you disturb me one more time, I'll throw *your ass* in *my* jail. Do we understand each other?"

Michael let his breath out slowly. The sheriff's reaction was both less and more than he had expected. It was several seconds before his mother responded.

"*Kiss my ass*."

52

"Who *are* all these people?" Tedric asked. He was in Scott Farley's barn—the same barn where all that remained of Scott's son Bo was a forgotten fingernail laying on a hay bale like a lost and forgotten piece of cheap jewelry. Tedric was tied up in a wooden chair.

Tedric had gone to the sheriff yesterday for help and at first the sheriff seemed pleased, even enthusiastic, to hear his tale. The sheriff had gone so far as to offer to take Tedric in his police cruiser out to the Sarasin's place in order to personally check in on their well-being. When they reached the Sarasin's property, however, the sheriff hadn't slowed or even glanced at the house as they raced past it. All of Tedric's questions from that point on had been met with silence.

A man was now coming out of the shadows from behind a large stack of hay. Tedric wasn't sure but thought he'd counted at least a hundred people in the barn. Most of them acted as if they were unaware of anything around them—staring fixedly at whatever was in front of each of them—be it a blank wall or a pile of straw. At first, he had tried to talk to several of them—but in each instance had been ignored. The people simply sat or lay on the bales scattered about the barn as if they were nothing but sacks of grain themselves.

"Well, hello, Mr. Bentley," the stranger said, repositioning himself so as to stand directly in front of him. Tedric immediately felt a dislike for him even though he was the first person to have said anything to him since he had been brought to the farm late yesterday.

"H . . . Hello," Tedric stuttered. Inside, he cursed his fear.

"Oh, pardon me. I don't think we've been introduced. My name is Larry Johnston," the man said but didn't offer his hand. Instead, he smiled. Tedric didn't like the man's smile; it was as if somehow he had too many teeth. "I have a few questions I would like you to answer, Mr. Bentley. If you do so, things will go easy for you. If you do not . . . well, let's just say I can be extremely unpleasant toward those who . . . upset me. Have I made myself clear, Mr. Bentley?" the man said and smiled again and when he did, his tongue seemed to slide about inside his mouth, running behind his teeth, bulging and rippling the surface of his cheeks.

Almost like he's got a snake in his mouth.

"Screw you," Tedric said and had just enough time to enjoy the fact his comment had erased the smile from the man's face when he was hit a stinging blow by a hand he never saw. When he turned back to face Larry, the sheriff was now standing beside him.

"Don't fuck with us, nigger," the sheriff said. "You better cooperate or it's going to get a whole lot worse. And I do mean a *whole lot worse*."

Now both men were grinning. Tedric glared at them.

"First question, Mr. Bentley. Do you know the location of the medallion?" Larry's voice was smooth and calm. Under different circumstances, he would have even sounded friendly—a grandfather inquiring of his grandson the whereabouts of his baseball glove so that they might play catch.

"I don't know—" Tedric began and was immediately hit again. This time he saw the slap come from Larry. Tedric couldn't believe how fast the man could move. And although he was positive Larry had only hit him with his hand, the slap felt like it had come from one of those three-pronged hand rakes gardeners use. The pain across the side of his face grew hotter as blood dripped from his cheek onto his chest.

"Like they say in the movies, Mr. Bentley, *wrong answer*," Larry Johnston said. There was no grin now. "So let's try this again. We have reason to believe that a gold medallion has come into the possession of one of the members of the Sarasin family. We would like to know who that person is and we believe you know the answer. So I will ask you once more,

Mr. Bentley. You would be well advised to answer us truthfully, I assure you. *Who has the medallion?*"

Tedric decided to say nothing this time, hoping a non-answer would go better than another denial. Unfortunately, it didn't. This time the blow came from behind him. He had barely enough time to realize Larry was no longer standing in front of him before the pain blocked everything out. It felt like he had been scalped and, being unable to help himself, cried out which only got him another head-jarring slap from the sheriff. As a result of this last blow, he blacked out.

He didn't know how much later it was when he regained consciousness but when he did, Larry Johnston was still standing in front of him as if he had never moved. There was, however, no sign of the sheriff. Tedric looked directly into Larry Johnston's eyes and at that moment knew, without doubt, that no matter how forthcoming he was, no matter how much he told him—it was never going to be enough.

53

August 7 & 8
Monday Night and Tuesday Morning

1

They had now divided into two teams: Michael and Richard concentrated their efforts on Dr. Woulfe's journals, searching for clues as to the method of opening the tunnel's door while Alan and Sam continued to search for Amanda.

Michael let Richard examine the first volume of Woulfe's notes, hoping his grandfather might find something he had previously missed. Meanwhile, he continued his own examination of the second volume. Although he found several promising leads, nothing afforded him the special insights he was looking for and so desperately needed.

Alan and Samantha began their search with an exhaustive scouring of the basement hoping to find some evidence of the door to "Michael's tunnel." Finding nothing, they proceeded to investigate the other floors, ending their search in the attic. From the house they went outside and searched the carriage house, barn and gazebo before moving into the woods. Alan walked the trail to the Stone Circle and back, while Sam walked to the claw-like willow tree before extending her search into the woods along the perimeter of the field. Neither found anything.

It was early in the afternoon when they regrouped at the house to discuss each other's discoveries but succeeded only in further depressing each other with their lack of results. Since no one felt like eating, they skipped lunch and returned to their respective tasks. Alan and Sam continued their search over a wider area of the woods while Michael and Richard intensified their study of the journals.

By dinner they still hadn't found any clues in the woods or within the strange pages of Dr. Woulfe's notes and so around 6:30, exhausted, they reluctantly broke off the search. In the kitchen, Richard and Alan prepared a meal of stroganoff, peas and tossed salad, while Sam took a nap. No one, though, was much in the mood for eating, so dinner proved to be a somber affair only punctuated at intervals by failed attempts at conversation meant to take their minds off Amanda's plight.

2

Later that night, they tried sleeping but it proved elusive, even for Michael and his grandfather who had been up the entire night before. From the basement, the sounds, not heard in weeks, had now become a constant murmur—at first frightening—then aggravating. To Michael, they no longer sounded like voices in need but rather voices contented . . . or even mocking.

Michael's mind continued to be preoccupied with thoughts of Amanda—something was still bothering him about the peculiar manner of her disappearance. He continued to search for the solution, wrestling with his bed sheets as if trying to wring the answer from them. He felt close to comprehending it—at least he knew the pieces he had to work with—only the job of successfully fitting them together lay ahead of him. But, at the same time, he couldn't shake the feeling that somewhere out there, there was still one large, critical piece of information he didn't have yet. His faith in his ability to acquire this crucial piece was made fragile by the fact that he still had no idea what it could be—and yet the possibility of its existence was strengthened because of his inability to put together what he already possessed into a cohesive, unifying whole by which he could complete the equation.

Why has Amanda been taken? What about the dreams—if they are symbolic representations of future events, what is their origin and why? Is Harvey Olds really Cecil George? If he's not who he says he is, who is he then and how much does he really know and why does he seem to want to help us? Are the animal attacks related to anything? What does Teufel want? Is his goal simply possession of Amanda or is Amanda only part of some greater plan? And what about the missing miners that set up sister cults in other areas of the country? Were the cults really using Teufel—or was Teufel using the cults? Who's making the noises under their house? If Sylvia's body was never found, could it be possible she's still alive and it's actually her, not some imaginary demon called Teufel, that is responsible for everything?

The conflicting feelings tormented him, keeping him awake, holding back the hands of exhaustion. Finally, he gave up trying to sleep and settled back to formulate a plan of attack for the following day. Of one thing he felt certain—to save Amanda he was destined to have to venture into the tunnels. Exactly how he would accomplish this he had no idea. He also had no idea how, once he came face to face with Teufel, he would ever wrest his sister from the clutches of some super-demon—assuming he could ever find him—and if indeed Teufel were even a real entity. Somehow, though, he knew Teufel was every bit as real as Harvey had told him . . . which meant Amanda's life would come down to a single confrontation, a confrontation Michael had no idea how he would win.

3

When Michael awakened and looked at his clock, he was surprised to see it was nearly eight. For the moment, he felt better, if only physically. His plans from the night before now seemed fuzzy, and so as he lay in bed, he went over again what he intended to do. His first step, he knew, would be to retrieve one of the backpack kits from his grandfather's car.

Once he had done this, he would somehow slip into the tunnels through the basement, find Amanda, free her from the clutches of the demon and return with her home to safety.

Simple, right? Like filling in the Grand Canyon using a strainer and a sand box.

The first thing he knew he had to do was determine how to open the tunnel entrance. Knowing he had already done it once though gave him some confidence at least that he could—somehow—do it again.

But then what? Once inside, how was he going to find Amanda in what he could only imagine would be a huge labyrinth of interconnected tunnels which ran only God knew how many miles?

And so, as he got out of bed, he determined to check the basement one more time, to see if there were anything, no matter how minute, they might have missed. Sneaking downstairs, he had assumed both his parents were still asleep. So, upon reaching the first floor, he was surprised when he ran into his father standing in the kitchen, drinking a cup of coffee. His father looked exhausted, as if he had remained awake all night.

"Hey, Michael, you're up early. Know where your grandfather is?"

"No. I just got up. Why?"

"He's not in his room. His car's here but he doesn't seem to be anywhere inside the house."

Michael could hear tired exasperation in his father's voice.

"Did you check the backyard? Maybe he went for a walk?"

"A possibility I suppose."

Alan drank the last of his coffee and set the cup down on the counter. Michael stood aside as he walked past him and headed outside. He waited a few moments, then followed.

Michael walked over to his grandfather's car, opened the driver's side door and found and pulled the latch that opened the trunk. The fact that his grandfather was missing didn't make an impression until he looked in the trunk of the Jaguar—and found only a single backpack remaining.

He's already in the tunnels!? But . . . how!?

He had no idea how his grandfather could have done such a thing, yet he was certain it had somehow happened.

Grabbing the remaining backpack, he returned to the house, and descended into the basement. Turning on the basement lights, he immediately saw, near the northeast corner, where once had been a smooth wall of white-washed cement and fieldstone, was now the gaping maw of a dirt passageway leading away and downward . . . into a tunnel.

For several moments, all he could do was stare into the yawning black mouth of that which previously had been so difficult to comprehend—until now.

Grabbing a piece of scrap paper from the work room, he penned a note to his parents:

Dear Mom and Dad:

I've gone into the tunnels to find Amanda. Please don't try to follow me. I think I know where she is. Try not to worry. I'll be back with her soon.

- Michael

He placed the note on the floor in front of the tunnel entrance. Then, taking a deep breath, he stepped inside.

He never saw the tunnel entrance close itself behind him.

4

Several minutes after Michael entered the tunnels, Samantha found his note. Even before she'd finished reading it, her tears had begun again and her entire body started shaking. A moment later, Alan arrived behind her.

"What's wrong?" he said as he put his arm around her. She handed him Michael's note. As he read it, he knew also where Richard must have gone. He surveyed the basement, but it appeared just as it had every other time they had searched it.

So where is this damn tunnel?

"So now my son is gone too?" Sam began, "And what about Dad, is he? . . ." Alan grabbed and hugged her tightly against him, stifling the rest of her words. He knew he had no answers for her.

In the space of twenty-four hours, three people had vanished and it had now come down to just the two of them.

But the two of us against . . . what?

But Alan could no easier answer his own question than that of his wife.

54

August 8 • Tuesday

1

Michael wondered how his grandfather had managed to open the tunnel when earlier, he had failed. Then he thought how it was he himself must have first opened it.

In a possessed state—my body under the control of Teufel. So, is my grandfather now one of Teufel's disciples—a mindless minion sitting in ambush in some dark crevasse somewhere?

The thought was frightening, but he knew worrying about it was useless.

The tunnels were as black as those of the Sedgwick-Davey Copper Mine and he needed the flashlight to safely guide his way. As he crept farther along, he wondered just how much longer the already well-used flashlight batteries would last. The fear of becoming lost in a total, unforgiving blackness now took up residence at the back of his mind like a hungry ghoul.

Although the tunnel had a dirt floor, Michael wasn't able to see Richard's footprints. Furthermore, the dirt, while obviously previously disturbed, provided no definitive path he could follow.

The passage was narrow, but tall—roughly three feet wide and seven high. He thought about how old it must be and wondered how it had kept from caving in during the last hundred years or so, and then he remembered the noises that had wakened him and his family throughout the last month—sounds which had been suggestive of digging . . . or perhaps construction and repair.

Then, as before, Michael knew there was nothing he could do about it now except continue to be careful. Putting the thought aside for the moment, he wondered again about his grandfather. Did Richard fully comprehend the level of danger he had walked into? And . . . was his grandfather still really Richard Knapp?

He continued his quest down the tunnel and could feel it descending and the air becoming cooler. Fortunately, so far at least, he hadn't come across any branches or junctures where he would be faced with a decision as to a direction. Originally, he had been expecting a huge underground maze, so when the real tunnel appeared to be no more than a single passage, at least so far, it gave him hope—hope that he would be able to find Amanda without as much trouble as he had initially thought—and that they might even be able to find their way back out again without difficulty.

Several minutes later, the dirt floor turned to gray rock while the air remained cool and surprisingly dry. After entering this section of the tunnel, he began encountering branches and junctures at almost every turn. However, as he continued, and his hope faded with each additional juncture, an unanticipated serenity settled over him—a calmness which also infused him with a strange and unanticipated sense of instinctual direction. He stopped and waited for the feeling to pass, but it didn't. He continued walking and as he came to each juncture and side passage, he discovered he was now able to choose a direction without hesitation, fully trusting in this inexplicable feeling which, he thought, might be nothing more than arrogant self-assurance, and yet he didn't think so. Somehow, in his own way, he believed he had tapped into some sort of special power of his own, perhaps even a supernatural power. As he came to this realization, though, he immediately attempted to cast it from his mind, feeling that to focus on such things at great length could ultimately push him over the edge, or, worse, cause him to lose his unexpected gift.

He then reminded himself that his first and only priority was to find his sister.

What his realizations did do, though, was bolster his confidence—that somehow and in some way he was indeed going to find the way to Amanda and when he did—that he would possess the knowledge, power and courage to save her. At the same time, as much as this new confidence had renewed his hope, the sweat on his brow and the growing wetness under his armpits in the midst of the mid-50-degree temperature inside the tunnel attested all too well that he was also very much afraid.

When Michael heard a sudden noise in front of him he stopped, cursing himself for walking so fast and with such recklessness. He wondered if whatever it was that lay in the tunnel ahead of him had therefore heard him first.

He switched off his flashlight and winced in the darkness at the sound of the switch sliding forward—in his mind, it had sounded as loud as a train engine coupling itself to a railway car. He waited and held his breath, but the silence remained as total and complete as the darkness.

2

They arrived in all manner of vehicles from almost every state: Florida, Texas, Oregon, Virginia, Maine, Tennessee, Alaska. They came in cars, trucks, RVs and motorcycles. The middle class drove their mini-vans and SUVs while the rich showed up in their Mercedes and even one black Ferrari. But no matter their vehicle or their station in life they all had come with the same purpose in mind—ironically, a purpose they as yet did not know or understand but at the same time knew that to refuse its Calling was as unthinkable an act as forgetting how to breathe.

As these people passed through town, Sheriff Bruce Kelly carefully observed them from his police cruiser. He was also watching and waiting for a message from Larry Johnston.

While waiting for the message, the sheriff or one of his deputies would periodically take a group of the arriving members out to the farm, which necessitated their driving past the Sarasin house.

Although the sheriff was not keeping track of the numbers, Larry Johnston was. At last count the sheriff had heard (and this had been more than an hour ago when he had taken a Mr. Victor Glime from Kansas out to the farm after Mr. Glime's 1990 Chevrolet Cavalier had blown a front tire not two miles from the Boyne City town limit) that the number of those in attendance had now reached two hundred forty-five.

The gathering of the membership, the sheriff realized, was nearly complete and the thought created a wide grin across his face, a face which had gone unshaven for four days.

55

1

"Who's there?" a voice called out from somewhere in front of Michael and he recognized it instantly. His palm was so sweaty that he nearly dropped his flashlight as relief and exhilaration rippled through him.

"Grandpa?" he asked hesitantly. "Is that you?"

"Michael?"

Michael turned his flashlight back on and almost instantly there appeared an answering glow from ahead. As he ran forward, he tripped on a loose rock, and nearly fell headfirst into Richard.

"Whoa there, son, not so fast. Darn near bowled me over."

"What are you doing here?" Michael asked as they shined their flashlights into each other's faces before redirecting the beams toward the floor. In the gloom which followed, he thought again of the question as to who the man in front of him really was—Richard Knapp, loving grandfather—or someone or something else.

"Well, I certainly could ask you the same question, couldn't I?"

"Sure, but I asked you first." As he waited for an answer, he studied his grandfather's shadowed face.

"I see. Well, I guess I'm here doing the same thing you are—looking for Amanda."

And then Michael felt something. In the same way he had been able to find his way through the tunnels to where he was now—he now felt an affirmation of his belief in his grandfather, confirming that what he'd feared hadn't happened.

But could he trust these new feelings? Were they even *his* feelings? What if his sense of direction and his feeling of trust in his grandfather were all part of a well-conceived plot—the first part of which would be to lead him to Teufel's lair and the second to become the instrument of his own destruction?

But right now there was no other choice. If what he had been feeling were all part of an externally-controlled illusion, then they were up against a force whose strength, he felt, they couldn't best no matter what. But in his heart he didn't believe this. He couldn't accept that what he was feeling was all just some sort of trick. He had to be able to believe in himself; for if he couldn't—who *could* he believe in?

As Michael arrived at this decision, his relief became complete—his grandfather was just who he thought he was. Because Michael *felt* so.

"Any clues?" Michael asked.

"No—nothing. The worst thing is, even if we do find her, how are we ever going to find our way back out of this maze?"

"Good question," he said and thought that this might be an opportune time to disclose his new abilities to Richard—but then decided against it.

"I did find something you might be interested in, though," Richard said and gestured for Michael to follow. "It's just up ahead here in the tunnel." Richard proceeded forward and Michael followed.

They'd walked about a hundred feet before Richard turned right down a side passage where they entered a dead-end cavern about fifteen to twenty feet in diameter. In the center of the cavern's floor rested the remains of a human body. Richard walked into the room and stood behind the body to give Michael a better view. Michael walked ahead slowly and stopped in front of the remains.

He could see there was little left but a rag-draped skeleton and the bones appeared to be nearly the same gray color as the rock on which they lay. Despite what little was left, Michael nevertheless immediately knew the dead person's identity.

"I think . . . this must have been Sylvia."

"I came to the same conclusion," Richard said. "No real way to know for sure though, but it seems logical to me."

"The newspaper reports stated she had been shot but her body never recovered. This might explain it. She was fatally wounded in the raid, but retained enough strength to drag herself down here where she finally died." Michael paused. Then, "Which reminds me. How did you open the tunnels?"

Richard gave a little laugh.

"I found them already open. I simply took it as an invitation."

Richard took a step back from the body to get a closer look at the walls of the cavern. Michael did the same and the first thing he noticed were several large roots coming out of the ceiling in several locations, some snaking their way down the walls and into the floor. And then, without doubt and needing no further proof or explanation, he knew they were now located directly below the great willow that grew in the field by their house—the twisted, gnarled tree in which Michelle Wilson had committed suicide and with which the young artist, Marcus LaSalle, had become obsessed.

"Makes you wonder how many ways there might be into this place," Richard said.

"Yeah. Good point," Michael replied, still fixated on the tree roots. "And makes me wonder how Sylvia managed to get herself all the way here from the Stone Circle before she died." Several uneasy seconds passed without either of them saying anything before Michael spoke again. "Anyway," he said, turning away, "I guess we go on then. There doesn't seem to be anything here that's going to help us."

Michael looked up from the body to see if his grandfather was ready to leave. In the sudden silence, he detected a faint sound behind them, a sort of light shuffling or sliding. He thought at first it was some loose dirt or rocks, perhaps dislodged by their recent passage, now falling to the tunnel floor. Richard was almost to the back wall but at the sound, he turned around. Michael felt vulnerable with his back to the entrance and so he began to turn as well but stopped when he noted the puzzled expression on his grandfather's face.

What? . . .

Michael yelled as something heavy and fast struck him in the back. He had only enough time to register the sound of an animal's snarl and feel a brush of fur against the back of his neck before his face was slammed into the cavern's floor, crushing his forehead and nose against the unyielding stone.

2

Alan watched curiously as for the third time that day, Sheriff Kelly drove past the front of their house. Each time, Alan noted, the sheriff seemed to have a different passenger or passengers with him, as if he had turned over his job as chief law enforcement official for that of chief tourist guide for Boyne City. Alan wondered if the drive-bys were perhaps some sort of surveillance of the family. This time as the car cruised past at a speed well below the posted limit, he noticed that every eye in the police cruiser was turned upon the front of the house. To compound the mystery, Alan even recognized one of the passengers. This particular voyeur was a young man, sitting in the back seat on the driver's side, his face pressed against the window like a suction-cup Garfield. It was the clerk from the hardware store.

As Alan turned away from the window he was startled to find Sam standing in the doorway behind him. He wondered how long she had been there. But, more importantly, when he looked at her, he didn't like what he saw in her eyes—not just fear—but the beginnings of a sense of hopelessness.

"Sam?"

"What's going on, Alan?"

"I think . . . something is about to happen—"

He left the window and walked over to where she was standing.

"What do you mean something's about to happen? Isn't it enough both of our children, and my father, are missing?" Sam said, her voice trembling and breaking on the last word.

"I don't know for sure . . . but I think the sheriff is in on it . . . probably several others, some of the other people in town."

"In on *what?* Are you saying they're involved in Amanda's disappearance?"

Alan paused and thought for a moment about how he should answer. "Yes . . . not directly maybe . . . but I think they're going to come here and try to stop us."

"I don't understand," Sam said, her voice cracking. "Stop us from what? We're not doing anything!"

Alan held her firmly by the shoulders and stared into her eyes.

"*We* may not be doing anything, but I think your father and Michael *are*. And I think they—the sheriff and the others—know about it. Somehow they know and it's of great concern to them."

Alan watched as his wife's face seemed to *change*—the lines of worry fading, eyes that had been dull and wet with tears beginning to sparkle. He was reminded of his son's sudden transformation during their trip to Mackinac Island and was initially nervous.

Then, without another tremble or shake, Sam said simply, "So what are we going to do about it?"

Alan smiled in relief at the return of the sounds of anger and defiance in his wife's voice, two qualities which in times past had often been a cause of trouble in their marriage, but to their detriment had been noticeably absent since Amanda's disappearance. He knew that she needed those strengths now more than ever and was relieved beyond measure to know she had "strapped" them on once again—like twin revolvers on the hips of a gunfighter, fully loaded and primed for battle. Sam was back. The acceptance of the challenge before her had been made, a crucial bridge had been crossed. And, instead of letting herself languish in self-torment and despair, she had chosen to cross the chasm—and was ready to fight. And that, Alan feared, was exactly what they might have to do.

He turned to her and said quietly, "Prepare."

56

1

When Michael struck the rock floor, his flashlight hit the surface even harder and its light immediately went out. At nearly the same time, the other flashlight went down, but stayed on, pointed toward the cavern wall, giving off a feeble, but nevertheless constant glow to about half the room. Michael tasted dirt, rock chips and blood.

Michael's attacker, now on his back, felt light, despite the incredibly heavy blow it had dealt him. It had attached itself to him with claws which had cut through his clothes like knives through paper. He surmised that the animal must have hit him on the run in order to have struck so hard.

He twisted aside and slammed whatever it was that had assaulted him against the rock. He heard a high-pitched squeal of pain and felt the creature relinquish its hold. As he spun around, another creature struck him from the front. Before it hit him, though, he was able to catch a glimpse of his grandfather on the floor wrestling with a hump on his back that looked roughly the size of a wolf.

Before the second creature hit him, Michael was able to raise his hands in front of his chest, to more or less catch the animal as it struck. He was unable to withstand the creature's momentum, though, and it pushed him over backward where he struck the rock floor heavily in the same spot he had just fallen. The fall made him lose most of his grip on the animal so that he could only retain a loose handful of thin wiry hair from the animal's side. Instantly, he felt claws shredding the front of his chest and grabbed at a hairy arm that felt thin and skeletal, yet incredibly strong. With a better grip on his assailant, he rolled over, pinning the creature on top of the corpse of Sylvia Woulfe. He heard and then felt the brittle rib bones of the skeleton shatter beneath him like dry sticks. Grabbing at the rotted skeleton, he managed to free an arm bone to use as a club. When struck, the animal squealed and thrashed, but then surprised Michael with a violent twist—suddenly bolting out from underneath him as if it had never been there. He heard it run down the tunnel, claws tapping against rock. He stood up and braced himself for the next attack but it didn't materialize.

He moved away from the corpse and sat down against the cavern wall to catch his breath. At the same time, he heard what sounded like his grandfather panting heavily from the dark side of the room somewhere in front of him.

"You all right?" he asked.

At first there wasn't a response and he feared that his grandfather might have been killed, and that the sound of the panting he heard was instead another of the creatures waiting in the shadows to attack him.

"Yeah . . . just a few scratches . . . not too bad," Richard said, but Michael could detect what he thought was the pain of more than a few scratches in his voice.

Michael got up and stumbled as he reached toward the wall where the one still functioning flashlight glowed like a waning candle. When he picked up the light and swung it toward the back of the cavern, he located his grandfather lying on the floor against the wall. Richard had managed to sit up and Michael could see that his face was covered with blood and dust. Michael lurched over to where he was and crouched down beside him. In the battle, Richard had indeed suffered more than Michael had. His face was a grid pattern of scratches, and his shirt was in tattered strips. Visible through his shredded shirt was a chest scored with a multitude of long scratches that started at his neck and reached down to his waist.

"Jesus," Michael said under his breath.

"If only He could help us now," Richard replied with a tired wheeze.

As if I needed any more proof of whose side he's on—I sure have it now.

Michael inspected his grandfather's wounds. Although numerous, none appeared deep. There was a lot of blood, though, but he thought—hoped—the bleeding would stop soon.

"What in the *hell* were those things?"

Michael paused a moment, then laughed quietly.

"I think the hell part is the key," he said, then helped Richard take off what was left of his shirt and tied it around his chest as a bandage. "Come on, let's see if you can stand up."

Michael took hold of one of his arms and helped him to his feet. Richard was able to stand, but groaned loudly as he did so.

"I guess they didn't do that much damage after all, but God these scratches hurt!"

"Can you go on?"

"Interesting question. But, do I really have a choice?"

When Michael looked at him, what he saw frightened him. He had been counting on his grandfather for help against Teufel. But now, though he hated to admit it, Richard had transitioned from an asset to a liability.

Richard took Michael's silence as his answer.

"That's what I thought. But then again, I expected nothing less from my number one favorite grandson."

"I'm your only grandson."

Richard smiled. "Yeah, that too," he replied in a whisper Michael barely heard.

Michael led the way out of the cavern, doing his best to support Richard. Fortunately, he could feel the instinct still strong inside him and was eager to get back on the trail. Furthermore, he felt a sense of urgency now, not only in locating Amanda, but also in being able to minimize their chances of running into any more of the creatures that had just attacked them. Although he wasn't sure, he thought that in the encounter there had only been three of them, perhaps four at the most.

And so what's going to happen next time, if instead of three or four, there're six . . . or a dozen?

He didn't want to think about it. One thing though, seemed certain—his grandfather wouldn't survive another attack.

2

At first, the sheriff watched the homeless derelict's approach down Main Street with indifferent contempt.

Harvey Olds, with an apparent disregard for the events that were transpiring, was riding his bike seemingly without a care in the world. About a block from where the sheriff was parked, Harvey stopped, got off his bike and parked it on the sidewalk next to one of the small trees that had been planted two years ago as part of a downtown beautification project.

Next to the sheriff, in the front seat of the police car, sat Larry Johnston.

"What's first?" the sheriff asked, all the while keeping his gaze on Harvey Olds. Harvey was now standing beside his bike as if trying to decide what to do next. Then he stared directly in the sheriff's direction.

Instead of answering though, Larry asked a question.

"What's the situation at the house?"

"Good. I've been by there several times already. I don't think we'll have a problem . . ."

"But? . . ."

The sheriff marveled at the old man's skills in perception—and swore at himself for underestimating him. This time the sheriff turned to look at Larry before answering.

"The kid and old man are still in the tunnels."

"Interesting," Larry said slowly, thoughtfully. "We'll have to come at them from both ends."

"You mean? . . ."

"They're loose, but *controlled.* In fact, it's more than likely the problem has already been taken care of. However, we'll confirm the situation tonight. What, after all, can just a boy and his grandfather do?"

The sheriff reflected on this for a moment then asked, "When do we start?"

"Nine thirty, just after dark. Have you arranged for transportation?"

"It's covered," he said and turned to look in the direction where Harvey Olds had been standing but he was gone.

"Is there a problem?" Larry asked calmly.

"No . . . no prob—" the sheriff started to say when something smashed into the back window of the police car, shattering it with a sound and force like a rifle shot. It sent the sheriff forward off his seat in surprise. A yellow fire brick had landed on the front seat between them.

"What . . . the . . . *hell?*" the sheriff began from his crouched position in the front seat. He drew his gun. With the big automatic in hand, he peered over the front seat and out through the gaping hole now prominent in his car's rear window. Larry also turned and they both scanned the street behind them but saw no sign of their attacker.

Then there was another crash and the windshield evaporated in a dense spray of glass particles, the projectile landing with a thud against the back of Larry's neck.

As Larry grunted and fell toward the sheriff, the passenger side door was thrown wide and Harvey Olds, grinning maniacally, lurched into the car, his knee forcing itself into Larry Johnston's back, pinning him. In nearly the same instant, Harvey put his hands in a strangle-hold on the sheriff's neck. The sheriff hadn't lost the hold on his gun, though, and brought the big Browning up between the arms that were presently trying to choke him and pointed the gun directly at Harvey Olds' forehead. Surprisingly, Harvey's grin spread farther, farther it seemed to the sheriff, than should have been physically possible. He held the gun pointed at Harvey's face for several seconds, giving him one final chance to release his hold.

As the sheriff's air supply depleted—he pulled the trigger.

The sound that reverberated inside the metal shell of the car was like thunder bouncing inside a coffee can. Before the echo died though, the sheriff had the strangest idea that he'd heard laughter just as the gun exploded in his hand and Harvey Olds' head exploded out the passenger side of the car, its remains making an abstract, gruesome design on the sidewalk.

57

1

Alan didn't notice the people until nearly thirty cars had lined up along both sides of the road in front of their house. Most of them seemed content to simply sit in their vehicles, as if waiting for a parade to go by. Others seemed to be aimlessly ambling up and down the road. A few had taken up sitting positions on the grass of their front lawn as if getting ready for a picnic. When Alan first saw them, he immediately questioned himself as to how so many people could have arrived without him having noticed them earlier.

"Sam?" he called, before realizing she was upstairs taking a nap. He left the library and went to the foot of the stairs where he called her name again, louder.

"Yeah?" came a sleepy voice in reply.

He hated to wake her as she had gotten little sleep over the past two days.

"You better come down here!" he yelled and, without waiting for an answer, returned to the library. He peered out the window again to observe the small, but growing group of people that were apparently setting up what he could only think of as a siege outside the front of their house. He didn't turn away from the window until he heard Sam pad into the room behind him. She looked drained. "Look," he said without emotion, holding the edge of the drapery aside.

Sam looked and observed the scene outside their house as if she were observing nothing more than the mail carrier dropping off their daily mail or their neighbor driving by on his huge dual-wheeled tractor.

Except that we haven't seen the mailman since Saturday and our neighbor is dead.

"But what do they *want?*" Sam asked and her voice seemed to catch on something and she cleared her throat.

"I don't know," Alan said, though he had a pretty good idea—but to tell his wife at this point would serve no purpose other than to possibly push her over an edge that she was already too close to. Besides, he thought, somewhere deep down in her own heart, she probably already knew the answer.

A knock at the front door startled them. Alan hadn't remembered seeing anyone approach the house. Whoever it was then had either come in from the opposite side by scaling the porch wall . . . or had been standing at the door the entire time. This last possibility sent a cold shiver down his back like a slow-moving ice cube.

Pushing his face against the glass of the bay window, he was able to discern the identity of the figure standing at their door. Alan wasn't surprised to recognize the young clerk from the hardware store again. The boy was even still wearing his name tag.

Before he turned from the window, Alan observed that the nervous smile that had been on the clerk's face that day in the store had now been replaced by a rigid look of apparent mindless concentration and focus.

2

As Michael continued to rely on his instinct, whose source he still couldn't fathom but which he was afraid to question, he sensed the air in the tunnel growing hotter—like a physical manifestation of the childhood game "hot-cold." As he followed what he was confident was Amanda's trail, the temperature seemed to rise steadily. Each time when he would come to a fork or a juncture involving side passages, cold air wafted out at him from the incorrect passages like the reek emanating from a stale mausoleum.

Their progress was slow and Richard, with each step, seemed to have little breath left in him, thereby necessitating their stopping frequently to rest. Michael was becoming ever more worried about him. To leave him behind however would be to leave him to his death, either at the hands of the creatures that had attacked them earlier in Sylvia's tomb, or from his becoming lost forever in the endless maze of tunnels. Guided now exclusively by Michael's instinct—to separate was out of the question.

They stopped to rest again, this time at a wide junction of five interconnecting passages. "I'm sorry, Michael; my strength seems to have left me. The attack . . . it's left me so tired," Richard said just prior to falling against one of the stone walls and slipping to the floor, his breath coming in wheezing gasps.

"It's all right," Michael said.

Michael listened to his grandfather's tortured breathing, knowing he had no way to help him.

"Do you know where you're going?"

"I think so. Don't ask me to explain how I know, though. It's like nothing I've ever felt before. But somehow, yes, I know where we're going. I also *know* we're on the right track to find Amanda. It's like . . . almost like someone is guiding me."

Richard said nothing, and lowered his head. His breathing had slowed considerably. Somewhere up ahead, Michael heard the distinct sound of dripping water. Ironically, the sound was like that of a ticking clock which made him more acutely aware of the passage of time, time he knew Amanda had precious little of if they were going to find her before it was too late.

When he looked again at his grandfather, Richard was still sitting huddled on the floor. Michael stared at the dried blood on the side of his face and on his shredded clothes.

"We need to keep moving," Michael said.

"Just a few seconds more."

Michael listened more closely to the sound of the dripping water, marking off the seconds by the rhythmic echoing of plinks and plops. The sound was becoming irritating and he was afraid he might lose his instinctual sense of direction while waiting for his grandfather to recover his strength. He started fidgeting, not only at his impatience to resume their trek but to make noise enough to drown out the incessant dripping of the water. He felt like the murderer in the Edgar Allan Poe story, *The Tell-Tale Heart*, pacing back and forth across the floorboards of his home in a maddening attempt to drown out the imagined thumping of his victim's still-beating heart buried beneath his feet.

"Okay," Richard said and stood up slowly. "I'm ready now."

They set off immediately. Michael was nearly fifty feet ahead of Richard before he looked behind to see how his grandfather was progressing. To help him, he forced himself to walk slower and a short while later, they passed the side passage from which Michael realized the sound of the dripping water was coming and then it was behind them. They continued marching, Michael moving as fast as he dared while still allowing his grandfather to keep up. They continued without hesitation—now through the middle corridor of a three-way branch, then unerringly taking rights and lefts into side passages that were now presenting themselves with almost clock-like regularity.

A minute later, Michael heard the first sound of pursuit.

58

1

"What do you want, Charles?" Alan inquired from the foyer. The hardware store clerk was a fuzzy shadow on the other side of the thin curtain covering the front door window. "You and your friends aren't welcome here. You're going to have to leave."

"You know we can't do that, Mr. Sarasin," the store clerk said but this time Alan didn't recognize his voice. It was a cold, mechanical voice—devoid of emotion—or even, perhaps, fear.

"What do you want?" Alan said and realized he had shouted the words.

The same dead, flat voice answered back, as if reciting a pre-programmed response, "You."

"Afraid not . . ."

"The time is nearly here. A new world and a new existence await those of us who Believe. It is however not too late for you to join—He is forgiving. Join with us and become a part of the New Freedom."

"Somehow, I don't think we can do that," Alan said, even as a plethora of questions blossomed in his mind—*New world? New Freedom? What the hell is he talking about?*

Confusion crept into the clerk's voice. "But . . . you must, it is the only way." And then, just as quickly, the confusion was gone, replaced by a cold command, "You must join—or you will be made Gone."

Alan had little doubt as to what the clerk implied by "Gone," though it made it no less easy to comprehend. He left the foyer and locked the outer door. Sam was standing in the archway to the library, her look of determination being all that he required to begin what he knew had to be done next.

2

"We're getting closer to her. I can feel it," Michael said.

He was leading the way, still guided by his unexplainable instinct which allowed him to follow what he was confident was Amanda's trail. They were running now as Michael tried to ignore the disconcerting sound of his grandfather's heavy gulpings of air behind him, knowing that they couldn't slow down and glad that Richard wouldn't let him do so simply on his account. They tripped frequently on the uneven floor—the tunnel construction continuing to alternate between dirt and rock which exacerbated the difficulty of maintaining their pace. The floor of the section they were in now was mostly dirt and Michael assumed they must be near the surface.

He thought they had probably been running uphill for the past twenty minutes. But as they ran, he had kept alert, listening for sounds coming from behind them. For the moment at least, there was nothing.

So maybe I didn't really hear what I thought I did. Maybe it was just more water.

They had now come to another fork in the tunnel, one branch leading right, one left. Michael's instinct, up to that point strong and unerring, was suddenly silent. It took but a moment for him to realize why—their pursuers had found them again. Although he didn't understand the basis for such reasoning, he knew the events were nevertheless connected. As he struggled to decide which direction to take, he could hear the creatures closing in on them—knowing for certain now the sounds for what they were. Richard still hadn't heard them, though, and so Michael forced himself to make a quick decision and turned right.

They were running again and Michael knew his grandfather couldn't continue the pace much longer without a rest. But he also knew that resting wouldn't help them find Amanda and would instead leave them as prey for their relentless pursuers—culminating in an inevitable clash sure to consume more energy than would the running itself.

"How far?" Richard tried to say, but it came out weak and choked.

"We're close," Michael said—for the third time in a row—and kept running. He didn't want his grandfather to hear their pursuers.

The tunnel continued to twist, turning right and then left in sharp bends and long curves and the only thing Michael was sure of was that they seemed to be traveling neither up nor down. The tunnel had become composed exclusively of dirt again and although he wasn't entirely sure, Michael thought he had noticed during the last several minutes some roots coming out from the ceiling and walls at several locations.

Then, without warning, Michael stopped. Richard nearly ran into him and as it was, had to put an arm on his shoulder to halt his progress thereby causing Michael to rock forward to maintain his balance.

Panting loudly in Michael's ear, Richard asked, "What is it?"

For the first time since their escape from Sylvia's tomb, Richard heard their pursuers.

"Oh . . . it's—"

"Quiet!" Michael hissed. Then in a whisper, "Come on! I think I hear her!"

They stumbled ahead half-walking, half-running toward a sudden light whose origin Michael couldn't determine but which produced a warm faint glow in what appeared to be a cavern ahead of them. They broke once more into as much of a full run as they could muster and within moments arrived at a small cavern which seemed to be glowing of its own accord, as if its dirt walls had been covered with the hot coals of a fire. And there before them, highlighted by a bright orange glow, a small form was lying in the middle of the floor.

Richard, despite his nearly overwhelming fatigue, was the first to her side, as much falling to his knees from his own exhaustion as from his attempt to crouch near Amanda's inert body. Amanda lay still on the ground with her arms crossed over her chest. Michael reached her next and knelt down beside her.

"Amanda? Amanda, it's Grandpa. Can you hear me?" His words however produced no immediate effect. Richard held her hand and though her arm was limp, Michael prayed that it was not the limpness of death.

And then, unexpectedly, but with a force that could not be denied, the memory of last summer's trip to Yellowstone suddenly came to him yet again. This was followed almost immediately by the memory of a pitiful, abandoned dog, dragging its broken leg behind itself and whimpering. The memories unreeled themselves like pieces of film. He squeezed his eyes shut in an attempt to drive the pictures from his mind.

"Amanda, it's Michael. Wake up, we have to get out of here."

This time there was a response—a response so sudden and unexpected that Richard stumbled back, lost his balance and fell down.

Amanda sat up, but not in the slow, groggy manner in which a sleeping person normally comes awake, but as if a rope, somehow connected to her head, had been suddenly yanked. She was sitting up in one instant—standing in the next.

Michael, still on his knees, looked up into a face that—while it possessed all the physical characteristics of the person he had known and loved—was no longer the face of his sister, Amanda Sarasin.

59

August 9 • Wednesday Morning

1

"Are they still there?" Sam asked Alan who was standing at their bedroom window. It was early morning, the sun having risen within the last few minutes. On any other day, the glowing red sunrise, displaying banded streaks of orange and purple would have been cause for a silent moment of peaceful reflection.

Because of the physical location of the porch, it was still cloaked in the remaining remnants of the night, and Alan could not yet see the full extent of the encampment outside. However, judging by the number of vehicles that he could see parked along the road, it was obvious the number of visitors had increased substantially since the previous afternoon. At least there had been no more callers at the front door.

Alan and Samantha had used most of the previous night to create a multitude of interior modifications—all of which were not yet done though. Not only had the preparations become a necessity for survival, but the work diverted their minds from the plight of their missing children and Richard.

From the basement, most of the sheets of plywood and other lumber Alan had purchased to repair the gazebo, as well as the extra lumber bought for as yet undetermined future projects, had now been put to use to barricade all the downstairs windows and doors. Presently, only the side windows in the living and drawing rooms were still not covered. The side door, rear porch door and front doors were all locked, nailed shut and reinforced with two-by-sixes. Sometime during the night, their phone service had been disconnected but for the time being at least, they still had electricity.

"Looks like they camped out there all night," Alan said.

"I still don't understand what this is all about," Sam said, her voice full of strain and exhaustion. "We're assuming they want in—but, what if instead, their intent is to keep us from getting *out?*" As Sam walked over closer to where Alan was standing, he moved aside to let her have a better view.

"Not if we believe what our good friend Charles had to say. No, I think what they want is *us*—for whatever reason. On the other hand, it could be as simple as them not wanting us to interfere."

When Sam turned away from the window and faced Alan, he could read the next question in her eyes before she spoke it.

"Interfere with what?"

"I'm not sure. Maybe Amanda? I think it's become pretty obvious though that all of this is somehow related, just like Michael was trying to tell us. And I think that maybe in one way or another it's all related to Amanda . . . or whatever it is they want Amanda for." The pained expression that crossed Sam's face encouraged him to rush on. "What I also see is that these people camped out in our yard are some sort of guard, waiting by our house to see if we get Amanda back—"

"And if we do—"

"Then they'll probably try to take her again," Alan finished. Now they both turned away from the window, looked at one another, then headed downstairs.

On the first floor, the covered windows made it look like it was still night. Furniture, once familiar, now appeared monster-like in the unnatural dimness.

Through a small aperture between two boards nailed across the library windows, Alan finally saw and realized the full extent of their dilemma. There appeared to be at least a hundred and possibly as many as one hundred fifty people camped out in their front yard. He continued watching them while Sam conducted a visual reconnaissance of the rest of the downstairs, checking the condition of each of the observation holes they had left in the boarded-up windows as well as the status of the remaining uncovered windows in the living and drawing rooms. She returned minutes later with her report.

"Looks like we're surrounded. Probably another fifty or seventy-five along the sides and in the backyard," she said, then added quietly, "Now I'm really scared, Alan."

"Yeah . . . me too."

"What about . . . guns?" Sam asked, her voice flat and sounding to Alan like someone in shock—a thought he wasn't prepared to dwell on at the moment.

"I got them out last night . . . after you went upstairs," he said.

As Sam's eyes drifted toward the floor he put his hand on her shoulder.

"We better hurry and get those other windows covered."

They made their way into the living room to conduct a closer inspection of the windows still left to be secured. All the while, Sam stood behind him, surveying the crowd surrounding their house. After he'd checked the windows, Alan glanced outside. He hated being afraid. The worst part of it was that he wasn't exactly sure *what* he was afraid of.

What did they want? Who had assembled them? What were they capable of? And was that what they were—a posted guard meant to keep them from running away with Amanda? Or to keep them locked in? If so, and if they were to eventually be reunited with their daughter, would they ever get through them—that is, assuming Michael and Richard were successful? Had anybody from town noticed what was going on here? Was the sheriff in on it?

But he could find answers to none of these questions and he realized that to guess at answers would only generate more questions.

Turning to Sam he said, "I'll get more wood." He kissed her lightly on the cheek as he walked past her on his way to the basement. But he hadn't traveled more than a few steps when she called out.

"Alan, wait!"

He turned and his gaze immediately moved toward one of the uncovered windows. Something was happening outside. There appeared to be some sort of shock wave rippling through the crowd. The people that had been sitting in the grass, on top of car hoods, or leaning against trees were all now on their feet and standing as if having been called to attention. At the same time, those already standing in the yard or ambling about—had become still. All of them appeared to be attuned to some far-off signal . . . or Calling.

Sam whispered to him, “What are they doing?”

“I don’t know.”

Then, just as suddenly, the people were moving again, assembling themselves with military precision into a single group. As the people lined up, Alan turned to leave the room again.

“Where are you going?” Sam asked after him, frightened.

“I’ll be right back.”

He returned seconds later carrying their guns—a 12-gauge double-barrel shotgun and a Colt .45 automatic, both of which he had inherited from his father but had, until now, never had a use for. As he handed the Colt to Samantha, the first attack began.

2

“Welcome to my lair,” the thing that looked like Amanda but was not Amanda said to them with a voice sounding as if it were coming from a metallic throat filled with crushed stone. The orange glow of the cavern seemed to seep out of the walls and alternately brighten and wane in sync with the inflection of the creature’s words.

As it spoke, time seemed to slow down for Michael, and each event now seemed to be occurring in precise, slow-moving detail. Surveying the outline of the cavern, he carefully noted each feature—every outcropping of rock—every shadow. And then of course there was the thing that looked like his sister but was not, though he immediately realized that this was not entirely true—for on the surface it *was* Amanda—but it was an Amanda possessed by a force he didn't understand. Without question, this was the creature Harvey had warned him about—the creature he had seen in his dreams—exact in every detail except for the white robe. He recognized the clothes the Amanda-thing was wearing—faded blue jeans with red-patched knees, and a blue and white Grand Teton T-shirt—as the clothes he had seen Amanda wear many times before. But, as he looked more closely into her face he noticed that her eyes blazed forth with an intensity totally alien to his sister.

For the most part, the cavern was not especially spacious, about sixty-some feet in diameter, and almost perfectly circular. In addition, it appeared to have only one entrance/exit—the tunnel through which they had just arrived. Suddenly, from this same tunnel behind them, came the unmistakable sounds of the approaching creatures—sharp claws clicking and scraping. In the floor near the wall to the left of the entrance he noticed a long, black crevice at least eight feet wide and fifteen to twenty feet long. He preferred not to care to guess how deep the fissure might be.

He felt as if he had been looking about the cavern for several minutes, while the reality was that Amanda's booming words still seemed to echo within the limited confines of the cave and his grandfather was only now making a response.

"Amanda! We know you're in there somewhere. We're here for you now. Try to talk—"

But when the voice boomed again inside the cavern, echoing and re-echoing, it was as if half a dozen people had spoken in unison, "She is beyond your touch, old fool. You'd do better to concern yourself with your own tenuous existence. My *unmenschlich* are nearly here and I fully intend for them to make quick work of you this time."

Michael looked around and realized they were standing up and had somehow managed to back up several paces from the center of the cavern where the thing that was in possession of his sister stood and talked to them in an inhuman voice never meant to be heard by mortals. Richard was now standing next to and slightly in front of Michael.

"What are you? And why have you taken over my sister?" Michael asked, hoping for what kind of response he didn't know. Some sort of answer he supposed, though what good it would do them under the circumstances he had little idea.

This time when the thing laughed, the sound was deep and rough—as if someone had put metal bolts and nuts into a blender and turned it on low speed. And then the thing which resided inside his sister answered.

"You need not concern yourself with such trivial matters little boy."

"Then take me," Richard said. "Take me instead, whatever you are. She's just a little girl; let her go." Then Richard surprised Michael by taking a step forward.

It took Michael a full second to realize what his grandfather had said. At first, he was angry that Richard had interrupted his questioning.

"Ah, yes, I forget how noble and heroic you humans think you are. You propose a trade old man? And what is the point? You are in no position to bargain. I can have you all just by thinking about it—or simply leave you as fodder for my unmenschlich. And furthermore, what would be the point of a trade—in a short time there will be nothing left for you to go back to—*none of you.*" Then the Amanda-creature grinned and Michael saw, for the first time, what looked like blood dripping from long, sharp, canine teeth. Immediately, he closed his eyes—and tried to drive the Image from his mind. "You have no comprehension of the magnitude of the power swelling about you—a force well beyond your ability to fathom. An unstoppable power that I alone now wield. As such, there will be no escape for any of you."

Richard took another step forward and spoke next in a voice that made Michael glad once again that he was with him.

"If what you say were actually true, then you would have no reason to say it. I think you're hurting—your long sleep has made you groggy and right now you're having trouble holding on. You're not yet as powerful as you think you are or trying to portray yourself as being. Perhaps in time you will regain such strength—but as yet you haven't. We have found you too soon. *I can sense your fear.*"

"Big words for such a pathetic old fool," the thing said. But Michael felt there was some semblance of truth in the words his grandfather had spoken.

Richard shouted, "Amanda! You have to listen to us now! You have to fight Amanda! You have to try to break free! We're here and we can help you. Try to concentrate on the sound of my voice. Just listen to my voice—"

The monster laughed, but Michael's heightened perceptions allowed him to see the momentary grimace which the creature used its laughter to try and conceal.

Michael joined in, "Amanda! It's Michael! We're here to save you, but you have to help us! You have to fight against it Amanda; you're going to have to fight hard, but you can do it; you're a strong girl. We know you can do it!"

And then, before his eyes, Michael could actually see a physical struggle—as Amanda's face bunched itself into folds and wrinkles with the strain. Her eyes seemed to swim in and out of focus, and, at the same time her hands continuously moved up and down, clasping and unclasping. Although Amanda was still a young girl, Michael knew that what mattered in this battle wasn't the strength of muscles and bones, but the strength of wills—an ability not necessarily handicapped by age. But, even as she seemed to be gaining ground, he could see that her will alone wasn't going to be enough. He knew she could put up resistance for a while perhaps but not indefinitely—and it would not be powerful enough for her to break free of the demon's control.

And then Michael felt, physically, a new terror—the cold breath of one of Teufel's unmenschlich at his back. He hadn't heard the creature enter the cavern and he wondered then how many might now be behind him. Richard, deeper into the cavern, turned toward the tunnel entrance—and held up three fingers. Michael could sense the unbridled anticipation of the creatures behind him, held in check, he suspected, only by the unspoken command of their leader standing before them, residing in Amanda's small, fragile body.

Richard Knapp made his next decision quickly and determinedly.

Faster than Michael would have ever thought possible, Richard lunged toward Amanda. The abruptness of the movement caught the creature by surprise and it was unable to react in a retaliatory manner as Richard firmly embraced it. The force of his momentum carried them both backward and together they stumbled several yards farther back into the cavern, falling to the floor, closer to the gaping fissure.

"Now, Amanda, NOW! . . . Come into *me* you bastard . . . come into *ME!*" Richard yelled and fought to hold on to Amanda's suddenly thrashing, fighting form.

Michael remained where he was, transfixed by the struggle—feeling powerless to help. The thing controlling Amanda was making her thrash and twist and struggle like some sort of mad animal. In an instant, they were erect again but Richard was still holding Amanda firmly in his embrace. Her small hands, curled into claws, were being used to grab and tear and scratch. Richard grimaced and cried out as his earlier wounds were reopened and new ones created. He realized however that he could do nothing but hold on and try to minimize the damage to himself. To fight back—to attack the creature—would be to attack and hurt Amanda.

Michael's concentration was abruptly broken when he felt the unmenschlich come alive behind him, the warning as much instinctual as physical. He threw himself to the left and forward in response—out of the direct path of the first creature which shot past him, the animal catching his shirt with a single claw, tearing a gash in the fabric and lightly grazing his back. At almost the same instant, Richard threw Amanda towards him. Caught by surprise, he was unable to catch her properly and grunted as she fell clumsily on top of him, sending him crashing to the floor on his back, and knocking most of the breath out of him. Immediately, intense pain exploded up his spine caused by the protruding rock he had landed on.

A second later, Michael forgot his pain as he heard Richard scream in agony. This sound was the most horrific thing yet—a wail of pain both physical and mental as his grandfather fought for control of his very soul.

As the scream seemed to fade in repetitive echoes, Richard struggled to shout, "Run, Michael! . . . RUN!"

Then Richard screamed again and this time Michael knew that this would be the last sound he would ever utter as Richard Knapp. As the pain of possession consumed his grandfather, he understood what Richard had been trying to do. And then, though it hurt him to do so, he made the only possible decision he could—to leave his grandfather behind. For to leave now would be he and Amanda's one and only chance at escape.

The unmenschlich, momentarily confused by the battle in which their leader was engaged, didn't try, or were unable, to further their attack. But instead of leaving as he had resolved to do, Michael found himself transfixed by the events happening before him. Standing, holding Amanda firmly against him, he watched as Richard's face seemed to elasticize—its features twisting and wrinkling in seemingly impossible configurations—and though his eyes could only see the body that was his grandfather's, some other sense was able to convey the duality of personality now locked in a battle for ultimate possession. His grandfather struggled as if he were actually wrestling with something physical, and as he did so, he moved even farther back into the cavern and it was then that Michael realized the final, horrifying intended culmination of his grandfather's plan as he could see that the gaping crevice situated at the back of the cavern was now less than a dozen feet from the place where Richard was locked in his internal struggle with Teufel.

Michael was undecided as to his next move. Amanda had been saved—entirely through Richard's heroism—could he now just leave his grandfather to commit what would be almost certain suicide? And for that matter, could any of them really know if such a sacrifice would be meaningful? Would it permanently damage Teufel, or would it be nothing more than a minor inconvenience?

He tried not to think about it. The idea that his grandfather might throw his life away in vain was something too horrible to contemplate.

As he wrestled with his decision, he saw Richard move still closer to the edge—the crevice behind him now less than eight feet away. Suddenly, someone spoke. It was Amanda—the real Amanda—now free from the demonic force that had held her captive for three days.

"Michael? Michael, where am I? What's Grandpa *doing?*"

In the sound of his sister's few simple words, words that were the most wonderful thing he thought he had ever heard, he found his answer.

"We have to leave now, Amanda . . . Grandpa's going to stay here . . . so we can get away," he said and it was as if he were listening to someone else talk—someone much stronger and confident than he had ever been. But it was what had to be. He knew there was nothing he could do for his grandfather now—to delay their departure would only make them spectators to something he didn't want to see—and something Amanda *shouldn't* see. They couldn't waste the opportunity Richard was about to give them, one he was going to pay for with his life.

They were somehow able to clamber over the hunched bodies of the nearly dozen unmenschlich that had now gathered behind them, creatures who currently seemed able to do nothing but squeal and growl at their passage. Several of the animals even nipped at each other in frustration and it was then that Michael knew he had gained still another important part of his puzzle. A minute later, he and Amanda found themselves racing down the tunnel—away from the glow of the cavern—back into the welcoming darkness of the tunnels.

At the instant Michael turned his flashlight back on, they heard a far-off scream which, thankfully, faded almost immediately. He tried not to think about what the scream signified and was especially thankful when Amanda didn't ask him about it. Then he wondered if perhaps she had realized the truth of it anyway.

They said nothing as they ran, hand-in-hand, and for the moment, he was able to find relief in the fact that he heard no pursuit. He knew, though, that this would only last a short time—time tragically paid for with their grandfather's life.

Finally, though he'd fought his best to hold it in—he felt a single tear leave his eye and trail coldly down his cheek. Clasping Amanda's hand more fiercely, he ran even faster.

60

The attack, when it came, was curiously without sound. There were no yelled battle cries or outbursts, only a silent, methodical plodding as half the cultists (as Alan now thought of them, though if asked he would not have been able to explain why) marched forward like some kind of army and began to tear, rip and kick at the house. Their actions at first were slow and systematic. However, as the minutes passed with little to no apparent progress, their efforts intensified, yet never exceeded what Alan could only describe as a mechanical, mostly mindless effort.

The cultists attacked without logic, hurling themselves indiscriminately against whatever obstacle was closest to them, ignorant of the fact that while most of the first-floor windows were boarded from the inside, several had not yet been covered. And so, as the attack continued, Alan worked quickly to board up the remaining unprotected windows. After first covering the two in the living room, he moved to the large bay window in the drawing room which by this time had suffered two broken panes. Sam was there, standing guard, so far holding off the cultists using nothing but a broom handle. While Alan worked, he happened to take notice of one of the attackers.

This particular cultist was an older man, of medium height and build, with a full head of thick, snow-white hair. Alan wondered briefly if he was someone's grandfather and this caused him to think momentarily about Richard and then Michael.

To clear his mind, Alan closed his eyes. When he opened them again, he watched as the white-haired man walked forward out of the crowd and started, with his bare hands, to tear at one of the living room windows Alan had just finished covering with several pieces of chipboard. The man began by first breaking the glass (impaling his left hand with several glass shards in the process) and then clawing at the underlying boards like an animal. Alan watched, dumbfounded, as within minutes the wood became slick with the man's blood, which poured freely from his ragged hands. The man seemed oblivious to his wounds though and continued clawing and tearing at the wood. Blood-soaked splinters stuck to his shirt and hair while others accumulated on the ground at his feet. As he continued relentlessly, scattered in the midst of the splinters, Alan could see what looked like fingernails; the old man didn't seem to mind this however for he did not stop, did not slacken his efforts, and did not indicate in any way that he felt even the slightest pain. When his fingers had become little more than bleeding stumps, he was shoved politely but firmly aside by another of the cultists, a black-haired man who looked no older than twenty-five, who took over where the older man had left off, employing the same, mindless modality of attack as his predecessor.

Once Alan had finished covering the bay window, he stood back. As he rested, he wondered why the cultists didn't simply pound their way in instead of digging at the wood like a bunch of rats. Then he remembered the sounds they had first heard coming from underneath the house and wondered if whatever it was that they had heard down there before was now responsible for the mind control of these cultists.

Mind control. Jesus.

It was mid-morning when the shooting began.

It started with a woman who on the surface looked like an ordinary forty-something housewife, complete with a floral print dress. She was slim and fairly tall and was the first to actually break in, entering through the window in the side door on the landing between the basement and first floor. Alan however was waiting for her as she crashed through the last of the plywood, large splinters of wood tangling in her brown hair. When she finally pushed herself through, she clumsily fell onto the landing in a jumble of arms and legs. After picking herself up, she cast a grin at Alan as he stood before her pointing the cannon barrels of the shotgun directly at her face, less than four feet away. But along with her grin came a knife, extracted from the folds of her dress, a dress Alan had time to think was probably hand-sewn. With the woman's second lunge of the knife, Alan fired the left barrel of the shotgun. The blast caught the woman full in the face, sending her backward in a wild flailing of limbs against the door. But, like Arnold Schwarzenegger in *The Terminator,* she merely picked herself back up, slowly, and without apparent pain. Alan even imagined that the grin was still present on her face, though what came after him next contained on its shoulders little more than a ragged hole where a face had once been. Barely recognizable, he could still see a single remaining tooth, a large molar, visible toward the back of the mass of red, dripping tissue. Impossibly, her right eye had somehow survived, though it was now canted downward, and it was at the precise moment when Alan looked into this single, glazed orb that he pulled the trigger on the second barrel, the second blast all but decapitating her.

Alan had never killed anyone before and so, staring at the blood on the wall and door, his hands and body began to tremble. As he remained standing and shaking, a dizzy, nauseous feeling seeped into him, as if he were a sponge slowly absorbing some thick, cold oil. The feeling lasted several minutes then faded into gray numbness.

With difficulty, Alan pushed the remains of the woman's body out the window and nailed on more wood to re-cover the hole. Almost immediately after reinforcing the barricade, there was an explosion. Instantly, he recognized the long-ago familiar sound of the Colt automatic—the shot, he realized, had come from the direction of the library.

In two leaps he bounded up the stairs from the landing and ran into the library where he found Sam holding the Colt with the barrel pointed at a dinner-plate-sized hole in the wood covering the bay window. She was shaking and crying as Alan went over to her and helped her lower the gun. She managed to stop crying but seemed barely conscious of his presence as she remained immobile, standing and staring at the hole. He walked over to the window and looked out. Lying on the porch was a body. The attacker had been a boy, probably no more than sixteen years old. He lay motionless on his back and Alan could see a bloody hole next to his nose, just under his right eye. A pool of blood was rapidly spreading across the porch from under the boy's head.

The boy on the porch and the woman at the side door were only the start. As the day progressed, the situation worsened. Their attackers were relentless, even as the bodies began piling up at the places where the cultists managed to gain a momentary foothold into the house. However, no sooner would Alan and Sam reseal one entrance, Sam doing the nailing and Alan keeping the way clear, then another break-in would occur somewhere else. For the rest of the day, they ran from window to window and door to door as outside, the dead bodies continued to collect in growing, sickening heaps. By late evening they estimated there were at least seventy dead, though it seemed to do nothing to deter the rest of the attackers who came on continuously and mindlessly, stepping on or pushing aside the corpses of their fallen comrades in order to enact their own personal assaults.

A few minutes after eight in the evening, the attack suddenly stopped. It was as if a silent order had been given, although neither Alan nor Sam could imagine how such a communication could have been delivered simultaneously to every one of the attackers.

Their respite, however, was brief. Within half an hour, the attack had begun again.

61

1

At the moment, Michael could afford neither the time nor the emotional energy to dwell on his grandfather's sacrifice; his grieving would have to come later. Now, he had room in his mind only for thoughts that had to do with finding his and Amanda's way out of the tunnels and back to the house. Already they had heard sounds of pursuit more than once but had managed to successfully evade the unmenschlich each time. Fortunately, he could feel the instinct strong within him once again, leading him in a direction he could only hope would lead back to their house. He had trusted his new instinct completely, even while not fully understanding it, to lead him to Amanda and in that instance it had worked. So, he felt he couldn't abandon it now—regardless of whether he felt he could still trust it.

Most of the time they ran, Amanda following behind him as best she could. She hadn't said much since her rescue and when Michael yanked her hand whenever she slowed, she didn't protest. He wondered briefly if the person whom he was rescuing was really still the sweet, full-of-life, little girl he used to know—and felt the anger inside him waiting to explode if any permanent damage resulting from her ordeal were later discovered.

Michael's thoughts dissolved like a dream and he halted when a group of six unmenschlich appeared in the tunnel before them. In an instant, the air became hot and Michael struggled to breathe. Upon sighting their prey, two of the animals in the front of the pack bared their teeth and growled.

2

At the house the battle continued to rage but was no longer as fierce. Abandoning their brute force approach of attacking against all fronts at once, the cultists had now regrouped and gathered their numbers together to strike en masse at a single point. So far, they had tried this tactic twice (the side entrance and the kitchen window)—and in each attempt failed—but only barely.

"How's our ammunition?" Sam asked as they waited for the next attack. They were now at the back of the house, sitting on the floor underneath the windows in the formal dining room. After the last attack, the cultists had fled into the woods behind the gazebo and there was currently no visible sign of them. It was almost nine-thirty and nearly dark.

"Well—" Alan began, hesitating.

"Tell me, Alan," Sam said, her voice now stronger and more controlled. Despite the visible devastation of the day, Alan felt that his wife seemed to have become more resigned, more accepting of what was happening to them—and somehow had managed to gain an inner strength from it—while at the same time he feared he was moving in the opposite direction. Through the broken windows, the stench of death was making him nauseous. He wondered if he would ever be able to eat again after what he had seen.

"It's not very good," he said finally, avoiding Sam's gaze.

"I have to know, Alan." She reached out and placed her hand lightly on his wrist.

He pointed to a box of ammunition on the edge of the dining room table.

"That half box for the Colt is the last . . . and for the shotgun . . . ten shells."

An uncomfortable silence followed his review. A moment later, it was broken by the sound of the half-hour chime from the living room mantle clock.

"I guess we're lucky . . . lucky we even had as much as we did," she said finally and looked over at him again. This time, though, he met her gaze and he was aware of so much strength in her voice and such a look of defiance in her eyes that he wanted to reach out and hug her—but exhaustion kept him where he was. Instead, he simply smiled.

Alan turned away and returned his attention to the carnage outside. More than one hundred bodies—what they calculated to be only about a third of the force that had begun the attack—lay strewn outside their home. Most of these were lying in haphazard piles. Others, farther away, remained where they had been cast aside by their comrades. The living seemed oblivious of the dead—walking on them, kicking them, or simply just shoving them aside.

Earlier in the afternoon, to gain a better assessment of their situation, he had stuck his head out one of the upstairs attic windows and surveyed the battlefield below, observing at the same time the side of the house—the once pristine white sides horribly stained by wild abstracts of splattered blood defacing the surface like red graffiti.

Although in his heart he perhaps already knew it, his acceptance of their fate that there would be no one coming to rescue them was made final when, just after one o'clock that afternoon, he had seen the sheriff cruise slowly past in his patrol car. The sheriff had stopped in front of their house for a brief moment, as if checking things over, then moved on with a grim, satisfied smile.

"We really should be watching outside right now," Sam said. She rose first to a half crouch, then stood up. She moved to take a position as an observer before the gap left between the two-by-sixes covering the window. Alan rose and joined her. As they surveyed the rapidly darkening forest, alert for any movement that might signal the next attack, he thought about asking Sam what would happen when they ran out of bullets, but couldn't bring himself to do it.

One of the possibilities for survival, which he'd foreseen, involved barricading themselves in the basement. Although he knew that by doing this they would be backing themselves into a dead end, such a position would be at the same time the easiest to defend with but a single way in or out. Another possibility involved the mysterious, as-yet unseen tunnel, but finding the means of opening it at this point made it too unlikely a prospect. And finally, there was the possibility he didn't want to think about, the choice of last resort. By trying not to think about it, though, he caused the opposite to occur, and, in fact, had been unable to shake it from his mind for most of the afternoon.

But what really bothered Alan, and was the main factor in the erosion of his own self-confidence which was, to his regret, inversely proportional to Sam's apparent increasing level of control and acceptance, involved simple *understanding* or the lack of. Despite all that had happened and what they had been through together, the *why* of it all had as yet eluded him and thereby fueled his unending frustration.

Why were they being so relentlessly attacked? What did this force, Teufel, have to gain by their destruction that he would be so willing to expend such monumental resources? Were the cultists really after them—or something else? If not them, what was in the house, or about the house, that was so valuable? And, of course, what was Amanda's connection, or use, in it all?

As usual, Alan had no answers.

"I'll be back in a minute," he said and turned from the window.

"Where are you going?"

Alan glanced at his wife—and didn't know what to tell her. Where *was* he going? He realized he wasn't sure; he just knew he had suddenly felt an inexplicable need to go and get something. Then, as he thought more about it, the answer came to him—the medallion—he had to retrieve the medallion. The need had now become a sudden, undeniable urge.

But why?

But he realized that he didn't know the answer to this question either.

62

1

Michael noticed that one of the animals near the front of the pack looked different from the others. Immediately obvious was the fact that it was the largest of the creatures present, but there was something more. When he looked more closely at the creature's grinning mouth, he saw not one, but two sets of sharply-pointed, shark-like teeth. This caused him to imagine those same teeth tearing into the body of his grandfather, slicing into arms and legs and then he thought that he could actually see a piece of blue flannel shirt hanging from one of the animal's large fangs. But then he blinked and it was gone, replaced by a suggestive shadow.

Then, as if a gate had been opened on a pack of wild dogs, the unmenschlich rushed them with bared teeth and extended claws. Without thinking or even cognizant of what he was about to do, Michael shouted at them.

"Frugh-har! An sam lur grag!" he said, uttering the strange and inexplicable sounds from the deepest recesses of his throat without conscious effort or thought, almost as if . . .

. . . almost as if someone had spoken for me.

Instantly, the creatures halted their pursuit and looked at him in confusion. Their mouths closed and in frustration they began batting and nipping at each other—but advancing no farther.

Without hesitation, Michael grabbed Amanda's hand and bolted down the tunnel in the direction from which they had just come. Before they had gone far, Amanda spoke, her words coming out choppy, in sync with her running.

"Michael . . . how did you . . . do that?"

Michael slowed, then stopped, pausing to catch his breath.

"I have no idea. Just when I think I've got some of this mystery figured out, something else happens that throws it all to the wind."

"Do you know what you just said?"

"Not a clue. And if you asked me to repeat it, I couldn't—I've already forgotten the words—if that's even what they were."

And then Michael realized something else—Amanda was, once again, Amanda. His fear about her having been *damaged*—was gone. His sister was going to be all right, though under the circumstances the thought brought only momentary joy.

(going to be all right? aren't we forgetting something here? like the small matter of being able to find your way back home, Dorothy?)

Before he could focus on this turn of events further, a sound—he couldn't distinguish whether real or imagined—made him turn and glance behind them. But when he shined his flashlight into the tunnel all he could see were shadows.

"Come on, we better keep moving. I don't think we should count on me being able to save us like that again."

They continued to run for what seemed nearly half an hour—the whole time trying to listen over the sound of their own footfalls and labored breathing for the sounds of pursuit—but hearing nothing. Michael felt that at least they were back on the right trail again. Minutes later he was sure of it—when before them he saw the tunnel rise up sharply—and end at a wooden door.

Michael remembered what his grandfather had said about the possibility of there being many different ways into and out of the tunnels.

He stepped forward with trepidation, put his hand on the doorknob and slowly opened the door. It swung out easily and without sound, and he took a deep breath as a refreshing tidal wash of sweet evening air poured down upon their exhausted bodies and into the tunnel.

It was evening, sometime around nine o'clock, Michael surmised when he helped Amanda climb out of the previously hidden tunnel entrance. They found themselves in the long grass of the field, several hundred feet on the other side of the tree—The Claw—on the side farthest from their house. When he looked at the house, though, any jubilation at having escaped the confines of the tunnels was swept away with sudden despair. Even from as far away as they were, he could clearly see the clustered hordes of encamped cultists. As they stood looking, the still air was interrupted by the sound of two muffled gunfire blasts.

"What are they doing to our house?" Amanda asked.

"I'm not sure . . . but I'd say it looks like we're going to have to go back the way we came," he began, but then was stopped by the realization of what he was witnessing. As more of the connections fell into place, he continued, "To get into the house we'll have to go through the tunnels in order to get back in through the basement. There's no way we can go through them," he said—despite being barely conscious of the sound of his own voice.

So this is what it's all about—the miners who disappeared. They were commanded to start cults of their own . . . and now when the troops are needed, they have obeyed the summons . . . obeyed the summons of The Calling and returned. Only question is . . . why? Why are they here, or what have they been Called here, to do? Why are they attacking our house?

He was jolted out of his brief reverie when he realized Amanda had said something. She repeated it.

"No!"

"Amanda . . . we have to. Mom and Dad are back at the house. The only way we're going to get to them is to go back through the tunnels and in through the basement."

"No! I don't want to," she said again, sounding like a petulant three-year-old.

Before he could think of a suitable response, he detected movement out of the corner of his eye. He turned, but saw nothing. Then, as he turned back to Amanda to tell her she had no choice, he glanced to his right—and saw him standing about a hundred feet away, still wearing the same dirty clothes and coat. Michael wondered at first how he could see him so well in the gloom, then realized it was because there was some kind of glow emanating from his body—like a single beam of sunlight coming from some unseen hole in the sky shining directly upon him.

"Harvey?" Michael began, not realizing he had spoken the name at a decibel level no louder than a whisper. Harvey's answer, when it came, was spoken softly as well, as if Harvey were whispering to him from a distance of no more than a couple of feet instead of a hundred. Furthermore, the sound of Harvey's voice was like nothing he had ever heard before—as gentle as that of a loving father when consoling his sick child, or of a priest extolling the virtues of one's dearly departed—a sound full of warmth and depthless compassion. The tone of Harvey's voice felt like magic in the air—even while it raised the flesh on Michael's arms.

"Yes, Michael, it's me. My work here is nearly done. You have done well—truly a hero by anyone's standards . . . but we both know the hardest is yet to come. I hope you realize now that my trust has always been in *you*—that I recognized your indomitable strength even when others—and even you—did not. But the potential negative consequences of my continued interference are now as great as those for failure, and so I'm afraid this is good-bye."

Michael's mind once again filled with questions and—for the first time—surprisingly with answers. But the questions, answers and realizations all mixed themselves together, creating a momentary chaos of inseparable emotions. It was all too much too soon, as the many and varied sections of the puzzle he felt his life had become, now clicked and locked themselves together at a frightening pace. When he once again opened his mouth to speak, he could see that the image of Harvey Olds was already fading and that waving strands of field grass were now visible behind him—visible *through* his body.

Is this another dream?

"Wait!" Michael tried to yell, but as before, it came out only as a whisper and was immediately snatched away by a gust of wind as if an unseen hand had plucked the word out of the air before it could travel any farther.

"I'm sorry, Michael . . . you're on your own now . . . there's no more we can do for you," he heard Harvey say, this time without seeing his mouth move. And then the words—that is, all except one—faded along with Harvey's image. The word that remained, though, kept repeating itself in his mind . . . *we . . . we . . . there's no more WE can do for you.*

He tried to say something more but the man he had once thought of as little more than an eccentric street wanderer had now vanished—just like the day he had in the Stone Circle. He continued staring at the spot where Harvey had stood—and disappeared before his eyes—and suddenly felt more alone than he had since his family had moved into their new house.

"I guess you're right," Amanda said.

"Huh?" Michael replied, turning his attention back to his sister.

"I *said*, I guess you're right—we're going to have to go back into the tunnels—as long as you know the way."

And I suppose I have you *to thank for this too, am I right, Harvey? Or whatever it is that you were . . . or are. So just how much of my sudden good fortune* do *I have to thank you for? Perhaps that little episode back in the tunnel with the unmenschlich—would that do for starters? And how about my amazing sense of direction? Was that a part of your bag of tricks too? So just what in the hell were you, Mr. Harvey Olds? Some sort of guardian angel?*

Michael almost felt like laughing, and maybe would have if he hadn't felt it was closer to the truth than he wanted to admit. Instead, he looked down at his sister.

"But . . . didn't you *see?*" he began, but already he could see the answer in her eyes.

As he glanced back at the house, he again heard the sound of distant gunfire. With each passing hour he seemed to be finding out more, and yet, at the same time, feeling like he knew less and less. One thing he knew for sure, though, and that was, as Harvey had indicated, things were going to get worse before they got better.

Yeah, and I can hardly wait to see what worse looks like. My grandfather is dead, our house is under attack and we're about to run back into an underground maze full of creatures from hell's abyss, and one powerful and nasty demon. Just how much worse can things get?

A moment later, Michael led Amanda back into the tunnel.

2

When Alan returned to the dining room with the medallion tucked safely into his pocket (for what purpose he still didn't know, but having it with him made him feel somehow reassured), he thought about the questions he had been asking himself before the sudden urge to retrieve the medallion had overcome him. Before he could ponder such questions further, though, a white flash caught his eye. Sam saw it also and latched onto his arm hard enough to make him wince. Immediately, he felt his muscles tense, preparing themselves for what could be the final attack ominously signaled by the flecks of color which were now flashing with depressing regularity among the black tree trunks.

And then he had the strangest sensation that something was terribly *wrong* and he frowned. The cultists were no longer advancing, just . . . moving around . . . not forward but simply back and forth. Their movement seemed too purposeful, too intentional, almost as if the cultists *wanted* Alan and Sam to see them.

But if that's the case . . . that could only mean . . .

He wasn't able to complete his thought as in the next instant an explosion rocked the house. It had come from upstairs.

"My God, what was that?" Sam said, obviously startled.

So, their distraction had worked, he thought as his gaze rested once more on the nearly empty box of ammunition that was all that remained for the Colt. Then he looked over at Sam—and saw his own suppositions become a terrifying reality.

The cultists had finally found a way in.

63

1

Following his instinctual sense, Michael was disappointed as, for the third time in the course of the last thirty minutes, his probing flashlight revealed yet another passageway ending abruptly at a solid stone wall.

When Michael turned around he was met by Amanda's stare. During the course of the last half-hour she had said less and less and he was beginning to wonder if she had slipped into some sort of post-traumatic disorder.

He remembered the desperate battle going on back at the house and the memory instilled a new sense of urgency within him. He turned abruptly, setting off back the way they had come. As he walked, he sensed the narrow confines of the tunnel pressing in on him almost as if he and Amanda were traveling inside a throat that was trying to close upon and swallow them.

They walked for another half-hour in silence, Amanda never falling far behind. At periodic intervals he would stop and listen for sounds of pursuit or anything that might indicate the presence of a waiting ambush: he was most concerned with the latter possibility. He felt reasonably confident that they would have at least some warning if they were being followed—but if the creatures were already somewhere up ahead waiting to attack them in a boiling, clawing horde . . .

And so as they walked, Michael passed each side opening and junction with trepidation, his body tensed for an attack that, thankfully so far, had never come. It was this constant up-down, roller-coaster ride between tension and relief that was taking the biggest toll on his body's resources—more it seemed than the miles they had covered within the maze of tunnels.

Passing by another opening, a small tunnel not even big enough for Amanda to walk upright in, he stopped when he thought he had heard a noise. He turned to Amanda and put his finger to his lips. She stopped also and, nodding her understanding, remained silent.

He listened carefully but the sound, if it had indeed been a sound and not something created out of his imagination, didn't repeat itself. He suddenly felt a chill—the cold seeping up from his feet all the way to his neck, as if he were being slowly immersed into a well of cold water. That they were close to *something*, he felt certain. Like his former instinctual ability that had enabled him to know in each instance the correct tunnel to take, it now seemed to allow him to sense the presence of something close by. Likewise, he somehow knew it was a presence, or proximity, that was not that of a waiting ambush or an unknown danger, but rather a presence of power—of a throbbing, emanating evil. To acknowledge this presence, he knew, could only mean one thing—that Teufel was near. He waited, listening intently for several minutes, hoping to hear the sound again, but there was nothing.

"What is it?" Amanda whispered.

"I'm not sure. Nothing, I guess." He took his sister's hand which felt cold and dry. "Let's go."

They continued through the tunnel more slowly than before, peering around each corner even more cautiously. They walked for another quarter hour this way, along the same passageway, when Michael began to experience doubt about his earlier feeling and a moment later, it had evaporated. As they continued walking, now at a faster pace, Michael felt that the tunnel was now widening. After a couple more minutes he was positive of it—the tunnel that they were in was now both wider and taller than any of the passages they had been in previously.

At the junction where a much smaller passageway led to their right at a sharp upward angle, he stopped again to listen—and this time was certain that he *did* hear something. It was a continuous tone—a sort of humming—or more accurately, a vibration in the rock beneath his feet as if somewhere close by there existed a heavy, throbbing piece of machinery.

This time the sound/feeling generated the memory of his family's vacation trip out West when they had gone to the Grand Canyon in Arizona. On their way, coming down from Utah, they had stopped at the Glen Canyon Dam, a large hydroelectric plant on the Colorado River. At the dam they took a self-guided tour of the facility, riding an elevator into the heart of the concrete edifice. Inside, while they looked upon the generator room where huge twenty-foot diameter turbines spun at incredible speeds he remembered a humming in the air and a rumbling electric vibration in the floor exactly like the sensation they were experiencing now.

Amanda had sensed it too and was looking at him strangely. Michael's feeling that something evil was close by suddenly came back even stronger than before—no longer a feeling—but a certainty.

Although apprehensive, they continued on; Michael's instinct once again insisting on the direction—a direction that would take them nearer to the sound's source—nearer to the rhythmic pounding that was like a deranged cobbler tapping madly on the bottom of their shoes with a heavy hammer.

The tunnel continued to widen, its size quadrupling in every dimension, when the appearance of a blue glow up ahead made them stop.

"Michael? What's that light?" Amanda asked, clutching his arm for support. The sound was so loud that they could no longer converse through whispers—the vibration a constant thudding that seemed to be literally rising up through their feet.

"I don't *know*, Amanda," Michael began, suddenly irritated at her question. He took a deep breath and, in doing so, thought the air felt warmer. "But . . . I think we need to go towards it," he finished hesitantly, as if the words were being put into his mouth, that he wasn't really creating or thinking about them; he was just opening his mouth to let out what had already been placed there.

"I don't want to . . . it's like the dream."

"I know," Michael said, pausing before continuing. "But I don't think we have a choice," he said, surprised to hear his own answer since every fiber in his body was screaming at him to turn back and run for his life. He disregarded this impulse though and took a step forward. It was definitely warmer in the tunnel now and he thought the heat was coming from in front of them—from the source of the blue glow—as was the vibrating sound that was now like a constant rumble of thunder that announces an approaching storm.

"Michael!" Amanda was pleading now.

He took a second step forward, then a third. Soon, they were both walking again toward the strange blue light. The vibrations coursing through the rock beneath their feet were like walking on top of a raging underground river of lava, its current faster and more turbid the closer they came to its source. Ahead, they could see where the tunnel opened into a cavern and knew that the source of the light and sound was located somewhere within it. Michael and Amanda continued their careful, determined walk forward. Once inside the cavern though, Michael was confronted by a sight that, although initially appearing unbelievable, he thought he had seen once before.

At the opposite end of the cavern was a blue fire roughly the size of the man standing next to it. The disturbing sound, though, didn't seem to be coming from the man or the fire, but from the cavern itself. The blue light also seemed not to come from the blue flames either, but rather from the walls, discharging from behind every rock and extrusion, and from out of every corner and crevice like a gas. It was as if the rock seemed to be bleeding blue light, leaving nothing untouched.

The man near the fire was standing with his back to them.

It was however this strange property of the light which, as the man turned around, allowed Michael and Amanda to immediately recognize his face.

From the far end of the cavern, where the blue light flickered and painted his skin in ghastly colors, they saw their grandfather, Richard Knapp, grinning back at them.

2

Alan was first up the stairs, taking them three at a time; Sam following closely behind. At the top, he turned and could already see four cultists in the room that served as his office. He reached the doorway just as a fifth was making his way into the room through the shattered window. On the porch roof outside, another dozen or so cultists were waiting their turn to step through. Moving quickly into the room, Alan opened fire without hesitation.

His first shot threw three of the four cultists already in the room back against the wall and window, immediately killing one of them. As the smoke from the shotgun cleared, Alan recognized Chuck, the hardware store clerk, as the man now lying dead against the wall. A second later, two of the other cultists—the one that had escaped Alan's first shot and the one that had just come in through the window—rushed him. He was able to fire the other barrel at the cultist in front, a middle-aged, overweight man sporting a ponytail. The man's head violently exploded in a red splatter which sent the ponytail flying away like a hairy snake. The other cultist, a young man with bright red hair and a mustache, caught Alan off guard, hitting him at full speed, knocking him flat on his back, and slamming the shotgun down sharply on his wrist.

Sam arrived next, announcing herself with a thunderous explosion from the Colt which made Alan's attacker disappear as if he had been picked up and yanked backward. As the red-haired man stumbled backwards, Alan noticed the dime-sized hole that had been made in the center of his acne-encrusted forehead. As the man fell away, the two attackers temporarily repelled by Alan's first shot were back up again. Behind these two, three more cultists—a boy no more than ten, an oriental woman and a tall black man—had just climbed in through the window to join the foray. Before Alan could react to the new arrivals, the Colt exploded from behind him three more times and the three newest arrivals all collapsed in a bloody, messy tumble.

Alan got up and rushed the remaining two attackers. Now employing the empty shotgun as a club, he made quick work of the two—both of them young men who did little to protect themselves. As the last one hit the floor with a loud groan, two more explosions from the Colt dropped the next two closest attackers while still outside on the roof. As they went down, a third became entangled with them and the three of them rolled off the roof together.

Alan reloaded the shotgun and scrambled to the window. Aiming at the densest conglomeration of bodies, he fired—sending two more cultists down, one of them rolling off immediately, while the other squirmed and convulsed at the roof's edge for several seconds before ultimately dropping away. However, there were still eight or nine cultists on the roof and as they came forward, Alan fired a second shot.

Meanwhile, behind him, Sam was reloading the Colt. As he retreated from the window, having taken out two more of the attackers with his second shot—and at the same time trying to reload the shotgun—another cult member suddenly appeared at the roofline. It was then that Alan realized the cultists were using a ladder.

"We've got to get the ladder!" Alan yelled to Sam, just as she'd finished reloading. "We're going to have to go outside onto the roof and pull the ladder up *here*, got it?"

Sam glanced outside, then nodded.

Alan went out first, once again using the shotgun as a club and swinging it as soon as he was on the roof. Sam remained crouched at the window sill and continued to shoot at those cultists who surrounded him. With his first swing, Alan knocked down an elderly man and a teenage boy with long hair who seemed to somehow retain his smile, even as the butt of the shotgun pulverized most of the bones and tissue along the right side of his face. The two of them fell down and rolled to the edge of the roof but did not immediately fall off.

Behind him, Sam's Colt had become a steady thunder as she dropped a large white man wearing a neon green tie; a blonde woman who could have been pretty enough to be a model until the Colt punched a ragged hole through the front of her neck; a teenage girl so freckled she looked like she had been splattered with brown paint; and finally, a young man with a grinning boyish face whose smile instantly turned to an open-mouthed look of surprise when the Colt tore his left cheek away and left it dangling from his face like a bloody fake beard.

With only four of the cultists still left standing on the roof, Alan made his move for the ladder—and found himself looking down on three more cultists climbing up from below. Fortunately, the topmost one was close enough for him to effectively bring the butt of the shotgun down on her head which made her let go. As she slid down the ladder, her fall managed to take the two cultists behind her down along with her to the ground where the woman landed hard on top of them. Alan saw her elbow ram into the mouth of a silver-haired man who looked to be in his sixties, subsequently shoving most of his front teeth back into a suddenly wider mouth which quickly filled with blood.

Alan turned his attention back to the edge of the roof and grabbed the ladder. When he pulled, the cultists on the ground were too slow to react and so he was able to lift it easily, yanking it out of one last weak-armed attempt to secure it by the same woman who had just fallen. As he was dragging it out of her grasp, she snarled up at him like a feral cat. By the time he'd successfully retrieved the ladder and shoved it most of the way behind him through the broken window and into the office, Sam had dispatched the last four cultists on the roof.

Alan successfully managed to push the ladder the rest of the way into the office, then fell in behind it landing on the floor in an exhausted heap. Sitting on the window ledge, Sam breathed heavily and wiped the sweat from her brow with the back of her hand which still held the smoking Colt. Alan noticed her hands were trembling. Before he could go to her, she got up, nearly stumbled across the ladder, and collapsed by his side.

"Are we having fun yet?" she said and managed a small laugh.

"You're getting awfully handy with that gun," Alan said.

"I had a good teacher."

And then, because they were still looking into one another's eyes, they were each able to watch the reaction of the other when downstairs they heard—and then felt—another enormous crash which shook the house as if some giant monster had picked it up and, finding it uninteresting, dropped it back to the earth again.

64

1

Michael pulled Amanda into a bear hug, tugging and twisting so her face would be forced against his chest that he might spare her the frightening sight of the grandfather who had given his life for her.

The thing that had once been Richard Knapp stood before them, covered in blood. Where his eyes should have been were two gaping holes. The thing that used to be their grandfather stood before them with arms crossed and feet spread. There was no evidence of the shirt Richard had worn into the tunnel and his jeans were nearly black with soaked-in blood and dirt. His chest was so covered with dried blood and grime it was impossible to distinguish the wounds from the dirt.

I just have to remember—that's not my grandfather anymore. Richard Knapp is dead. It's only Richard's body and nothing more.

(quoth the Raven, nevermore?)

Then the Richard-thing spoke to them, "Welcome children. I'm so glad you could make it," it said, its voice somehow able to project itself above the thunder inside the cavern with a resonance louder and more powerful than anything Michael had ever heard his grandfather utter.

After the thing had spoken, Michael realized that he was now better able to accept the fact that what he was seeing was simply the resurrection of his grandfather's body as a vehicle for the physical manifestation of Teufel. Then he thought of how it had previously possessed Amanda and yet . . .

. . . and yet this is a dead body. How can it possess and use a dead body?

Then he thought of the other body they had found earlier—the one which they had presumed to be Sylvia Woulfe—and which had been located directly underneath The Claw.

What a fitting name, The Claw . . . because that's exactly what it was . . . the claw of Teufel reaching above the ground to snatch at anyone unlucky enough to venture too close. And so that's how he must have lived—by using Sylvia's body as a host. But since she was dead, he was no longer able to extract enough power—or perhaps extract it fast enough—in order to secure a new host . . . until now. Until Amanda. That's what my two-week blackout must have been—Teufel's initial attempt—which failed probably because of my leaving the house and/or Teufel not being strong enough yet to overcome me.

"Why are you here?" Michael shouted, trying his best to sound strong and unafraid. Instead, his voice betrayed him, cracking on the last word like a pubescent teenager's.

The grandpa-Teufel thing merely chuckled, with a sound dry and rough, like the splintered edges of two broken bones sliding against each other. The eerie sound made beads of ice-cold sweat erupt across the surface of Michael's forehead, even as he wondered again how Teufel was able to make his voice heard above the cacophony that dominated the cavern.

"You think you can stop me *now?*" the thing said and laughed louder. "You are as foolish as you are stupid, my young naïve, Michael. You still do not fully understand."

Michael was still trying to keep Amanda turned away from the sight, but it was not to be as she suddenly wrestled away from his grasp to get her own look at the creature with whom he was conversing.

"Grandpa?" she said.

"That's not grandpa, Amanda," Michael said quietly. With the constant booming, it would've seemed there should have been no way the thing could have heard him—and yet it did.

"Oh, but you're right, my little darling, don't listen to your brother. I am indeed your grandpa. And I gave myself willingly because I know who will soon be in charge. Join us, my darling, and you will see."

"He's lying, Amanda, don't listen to him."

Teufel laughed.

"Oh, all right then, you got me, Michael. No, Amanda, I am definitely not your pathetic little grandfather. I'm just *borrowing* his body for a while. In fact, you might even go so far as to say a *permanent* loan, if you *get the drift* as you young folks say. A foolish and useless sacrifice, I might add. Hope you don't mind," Teufel said, his voice laced with thick sarcasm.

At the end of this diatribe, Michael noticed that the fire next to Teufel had expanded, growing fatter and at least a foot taller, its flames now wavering well above the head of Richard's re-animated body. The sight of the fire's noticeable increase in size made something come together for Michael—more of the puzzle snapping itself into place—even while the overall picture remained unrecognizable.

But he felt he was close. Very close.

"Ah, yes. I feel your little mind working, Michael—searching and groping for answers like some insect feeling along with its antennae for the slightest crumb of nourishment. To be honest, I find it amusing—and yet so pathetic. To think that a *child* could have even the faintest comprehension of the events unfolding before him—events anticipated, planned and designed almost since time's beginning—yes, I must say, amusing indeed."

"Is that what you wanted my sister for, as a . . . a *vehicle*, to contain your form? No, Teufel, you're the only one deserving of pity here," Michael said.

Teufel didn't merely chuckle this time, but emitted a gush of crazed laughter that seemed to rattle the entire cavern—gobbets of it bouncing from wall to wall, unaffected by the cavern's rhythmic booming, the laughter bursting and splattering over their heads in a shower of thick, vile sound.

"Oh, Michael, I find you so entirely entertaining. It will be such a shame to destroy you with all the rest. You continue to insist on trying to break everything down into petty *wants* and *desires*, as if it were all nothing more than some individual agenda of self-gain. But it is so much more than that, my dear child. I'm afraid, Michael, that the grand events you so unwittingly fell into the middle of are quite beyond the limits of your tiny mind to imagine, its sheer magnitude incomprehensible for *any* human mind to grasp—let alone yours."

"Such an overwhelming display of confidence only proves you're still afraid, Teufel," Michael said, his mind racing to put the final pieces together. *He felt so close!* "So, what is it? What are *you* afraid of? Afraid I'm going to stop you?"

When the creature smiled, the sight of his grandfather's smiling, eyeless face was suddenly too much for him and he turned aside.

"I see your friend has been most helpful to you—pity it doesn't matter now."

Somehow Michael found the courage to confront the horror before him once more.

"Come, come, Michael, don't attempt to play the fool with me—even though, ultimately, that is what you are. Yes, your eyes betray the one I speak of—the one who calls himself Harvey Olds. I must admit though that I applaud his guardianship of the south field tunnel entrance—most admirable—but I assure you even *he* can not stop what is about to be unleashed now."

Suddenly, the last piece of the puzzle clicked into place—and Michael's understanding became complete. Michael thought he finally knew what it was that Teufel was up to—the essence of what he immediately thought of as Teufel's Grand Plan. It had come together so quickly and easily, that he wondered why he hadn't realized it before. But with this revelation, there came additional doubt.

But . . . did I just figure this out on my own . . . or did someone show me? How can I know for sure?

(does it make a difference?)

"Ah, suddenly I sense a certain degree of understanding in you, Michael. Perhaps I have misjudged you after all—if only just a little bit. You think you understand now, do you? You believe you sense the truth? You sense nothing. You know nothing. Even what you think you know is wrong. And whatever truth you feel you've found is based on lies based on misinformation based on deception and deceit from those you naively call friends. You have been played a fool, Michael. Used and led. For amusement, for entertainment, for selfish formulas you do not understand, cannot understand, and will never be *allowed* to understand. You're a puppet, Michael. Pity you do not see the strings. Though you cannot understand this either, I will tell you that I have not nor will I ever deceive you. *I* have nothing to hide. *I* am not here to misguide you or let you flounder with incomplete information. Here, let me show you. Do you *SEE?*"

And then Michael *did* see . . .

the gaping black throat of a hole in the cavern wall, Teufel standing before it, no longer as the reanimated body of his grandfather, but as an indescribable creature made of stitched together body parts—some human, some not—standing and beckoning to something enormous lurking inside the darkness of the hole, hidden by a curtain of twisting, dancing blue flame

. . . and then the Image was gone, not fading, just simply gone. The effect disoriented him for a moment. To regain his bearing he struggled to refocus his eyes on the objects in the cavern—and on Teufel.

"Yes, I'm beginning to see now," Michael began, "I finally understand what this has all been about. What it's been about since the beginning . . . from the time of Dr. Woulfe's cult . . . how cleverly you used him . . . how you used *all* of them, who in turn used more . . . how everything has been used for your own purposes all along."

Teufel began laughing again and Michael noticed—although he didn't know if it had been there before or if he were only now seeing it for the first time—a light, deep within the empty eye sockets of his grandfather's face. It was a blue light, the same as he'd seen earlier inside the cavern itself.

"Go on, my child," the monster said, like a father prodding his son to complete some important task.

"That's what you're doing now, isn't it? You've finally accumulated the power to create your *own* gate, the ultimate gate . . . a *permanent* doorway between our world and yours . . . big enough to let . . . them through"

"Oh, but there's more, much, much more, Michael. The hordes I shall soon command are not simply an army—but an army of armies! A vastness of strength your world has never seen nor imagined—a force it will be utterly helpless before. Just try to imagine it, Michael! An army that has been growing since the beginning of time, built of discarded souls desperate for freedom—and revenge and *power*—and one so vast that but a fraction of it would be more than sufficient to wreak destruction across the expanse of your entire world. And all of them will be coming . . . now . . . *here. And it is I who will lead them*."

"And what happens to those you've already used and those that came before them?"

"You still do not grasp the magnitude of what it is that is about to be unleashed—and the extent of the destruction that will soon commence. The lives of those to whom you refer are but a single grain of sand along a beach—a beach that represents all the lives of your world. But it is, after all, only a single beach. Those that I shall command will comprise a force like all your world's oceans gathered into one and formed into an unstoppable tidal wave that will wash everything in its path away."

Michael reeled with the terrifying implications. What Teufel was attempting to enact was nothing short of the invasion of the earth by all the forces that'd been kept in check since time's beginning—"discarded souls" as he'd called them. And worst of all—he'd found the monster's analogy of a beach before an enormous tidal wave all too believable.

. . . desperate for freedom . . . and revenge . . . and power . . .

And now such beings were to be loosed upon the world, driven by a vast hatred and a revenge nurtured since the beginning of time . . . all of them about to be set free . . . not just a throwing wide of the gates but the collapse of the entire wall at once before one enormous, unstoppable onslaught.

So maybe Teufel's right—maybe such a horror is incomprehensible. And even worse, I seem to be the only one who can do anything about it. And so can anyone please tell me, how one teenager is supposed to go about stopping the legions of the undead from destroying the earth as we know it?

2

Too exhausted to move, Alan and Sam sat and listened, trying not to breathe too loudly as the sound of countless pairs of feet shuffling and trudging downstairs made it clear they had finally been overrun.

"We've got to try for the basement," Alan whispered. Sam looked at him with watery eyes which seemed to say, *What's the point?* Nevertheless, when he got up, she followed. They literally tiptoed out of the room. When they'd reached the top of the stairs, they stopped and listened again.

"You better reload," he said, "we're going to need all the firepower we have."

Sam nodded and they returned to the office to minimize the sound. While Sam was reloading the Colt, thereby emptying their only box of ammunition in the process, he put two more shells in the shotgun—leaving him with only four.

"So what happens when we reach the basement?" Sam asked.

"We defend it with our lives. The stairs are the only way in or out and we've got one hell of a solid door down there that should slow them up pretty good. I just hope they haven't found it yet. But, it sounds like they're moving pretty slowly. And besides, we need to be by the tunnel in case Michael and your father . . . with Amanda . . . return that way."

At the mention of Amanda's name Sam seemed to cringe momentarily.

"It's the only hope we've got, Sam," he said and when he met her gaze he was relieved to still see a smoldering defiance there.

Back in the hallway, they proceeded immediately down the steps. They had no way of telling how many of the cultists were now inside the house, but Alan was hoping that some element of surprise was still on their side. As they reached the landing halfway down, Alan came face to face with the first of their invaders. There were four of them. When they saw Alan and Sam they looked at them without surprise . . . even when the roar of the shotgun sent a hot blast of pellets into the man who appeared to be leading them. As the man flew backward, he took the three other cultists behind him down the stairs with him in a pile of tumbling, intertwined limbs, the only sound that of flesh connecting with wood.

Alan ran down the rest of the stairs, stepping on and over the bodies of the fallen cultists who were already trying to paw their way back up. As Sam followed, one of them reached up and grabbed her ankle. The cultist was only a girl, no more than twelve, and for a brief moment Sam hesitated with the Colt pointed at the girl's forehead. So, instead of pulling the trigger, she tried pulling her leg free. The girl seemed amazingly strong though and Sam wasn't able to get away. She started kicking at the girl's arm with her other foot and finally managed to break free.

Sam rejoined Alan and together they turned the corner on the stairs leading to the basement. At the same time, they encountered the back of one of the cultists who was on her way down the stairs ahead of them. She was an older woman—they could see her white hair done up in a chignon—and when Alan crushed the top of her skull with a hammer-like blow of the shotgun stock, she instantly fell onto her back in a crumpled heap on the floor only to stare up at them with a strange, twisted smile on her face, reminding Alan of The Joker from the first Batman movie.

The door at the bottom of the stairs was still closed. Alan hoped it meant that none of the cultists had entered the basement yet. He reached the door and swung it wide onto a room full of blackness. He rushed in first, and then, as he turned to pull Sam in after him he saw the young girl Sam had spared a moment ago, flying down the stairs behind them. Sam never saw her . . . or the kitchen paring knife the girl had raised above her head.

"Sam!" he yelled, but it was too late. She had started to turn at the last minute though—and it turned out to be enough to save her life—for as the knife came down with the full weight of the girl behind it, instead of impaling the back of Sam's neck, it went into her shoulder instead. Sam screamed and fell sideways down the stairs, the girl on top of her still firmly holding the knife into her shoulder, even after having come to rest against the wall halfway down the stairs. Alan crouched low to the floor and lined up the sights of the shotgun before realizing he would never find an opportunity to get off a clean shot.

The girl pulled the knife out and—while still lying on top of Sam who was struggling to bring the Colt out from under her and around—slashed at her again. Sam turned as much as she could within the restrictive confines of the stairwell, screaming again when the knife struck, this time opening a gash down the length of her forearm. Immediately after the knife completed its arc, there was the thump of flesh and bone on wood as Alan swung the shotgun down, connecting squarely with the top and side of the girl's head. The girl flew sideways, bounced off the wall of the stairwell and rolled down into the basement.

When Sam was eventually able to get her feet back underneath her she lurched the last few steps down, leaving a splattering of blood in her wake. After Alan had pushed the young girl's body back up the stairs, he slammed the door shut behind them and locked it. Just as he turned on one of the bare bulb lights, Sam collapsed at his feet, exhausted and in shock. Alan tossed the bloody shotgun aside and picked up his wife and carried her over to the middle of the basement where a single throw rug lay. He laid her gently down, then went to search for something to use to stem the pulsing flow of blood which was still pouring forth prodigiously from the two knife wounds she had sustained.

The door to the basement was solid oak and at least three inches thick and while Alan bandaged his wife using clean rags from a box he'd found by the clothes washer, he prayed the door would hold. Already one of the cultists had begun pounding on it, the sound reverberating throughout the basement.

Alan knew Sam was in bad shape; her skin had the pallor of a ghost, blood covered both arms and had made a splattered mess down her chest and along the sides of her legs. He thought she was dangerously close to passing out.

When he'd finished dressing her wounds he looked into her eyes. The pounding on the door had now intensified to a rhythmic booming which was shaking the entire door and the walls on either side. He couldn't help but think of the possibility he had considered a few hours before, a possibility he hadn't wanted to think about at the time and had therefore shoved into a back corner of his mind. Now, though, almost on its own, it had come into the light again, demanding to be seen and heard.

Looking down at his wife, he sensed Sam reading his mind. He looked from her eyes to her hand where she was still clutching the Colt and, as he watched, she brought the gun up and laid it on her chest. Alan continued staring at the gun for a moment, then looked once again into his wife's face. As their gazes met, he put his hand firmly on top of hers—and on top of the gun—and squeezed gently. A single tear rolled down her face, hung for a moment at her jaw as if trying to decide whether it was willing to take the plunge or not, and then did, falling to the floor, creating a small, dark circle.

Behind them, the booming on the door continued as if it were a huge clock thundering out the final pulses of their lives.

65

1

Michael looked down at Amanda. She was clinging to him and staring at the thing known as Teufel currently residing in the body that had been the only grandfather she had ever known. Michael felt powerless to protect her and his helplessness made him furious. He took a step forward . . . and discovered it was like wading through knee-deep quicksand. He tried taking another and found that he couldn't. Something was holding him back—Teufel apparently keeping him at a distance. But, instead of being discouraged, it gave him hope.

He's afraid of me. Somehow, and in some way, he's afraid of me . . . which means there must be something I can do; some way I'm a threat to him despite all his bravado.

He reached down and grasped Amanda's hand. As he did so, the fire in the cavern seemed to *lunge*, growing several feet taller and larger in diameter. And although he realized they didn't have much time, he knew there was nothing he could do at the moment. It was while thinking that it would be best to try and leave, that the Image overwhelmed him like a transfusion of consciousness—in an instant everything around him was gone and he saw nothing, heard nothing, felt nothing that was not the Image . . .

of his mother, her eyes closed, her eyelids wrinkled waves of bunched skin . . . his father holding a gun with a trembling hand, the tears streaming down his face as he raises the gun to her head

. . . and so he struggled against the Image and in doing so, felt beads of sweat burst out across his forehead and then he saw . . .

his father's finger on the gun's trigger depicted in excruciating detail, like some extreme close-up in a movie, and he can see the muscles underneath the skin of his father's finger tightening, the finger bending and squeezing the trigger—springs inside the gun expanding, the hammer pulling back, poised to slam home and

. . . nothing but the Image which Michael knew was not real, that it was a false image—a fantasy—a picture conjured by the demon as he realized in some far-off corner of his mind that another answer resided here, the answer to the dreams—dreams he suddenly knew had been instilled within each of them by the image-casting ability of the demon which called itself Teufel, and then . . .

he watches helplessly as his father's finger squeezes harder and he can see the skin creasing at the inside joint; turning white on the outside knuckle . . . the details coming to him in dream-like slow motion . . . and then he can smell his father's sweat—the smell made up of the sharp tangy metal of fear and the musty thick rottenness of hopelessness as

. . . he fights with renewed vigor against the Image, pushing against it—and succeeding—only to have it crash against him even harder, forcing him physically to the ground onto his knees and . . .

he watches the finger complete its pull and sees—but does not hear—the gun's explosion—the brilliant sun-like flash followed by the white-gray cloud of smoke . . . the scarlet eruption

. . . and then he heard shouting and a pleading, desperate yell . . .

"Michael! Wake . . . up . . . please! . . ."

. . . of his sister's voice and realized this was not part of the Image, that the Image was fading and he could once again see the blue glow of the cavern and his sister's tear-covered face—and beyond this—the oozing face of his dead grandfather, animated through an abomination of hell-born nature.

"Come on, we're leaving," he said.

"Yes, my children, leave me now. I have work to do and it would be best that I be left to do it alone."

Michael halted, sensing that something had changed. A moment later he realized the booming from inside the cavern had stopped, the sound replaced by the blue fire which now raged as if it had become a demon of its own . . . and then he wondered if it had.

Should he believe Teufel? Why would he simply let them go? Was he that confident or was this some sort of trick?

And what had been the purpose of the Image? Surely a fantasy, but why? Or is Teufel really afraid of me, afraid I might interfere in the next stage of his plans? But why not just kill me—us? Is he not yet powerful enough to do so?

But to these questions Michael could find no answers—and felt precious time slipping away the longer he delayed. If there were actually some sort of chance he could stop Teufel, then time was of the essence. Yet, though he recognized the urgency of the moment, he also somehow knew that now was not the time for defeating him because there was still something missing—like the corner piece of the puzzle—one last thing essential to locking it all together.

Michael looked again at the demon, but already he had turned his back to them, his attention re-focused on his ever-expanding fire.

It's his Gate. The fire is the final phase. From what he was boasting of though, it's going to have to be huge. So there's still time.

Then Michael, with Amanda in hand, began slowly backing out of the cavern. The caution, though, seemed unwarranted—Teufel seemed to be making it a point to ignore them.

To hell with it!

They turned—and ran.

Behind them, the rhythmic booming began again.

2

They ran until the blue glow of the fire could no longer be seen behind them and the thrumming of the rock beneath their feet had become nothing more than a dull, half-remembered vibration. As they slowed to a walk, Michael noticed that as they had removed themselves from Teufel, his instinctual sense had returned and was growing stronger by the second. After several minutes of brisk walking, he found he was following it unerringly once again and after another half-hour of not reaching a single dead-end, he was confident they were back on the right track.

As they walked, Amanda said little and for this Michael was thankful. He nevertheless continued to think; it was, as he had told Teufel, all finally coming together for him. The cult, far from serving its members through bonding with the demons of the underworld in the hope of guaranteeing their passage to an immortal afterlife, were nothing more than pawns in Teufel's grand game of invasion—an invasion that would ultimately turn the world upside down.

Teufel's unwitting victims had been bonded—or possessed—with demons not to secure for themselves a guide to the afterlife, but rather to function as an expendable pre-invasion force.

But why send them to attack our house? If it was only to kill us—then why did he let Amanda and me go? Something still doesn't add up!

As Michael looked down at Amanda he saw that she was walking beside him while looking at the floor and holding the flashlight. He wondered again how much longer the batteries would last—and what he and Amanda would do if and when they finally ran down.

So if I assume Teufel is afraid of something—afraid of something because it could be used against him or even to stop what he's doing—and he's using what looks like all his current force to break into our house—then that at least narrows things down a bit. So, something about the house then? Or something in the house? The journals? Something to do with my parents? What am I missing? What is Teufel after? What is it he's afraid of? Meanwhile, while I struggle to find the answer, he's walking up to the fiery gates with key in hand—about to unleash the hordes of hell—and I'm the only one that can stop him.

66

1

Michael had been holding on to Amanda's hand for the last half-hour, mostly using it to drag her along. She stumbled frequently and would often sit down, exhausted, on the tunnel floor until Michael pulled her up again. She felt heavier each time he lifted her and soon, he thought, he would be carrying her and wondered where he would find the strength.

Michael's sense of urgency was fueled by a feeling that they were getting closer, that at any moment they would be turning a corner and walking back into their basement.

And finding what? Our dead parents? Or something worse? How about Mom and Dad, their arms outstretched not in loving welcome, but in groping, mindless want—human automatons possessed by demons—their empty eye sockets reflecting the blue flame of Teufel's Gate?

Michael swept the vision from his mind and stopped when he heard a booming sound in the distance. At first he despaired, thinking they had somehow mistakenly come full circle and were heading back toward Teufel's cavern. Then he realized it was a different kind of sound, a *real* sound, rhythmic and constant.

"Come on, I think we're almost there!" he cried and took off at a half-run, half-walk pace, pulling Amanda behind him like a beloved, if somewhat abused, teddy bear. They ran in the direction of the sound and then slowed when they came to what looked like a dead-end until the rock wall in front of them suddenly dissolved into a glorious and familiar light.

They had finally reached the basement.

2

"Mom!" Amanda screamed, nearly knocking Michael over in her rush from the tunnel. Michael tried to shade his eyes against the sudden glare. After having been so long in the tunnels with nothing but a flashlight for illumination, the bare bulbs hanging from the basement ceiling shone like tiny suns.

Squinting against the light, he was finally able to recognize his mother sitting on the floor with his father standing next to her. Michael couldn't tell whether Alan looked like he had seen a ghost or was merely bewildered at their abrupt return.

When Amanda threw her arms around her mother, Sam winced in pain and began to cry—both from the pain and from joy. At the same time, Michael noticed the blood-soaked rags wrapped around her arm and shoulder.

While Sam and Amanda sat comforting one another in the middle of the central room, Alan stood off to one side, still looking as if he didn't quite understand what had just happened. On the opposite wall, the big oak door was shaking—but holding—as the cultists increased their efforts and battered themselves even more fiercely against it. Michael wondered how much longer it would take before they were finally able to break it down. He also knew it didn't really matter at this point—they would be going back through the tunnels again and not just because it was the only way out—but because there was still unfinished business to attend to.

"Wha—What did I do?" Amanda cried, sensing her mother's pain and letting go.

"It's . . . all right, Amanda," Sam said. "Just a couple of cuts on my arm. Nothing to worry about. It's okay. I'm much more worried about you. I never thought I would see you again!" They hugged again, but this time more carefully.

"Boy, are we glad to see you!" Alan said finally, nearly shouting in order to be heard above the noise of the pounding, then walked over and embraced Michael, taking him by surprise.

"Feeling's mutual, I assure you," Michael said tiredly, holding on to his father tightly and finding, strangely it seemed, that he didn't want to let him go.

When Alan released him they stood looking at each other for a moment, not understanding why at first.

"The pounding's stopped," Alan said. He looked away from Michael towards the door and then back to Michael again. "I don't like it. We've had enough experience with these people to know it means only one thing—they're up to something new. The last time this happened, they broke in and overran the house."

Then Alan turned and pointed past Michael to the tunnel they had just come out of. "Can we get out that way?"

"Sure, if we can find our way again," Michael said. "About a half a mile south of here there's another entrance that opens into the field."

Alan went over to the workroom shelves and grabbed a big lantern light.

"Good. Then let's go—and I mean now. I don't want to wait around to see what they have up their sleeves this time," Alan said, then came back over and bent down to help Sam to her feet. Gritting her teeth against the pain, she allowed herself to be helped up.

"Michael?" Sam called out suddenly. The sound of her voice instantly stopped him, as he knew what she was going to ask.

"Yes, Mom?"

"Where's your grandfather?" She stated the question simply and seemingly without emotion, yet he could sense the fear in her voice, a fear he knew meant she was already anticipating the answer.

"He . . ." Michael began and then forced himself to look her in the eye.

But how should he answer? Sorry, Mom, but your dad threw himself into a crevice wrestling with a demon that is now using his body? Or, sorry, Mom, but your dad threw his life away for nothing, thinking he could kill a demon?

". . . gave his life so that Amanda . . . and I . . . could get away," he said finally. She put her hands to her face and closed her eyes against the welling of more tears. When she pulled her hands away, however, she seemed at first to have calmed herself.

"No," she said suddenly, quietly. Then her voice rose, "No, no, NO!"

Alan turned toward her and started to put his hands on her shoulders, then stopped, putting them on her waist instead, "It's going—"

But she never gave him the chance to finish, forcefully yanking herself away from him in the process. "When's it all going to *end,* Alan? And *where*—when we're all *dead?* And for what? That's what I want to know—*what in the god-damn hell is this whole thing ABOUT?"*

She looked at each of them in turn: Alan, Amanda, and finally Michael. She was waiting for some kind of answer and when she received none, her body began to tremble, and then the tears came again—at first slowly and then in a rush accompanied by a cry of anguish.

Alan went over to her and this time she let him take her into his arms. She cried against his shoulder and then Amanda started crying with her. Hearing this, Sam lifted her head.

"Come here, honey," she said, extending her good arm from around Alan's side.

Amanda ran over to them and put her arms around her mother. Michael suddenly felt left out and somehow embarrassed.

A moment later, regaining control, Sam turned to face him again.

"I guess that's what he would have wanted. He felt he owed me . . . owed you and Amanda. He probably thought he had to pay for . . . for all the years . . . he wasn't here."

"He saved our lives," Michael added quietly. "If he hadn't done what he did, Amanda and I wouldn't be here right now."

She nodded, wiped at her eyes and then indicated to Alan that she was ready to leave. The reunited family shuffled toward the tunnel entrance with Michael in the lead and Alan supporting Sam who was holding Amanda's hand. "Are you sure you know the way, Michael?"

"Well . . . pretty sure . . . but, Dad?" Michael said, and hesitated at the mouth of the tunnel. "There's something we have to talk about."

Before Michael could say anything more there was an enormous crash, so heavy they felt the cement floor beneath their feet shudder as if they had been perched atop some huge beast that had suddenly shaken itself awake. They turned in time to see the basement door explode inward in a shower of flying splinters. They turned and ducked, but not quickly enough as Michael heard both his father and mother cry out as they were struck by flying debris, and then Amanda screamed.

"Come on, let's go!" Michael yelled and grabbed Amanda before taking off on a blind run into the tunnel, not knowing if she or his parents had been hit, or if they would follow, or how the cultists had finally managed to breach the heavy door.

3

But Alan did look behind him. What he saw made him wish that he hadn't. For, standing in the shattered doorframe, was the grinning specter of Sheriff Bruce Kelly. And yet it was not so much the sight of the sheriff that made him hesitate and wish he had run into the tunnel with the rest of his family—but the sight of the man standing behind the sheriff. A man with dead eyes. Eyes that were not only dead, but appeared capable of draining the life out of whatever they stared at. But stare into them, Alan unfortunately did.

Immediately he felt lost and confused, like an animal mesmerized by the headlights of an oncoming car. And then he felt the eyes *pulling* him. With the pulling, draining sensation, he felt the joy that being reunited with his children had brought suddenly *yanked* out of him . . . and his newfound hope that they were all going to be able to escape, flowing out of him as if he were an insect whose body that, having become entangled in some spider's web, was now being sucked dry.

And, just like the tangled insect, Alan found himself unable to move.

67

When he opened the sixth seal, I looked, and behold, there was a great earthquake; and the sun became black as sackcloth; the full moon became like blood, and the stars of the sky fell to the earth as the fig tree sheds its winter fruit when shaken by a gale; the sky vanished like a scroll that is rolled up, and every mountain and island was removed from its place.

- Revelation 6:12-14

The cavern throbbed with the blue light and the sound of wrenching, moving, transforming rock—the Prime Gate was nearly complete. The fire which Michael and Amanda had once seen as but a bonfire was now a consuming mass covering, from floor to ceiling, the entire south wall of the long cavern. Behind the wall of blue fire, which made neither sound nor emitted heat, the rock wall seemed to be in fluid motion. The once rough-cut stone had smoothed and seemed to have come alive, its glassy, creviced surface writhing and buckling like rough skin stretched over moving muscles straining against a weight too heavy for them.

The wall was in a state of elastic transformation, becoming a fluid corridor between two sets of disparate worlds—evil and good, religion and science—separated by an eternal gulf that at its essence was a chasm gouged by Time; though other things, things perhaps not quite imaginable or even understandable, added to its depth and magnitude. It was a barrier never meant to be crossed, let alone dissolved or circumvented, if even at a single point. However, the flow of energy, as dictated by scientific principles never meant to be applied to such an event, would soon traverse between the opposing energies from that of the stronger to the weaker. The resulting mixture, though containing both components, would thereafter be defined by the larger and more dominant of the two.

The thing that called itself Teufel stood before this transformation—admiring the event it had taken him millennia to enact—and was awed at his creation. He could feel the hunger and yearning; the lust for power, freedom, redemption and revenge of the countless hordes previously entombed, emanating from behind the Gate like a surging sea of barely contained emotion lapping at the spout he was creating. He marveled too at the simplicity of it all and knew that the force, once unleashed, would be unstoppable—even by him.

Teufel's stolen body convulsed and shuddered in anticipation of the Feeding that would soon commence.

68

Now war arose in heaven, Michael and his angels fighting against the dragon; and the dragon and his angels fought, but they were defeated and there was no longer any place for them in heaven.

- Revelation 12:7-8

1

The sheriff and the man with dead eyes had now covered half the distance from the door to where Alan stood. It was at this moment that Alan felt something grab him. At first, he tried shaking it off, but it was too strong and wouldn't let him go—it felt like a claw on his arm, dragging him backward and he was suddenly conflicted again—he wanted to be pulled, but at the same time he wanted to stay. The eyes were getting closer and he felt a nearly undeniable need to see them and it was this need which kept him from looking away.

When the thing on his arm pulled again, he finally allowed himself to be moved.

The eyes were now less than ten feet away and he could feel them probing him, as if they were looking for something, delving within the depths of his being to examine the very fabric of his soul, seeking out the deepest and perhaps even darkest secrets of his mind. His concentration was suddenly interrupted by a sound—someone's voice—calling out to him as if from a great distance. It wasn't until then, though, that he realized everything had once again become quiet—that while the sheriff and the man with dead eyes had been walking toward him across the broken pieces of door, he had been unable to hear their footsteps.

Again he tried listening to the voice, but the exact words were still only a far-off and undecipherable whisper and he didn't know whether he should listen to or even trust them.

Run, Alan, run!

Who or what was telling him to run? And where was he supposed to run to?

He turned and looked behind him and instantly the world *turned on* again—the sounds assaulting him like a stereo suddenly cranked to full volume. He could hear everything at once—the people in the basement, the pounding, thudding footfalls of a steady stream of cultists pouring down the basement steps—then he looked down and saw that it was Sam holding and pulling on his arm, screaming at him to run.

And so he ran.

2

Michael led the way into the tunnel using the lantern light his father had been fortunate enough to grab before plunging into the subterranean maze. Safely inside for the moment, the once again reunited family ran hard—the sound of the pursuing cultists leaving them no alternative. Behind Michael came Alan, followed by Sam and Amanda.

Michael wondered just how long they could keep up this pace. Back in the basement he had seen the exhaustion in his family's eyes—while also being acutely aware of his own. He knew it would take them at least an hour to reach Teufel's cavern, assuming he could find the way again without error. And if this weren't enough of an obstacle with the cultists close on their backs, there was the potential of additional, potentially deadly, encounters with unmenschlich ahead of them.

Yeah, and what happens then? What if around the next corner there's half a dozen of Teufel's pets waiting for us? Am I once again going to suddenly utter a bunch of magic words and make them all turn tail? The likelihood of me performing that miracle again is probably about as likely as me making Teufel go away by saying pretty please with sugar on top.

They ran on, through countless tunnels, passing numerous secondary passages and caverns both large and small and where his family's energy was coming from Michael had no idea. The constant pounding on the hard surface had made his mother's wounds bleed more profusely and they stopped twice to retighten her improvised bandages. They had run for close to three-quarters of an hour but during the last quarter hour they had heard no further sounds of pursuit. They couldn't, however, quite bring themselves to believe they had so easily escaped the cultists. Michael, though, had another theory.

Coming into a wide four-way junction, they stopped again to rest and check on Sam.

Alan, now panting from the exertion of the escape which had been piled on top of the last twenty-four hours of life-threatening turmoil, looked wearily to Michael. "Michael? Back in the basement—you'd started to say you wanted to tell me something . . . what was it?"

Michael looked again at his family. Never, he realized, had he seen a more desperate group of people. Without a doubt, based on what they'd all been through to this point, they definitely deserved the truth—as difficult as it might be for them to hear it.

"We're not leaving the tunnels—at least not yet."

His unanticipated declaration was met with silence.

"Where are you taking us then?" Alan asked, too tired to sound either surprised or angry—the two reactions Michael had anticipated.

"I can hardly wait to hear the answer to this one," Sam added.

"To Teufel . . . to his cavern. We have to try and stop his creation of the Gate," he said and, without waiting for his parents to ask what he meant, he went on to explain what he had figured out about the cult and Teufel's plan.

Only blank, silent expressions greeted him after he'd outlined what he thought was the demon's plan to invade the earth with nothing less than the countless legions of the undead. He anxiously waited for a reaction, but either they were too tired, didn't care—or were too tired to care.

"And you think *we* alone can stop such a thing?" Alan asked. He shook his head, leaned back and looked up at the ceiling. Then he sat down on the floor and buried his face on top of his knees.

"There's no one else. And because of that, yes, I think we have to at least try," Michael replied and stared at the floor where he saw a set of footprints visible in a low spot containing an accumulation of rock dust—two and part of another—one of them his, the other part, Amanda's.

"He's right," Samantha said. Michael stared at his mother with a confused look on his face, not quite believing what he had just heard. "We've got to try and stop this thing, whatever it is," she continued, then turned to Alan. "If we run now, we'll be lost . . . it's time to stand our ground."

An uneasy silence followed. Then it was Alan's turn to speak.

"It doesn't look like we have a choice anyway," he said wearily and stood up, grimacing from the pain of muscles protesting his sudden end to their short rest. "We better get going then—from what you say, Michael—we might already be too late."

They continued their trek at what could best be called a fast walk, Michael guiding them with nothing other than his instinct. Even if they'd had a choice, he thought, they never could have found their way out on their own.

Whatever the source of my guidance, it's determined this journey and destination as well.

Twenty minutes later, they had all begun to feel a presence in the floor—a deep, steady vibration, like the precursor to an earthquake. And in a sense, Michael thought, that's exactly what it was, an earthquake of global proportions that threatened to tear their world apart.

"What's that sound?" Sam asked.

"It's coming from the cavern," Michael said. "I'm not sure exactly what it is, but it has something to do with the creation of the Gate. You'll understand better when you see it."

And so they continued on, and soon were able to see the blue glow, like a photokinetic fungus, rippling and dancing on the walls of the tunnel which led into the cavern. As they got closer, they slowed their pace, the throbbing vibration of the floor disorienting them and making walking difficult.

The effect was stronger now, Michael realized—somehow deeper and more powerful.

From the cavern, whose entrance they could now see as a blue disk of dancing stroboscopic light at the end of the tunnel, they heard nothing but the dull pulsing of the rock. Michael had maintained the lead and didn't falter as he approached the cavern entrance—the cavern where at any moment the fabric of existence between that of the living and that of the damned was likely to rip asunder in a cataclysmic wrenching of time and space.

And then, like a diver, Michael held his breath . . . and plunged headfirst into hell.

69

It took Michael several seconds to realize that the sound he was hearing above the thundering rock was the sound of Amanda screaming.

He looked behind him and wondered at first how he'd managed to travel so far into the cavern. He was now at least twenty feet from the entrance where the rest of his family still stood—but this was but a passing thought as he realized what was happening. He cursed himself for not having had the foresight to warn them.

Teufel was attacking his family.

His first reaction, of course, was to go to them. Teufel, though, had other plans—Michael discovered he couldn't move. He tried to lift his leg but it refused to obey. He could turn his head and move his arms—but everything else was held as firmly in place as if he had been turned into an extension of the stony floor.

So what other tricks have you got up your sleeve?

Amanda stopped her screaming . . . then fell to the floor and began writhing like an epileptic in the throes of a grand mal seizure. He watched in agonized horror as she clawed and scratched at her head as if she thought she could somehow rip the Image from her mind and he remembered from his own experience the feeling of intrusion and personal violation that she must now be feeling.

His father was now the only one still standing—though his hands were tightly clamped over his ears and his mouth was open in a silent scream of pain. His eyes were squeezed shut against the horror that undoubtedly filled his mind, and then he began tearing at his hair, pulling and yanking on it, making Michael think of an animal being attacked by a stinging horde of red ants.

But it was when he saw his mother's situation that he himself actually began to scream—crying out in one single, long peal of grief, torment and frustration as his mother had now sunk to her knees and begun ripping away the bandages on her shoulder and arm, making the blood—blood she could ill afford to lose—flow freely in winding red rivulets down her arm, soaking into her already-stained blouse and jeans. He knew that if she continued, it would only be perhaps a matter of minutes before she eventually lost consciousness.

Seeing his mother attacking herself made him try once again to move his legs, his foot, even a single toe—but he couldn't.

It's Teufel who's in control now. And he's apparently decided it's my turn to watch.

With this realization, he turned his attention away from the torture of his family to confront the creature at the other end of the cavern and saw Teufel standing with his back to them in the same position as when he and Amanda had left him.

"LET . . . THEM . . . GO!"

When he screamed the words it was somehow at a decibel level above that of the thundering pulse of the rock—yet there was no reaction from the demon. As he contemplated his available options, despair seeped deeper into his thoughts, inviting him to abandon his hope—and his family.

So is this it then—the end? First he's going to kill my family in front of me—making sure I'm able to watch—and then take care of me? Is this what it's all been for?

Harvey, where are you? You have to help me! And I don't care what rules you think you have to play by here! I know you think I have a chance of stopping this—but I don't know what to do. How am I supposed to fight this? HOW?

He waited for an answer. Waiting and not knowing exactly where to look as he did so, he stared up at the ceiling, refusing to turn away even as he heard his mother and father cry out in horror behind him. To truly help them, he knew, required an understanding he did not yet possess—yet somehow needed to quickly find.

Harvey? Are you there? Harvey!?

He screamed again—as much to drown out the sounds of his family's anguish as to express his own pain and frustration. It was shortly after he had closed his mouth, that he was finally confronted by the realization of why Teufel had let him and Amanda go earlier.

Because he knew I would bring them—he tricked me into bringing them here by letting me hope that together we could somehow defeat him. And all along, it was his plan from the beginning—he knew there was nothing we could do to stop him—but he wanted to enjoy the satisfaction of destroying us all together! So he used me to lead them to him. There probably is no Harvey Olds . . . he was probably just another illusion like the Images and the dreams . . . just one more party favor to make the celebration complete.

What a fool I was—and now we're all going to pay for it.

"Michael."

Michael heard the voice—a sound like wind, and barely above a whisper—and wondered where it had come from and how it should happen that he'd been able to hear it above the pulsing thunder within the cavern. He looked around but nothing within the cavern appeared to have changed. Then he realized that the voice had come from inside his mind. When, finally, he recognized this, it spoke again.

"Michael, it's me."

70

When Alan entered the cavern behind Michael, he had just enough time to obtain a glimpse of something which he perceived as a living wall of blue flame before the Image took over his mind and he saw . . .

his father—wearing the same jean coveralls he had seemed to wear every day of his life—walking toward the barn, then reaching it, finding the power off, walking to the old circuit box mounted on the outside wall—the circuit box he had always meant to enclose somehow but had never seemed to get around to—reaching toward the box, opening the cover, the bright flash of light and sparks, the sound of humming and crackling current let loose from its metal lair, the smell of burning meat, his father's blackening hand, the blood vessels boiling and erupting, the blackness reaching, spreading like a shadow up his arm

. . . and then he tried shutting the Image out, squeezing his eyes until they hurt but the Image prevailed and he saw . . .

a shadow black as night, painting what it touched not only with darkness but with the absence of life as he saw his mother running from the hog pen where she had been shoveling, running past him as he screamed at her—knowing no sound was being generated—his mother grabbing onto the smoking, blackened thing that used to be her husband and at the point of contact being grabbed and then slowly absorbed by the same black shadow and

. . . he tried willing the Image out of his head, aware of what it was even as his consciousness was being consumed by it . . .

then he was screaming as he saw himself walking toward the shiny black and red mounds—walking with one hand outstretched, reaching for the unrecognizable things that had once been his parents—and before he was able to touch them they stood up and he screamed again and backed away as they walked toward him and then he was running but he could still feel them behind him, reaching out to him, pulling at his hair as

. . . then he tried pushing the Image away and tugged at his hair where the black thing that was, but was not, his mother had touched him.

71

Harvey?" Michael said, speaking the name not aloud, but from within his mind.

"Yes Michael, I'm here."

"Can you help us?"

"Your father has what you seek."

"What does he have?"

"Your father will know."

In Harvey, Michael's helplessness found release. His family had been through too much—the loss of Richard, the fight with the cultists—his mother lying on the ground behind him bleeding to death.

"Fine! Play your *fucking* games then! But count me out. I'm tired of caring."

But Harvey's voice continued, its smooth melodic tone in his mind calming him—melting away his hostility.

"This is not a game, Michael. You have to believe me that everything depends on you now. The price for failure is unfathomable, untenable . . . unacceptable."

Michael stared at the wall in front of him, its blue coating a writhing sheet of luminescent disease.

"Yeah, I heard the same thing from Mr. Demon-kind over there. So try telling me something I don't already know. Like what the hell are you? And why should I trust you?"

"It is for what your father has that your house was attacked and you were pursued through the tunnels. As for me . . . you must think of me as a friend. I'll do what I can but there are limits over which I have no control."

"Damn you! Why is everything always a secret with you?"

Then he had a sudden thought.

"You're not . . . *alive* anymore . . . are you?"

"You have presumed correctly, Michael. I allowed my earthly form to be killed so that I could help you."

"Jesus."

"Not quite."

"Oh my God, that's it, isn't it? You're like an angel or something. Am I right?"

"I can only answer that you are a very smart and very brave young man, Michael Sarasin. You deserve not the responsibility that has been thrust upon you, yet you have excelled most admirably and endured more than most while refusing to give up."

Michael could think of nothing to say.

"I have to go now. Remember what I said about your father. You must go to him—he has what you need in order to defeat Teufel and close the Gate."

"Wait! But how am I supposed . . . I can't even move!" Even as he shouted this in his mind, he knew that Harvey was already gone.

Well . . . at least things are a little better than I thought—if I can trust him. There's still a chance; though I don't know how much good it does me if I can't even move.

(but maybe he *can)*

But as he turned to look back at his father, he felt something strange—something he could define no more precisely than as a presence—but a presence whose nature he seemed to recognize. He was too late though in trying to hide his thoughts as he felt the unwanted presence enter his mind like fingers probing around the edge of a doorway, before roughly pushing it open.

Teufel had successfully penetrated his mind . . . and discovered all that Harvey had just told him.

72

Even before Michael had time to regret what had transpired—that perhaps Teufel had learned that Alan might be the more real threat to him—the first Image assaulted him . . .

body parts—arms, legs, hands—falling over a hillside in a waterfall of severed flesh—arms writhing and jerking spasmodically, hands clasping and unclasping, heads slobbering and biting as they roll in a tumble against each other

. . . and he slammed his hands against the sides of his head to cover his ears, as if the Images were a physical stream of matter polluting his brain and that by covering these openings he could somehow shut off the sickening flow . . .

then Amanda's head, white and misty, like a bust created out of chunky fog, the face soft and smiling—then exploding—tangled strands of ropy, wet flesh ejecting outward in pulsing colors of red, white and gray

. . . but his hands could not stop the torment—even as he realized he had now learned to see through the Image to the world outside—to see the effects of Teufel's projections on his father, mother and sister, able to see them through the Image like the video of two TV stations overlapping each other—his family no longer suffering—perhaps because of Teufel's re-directed interest in him. Then he noticed a small shadowy figure being helped up by a larger figure and wondered how he was able to continue to fight against the demon's attack—wondering if it was Harvey that was somehow lending him the strength . . .

and after the explosion of Amanda's head, his grandfather's disembodied face appears, mouth open, a look of terror in his eyes as a hand slithers out of his throat, reaches up the front of his face and begins to gouge first

. . . and he tried desperately to shut out the Images that were increasing in intensity—Images more powerful than anything that had afflicted him previously—and the world beyond the Images faded under their power as a part of his mind uttered something about the proximity to the source, but he was unable to concentrate on this for long, the Image screaming its presence through the vibrancy of its projection—and when he realized he had been holding his eyes shut he opened them adding another layer of visual pressure on top of his already overloaded mind—but he forced himself to do it, balling his hands into fists to accentuate the effort, his wrists aching as if someone had been pounding out a steady rhythm on them with a hammer—and he looked fiercely around, concentrating on the objects he saw, realizing he had unknowingly turned around again—seeing the fire and the rock, then his mother and Amanda—and he attempted to focus on these objects in the real world in the hope of overcoming those in the illusionary—and looked to the far wall and heard himself gasp involuntarily at the sight of the Gate before which Teufel now stood, arms outstretched in front of it . . . and . . . the . . . Image . . . fading . . . becoming dark . . . then suddenly, mercifully gone.

Michael sank to his knees in exhaustion and bowed his head. He remained in this position for several minutes and then, when he found the strength and courage to look up once again—saw why Teufel had abandoned his interest in them.

In the wall at the end of the cavern—the Gate was opening.

73

By now the Gate had consumed nearly half the cavern wall, turning it into an indistinct mass of what could best be described as *nothingness*, neither black nor transparent, more a void without color distinguishable only by the absence of color—a hole in the fabric of human existence leading to a world of unimaginable horrors. The Gate was like a mouth, stretching itself wider as Michael watched, consuming everything around it—and soon perhaps—everything before it.

Teufel stood before his creation, his arms outstretched in apparent welcome to that which would soon come through. His back was to Michael and his family, confident it seemed, that they could do nothing to stop him.

The throbbing protest of the rock was deafening. When his father's voice broke through, Michael at first thought it was a sound from a dream—quiet, far away—dismissible as imagined. But, in a moment, he knew it was real. And so he listened, sensing a unique urgency in the small, quiet voice. As he was better able to recognize the tone, the voice seemed to move closer.

"Michael!" he heard, still barely discernible as if from miles away. Then, "Michael!"—still incredibly small and faint, though now more like someone whispering to him from another room. "Michael!"—and now he was certain it was indeed his father's voice speaking to him distinctly from the tunnel entrance—less than thirty feet away.

"How do we stop it?" his father yelled.

He didn't know how to answer his father's question, and in another second he knew why. Another Image was now revealing itself to him, but, just before he resolved to try and block it, he felt—*knew*—somehow, that this particular one had not been sent by Teufel but by someone—or something—else.

Gradually, and cautiously, he willingly opened his mind to it . . .

and sees a gold medallion on a chain lying in the dusty confines of a wall—the basement wall of their house

. . . which sparked a sudden recognition and memory, though he could not . . . quite . . . grasp what they were . . .

and watches a hand pick up the medallion, lifting the circle of gold metal up into the light where it burns like a fledgling sun

. . . and then it came to him in a rush, a wave of actualizing pleasure . . .

and he sees the dusty hole—where his father has removed the first notebook that is the journal of Dr. Woulfe—and watches the small sun being removed as well—and then concealed—dropped into a pocket while the notebook is replaced in the hole

"Dad!" he yelled.

"Michael? Can you hear me?"

"Yes! Do you have the medallion?" he called, but the words seemed to take forever to reach his father—precious seconds creeping by with the slowness of minutes—almost as if he could *visualize* each word as an individual sound floating through the air like a lazy cloud toward his father.

Alan appeared confused or perhaps surprised that Michael had discovered his secret.

But how was he going to make him understand? And was Teufel aware of what he was doing? If so, was he prepared to stop it? And how might he accomplish such a thing—with another Image—or something worse?

Michael's hope began to wither. His despair, held in check since his last communication with Harvey, was now testing its restraints—the chains (Harvey Olds' confidence) and ropes (Amanda, his family, his own self-assurance) starting to come apart one by one . . . when he thought he recognized the first inkling of understanding start to transform his father's face.

"Yes!" Alan yelled back.

He watched first in relief, then trepidation, as his father thrust his hand into a pocket—and searched for something.

The medallion is the key to stopping Teufel! A medallion his father had found—and never told anyone about.

At first, he felt angry—then realized why its knowledge must have been kept from him. To know of the medallion before this moment would have involved too great a risk.

Now he could finally see and feel the last piece of the puzzle. Within his mind, he tenderly caressed its contour—learning, exploring and understanding its shape—before placing it on the table of his working consciousness. By turning and rearranging the other blocks . . . he was finally able to lock the rest of the puzzle onto it, creating—for the first time—a single, completed whole.

As Michael watched, his father finally produced the gold, sparkling medallion, which shone with a brilliance which exceeded that of the blue cavern, emitting a light of its own, a golden light, pure and untainted by the sick glow which saturated the rest of the cave. Then his father swung—and threw—the medallion toward him. The medallion sailed through the air in apparent slow motion, floating up and out of his father's hand in a graceful, upward arc. Michael watched each revolution of pendant and chain revolve in micro-orbit around each other—and held his breath as the medallion floated downward towards him. He counted the revolutions: one, two, three, four, five and on the sixth the medallion fell heavily and warmly into his hand.

Immediately, he felt a spasm of white hot energy course throughout his body, as if his blood had been replaced by a liquid fire which was both hot and cold at the same time. He closed his eyes . . . and clamped down upon the medallion in his hand to bear against the sudden consuming pain.

And then the excruciating pain, as suddenly as it had come, was gone. But the power remained and within it was a voice . . . the voice of Harvey Olds.

Michael, I'm here with you. We can do this now . . . together.

A sense of serenity spread throughout his body and he felt himself relaxing, the tension and fear draining out of him like sand out of a rent gunnysack. In his mind, he asked—"But, now what do I *do?*"

Believe . . . and accept . . .

"I do believe, you know I do. I've believed all along."

But you must also accept. Accept your destiny . . . accept and allow yourself to be Our channel . . . through you—and the instrument of the medallion—the Gate may be closed.

"Doesn't sound too bad."

There is however one thing you must know.

Even in his mind, Michael could sense a purposeful hesitation.

"So just tell me!"

He heard a sigh—like the whisper of wind through a stand of aspen in the fall—a warning to the trees of the impending winter.

You may not survive the channeling.

As he strained to assimilate what he'd just been told, he stopped breathing for a moment as understanding coursed through him like an unstoppable river suddenly let loose from behind a broken dam. And then he exploded.

"So that's it! That's why you were always so damn secretive about everything! You didn't want me to know! You thought if I knew—that I never would have made it this far. That I might have turned tail and run. You tricked me into thinking I had to do this all on my own! You tricked me into being your willing pawn . . . your unknowing sacrifice . . . *YOU FUCKING BASTARD!*"

Tears blurred his vision as he decried his fate.

You must understand, Michael, that it had to be this way.

"Oh, I understand all right. I understand a lot of things now—you might even be surprised at how much I understand. And now I have a question for you, Mr. Harvey Olds."

Yes?

"What if I refuse?"

74

"So I'll ask you again—what if I refuse?" Michael said, almost shouting the words in his mind. "What if I just turn around—right here and now—and walk? Huh? What then, Harvey?"

You don't need me to tell you the answer to that, Michael. I'm sorry it had to be like this—you have to believe there was no other way—it was too important. You must try to understand.

"I don't have to *try* anything. And I *do* understand—I already told you I understand perfectly. You didn't think I could handle it. Didn't think I could handle the truth. *You never trusted me."*

You're wrong Michael. Search your feelings—you'll find I had no choice. There are things going on here about which you do not know and cannot comprehend.

"Oh yeah, well *fuck you!* Who the hell ever asked you anyhow!"

You're better than this, Michael. Time is short. The Gate is nearly complete.

"But why *me?* How can the responsibility for saving the world all be resting on *my* shoulders? I'm just a teenager. Of all the places and people in the world—why this place at this time and why me as being the only one able to save mankind? Why not my father? If he's had the key to this thing all along, why isn't it him?"

This time Michael had to wait several seconds before receiving an answer from Harvey.

You remember how Teufel . . . attacked you first?

"Yes."

But then you were able to reassert control and so, unfortunately for her, he then went after Amanda?

"Yeah, so?"

It was because you were too strong.

"I thought it was because we left the house."

Distance played only a small part. It was you, Michael—in the end it was you who thwarted his design. He hasn't forgotten that. So now it has *to be you.*

"Wait a minute—are you trying to tell me he's actually *afraid* of me?"

It is possible. The point is, there is something about you which makes it difficult for him to . . . use his powers against you. It is for this reason you were chosen.

He thought about what Harvey had said—wondering if he wanted to believe it. It all sounded too simple.

Time is running out, Michael. You must decide now.

"But you did say it was a chance, though, right? It was only a chance . . . I *might* survive?"

Yes.

This was followed by a long pause.

But not likely.

"Life sucks, you know?"

He looked at Teufel, the Gate, the wavering sheets of blue light in the wall in front of him.

"So if I die—which you seem to think is inevitable—what happens to me? Is there something beyond this—something else beyond that which is about to come pouring through that Gate?"

This time there was no answer.

"You want me to be your channel—to trust you with not only *my* life, but that of my family's—and you still can't answer my questions?"

No, Michael. I'm sorry. You must be able to appreciate—and accept—that the decision is not wholly mine.

"What a bunch of crap."

Michael, it is time. In a little more than a minute the Gate will be complete. Once it is finished, it will be too late. All you have worked and lived for in your lifetime will be lost forever.

Michael looked over at his father, who was staring intently at him. He wondered how much time had passed since Harvey's voice had come back into his head. He looked next to his mother but she stood oblivious; mesmerized by the creation of the Gate at the other end of the cavern, fresh blood continuing to run down her arm. He then turned to Amanda, now standing only a few feet away. She was also looking at him—and in her eyes he saw a world of understanding—and the strength to accept the only answer he knew held any hope for them. Finally, he looked at Teufel—and remembered the person his grandfather used to be.

"I'll do it."

You have made the right decision.

"What other choice did I have? Anyway, I'm ready . . . ready to *accept* this—but only because there's nothing else I can do."

He turned back to his sister and was gazing into her eyes when, in the next instant, the medallion in his hand seemed to reach the temperature and brilliance of the sun.

A second later . . . his mind exploded.

75

Alan watched his son's transformation, believing it at first to be yet another of the demon's Images. Then he thought that this was The End—that he was watching his son being burned alive and that in the next instant it was going to be his turn followed by Sam and then Amanda. And yet at the same time he felt he was wrong—that what he was seeing was conversely something good. Watching his son no longer filled him with sadness but with a strange sort of hope.

He watched in fascination as Michael turned incandescent—Michael's body continued to glow brighter and brighter before exploding magnificently in a burst of sun-bright brilliance that for a moment turned everything in the cavern white. Due to the incredible intensity of the light, he was forced to look away and even had to shield his eyes from a light which seemed to come from all directions. The burst subsided almost immediately, though, and when he looked again, he saw what he could only describe as a human statue made entirely of light. Then the statue that Michael had become held out his hand and against the overwhelming whiteness the medallion's gold circle was a dull yellow speck.

At the far end of the cavern, the wall of fire continued to throb and burn while the blue surrounding the gate had now turned to a silvery blackness—like liquid night mixed with mercury. In the center of this conflagration was the Gate itself. At least ten feet in diameter, the portal was a passageway into blackness—and yet a hole more dark and more black than any shadow had ever been. In the center of this blackness, Alan now sensed movement. Then Teufel beckoned to something inside the black well. Afraid of what he might see, Alan turned back to his son.

From Michael's outstretched hand, a white beam suddenly projected. On the surface, it appeared to be nothing more than a light. As he studied it at length, though, he thought he could distinguish a multitude of individual elements of light, or perhaps something else, contained within the stream. The elements of the light were a fine dust but much brighter and shinier than the material of the beam itself. And when he looked closer, he could see that each element was moving independently, in a somewhat random, but continuously forward direction.

The beam did not strike like a laser but grew slowly, continually inching its way from Michael's hand toward the wall of fire, the Gate and Teufel as if it were a growing extension of his arm. The beam had presently covered but a fourth of the distance between Michael and the Gate.

As Alan looked in the direction of his wife and daughter he saw them clinging to each other, heads bowed, huddled in the corner against the wall. They were apparently no longer able to look upon the events taking place before them, resolved instead to accept whatever it was that was about to happen. Alan willed himself to move toward them but found he couldn't.

The beam was now halfway to the Gate and he wondered what the beam's target was—the Gate—or Teufel? Teufel stood about a dozen feet directly in the center and in front of the Gate. Alan wondered what the eventual effect would be when the beam reached the demon who, so far, seemed not to have noticed it.

At the same time, Alan no longer had any doubt that, at the Gate's center, some sort of activity was taking place. Within the blackness were shapes, outlined in deep red, that swirled and glided. The shapes were too numerous to count and too indistinct for him to have any sense of what they might be, which, he thought under the circumstances, was probably just as well. He thought that to see what lay beyond the Gate might very well take his mind to a place from which it would be unable to return.

He turned back to look at his son.

Michael's form seemed no longer human, but instead had become a more or less shapeless mass of white, having grown both taller and larger around.

In the next instant—the beam reached Teufel.

76

Michael thought he had been struck by lightning. The strange feeling, like a white-hot explosion, began inside his head, then traveled down into his body creating an inferno blazing from the inside out. The explosion had also produced an intense, numbing pain, though this faded almost immediately, leaving behind it only the heat and whiteness and a welcome surge of energy.

He felt like a pipe through which the flood waters of a river had been diverted and pressurized—a constant feeling of flow—the influx and the release balancing each other's intensities and pressures. He realized that he no longer had any sense of body, time or environment—only a hazy, dream-like consciousness of surging, gushing power flowing through his mind and out whatever it was his body had now become. He felt fragile in comparison to the magnitude of the forces flowing into and through him—like a garden hose attempting to channel the combined flow of all the world's rivers.

In the next instant his awareness reached outward and he discovered that he could see. *In front of him stood Teufel, still in possession of his grandfather's dead body—and beyond this—the Gate.*

He concentrated his energies on Teufel, who stood with his back to him, still in apparent awe of his creation and waiting to welcome the hordes soon expected to come pouring through.

Michael, however, felt no immediate fear as he reached forward, only a yearning to unleash the energy he felt contained and waiting within himself. He wasn't even sure yet what he was going to do with this energy, but there was no doubting his emotions. As he traveled forward, it were these same emotions that he let assume control—anger, frustration, then love—for his sister, his family, his grandfather—in the hope that they would serve as the instrumentation through which he might direct the power being channeled through him.

In the next moment, Teufel realized his presence and at his instant of contact with the demon, Michael felt a sudden push*—a feeling of something stopping his outward flow of power. Immediately, there was a painful pressure—a pressure he knew was the power that, instead of traveling through him, was now backing up inside of him. He felt he wouldn't be able to contain such energy for long—that its unchecked buildup would quickly destroy him.*

He willed himself to push, *even while not quite understanding exactly what he was doing. After a struggle he seemed to win too easily, the pent-up energy exploded out of him like an erupting volcano, the pressure draining out of him in a relieving gush.*

He knew he had little comprehension of what he was doing or even what was happening to him. He was simply a vehicle for some undisclosed force. But its origin? Its purpose? He knew he was there to stop Teufel and, more importantly, the creation of the Gate—but how? Was he even supposed to know? Was he supposed to control and thereby direct the power that he had become the instrument for? If so, how?

A sudden darkness made him turn his attention towards Teufel. At first he thought its source was contained in the blackness of the Gate—that already he was too late and the Gate had opened. But it was not the Gate—it was Teufel who was the source of the sudden black cloud. At the same time, he felt another push*—stronger this time. As he fought to push back, he realized that not only could he see everything around him, but he could see it with an awareness unlike anything he had ever experienced before. It was like not only having eyes on the back of his head, but on the sides, top and bottom too. He could clearly see* everything *that was around him—Teufel and the Gate, his parents and his sister—even himself—simultaneously and with what felt like the detail of a microscope.*

Against the white beam Michael had become, Teufel had now created a similar, ebony force that was now pushing, mixing and attempting to disrupt it. For a moment he found it amusing to see the classical representations of white and black portraying good and evil. But then he suddenly understood, though how he didn't know, that what he was seeing was actually a manifestation of himself*—of his own ideas and thoughts about the true representation of the world. He was seeing his and Teufel's struggle in a modality that his consciousness was most capable of understanding and accepting. What he saw wasn't real—not in the sense that two beams of white and black light were coming together in some kind of battle—but that this was an artificial representation created for, or by, his own perceptions and thoughts turned into physical manifestations.*

As he pushed back, he tried to change its symbols—imagining instead of black and white, two dragons instead. And, as soon as he had conceived this, two dragons instantaneously appeared in the room—a magnificent white one locked in claw to claw combat with another, shiny red creature of similar form. Immediately, he manipulated the new representation of himself to increase the intensity of his push—and actually succeeded in pushing the red dragon down, pinning it beneath the legs of his white one. But before he had the opportunity to seize his victory, the red dragon twisted, spun and was up again, lunging at the white. The red dragon, striking quickly, sunk its teeth deep into the thick flesh of the white dragon's neck. At the same time, Michael felt a bolt of pain penetrate his body like a hot knife.

Fortunately, he was able to recognize the similarity to the effect voodoo dolls were supposed to have, before he mounted his counterattack—and watched as it was perfectly executed by the white dragon—the animal turning its head behind it while using its tail to sweep the red dragon off its feet. Before he could make the white dragon take full advantage of its dominant position, however, the red dragon was gone—replaced by a giant squid that, before Michael was able to comprehend that the structure of the game had changed, immobilized the white dragon within the grasp of a dozen tentacles each at least twice the length of the dragon's body.

Instantly, Michael felt himself being squeezed while a paralyzing, almost poison-induced like numbness rapidly soaked into his body followed by an indomitable pressure crushing him from the power of the constriction. The pressure and pain seemed to magnify themselves exponentially, making it almost impossible to concentrate. As the pain rapidly consumed his awareness, his ability to visualize the scene in the cavern degenerated.

Michael imagined himself as a hydra.

The hydra appeared instantly, its large, round body supporting twelve necks upon which twelve heads rose, each with a long, alligator-like mouth filled with pointed teeth. The heads worked in concert, biting into and cutting through the tentacles of the giant squid. Then, as the tentacles relaxed their grip, he felt the pent-up power within him surge outward again. This time, he funneled the initial energy burst into the hydra and watched as the creature nearly eviscerated the giant squid.

But then, in the next instant . . . the squid was gone.

Gone, he knew, but not vanquished. He searched the cavern, able to see everywhere at once, looking to see what form the demon had now assumed. But he was unable to find him.

Then, without warning, the Image slammed into him. From his awareness of the cavern and the hydra—in an instant too short to be measurable—he found himself transported into the world of the Image . . .

and here he saw his sister on the ground, his father above her and holding in his hands a rock the size of a coconut held above her head and

. . . within the Image, Michael tried to cry out at his father to stop, but heard nothing and in the next instant . . .

the rock came down, striking without sound, pulverizing Amanda's head as if it had been nothing more than a soft cantaloupe—and where Michael had expected to see the gray paste of brain matter, there oozed a white, syrupy-like substance that appeared to be alive, and in the next instant he was there, standing above his sister's crushed skull, looking down at a wet writhing mass of stringy white worms

. . . and tried using his power to stop the flow of the Image into his mind, using it to close and block and push back—and finally succeeded in making the Image stop . . . and then fade away altogether.

As he waited to see what form the next attack would take, he thought about what he could do to initiate his own offensive, knowing that only by devising his own attack would he have any chance of stopping Teufel. He also knew, that while his defenses against the demon were adequate, they were not capable of preventing the Gate from continuing the process that would ultimately result in its opening—a process that was threatening to be complete at any moment.

When the idea initially came to him, it at first seemed too simple to even be worthy of consideration and so he almost dismissed it. But then he thought he heard a voice. He couldn't recall any words specifically, or even be entirely sure he had actually heard something, let alone a voice—and yet it was enough to make him stop—and reconsider. He remembered the sudden gush of energy he had been able to unleash when he had created the hydra . . . could it really be that easy? And yet . . . why not? There had been enough craziness in everything else—why not something that simple? And so, maybe he had *heard a voice? Harvey's voice, trying to give him some sort of signal?*

(but a signal of encouragement . . . or warning?)

Encouragement. And why? Because it feels right. And through so much of this, all I've ever had to rely on are my feelings. It was my feelings that got me—us—this far. And as illogical as it seemed at the beginning to have relied exclusively on them, it would be equally impractical to abandon them now.

(hey, it's your world)

And just like it's been all along—what other choice do I have?

In the next instant, he felt it coming. This time he was able to sense Teufel's impending attack—as well as know it would be in the form of another Image—and yet there was something more . . .

and the Image of a dog was thrust into the center stage of his consciousness

. . . as he recognized the dog and . . .

it began to speak to him,

. . . he knew the voice could only be that of Teufel . . .

the dog dragging its broken legs behind it like a burden that, while heavy to bear, could not be abandoned as the pitiful creature said, "You think you're Good—the Innocent who can slay the forces of Evil. But you and I know differently—don't we, Michael Sarasin—you and I know what you did to this poor, broken little dog

. . . NO! . . .

that instead of saving it, instead of helping it as sole witness to its distress—what did you do, Michael Sarasin? WHAT DID YOU DO?"

. . . he yelled, the emotion overwhelming him . . . he hadn't expected anything like this—the incident in his life he was the most ashamed of, the most guilty of . . .

"Tell us, Michael, tell THEM what you did to me," the dog said, and beyond where the broken dog sat near the edge of the road stood his grandfather—his clothes torn and bloodied—and beside him Alan, Sam and Amanda—all of them wearing shredded clothes soaked with blood and dirt, their faces streaked with black and red as they looked imploringly at him with sad, waiting eyes and

. . . then Michael remembered his plan, knowing the time had come to enact it, that the Gate even now was beginning to open, finishing its formation as the bridge between two worlds never meant to be joined . . .

they began speaking to him, pleading for him to tell them what he had done and

. . . so he told them . . .

"I killed it, that's what I did. I killed it . . . OKAY?"

. . . even as he began to prepare . . .

"It'd been hit by a car and I found it on the side of the road next to the bridge where Haversham Creek went under Filmore Street

. . . stalling for time to prepare the trap . . .

I found it . . . its legs were broken and it was crying—whimpering—and I, I couldn't stand

. . . the building pressure . . . .

it! I couldn't stand its crying, it was hurting so much! What could I do? What? I had no way to help it. There was nothing I could do! And so I . . . I killed it . . . I . . ."

"HOW did you kill it, Michael Sarasin?"

"I . . ."

"HOW DID YOU KILL IT, MICHAEL?"

"I BASHED ITS BRAINS OUT WITH A STICK! I just kept hitting it . . . and hitting it . . . until it stopped making that God-awful whimpering, pathetic cry . . ."

and then he saw the horrified looks on the faces of his father, mother and sister within what he knew was only the Image . . . and with this in mind it was then that he PULLED *and using the vehicle of Teufel's own Image—he began pulling the demon inside it—inside what he suddenly thought of as HIS stage—a stage where Teufel had only been granted the right to perform—and he funneled the tremendous power he had allowed to build within him almost unendurably during the Image—and used it all—used it to pull Teufel from the world outside into the world inside and in doing so, prepared to endure the demon's struggles . . .*

Images and sounds and feelings coming at him by the thousands—then by the thousands of thousands as

. . . initially he felt himself losing control as the massive bombardment nearly overwhelmed him . . . until he decided to quit fighting against them and began to pull *them within himself as well . . . the sounds deafening in their shrieking roar, the Images like a hurricane of swirling pictures—each one a dagger of stabbing, destructive emotional energy—as he fought against a frenzy of competing feelings—loss, guilt, sadness, hopelessness, despair, anguish, pain . . . love . . . but as he held on, exerting an increasingly tighter and tighter hold, pulling it all further and deeper within himself—pulling it within the power storm of channeled energy he had become—he felt the bombardment slowly slackening, the Images lessening in their intensity, the sounds fading in their harsh wail . . .* and he understood his purpose . . . *and so he continued pulling the forces of evil within himself, the power inexorably and relentlessly flowing into him, no longer leaving but remaining in order to contain that which he was now gathering, then wrapping and holding it fast so that it could*

not escape while he continually drew in all that still remained outside . . . pulling it inward, the stream of all that had been Teufel . . . an unbroken thread . . . a thread that while it was pulled and stretched . . . could not be broken . . . its many parts merely facets of a single whole . . . and Michael knew his purpose was to be the container which would hold the power now being channeled into him . . . the power to act as the vessel to hold all that he was gathering from out of the cavern . . . that within him it would be captured . . . and contained . . . and now he understood . . . why Harvey had told him that he would not survive . . .

77

1

Alan, now with Sam and Amanda wrapped protectively against him, watched his son's battle with the demon without understanding the ramifications—or potential consequences—of the struggle.

What he visualized before him, he perceived as two opposing storms—one made up of a brilliant and sparkling whiteness that he knew somehow embodied goodness—the other a black, impenetrable cloud of evil in its darkest, most powerful form.

The clouds began their struggle by pushing and pulling at each other in an unyielding conflict before mixing together to create a swirling whirlwind and Alan felt it absurd when he was reminded of chocolate and vanilla swirl ice cream.

When the two opposing storms mixed, it was in a frenzy of activity that occurred too fast for him to follow. From what he could see, which was little more than a blur of indistinct color, there was no way to determine who—or what—was winning.

At the same time, beyond the battling storms, Alan noticed that the Gate was widening—having consumed all but a few remaining feet of the back wall of the cavern and he knew, without any reflection about the why or the how, that when the wall became covered in its entirety—the Gate would be complete and the "game" forever lost.

Alan returned his attention back to his son's battle and saw that something had changed. Although he couldn't be certain, he thought that perhaps the white storm had grown in size. At the same time, the chaotic mixing, swirling actions of the two forces seemed to have slowed.

"My God, Alan, what *is that?*" Sam shouted, struggling to be heard above the still present thunder permeating the cavern.

Before answering, Alan wondered if the deafening pounding might not be diminishing as well—and, for the first time, dared to hope.

"Only God knows!" he replied.

In the next moment, he was sure—the white, shapeless mass of sparkling energy that his son had become had now grown larger than its black adversary and seemed to actually be pulling the black substance inside itself.

And then he knew that the sound in the cavern was not just lessening in its intensity—it was changing. As he looked past the battling storms to the back of the cavern, he could see why—the void of nothingness that was the Gate had now completed its consummation of the wall.

The Gate . . . was finally opening.

Only a few yards in front of the rapidly opening Gate, the direction of the battle between Michael and Teufel had now swung clearly in favor of Michael, or of that which Michael had become—the white maelstrom having all but completely consumed the black. Then the entire mass of unified power and energy began moving backward—moving toward the open Gate.

Next, as a solid, tidal wave of indescribable black shapeless masses began toppling into the cavern, the newly formed tornado of white and black power . . . exploded. But instead of sound, the explosion was marked by silence, stunning in its abruptness . . . the thundering roar within the cavern coming to a halt as if a switch had been flipped, and from out of the ball of energy exploded a spherical mass of blackness which was hurled into, and then through the Gate, while at the same time pulling the fabric of the opening in behind it. Alan watched in astonishment as the void which had consumed the wall began pulling back within itself, becoming smaller and deeper . . . then spinning like the Charybdis of Greek mythology . . . consuming itself and collapsing toward its center . . . pulling that which had started to come out of it, back within it . . .

And that's when the screaming began.

2

As the Gate dwindled to a sphere no greater than a yard across, there came from within it an immeasurable onslaught of high-pitched inhuman screams—sounds so immediate and of such piercing intensity that Alan, Sam and Amanda had to slam their hands over their ears once again—and still it was but a fraction of the requisite protection they needed to save themselves from the tortuous affliction of sound that drove a hail of pain shards into their heads.

Alan stumbled, his sense of balance destroyed, and fell to the floor. His knee landed on a stone, a pain for which he was thankful, as it dulled, if only momentarily, the much worse pain of the howling driving itself into his skull in an unceasing torrent.

Because of their preoccupation with the pain inflicted upon them by the screaming, none of them observed the final closing of the Gate. The black void of the circle contracted to nothingness, the flames of the bonfire—all but previously eclipsed by the Gate and the storms—faded and died, and the wall at the back of the cavern became, once again, nothing more than gray, lifeless rock.

But, more importantly to Alan and his family, at the same time as the last trace of the Gate disappeared, the screaming ceased. Incredibly, it seemed, the "thunder" of the ensuing silence was nearly as deafening. As a result, Alan's ears conveyed a constant ringing inside his head that now ached as if he had been pounding it against the rock. When he finally pulled his hands away from his ears he found a drop of fresh blood on the dirty surface of his right palm.

When Alan looked up, he saw that the white storm was still within the cavern and was, in fact, presently their only source of illumination. He searched what he could of the cavern from his position on the floor and was relieved to see no remaining evidence of Teufel or the Gate. Even the body of Sam's father had mercifully disappeared.

Alan dragged himself over to Sam and Amanda who had huddled themselves into a ball on the floor behind him. When he reached them, they jumped at his touch, then welcomed him with warm, desperate embraces. But as they were busy hugging one another, they sensed an atmospheric change in the conditions of the cavern and let go to see what was happening.

The cavern—or more specifically the vaguely human-shaped white form currently illuminating it—appeared to be darkening. They watched as the light faded—the bright specks within the cloud-like mass disappearing first—ultimately followed by the cloud itself.

An instant later, it had disappeared completely . . . and the cavern was plunged into darkness.

78

August 10
Thursday Morning

As Teufel's Gate, located hundreds of feet below the surface of the earth, was suddenly sealed, a mini-apocalypse began on the portion of the land which included Woulfe House and the town of Boyne City.

It started with a massive cave-in of the Sedgwick-Davey Copper Mine, with the primary tunnel disintegrating along the first thousand feet of its entrance, the rock collapsing in upon itself in an earth-rumbling tremor that awakened nearly every resident still left in the town and was later found to have been heard as far away as Boyne Falls, six miles to the east.

A moment after this cave-in, the house built by Dr. Robert Benjamin Woulfe imploded in an anonymous, muffled collapse that no one, save perhaps a few curious denizens of the surrounding forest, heard.

Finally, the tunnel leading from the basement of this same house similarly collapsed upon itself, leaving a visible, winding depression snaking out into the backyard and off into the field to the north looking like the cave-in of an enormous mole's underground empire.

In the center of this same field, the strangely-twisted tree—The Claw—tipped by several feet at its base, its hand-like formation stopping to rest in a position where it would continue to lean for years thereafter as if struggling to reach something in the distant southern sky.

79

From out of the darkness, a light erupted somewhere in the distance. Alan, Sam and Amanda tensed, then clung more tightly to each other. From their vantage, they could tell that it was a small light, but it was too far away for them to determine if it was a flashlight or something else.

Alan, despite everything he had seen so far, somehow felt confident that his son had somehow survived. But then, he reflected, the concept of survival could be interpreted in many ways.

A tentative voice floated toward them from the direction of the light.

"Hello? You guys all right?"

"Michael?" Alan took a cautious step forward. "I . . . I think *you're* the one we need to be asking that of."

With what they presumed to be the light from a flashlight, Michael found them in the darkness. As the light, and Michael, moved towards them, Alan—despite his genuine joy at having confirmed that his son was still alive—remained apprehensive as the light bobbed toward them.

Was he all right? Was he still the same Michael?

And so, just before the light, and whatever it was that was holding it, reached them, Alan tried to convince himself that his concerns were based on his fear at having borne witness to something he didn't—and probably never would—understand.

2

As Michael attempted to rejoin his family near the front of the cavern, his gait was unsteady but still functional enough to allow him to negotiate the distance required to reach them.

"I think I'm all right. Just don't ask me how I survived that, because I'm not sure I know."

"Well," Alan said, "whatever it was, it was . . . incredible."

His mother hugged him fiercely, burying her face deep into his shoulder and Michael realized that her grip was weak and her skin cold. He put his arms around her and did what he could to soothe her trembling body, and as he did, he could detect fresh blood and knew they needed to get her to a doctor immediately.

"I'm sorry, Michael," she managed, her voice shaky and faint. "I'm sorry I ever doubted you."

Never before in his entire life had his mother apologized to him.

"It's okay now, Mom. It's okay, we made it," he said.

She lifted her head off his shoulder, then held him at arm's length, as if inspecting him. He could still feel the trembling in her hands and arms as they rested upon his shoulders.

"I know, Michael. I don't know how or why . . . but . . . I guess it's over."

"Yes," he said, "it's over."

"You saved us. Saved us all."

And then Amanda spoke. "You turned into an angel."

Michael would have laughed if he wasn't so tired and if his sister hadn't sounded so serious.

And then she added, quietly, almost as if she were whispering a secret to an invisible friend, "Look at his clothes."

When Michael shined the light upon himself he noticed that his shoes, jeans and shirt had all turned immaculately white and become nearly diaphanous.

"Maybe I did," he said. "Maybe that's just what I did."

An uneasy, though obviously relieved, silence followed. The flashlight dimmed for a moment, then brightened again.

"Do you know how to get us out of here?" Alan asked.

Michael didn't answer immediately—realizing he didn't know. But then he concentrated, probing the depths of his mind for the instinct that had previously led them all here . . . and found it. Like a reassuring hand on his shoulder—he felt it once again guiding him, only this time, in a direction out of the cavern—a direction he knew would take them, finally, out of the tunnels once and for all.

"No problem," he said, and despite himself and all that had happened, managed a grin. "Just follow me."

3

From the cavern, Michael led his exhausted family to the uncollapsed tunnel entrance he and Amanda had first found, located south of The Claw. They emerged from their confinement looking like rats that had spent their lives underground—with hooded eyes and wincing, dazed looks.

It was now dawn, the sun having not yet risen above the horizon. The sky was aglow with red and purple bands—putting on a magnificent show, Michael thought—in thanks perhaps for the ability to do so once again.

After they dragged themselves out of the tunnel, Michael turned back to the hole they had just come out of, and, without thinking about it, held forth the medallion—surprised to discover that he still possessed it. Immediately, the tunnel collapsed, the ground sinking in a back and forth line across the field for nearly a hundred feet behind them.

Michael turned to look at the house, wondering what had become of the sheriff and the cultists—before realizing that he didn't really care.

It was Amanda, though, that was the first to realize that their house was gone.

80

The sun was just beginning to peek above the horizon through the trees as they wearily trudged their way back to investigate the remains of what had once been their home. They shuffled slowly, in pain and exhaustion, their trek leading them past the now repositioned Claw Tree and, eventually, to what was left of their house.

Woulfe House had collapsed in upon itself, sinking into the ground and descending within a crater nearly three times as deep as the original basement had been. The tallest piece of the house which survived, a lightning rod, was at least a yard below ground level. Sounds of hissing gas and dripping water could be heard despite being muffled by covering rubble.

Michael, Alan, Sam and Amanda walked around the perimeter of the bowl-shaped ruins and as they studied the remains, no one said anything. They noticed that the carriage house had somehow survived the ordeal; however, the gazebo in the backyard now lay canted almost completely on its side from the impact of the tunnel's collapse. To their unexpected delight, they located their Jeep Cherokee sitting unscathed in the driveway. Richard's Jaguar sat nearby but appeared to have been damaged from falling debris. At nearly the exact moment that they regrouped, the eerie chime of their mantle clock announcing the half-hour floated gently up from the hole like a sound drifting from a dream.

"So much destruction," Sam replied. They were now standing next to the Jeep, preparing to leave, but still wanting to take one final look at what had once been their "dream" home—and their hope for a new life. The house, they all knew, had, when they first moved in, been more than a building—it had been their opportunity for a fresh start in a new town—a dream that had tragically collapsed, much like the house itself, into an unrecognizable jumble of nightmare and death.

"Come on, we need to get you to a doctor," Alan said to his wife. Sam nodded, but couldn't stop looking at the remains of the house; then she leaned on him. He put his arm gently around her.

"But . . . Alan?" Sam said. "What happened to the bodies?"

No one said anything while somewhere overhead, a jet rumbled.

"I don't know," Alan said.

They looked about again, as if believing that somehow they could have missed this particular detail. They stared once again at the hole, the backyard, the surrounding woods, but saw nothing of the piles of dead and wounded they had witnessed accumulating on all sides and at nearly every point surrounding the house but a few hours before.

"I . . . I don't know. It can't be—it's impossible . . ." Alan said, sounding lost and confused.

"Could we have . . . *imagined* it all? Like . . . some of those things in the cave?" Sam said. She frowned as she looked first to Alan, then to Michael for some type of reassurance.

"No. No way," Alan said with conviction, but paused as he seemed obligated to offer further evidence. "Well . . . look at your arm! That's not imagined, is it? I *saw* that girl stab you. And in the office—I *felt* that man slam me to the floor. I'll probably have the bruises for a week."

After this, no one said anything, but this time the silence was not uncomfortable. They continued staring at the wreckage . . . and that's when Michael noticed it. Down through a hole between several splintered boards and broken pieces of furniture, he saw a circle—one of the basement floor drains. The drain's cover was missing and around the edge of the hole he saw something dark, like spilled oil. With a start, he realized that he was looking not at oil but at dried blood, and at that moment *knew*, though he didn't understand how, where all the bodies had disappeared to.

"You're right, of course. But . . . how?" Sam persisted, unknowingly echoing Michael's introspection, as much asking herself—seeking some kind of understanding to calm the unanswered questions which she knew would probably never allow her the peace she so desperately craved—as needing to solicit an answer from either Alan or Michael.

"I think," Michael began, "that we're probably never going to understand all of what happened to us here. Harvey Olds told me . . . and so did Teufel for that matter . . . that we had stumbled into the middle of something beyond our comprehension. And in time, I think, there's going to be even more than there is now that we won't be able to understand, explain . . . or even accept. We believe what's before us now and understand at least certain events that occurred because we've just witnessed and lived them. But a year from now? Or five? We'll have a different perspective. And as incredible as this all seems to us now . . . we'll start to forget . . . it won't be so much that we'll want to . . . we'll *need* to . . . in order to go on."

"Well, well. My son the philosopher," Sam said and was able to smile for perhaps the first time in a week. "Maybe some of my father rubbed off on you after all."

Michael smiled also and together they hugged. The moment lasted only briefly, and when they let go, it was obvious to them all—that the rebuilding of their lives had already begun. Their ordeal, as traumatic and harrowing as it had been, would in time provide an even stronger foundation on which to build their future than might have existed before.

They clambered into the Jeep, Alan taking time to help Sam before taking his position in the driver's seat. The vehicle started at once and Alan eased it out of the driveway. They turned onto the road which would take them toward town and as they drove past their front yard, they couldn't help but gaze once more at what was left of their house, but were unable to see anything above the crater's rim. A moment later, they stared without emotion at the specter of The Claw, its fearsome appendages painting a vivid black silhouette against the morning sun and red sky behind it.

“Anyone have any idea how we’re going to explain all of this to our insurance company?” Alan asked and was greeted at first with silence. Then, without any prompting, they all began laughing together—a gushing, uncontrolled flood—a final, welcoming release.

It was a long time before the laughter subsided.

Epilogue

From the Journal of Michael Sarasin
Entry for Friday, July 4, 1996

Well, it's been a year now and I haven't written in here for a long time, so I guess it's about time I did.

I sure miss Grandpa. At least I think he was finally happy with himself at the end. He rediscovered a family that loved him and gained, maybe for the first time, the respect of his daughter, something I know he must have wanted desperately. I miss him a lot. The money he left mom sure helped too! Wow, what a surprise that was!

Newspaper stories about what happened at Woulfe House have for the most part calmed down now and we're only getting calls from reporters about once or twice a month. Even though the story went national I don't think anybody ever made the connection between the disappearances from all over the country and what happened in Boyne City.

The new house we're building, just north of Boyne City is nearly done. Dad said we could be moving within the next two weeks. With the help from the money Grandpa left us, mom really went all out. I guess the insurance companies came through also. We haven't been able to sell the land yet of course—I wonder if we ever will.

The medallion's gone. I realize now that it was really me all along—that the medallion was only a symbol—I was the real tool Harvey used. I threw the medallion in one of the rivers on our drive downstate to Grandpa's memorial service, but I kept the notes—Dr. Woulfe's journals. Don't ask me why I've kept them because I'm not sure myself. I probably should destroy them. But something's kept me from doing it for a year now, and if there's one thing I've learned through all of this, it's to listen to my feelings. So when we move in the next couple of weeks I guess they'll be coming with me. I know what Dad would say if he knew, but I'm pretty sure they're safe—at least for now.

Remembering back to those events of more than a year ago, I swear it feels like it all happened only yesterday. A common thing I guess—to see events that have had a major impact on our lives as belonging closer to our present memories than what the calendar tells us. Events so monumental they never stray far from our mind—they seem to always be there, to always be current, part of today or last week or last month. They just won't let themselves sit around up there, pushed off into some dark corner, covered up with a sheet and left to gather dust and be forgotten. Instead, they're like our favorite chair in front of the TV. It's the chair that's always there—always welcoming us into its warm, comfortable and familiar embrace and when we walk past it a dozen times a day and every evening we sit down in it we never notice if it's sagging a little more than it was last night or whether there's a new wrinkle in the leather that wasn't there a week ago. The changes are so slight from one day to the next that we don't notice them; they're too insignificant. And that's the thing about what we see every day—we don't notice when they change—they seem to always be the age they are today and for us to think about what they looked like even a year ago—we just can't do it. Our old leather chair in front of the TV just keeps sitting there and getting older, collecting its wrinkles and sagging a little more each day and still we don't notice it because we're too *close*. But then Christmas will come and Aunt Marion will visit for the first time in two years and when she walks into the living room to find a comfortable place to sit and talk, you'll notice how she looks strangely at the old chair, your favorite old chair parked in front of the TV, and you'll see her make a slight frown. It'll only be there an instant, but you'll see it nevertheless and immediately you'll *know*—as she takes a seat on the sofa, a new contemporary you bought just two months ago—you'll know at *that* moment that your favorite chair is indeed old and wrinkled and sagging.

Well, it sounds like Mom's home—and I think Dad's got supper ready, so I better quit now. Hopefully, of course, it won't be as long before I visit you again, Journal. It seems like not that long ago that to miss a day of writing in here was unthinkable, but, there you go again—things change.

Amanda's really looking forward to the fireworks tonight. I guess they're going to shoot them off from the edge of Lake Charlevoix in the park. We may get rained out though; the weather people are calling for a storm. It could be a pretty big one they said. But, I think we can handle it. We've been through a few big ones before.